"We killed every one," Yahnosa spat with fierce pleasure. "You gave us warning enough to grab bows and rifles."

Jacova felt very nauseous and even dizzy. Her lips were thick and she knew that her face was badly cut and swollen. That meant nothing. All that mattered was Yahnosa and the child of three bloods resting in her womb.

"Jacova? Are you shot!"

"No."

Her husband relaxed. "Kiati is dead. The old woman tried to reach you, but she ran across the Mexican soldiers' charge and was lanced."

Jacova bent forward and vomited. Retching and weeping, she would have collapsed except for Yahnosa's strong arms, which pinned her against his bare chest. It was then that Jacova felt a wetness on the back of her neck and knew that her husband, despite being Apache, wept too.

THE GILA RIVER

RIVERS
WEST

THE
GILA RIVER

Gary McCarthy

BANTAM BOOKS
NEW YORK • TORONTO • LONDON • SYDNEY • AUCKLAND

THE GILA RIVER
A Bantam Domain Book / November 1993

ISBN 0-553-29769-4

Published simultaneously in the United States and Canada

Bantam Books are published by Bantam Books, a division of Bantam
Doubleday Dell Publishing Group, Inc. Its trademark, consisting of the
words "Bantam Books" and the portrayal of a rooster, is Registered in
U.S. Patent and Trademark Office and in other countries. Marca Reg-
istrada. Bantam Books, 1540 Broadway, New York, New York 10036.

PRINTED IN THE UNITED STATES OF AMERICA

RAD   0 9 8 7 6 5 4 3 2 1

*For my bright,
blue-eyed girl,
BRIDGET MAUREEN*

Special thanks to the Pima and Apache people who freely gave me their time and history. To the Arizona and New Mexico Park Rangers who aided and directed me in my Gila River research and travels. And most especially, thanks to my dear writer friend and renowned Southwestern historian, Jeanne Williams.

Book I
MIGUEL—THE SPANIARD

Chapter

ONE

L ost in the sun-blistered Sonoran desert, the two dozen
Spanish soldiers marched in a thin wavery column as
they struggled north through the dense mesquite and
cactus. They were strung out for half a mile, first the
stronger soldiers, then the weaker, and finally the emaci-
ated Jesuit priest, Father Francisco Tomas Castillo. The
padre's body rocked to the motion of his staggering burro.
The Jesuit had fashioned a hat of creosote bush to shield
his brow, but the shrub's tiny leaves afforded little shade,
and rivulets of sweat ran down his face and neck to soak
into his black woolen robe. The padre's burro was very
weak. Its stride was choppy, its head and great ears angled
downward.

Sixteen-year-old Miguel Diego Santana led the burro
through the heavy vegetation, especially careful to avoid
the hated "jumping" cholla cactus. Among the entire expedition, his were the only light steps and he alone seemed
resigned to the punishing heat and desert surroundings.
The boy's eyes missed nothing. Not the quick and deadly
diamondback rattler, the fat, colorful Gila monster, or the
roadrunner that darted through a forest of prickly pear

cactus and flushed the long-eared jackrabbit into an erratic footrace.

Unlike his brother's soldiers, most of whom still wore their heavy bullhide leather jackets, Miguel wore only garments of loose cotton. However, there was a fine Spanish dagger at his belt, and his boots reflected quality. Under the protection of a wide-brimmed straw hat, Miguel's lips were cracked, but smiled whenever he overheard one of the suffering soldiers curse this New Spain.

It was mid-afternoon and the heat was unbearable. The Spaniards would have sought shade beside the lofty saguaro cactus whose dull green trunks were riddled by birds and rats, except that they were dying of thirst. Earlier that morning, dust devils had attacked their column. The wind-whipped sand and stickers had blinded them during those suffocating moments while the last pack burros had stampeded into the desert with the precious few remaining goatskins of water. Now, what water they had left was pooled inside their small skin bota bags. They would all die if they did not find a spring or the Gila River, signified by a ragged scratch across the parchment of their crude map. Dear God, if they had not been attacked by Indians on the Santa Cruz River and lost their horses, they would be resting at Tubac by now. As it was, they had been forced to march overland across this terrible desert.

The heat was so intense it radiated in thick waves across this steaming valley rimmed by sterile volcanic mountains. Where was the Gila River? If they did not find it this day or this night, it would not matter even if they located the three-story adobe castle marking one of the Seven Lost Cities of Cibola, whose storied streets were paved with gold.

Miguel could hear the padre praying. Maybe for the burro, perhaps for his sins and those of the profane Spanish soldiers. Or maybe even for his death and the long anticipated meeting with Jesus and Mary. Miguel did not wish to leave this world, not even for the promise of the Kingdom of Heaven. Like his brother, Captain Hernando

Diego Santana, Miguel desired only to find gold, silver, and precious stones. He knew this was wrong, that he should have burned with passion to spread the word of Christianity, to help the padre save heathen souls, but it did no good to lie to himself, because God knew his true thoughts. Miguel reasoned that if he found riches at this first lost city of Cibola, he would then do all that was in his power to help Padre Castillo. That way, he would satisfy both his spiritual and his temporal worlds.

"Miguelito?"

He turned to see that the padre was no longer bent in prayer. "Yes, Father?"

"Stop this poor burro. I will walk."

Miguel looked ahead to his brother, who had ordered him not to allow the padre to dismount in order to minister to his burro. A protest formed on Miguel's lips. "But Father, you are not strong."

"I am stronger than this burro. Stop."

Miguel had no choice but to obey. He knew what would happen, though. The padre would minister to the burro and pour his own precious water into the cup of his hand for the burro to drink. But the animal, in its great thirst, would only spill the water and then bray piteously for more. And Miguel also knew that Hernando would blame him for stopping the burro and letting the padre waste their last few drops of water.

"Father," he argued. "I think the river we seek is just up ahead. We will reach it by sundown and then your poor burro will have all he wishes to drink."

"If he does not drink now, he will not live until sundown. Stop the burro, Miguelito, and let me down."

Miguel sighed. His brother and the soldiers were still plodding mindlessly north. Perhaps after Father Castillo spilled his water into the sand, the burro could be muzzled and would not bray so loud. Maybe, too, the padre would remount and Hernando would be none the wiser.

"Yes, Father."

Father Castillo lifted his heavy black robes and dismounted. He was fortyish, a tall, awkward man made even more so by his alarming frailty. The padre's hair was white, the color and texture of corn silk. All his teeth were in various stages of decay. His cheekbones jutted outward and his pale skin was burned red. His nose was a peeling blade of flesh, often running. Only his eyes were still bright and beautiful. They were green, the color of emeralds flecked with gold. From them the padre directed a steady, unblinking gaze capable of penetrating a man's mind or heart. But most of all, the eyes were kind, a little sad and very forgiving. Miguel knew that the padre could forgive anything and anyone except himself.

Sweat dripped from the Jesuit's pointed chin. When he dismounted, Castillo was so weak that he had to lean against the poor burro for a moment to stop the trembling in his thin legs. Miguel was shocked at how feeble the padre was becoming and the toll that this Sonoran desert had already taken on his health. In less than two months the priest's magnificent eyes had retracted back into his skull. His once broad shoulders now drooped as if barely able to support the weight of his black robe.

"But please hurry, Father," Miguel begged, one eye on the padre, the other on his implacable brother and the plodding soldiers. "The soldiers must not be allowed to get too far ahead."

Castillo smiled tolerantly. "They rush into Hell seeking a city of gold, yet they would not pause a single moment for the promise of eternity. I fully realize that Captain Santana is your brother, but Jesus—not a soldier—is the one to follow."

"Yes, Father."

"Did you say your rosary this morning?"

"Yes, Father."

"I have not heard your confession lately."

It was an effort for Miguel to quell his mounting exasperation. "Please. We must not fall too far behind! This is Apache country."

The Jesuit's bony finger wagged. His voice trembled. "And Pima who once heard the word of God!"

"Yes, Father."

The Jesuit reached for the water bag fastened to his rawhide saddle. As he untied it, Miguel caught the flash of his golden crucifix. After all these months of travel up through the great wilderness of Mexico, the sight of that adornment still took Miguel's breath away. The crucifix was unlike any he had ever seen before. It was large, as big as the padre's outstretched hand. The cross was of heavy gold. Buried in the head of the cross, just over Jesus' crown, was a bloodred ruby. The crucifix hung on a golden chain that was itself a work of art.

Weeks had passed before Miguel had dared to ask the padre about the crucifix. All he would say was that it had been a "family" gift handed down among the priests of his family for generations. The Castillo crucifix was the padre's only possession of value, and he believed with all his heart that its beauty would surely reveal to the Indians that Christianity, bought with the blood of Jesus, was the price of eternal salvation.

The padre poured water into the cup of his hand and extended it to the burro. The thirst-crazed animal bit the hand so savagely that Castillo's fingers splayed, spilling the water. Blood seeped into his palm and replaced water.

"Father!"

"Miguel, you must pour out the rest," Castillo ordered, now cupping both hands so that the burro could drink.

"But—"

"Pour!"

Father Castillo's angry voice shocked Miguel. He poured, sure that the burro would refuse the water tainted with blood or, worse, even bite it again. But the burro did neither. It gulped greedily, and the padre ordered Miguel to empty the last few drops into his hands. The burro began to lap furiously, great brown eyes rolling. Its tongue was thick and swollen from thirst, coated white, but now pink with the padre's blood. If Castillo noticed, he said nothing as he stroked the beast's fevered muzzle.

"Father, your hand. I will find a bandage."

The padre made fists and dropped them to his sides. He swayed on his feet, and Miguel reached to steady the Jesuit before he toppled. "Father, the burro is stronger now. Please ride."

"Confession tonight?"

"Yes, Father."

"Then I will ride," Castillo said, satisfied with this bargain. Miguel held the burro while the padre mounted, then raised his face to the sun. Head tilted backward, lips silently moving, the padre closed his eyes and began to pray. Miguel, eager to push on before his brother realized their transgression, yanked the burro forward. He also said a prayer that the animal would be refreshed by the water. However, after only a few dozen yards the burro again began to weave and stagger.

Miguel lost track of time. His mind escaped the desert like its animals, slipping into the coolness of shadows and dreams. The hot, clutching sand fell away, slick as water. Miguel envisioned himself drifting like smoke toward a veil of magenta and silver which floated before him like the great curtains he had once seen at the famous opera house in Madrid. Now, as then, a beautiful dancer appeared. Her hair was as black and shiny as obsidian, her teeth whiter than sun-bleached bones. The girl was dressed in red and she danced.

"Miguelito!"

The dream evaporated like mist in fire. Miguel was jerked into reality as the rope in his hand spun him completely around. He lost his balance and almost fell as the burro broke at the knees and collapsed, its side crushing down against the terrible cholla cactus.

Father Castillo's robe split and his bare left leg was pinned. He did not cry out. Instead the padre lay still while the burro thrashed, eyes rolling with terror. Miguel leaned against the rope, desperately attempting to drag the burro off the priest. Unfortunately, that meant pulling it deeper into cholla. The burro fought crazily, making matters far worse. The padre's face drained of blood, like a corpse.

"Damn you!" Hernando bellowed as he rushed back from the head of his column. "Miguel, what have you done now, you worthless fool!"

"Father Castillo is hurt!"

"Here!" Hernando growled, tearing the lead rope from Miguel's hands.

Captain Hernando Santana was a big and powerful man. He threw his weight and muscle against the rope and dragged the burro deeper into the cholla. The animal went insane, and when the padre groaned with pain, Hernando drew his long Spanish dagger. Before Miguel or the priest could react, steel flashed and the burro's throat opened and poured like a flagon of wine. The burro stiffened, then quivered like a spent bowstring before it sighed and went limp.

"Don't just stand there, drag Father out!" Hernando roared at his men as he grabbed the burro's foreleg and lifted the beast's weight.

Miguel had seen much death since coming to New Spain. But never without reason. His reaction was instinctive. "You didn't need to do that, Hernando!" he cried, struggling to free the priest.

"Father's leg is broken!" Hernando said bitterly as the Jesuit was pulled free.

"It is a good thing that he fainted," said Sergeant Ortega.

"It is a bad break," Hernando answered after a quick examination. "See here where the bone violates the flesh? He may die."

"We could cut off the leg," Ortega said dubiously.

"Then he would die for sure."

"What do we do, Captain?"

"We will *all* die if we do not soon find water," Hernando snapped.

Miguel could not tear his eyes from the padre's broken leg. He knew that when bone pierced flesh, a man's life was in grave peril. And with the padre already so weak, what chance did he now have to live and do God's work? Almost none. Nearby, a cloud of buzzing black flies was already scenting blood and swarming to the burro.

"Move the padre over here in the shade of that spreading palo verde," the captain ordered.

This accomplished, the soldiers seemed to lose interest. Only Miguel stayed close by the Jesuit's side to minister to his needs. Where the padre's robe had split and his pale legs were exposed, Miguel could see that they were thick as fur with cholla spines. Miguel was ashamed to think that it might be better if the priest did not awaken. It would almost be a mercy if Father Castillo's soul were already winging out of this hellish desert and into the arms of Jesus.

Hernando wiped the blade of his dagger across his sleeve, then pivoted to gaze south along their back trail. Miguel, despite his anger, could read his brother's desperate thoughts. Should they retreat and attempt a return to the distant Santa Cruz River before they died of thirst? And even if they did, what then?

Casa Grande, as Padre Kino had described it many years ago, was somewhere up ahead in this huge, baking valley fed by a great river running east to west called the Gila. And although Casa Grande was deserted now, the legends promised that, hidden under its hard adobe floors and at the bases of its walls, were treasures of gold, silver, and jewels.

How much treasure? It was impossible to say. These two dozen privileged soldiers, secretly chosen and outfitted by their wealthy Spanish patron, believed that a fortune awaited them under Casa Grande. Father Castillo, however, gave no credence to the buried treasures. His mission was to make converts to the Church, and his idols were all the saintly padres who had gone on before him, especially the great Eusebio Francisco Kino, an account of whose life and travels he had painstakingly copied and used as a daily inspiration.

Father Kino, the "Padre on Horseback," was worthy of sainthood. He had almost single-handedly converted thousands of Pima Indians before their eventual uprising and the destruction of his churches and missions at Caborca and Tubutama, at Imuris, San Ignacio, and Magdalena. More than fifty years ago, all Kino's padres had been martyred, their missions sacked, the beloved chapels razed, the livestock slaughtered and stolen. The work of saints all lost in one bloody uprising, caused in part by the greed and inhumanity of a few cruel Spanish soldiers. But now Father Castillo was returning to the Pima armed with only a Bible, a crucifix, and Father Kino's words of hope and devotion to God.

In private Castillo had confided to Miguel that he expected death—even prayed for it as a reward for his priestly services. Furthermore, the padre prayed that if there were no worldly treasure buried at Casa Grande, that he might then be afforded the opportunity to save the souls of the greed-driven soldiers. Perhaps only in failure would such men fall to their knees and bend their wills to God.

"Captain Santana?" the Jesuit whispered.

They all turned to the padre. "Captain, we will die trying to return to the Santa Cruz River. Look forward, never back."

Hernando and Miguel knelt at the padre's side. The captain said, "You are badly hurt. This leg will probably kill you."

"Then my prayers will finally be answered."

"But what of the Indians?" Miguel pleaded. "What of their souls?"

Father Castillo opened his eyes to stare at Miguel. "If I leave this wicked world, then you must minister to the Indians."

Miguel shook his head. "Father, I am unworthy!"

"We are all unworthy. Even the twelve Apostles of Christ were unworthy. Yet they did as the Holy Spirit directed. You too can do this, Miguel Diego Santana. Have faith!"

"We will *all* be messengers of Christ," Hernando said with irritation. "That is part of this mission."

"It is the only part worthy of this mission," Castillo breathed. "But you must go on to the ruins. To turn back now would serve no useful purpose."

"He is right," Sergeant Ortega said, shielding his eyes and gazing north with ill-concealed impatience. "If this is the valley of Casa Grande, both river and ruins must be close. Those black mountains to the north cannot be more than another day's march. We will find Casa Grande soon."

"Make a litter," the captain ordered his sergeant. "We will carry the padre to Casa Grande—or to our graves—whichever is nearer."

"Now that the burro is dead," Miguel asked his brother, "what shall I do in our king's service?"

"Weave a fan to shield Father Castillo's face from the sun."

Miguel nodded and went to cut some brush. Back at the Santa Cruz River, there had been stands of water-loving cottonwoods whose leafy boughs would have been ideal, but what good did it do to think of such things now? In a few minutes his dagger made quick work of the task, and the soldiers were almost finished with their crude litter.

The padre's eyes tightened with pain when he was shifted onto the litter. In one hand he held his family crucifix, in the other a fine leather pouch containing his vestments, holy water, Bible, Kino letters, and things sacramental.

It bothered Miguel very much to see all the cholla stickers protruding from Castillo's flesh. So much so that he blurted, "Can't we remove some of the barbs?"

"No time." Hernando's voice was rough with impatience and authority. "It would take hours, and we cannot even spare minutes."

"He is right," the padre agreed. "Let us go either to our deaths or to Casa Grande."

"It had better be the latter," Sergeant Ortega growled.

In reply the padre just smiled, closed his eyes and began to pray.

Captain Santana set off at a much faster pace, causing Miguel to realize that his brother had actually been holding up the column of soldiers so that the burro and the padre did not fall too far behind. Now, without that encumbrance, the soldiers marched straight at the treeless black mountains. They advanced through the shimmering heat waves cursing and grunting and angrily hacking the ears off the prickly pear cactus as if they were the heads of the hated Apache. Surrounding them like tribes of tall, mocking giants towered the saguaro cactus, arms raised in supplication to the burning sun.

Miguel, holding his brush fan over the padre, stumbled along. It was, of course, nearly impossible to keep the circle of shade exactly over Castillo's already blistered face. And sometimes, despite himself, Miguel could not help but look down at the sharp protrusion of leg bone. It was flecked with blood, like a broken tooth poking through pale gums. The leg was already bloated and turning purple.

Miguel was staring at it when his ankle brushed a low-lying cholla cactus and the sharp sting of spines made him yelp.

"Give it up to God as a penance," the padre whispered without opening his eyes.

"Yes, Father!"

"We will find the Gila River and Casa Grande," the priest assured them. "I know this because the Lord has just told me so."

"I believe, Father. That makes me very happy."

"Me too," one of the sweating, litter-bearing soldiers grunted.

The Jesuit opened his eyes, squinting with pain, or concern. "You are a fine young man, Miguelito. And, because I am the last priest in my family, if I die, you shall have my cross to take among the Indians."

"But, Padre," a soldier cried, "it would bring a thousand pesos in Mexico City."

The padre twisted on his litter, fingers shielding the crucifix. "It would carry you to Hell, Señor Escobar! You and any others who did not use it in New Spain to advance the work of God."

Escobar scoffed, then winked at his companions and said, "Maybe much, much more than a thousand pesos, eh compadres?"

Outrage which quickly dissolved to pity clouded the padre's magnificent eyes. He turned back to Miguel. "Do not be afraid of this talk, Miguelito. God is with us always. You shall have this blessed crucifix when I am gone."

Miguel shivered despite the terrible Sonoran desert heat. Of course he wanted the Castillo crucifix—but not at the price Father Castillo was asking. "I ... I, forgive me, Father, but I would return it to Mexico and give it to your Jesuit order."

The padre's expression softened. "No," he said, rolling his head back and forth on the litter. "You will remain for the rest of your days in this land among the Indians. You will teach them of God, Jesus, and Mary—and they will believe."

Miguel did not wish to argue with the padre. After all, he was barely sixteen, still growing, not quite yet a man. And although he had come from a good family in Cadiz, Spain, and his brother was already a captain, Miguel realized his own true insignificance. His accomplishments, until this expedition, were unworthy of notice. His desires were worldly, just starting to focus on women. He was a Christian, but the love of God did not burn in his breast and he would never be a disciple or an apostle. He would fail this saintly priest and end up selling the crucifix or having it taken from him by force for others to sell. Either way, it would be a sacrilege. An abomination to God and to the memory of this poor man.

Miguel decided that later, when they were alone, he must explain all this to the padre. He would tell Father Castillo that if Hernando allowed and approved, he himself would also become a soldier loyal to the King of Spain. Right now he was just a boy without a burro or cattle to tend, and an ankle that stung like blazes.

"Look there!" Sergeant Ortega called. "Do you see them?"

"What!" everyone cried, shielding their eyes from the dying sun and gazing north.

"Casa Grande!" Ortega choked, breaking into a run.

Miguel did see the great adobe casa now. Through the sting of salty sweat, he saw, and he knew that they had found the ruins of an ancient and vanished civilization. And maybe, God willing, this was only the first of the Seven Lost Cities of Cibola. If that be the case, they would all return to Mexico City wearing rings of gold, and the soldiers would feel generous enough to allow poor Father Castillo to be buried with his family's blessed crucifix.

To sell the image of Christ would surely condemn them all to everlasting Hell and damnation.

_____ Chapter _____

TWO

_____

When the soldiers who bore the padre heard the cry "Casa Grande," they dropped the litter and bolted forward. Miguel heard the padre grunt with pain, saw him roll sideways off the litter into the hard, pebbly dirt.

"Father Castillo!" he whispered, kneeling at the man's side. "Forgive them!"

"Of course I forgive them. They are dying of thirst, Miguelito."

"But you know that it is not water that makes them run."

Miguel was filled with disgust at the sight of the soldiers throwing off their heavy leather vests and racing headlong toward the huge adobe ruins. "They are crazed and scrambling for gold."

"They will find nothing but bitterness and disappointment."

Miguel noted that his own brother was the first to reach Casa Grande. Hernando disappeared into the three-storied ruins. Miguel could well imagine Hernando falling to his knees and using his dagger to rip at the floor, an officer in the army of Spain with no more dignity than a

16

common soldier born of the lowest social order. Miguel looked away, eyes tight at the corners.

"Do not be too hard on your brother," the padre counseled, resting his injured hand on Miguel's shoulder. "The captain will soon have all the disappointment and trouble he can bear. You must defend him."

Miguel looked back at the priest, not understanding. "What do you mean?"

"I mean that there will be no buried fortune at Casa Grande."

"How can you say that!"

The priest was slow in answering. Finally, he seemed to resolve some inner conflict and his shoulders drooped. "Miguelito, you know I am a student of the great Father Kino."

"Of course. Of course, but—"

"In one of his letters, lost in the archives in Mexico City, I discovered a reference to this ancient ruin. A reference that made it very clear that there is no buried treasure at Casa Grande."

Miguel staggered, unwilling to believe what he'd just heard. "But Father, if you knew that—"

The priest placed a forefinger over his lips, then murmured, "I have not lied, Miguelito. In fact, I have repeatedly explained to everyone that there is no treasure. However, the soldiers refuse to believe."

"But this is the very first I have heard of Father Kino's reference to Casa Grande!"

The Jesuit shrugged his bony shoulders. "It was a very *personal* letter, and the reference to the absence of Casa Grande gold has no importance to a soldier of Christ. Father Kino scarcely mentioned the search for gold among his own soldiers. I also thought it unworthy of great consideration."

"But—" Miguel swiveled around toward the ruins. He could hear the soldiers shouting.

"Miguelito," the priest intoned wearily, "we must ask God to forgive their greed and show them through this dis-

appointment that the real treasure of life is in virtue
and—"

"No!" Miguel cried, taking a step toward Casa
Grande, mind unwilling to accept that there was no trea-
sure after all the suffering they'd endured since leaving
Mexico City.

Perhaps the great Father Kino had not even searched
for buried treasure. Why would he have? Like Father
Castillo, he was after souls—not gold. Miguel closed his
eyes and willed himself to behold the image of a fortune
that was most certainly being ripped from beneath Casa
Grande's floors by Hernando and his soldiers. A fortune
he could not resist.

"Miguelito! Please, stay with me."

"No!"

Miguel was out of breath by the time he reached the
huge crumbling adobe. It was as big as a cathedral, but the
sun and the gritty desert wind had taken their toll and, in
addition to the roof, many of the towering walls had collapsed. The door through which Miguel entered was very
narrow, and the high, worn adobe walls were bathed in
cool, dusty shadows. The sudden darkness blinded him.
Miguel tripped and landed hard on his shoulder.

"Get out of here!" a soldier raged. "All this room's
treasure is mine!"

The shoulder hurt so bad that tears stung Miguel's eyes
and he was grateful for the shadows. He retreated, sliding
along a wall until he almost fell through a doorway. A bold
shaft of sunlight, thicker than the body of a horse, spilled
and flowed like honey across the floor of another room.
Miguel hurried across the room into a hallway where narrow
staircases fed into what had once been upper floors but were
now only patches of empty blue sky. He passed small rooms
and saw other sweating soldiers bent over the floors, howling like fiends. Each man appeared to have staked his claim
and was attacking the rock-hard floors with daggers and
even swords. Chinks of adobe were flying thicker than
curses, and when Miguel found his brother, Hernando had

broken through the crust and was slinging dirt up between his legs like a digging dog.

"Hernando?" Hernando was lost in his quest to unearth gold. "Hernando!"

The captain looked up, eyes hooded by heavy brow, face streaming mud. "Here!" he shouted, tearing his sword from its scabbard and bouncing it off a wall. "Find your own room and start digging!"

Miguel snatched up the fine weapon. Many times over the years, he had marveled at its weight and balance. Hernando had always taken great pride in this, his favorite weapon of Spain. But now it was a mere digging stick.

Miguel took the sword, fled from the room and back down the hall, head swiveling from side to side as the soldiers ripped at the underbelly of Casa Grande like wild, burrowing animals.

Miguel raced up a stairway that ended in sunlight. His heart was pounding and he was dizzy with confusion. He collapsed on the staircase and, hearing the sounds, twisted around. He arched his head back and stared up through the casa's missing roof at the cloudless blue sky.

The padre was right—there was no buried treasure at Casa Grande. Miguel realized this now, and wondered what the soldiers would do to Father Castillo if he also revealed to them the reference made in Kino's old letter. A reference that would have aborted this entire expedition. Even though Father Castillo had tried to persuade the soldiers that there was no buried treasure at Casa Grande, the Jesuit had not worked hard to be convincing. The soldiers might very well blame him, rather than their own blind greed, for all the suffering they'd endured to find this old ruin. They would be furious and, in their despair, might quarter the padre!

Miguel snatched up his brother's sword, rushed back down the staircase and found his way outside. To the west, the sun was dying, and he could see a good many other smaller adobes whose walls had worn down to no more than the height of a man's shoulders. The ancient city glowed in a rosette even as it was being defiled.

His eyes reached out across the sage to Father Castillo. The padre was lost in prayer, his upraised crucifix sparkling in the sun. Miguel hurried to his side.

"Father!" he cried, looping an arm around the priest and bringing him erect. "They might turn against you! You *must* hide!"

The priest struggled to his feet. "No, the soldiers must finally turn to God now. He has given them water. Look!"

Miguel followed the padre's gaze north and, for the first time, saw the low line of dark trees just above the cactus and brush. It was the sure and unmistakable sign of a watercourse.

"Let us drink, Miguelito, before the waters are muddied." Castillo glanced down at the officer's sword clenched in Miguel's fist and reacted by raising his crucifix. "This is our only protection."

"I know, Father."

Shifting his brother's sword to his left hand and stepping over a discarded Spanish musket, Miguel wrapped his arm tightly around Father Castillo's narrow waist, and together they limped on toward the Gila River. The wild ranting of the soldiers still boomed from the belly of Casa Grande.

It was sunset before the priest and boy reached the warm, healing waters of the Gila. The river was not large, or deep. But it was clear and cool and it slaked their thirst better than French wine. Miguel pitched headfirst into the river and buried his face in the current, sucking up the water like a sponge. The padre floated in the shallows on his back, face half submerged, eyes mirroring the magnificent firestorm of sunset that gilded the mountaintops.

"Look, Miguelito!" the priest whispered, his expression radiant with joy. "See how God so loves the desert! He has given it the most beautiful of all sunsets."

Miguel pushed himself into sitting position. The Gila

River washed away his pain and buoyed his spirits. The padre's words were true. Even in Spain, even over the Mediterranean, he had never seen such a spectacular sunset.

"Father, what will we do when the soldiers realize there is no treasure? That all their suffering was for nothing?"

"Nothing is for nothing," Castillo explained. "All things have purpose. Even suffering and death, although our minds are too small to comprehend these great mysteries. As for your brother and his soldiers, we will pray and let God do His will. They will not harm you, Miguelito, and although I will soon die of this leg, I believe they would never martyr a priest. Even if they knew of Kino's secret letter."

"You must never tell them."

"Oh," Castillo said, shaking his head, "but I will."

Miguel had dreaded this answer. The padre feared sin, not death. The man did not have any conception of personal danger.

"But Father," Miguel argued, "the soldiers will be very, very angry."

The padre cupped water in his hand and doused his face again and again. "I would like to die right here," he said, more to himself than to Miguel. "Right here in this fine river."

"That is ridiculous!" Miguel was shocked. "You have taken too much sun or you would not say such a crazy thing."

The padre actually laughed. "Oh, but I mean it! Watch!" As Miguel stared, the padre retrieved his crucifix and raised it to the full length of its chain. And then he blessed the entire river.

"See?" The Jesuit laughed again. "I think it would be very fine to die in a blessed river."

Despite his shock, Miguel was cheered by the happiness in Castillo. It gave him hope that perhaps the priest was not really going to die. That Father Castillo's leg would mend and that he would live long enough to save many souls—if the conquistadors did not put him to the sword in a fit of rage.

"I love this blessed river!" the Jesuit proclaimed in a loud voice that echoed across the water. "I love it so much I will sleep in it tonight."

"I will sleep on that sandbar, Father."

"As you wish. But first, confessions."

"But Father, you know very well that I cannot hear your confession."

"True." Castillo cocked his head like a bird. "But you know, even though you cannot absolve me of my sins, it still pleases God for me to admit them."

Miguel twisted his head around to see if his brother or any of the others were coming. They would be here before long because thirst would soon overwhelm even their consuming greed.

"Father, I want to move a little downriver."

"But why?" The padre slapped the water, making a big splash. "What is the point of moving?"

"So that our confessions will not be interrupted if the soldiers come to drink."

Castillo accepted the wisdom of this suggestion. "Very well. But just in case my powers are weak, I will have to re-bless the place where we sleep tonight."

"I thought you blessed all of the Gila."

"I did, but I am not at my best these days," the padre confided with a gentle smile. "Come now, help me up, Miguelito."

Miguel helped the padre back to his feet. "Does the leg feel better?"

"Much."

"And the barbs of the cholla? I will pull them out by the light of the moon before they all break off and do even more damage."

"Do it while you make a confession. Afterward, I will tell you of *my* sins."

"The barbs are many, Father, and it will take a long time to remove them."

"My sins are also many. It will take time to confess them."

Miguel didn't know why he was trying to argue with this man of God. Father Castillo was wise, pious, and a man to be admired. The trouble was, Miguel could really not think of any sins of his own that he could confess. After all, what mortal—even venial—sins could anyone commit leading a burro across the desert?

Miguel decided he could reveal his vision of the dancing ballerina. Perhaps he could confess some outrage against that beautiful dream girl. Well, not an outrage, but an indiscretion. After all, he did not want to offend the padre, who was already in a fragile state of mind and body. He could just say that he had admired her form, her legs. Nothing more, because imagination would do the rest. Yes, Miguel thought, feeling better. He would describe the dancing ballerina and his sordid musings.

That done, he would listen to the padre's confession. What could it amount to? Would Father Castillo consider it a mortal sin if his poor, stumbling burro had crushed an ant?

Probably.

But Miguel was in for a surprise. After they had found a more distant sandbar upon which to spend the night, he made a quick but passionate confession about the dream dancer, which hardly even elicited a comment from the Jesuit. Then Castillo said, "Today, when your brother cut the burro's throat, I felt anger toward him, Miguelito. I wanted to ... to strike him. Yes, to cause Hernando physical pain."

"So did I."

"Hssssh! This is *my* confession. You have already said yours."

"I am sorry."

"Miguelito, you have no experience in hearing confessions," the padre explained, "but you must remember that it is *I* who am supposed to be sorry as you listen."

"Yes, Father."

The padre smoothed the calm surface of the Gila as if it were a silken vestment. "Now, as I said, I wanted to cause your brother pain. And when Señor Escobar smirked and said that my family's crucifix could bring a thousand pesos, I became even more angry."

"You had reason to be," Miguel said with indignation. "It would bring much more than a thousand pesos."

The Jesuit rolled his eyes with exasperation. "No, no! You entirely miss the point! I thought ill of Escobar and the others. I wished them a punishment. I was angry twice this day—once at your brother, and again at Señor Escobar, who was struggling to carry my own litter!"

"They only did that because of the orders. You should not feel guilt at being angry at them."

"But I should! And . . ." The padre struggled.

"What?" Miguel asked, leaning closer.

"And I felt angry at the burro for falling over right into the cholla and breaking my leg." The padre raised his dripping hands in supplication. "Can you believe this! The poor beast was almost dead on its feet, using its last ounce of strength to carry me, and *I* was angry."

Miguel could see the point, but he wanted the priest to feel better, and so he said, "Sometimes we do things we should not in order to do even greater things. You used the burro to conserve your strength to save Indian souls. That was no sin."

Father Castillo cupped his hands and poured water over his sweating head as if baptizing himself. "Miguelito, I have to say that you are far too lenient to be a priest, especially a Jesuit."

"I do not want to be a priest."

"Few are called, fewer still answer. But you must serve God anyway. And the greater your struggle, the greater your reward."

Miguel did not want to hear such depressing talk. He

did not want to struggle, and could not even conceive of saving souls. He wanted to be rich and famous. To return to Spain and make his father and mother proud and happy in their old age. To grow long in years with dignity and family. To live well.

But even as he thought this, the padre's words penetrated his own selfish thoughts as the man confessed how much it had hurt him to be angry at the burro. Castillo also admitted to wishing the sun would not be so hot—a sacrilege because the sun's heat was a gift of God.

After a long, impassioned discourse on the gifts of God, Father Castillo mentioned that his poor burro had squashed a horned toad sunning itself on the trail. "That horned toad had a God-given life," Father Castillo said, looking extremely despondent.

To Miguel, the priest's so-called sins were trivial, but he could see that the padre felt otherwise, and so he tried to look very wise and slightly concerned.

At last the Jesuit said, "We will say four Hail Marys together before we sleep and both ask for forgiveness."

It was late when their prayers were over and they lay back, a sandbar for their pillow. They could hear the soldiers prowling and splashing about downriver, then breaking brush as they hurried back to resume digging at the floor of Casa Grande. They also heard many angry curses.

"They are disappointed, and will be much more so by tomorrow," the padre mused. "At least we will be well-rested."

Miguel gazed up at the stars, feeling the hot wind of the desert on his cheeks and the cold, wet water of the Gila on his back. All his pains were gone. He could not bear the idea of leaving this river to again cross the searing desert, even to return to Mexico City and then to his family in Spain.

"Father," he said with a yawn, "I forgot to pull the cholla barbs from your poor leg."

"Wait until tomorrow. If they do not kill me and I do

not die tonight of the broken bone, *then* pull the barbs out. Otherwise, what is the point?"

"Yes, I understand," Miguel said, closing his eyes and feeling safe in the womb of this blessed river. It filled his senses; he even loved its heavy scent of mossy decay.

Perhaps tonight, nestled in the wet sand, his ballerina would reappear and he would have a very sensuous dream. If so, he would have a better confession for the padre tomorrow. Unless, in the cold light of dawn, the betrayed soldiers impaled Father Castillo on the tips of their Spanish swords.

Chapter
THREE

"**M**iguel! Father Castillo!"
Hernando's angry voice slashed across the
surface of the Gila River. Again he bellowed,
"Miguel! Father Castillo! Damn you both! I *order* you to
come out of hiding!"

Miguel jerked out of a sound sleep into a sitting position. He rubbed his eyes with the palms of his hands and
squinted into the bright orb of sun already scorching the
eastern bowl of this awful desert. Hearing the sound of
crashing brush and the approach of the soldiers, Miguel
splashed water into his face, trying to collect his faculties
even as he wished his brother's angry voice would go
away.

"Miguel, answer me!"

Miguel jumped to his feet, but the wet sand betrayed
his footing and he lost his balance and fell. Beside him,
Father Castillo said, "They are just around the bend and finally moving in the right direction. I suppose you should
answer your captain."

Panic seized Miguel as he remembered the circumstances of the night before. Now his worst fears were

about to be realized. "Father," he cried, rushing over to the padre, "we can still hide!"

"No. I have decided that discretion is called for with your brother and his angry soldiers."

"Thanks be to God!" Miguel breathed. "Then you won't tell them about Father Kino's secret letter?"

The priest was sitting on a slight mound of sand, one foot tucked under his broken leg. Despite what must have been terrible pain, he looked serene. The amber glow of the early sun was kind to his suffering face. "I am not sure exactly what I will say—only that it will be the truth, my son. I will not lie."

"Of course not, Father, but—"

Whatever Miguel was to say next was forgotten as Hernando and his soldiers splashed into view, knee deep in the river. One look at Hernando's dirty face contorted with fury told Miguel that he was in serious trouble. His heart quickened and he was ashamed to note the way his hands trembled.

"Do not be afraid for me," the padre said. "My fate is in God's hands."

"It is *my* fate that concerns me," Miguel admitted. "They look very angry."

"Help me up," Castillo ordered. "Quickly!"

Miguel scooped the padre into his arms and balanced him on one foot as the soldiers' advance created sparkling river rainbows.

The priest held up his crucifix, and when he spoke, his voice was as patient as if he were addressing children. "Captain Santana. My friends in Christ, what is wrong?"

"You know what the hell is wrong!" Hernando bellowed. "We have been deceived by you, Padre! And by the Lord our God we will have our vengeance!"

"Vengeance is mine, sayeth the Lord," the Jesuit reminded them.

"Enough, damn you!" Hernando shouted, drawing back a clenched fist.

"No," Miguel cried, stepping between his brother and

the priest. "It will only bring shame and more misfortune if you strike him."

The fist shot forward and lights exploded behind Miguel's eyes. He momentarily lost consciousness, but the river revived his senses and he managed to jump back to his feet. His brother struck him again, this time with the flat of his hand. The blow spun him completely around, and he heard the priest cry out in protest and anger.

Miguel reached for his brother's sword, but Sergeant Ortega pinned it to the sandbar with his boot as his hand went to the knife at his side.

Hernando grabbed Ortega's arm, drew his dagger and said, "Lay a hand on my brother and I will slit your throat like the burro's."

Ortega's cheeks flushed the color of wine. He was a big, ruddy-faced man and said to be very, very good with both his sword and his dagger. For a moment Miguel felt the two men contest wills, and then Ortega's bended. "Of course," he said, yanking his arm free. "But what about the padre? He has some explaining to do, eh?"

Hernando relaxed and sheathed his dagger. Miguel hardly recognized his brother, who was bare-chested and streaked with dust and dried sweat. Hernando's hair was filthy, and the knees of his pants were torn and caked with dirt. He must have been digging all night for treasure.

Hernando said to the priest, "There is no treasure under the floors of Casa Grande, is there?"

"No," Castillo admitted. "But I have been telling you that since we left Mexico City."

"What else does he have to tell us!" one of the soldiers snarled.

"Shut up!" Hernando ordered, whirling about and taking a menacing step toward the soldier.

The man retreated, stark fear dominating his swarthy features. He was unarmed, as were most of his fellow soldiers. "Forgive me, Captain Santana."

"Speak again and I will cut out your stinking tongue!"

"Yes, my Captain!"

Hernando pivoted back to the padre. "Now," he said, "tell us where the treasure is *really* buried."

"How should I know?"

"Because you alone have read all of Father Kino's diaries and the records of his journeys."

"Father Kino always said that the Seven Lost Cities of Cibola were just legends. He believed that the only treasure to be found in New Spain was in the salvation of Indian souls."

"No!" Ortega growled. "I too have studied the records, and many of Kino's soldiers swear that the Cities of Cibola exist!"

"Only in their fevered imagination, my son."

"If you are so certain of this, why didn't you tell us!"

"I tried. Many times."

"But not very hard," Hernando argued, his eyes cold and unforgiving. "Not once, in all the time we have suffered this journey, have you ever spoken the entire truth. You said that there was no treasure ... yet your eyes and your expression always gave lie to your words."

"I cannot speak except with my tongue," the padre countered.

"That is not true," Hernando said, "as you know much better than I." He leaned in on Miguel. "And what about you, brother? Did you also deceive us?"

"No!" Miguel protested, tasting blood and hearing a loud ringing in his brain, as if he had placed his head under a cathedral bell. "I left the padre and came to dig for gold with the rest of you. Remember? But you had each claimed a room and the entire floor of Casa Grande, leaving me no place to dig. So I watched and then I took your sword and came to protect our padre."

Hernando studied him very closely, then dipped his chin with remembrance. His eyes flicked to the sword and he blushed with shame. "Give it back to me."

Miguel picked up the weapon and held it out with both hands. His brother would not meet his eyes but took

the sword, then wiped its blade on his ruined pants leg before jamming it into his scabbard. Turning back to the padre, Hernando said, "Did Father Kino ever go north in
search of the Seven Cities?"

"No. He knew they did not exist."

"How could he know that!"

The padre shrugged. "He knew. And remember, Captain, the great padre journeyed west, not north."

"I have forgotten nothing," Hernando said with bitterness. "And even if Kino never ventured north of this river,
we cannot forget that Francisco Vasquez de Coronado and
his expedition marched many leagues north. And before
him went Cabeza de Vaca, who told of the great wealth of
the Seven Cities."

The padre sat down heavily. He pulled up his robe
and stared at his discolored leg. Miguel blanched. When
he looked up, he could see that everyone was shocked.
The leg was so swollen that the piece of white bone was
no longer a protrusion. It had been completely engulfed by
the discolored flesh.

Hernando towered over the padre, ignoring Miguel's
accusing eyes. "Father," he demanded, "did De Vaca lie?"

For a long moment the padre stared at his leg. Then
he looked up at the captain and said, "If I told you again
that there are no Lost Cities of Cibola, would you believe
me, Captain Santana? Would any of you who are con-
sumed by greed finally be willing to believe me?"

Hernando studied the padre with such intensity that
even Miguel squirmed. Finally, his brother gazed off toward the ring of dead black mountains and he clenched his
fists. "Father, perhaps it is God's will that we discover no
treasure in this cruel wilderness. And that I may never
equal the glory of Spanish giants like Francisco Pizarro,
who gave the Spanish throne the wealth of the Incas of
Peru. Or the magnificent soldier Hernando Cortez, con-
queror of the Aztecs of Mexico and whose name I carry
and cherish. Maybe it is God's will that I do not share
such glory."

"Bloody glory," the padre dared to say.

Hernando was caught up in emotion. Miguel knew that his brother worshiped both Pizarro and Cortez, just as the padre worshiped his predecessor, Father Kino. Hernando's eyes misted as he stared out at the line of cobalt mountains which seemed to hang over the waves of heat. "Padre, I don't ask for glory for myself, but for my king and for God!"

Castillo started to say something, but Hernando, his voice shaking, blurted, "Father, this land is just too big to be without mountains of gold and silver. Or at least a few outcroppings of jade, turquoise, and other precious stones!"

"That might be true," the padre gently admitted, "but if you go north and search for it, you and your soldiers will die."

"Then we shall all soon stand before the throne of God."

Hernando addressed his angry, exhausted men. "Listen to me. We came in search of gold and silver, precious stones and rare works of art from an ancient civilization of people who once built places like Casa Grande. But the people abandoned this place for better lands. If we discover these new lands, then we can still have their treasures."

"Captain Santana," the padre interrupted, his voice a soft entreat, "if you go on, you *will* die! Stay here and help me find the Pima that were converted by Father Kino! Become a servant of the Lord and do His work! If you do—"

"Then we will be *poor*!" Escobar spat.

This opinion was loudly echoed by the others. There was no doubt that the soldiers would not remain at Casa Grande, nor were they willing to call off their search for ancient treasures.

"Will you bless us in our travels?" Hernando asked.

"I will."

"Then do so," he replied, "for we rest this day and

leave you behind this night. We will follow this great river northeast to its headwaters."

"Why?" Miguel blurted.

For a long moment his brother seemed lost in thought as his eyes drank in the dark mountains cloaked in layers of heat. At last Hernando said, "I don't know. It is just a hunch."

"A hunch? You would risk all our lives on nothing but a hunch?" Ortega repeated, his voice openly contemptuous.

"It is more than just a hunch, Sergeant. If you were an ancient people, which way would you go?"

When Ortega shrugged and no one else answered, Hernando continued. "As anyone can see, a great civilization built Casa Grande and then abandoned it. Why? I think either because stronger enemies drove them out, or perhaps the river threatened to go dry in times long past. That being the case, if we were those people, it seems logical that we would seek the headwater of the river instead of following it into a dry sink and perhaps dying of thirst."

Hernando looked around, seeking agreement. It came quickly as his men began to nod their heads. Even the argumentative Escobar said, "That makes good sense, Captain."

"Of course it does. So the people who fled these ruins went in search of grass and water. And we all know that rivers start in mountains. So there must be high, green mountains to the northeast, and that is where I think we will begin to find the Seven Lost Cities of Cibola."

"Your words show wisdom," Sergeant Ortega admitted. "What kind of fools would go west? Don Juan de Onate went west in 1604, and he almost died. He said there was nothing that way except another great river that this one feeds."

"That is true," Hernando replied. "As you, I have also read his accounts. There are no cities of gold to the west."

"Northeast, then," Ortega said, nodding his head in agreement.

Miguel's attention had been shifting back and forth between the priest and his brother. His loyalty was badly torn. But the taste of blood in his mouth and the ringing of his ears gave him the courage to say, "I will remain with Father Castillo."

"No!" Hernando shouted.

"Yes."

Hernando's face darkened with anger. His hand fell to the hilt of his sword. "You are under my orders! I command you to march north with us!"

"And if I do not?"

"You know the penalty for disobeying an officer of the king's army."

Miguel *did* know the penalty—it was death. But when he looked down at Father Castillo and the leg that, baring a miracle, would soon kill him, death seemed almost worth the disobedience. Besides, Miguel was not sure that his brother would really carry out the full penalty. On the other hand, he had not the true courage to find out. Ashamed of himself, Miguel knelt beside the priest. "What shall I do, Father!"

"Go with them, Miguelito. I will be waiting for your return."

"You will die first!"

Castillo shrugged his thin shoulders. "If it is God's will, then I will die. We all must die sometime. That is how we enter the Kingdom of Heaven."

"I will spend the day hunting food for you," Miguel vowed, to assuage his guilt. "And then I will leave you a musket."

The Jesuit smiled. "And what would I do with a musket? Kill a living creature?"

"Just a snake if it tried to bite you."

The padre shook his head. "I will not use musket, sword, or dagger."

"Then you deserve to starve before your blood turns to poison and you go crazy with pain," Escobar sneered. "Then you can scream yourself to death crying out to God!"

Something snapped in Miguel and he threw himself at the soldier. His fist caught the larger man square in his big nose and it broke with a sickening pop. Blood cascaded into Escobar's beard. The soldier's hand stabbed for his dagger and he would have skewered Miguel, except that Hernando's own knife flashed.

Escobar cried out in pain and grabbed a deep, gushing wound in his forearm. Hernando could have taken the sergeant's life, but instead he wheeled about and marched back up the river with his soldiers slogging along behind, while Escobar tried to stop the flow of his blood.

"I will kill him!" the soldier choked.

"Then I will kill *you*," Miguel vowed.

Escobar turned his face toward Miguel. It was so mottled with hatred that even the priest looked quickly away. A moment later the soldier was staggering into the willows back toward Casa Grande.

Later that afternoon, when the sun was very high and there was no breeze, Miguel and the padre lay under the shade of a cottonwood tree, up to their chins in the Gila River. Miguel could feel the desert's terrible heat on his face, but the river was a balm, causing him to say, "Father, this must be what Heaven is like, and the desert is like Hell."

"No, Miguelito, Heaven is much better than this, and Hell infinitely worse than any desert."

"How do you know?"

"Because the Holy Bible tells us so."

Miguel was silent for a long while. He watched as leaves from the cottonwood trees floated past. Occasionally he saw the river ripple to the passage of a big, lazy trout or catfish. "Soon, I will catch a great fish for you."

"I would be grateful. Do you have hook and thread?"

"No."

"Then how can you catch fish?"

"I don't know," Miguel admitted. "Who would have thought there would be any in such bad country?"

"I have a needle and thread. God willing, I will catch my own fish when you are gone."

"Then I will kill you some lizards and make you a rabbit trap."

"The fish will be good enough," the priest decided. "Either way, I will die before long."

Miguel glanced sharply at the man. "We need you, Father. You should not be so ready to die. It would not be fair to the rest of us."

Father Castillo's fingertips brushed Miguel's cheek. "You are a very smart boy, Miguelito. I shall watch over you if I reach Heaven before you die. But you must not die until you have found the Pima and explained that God has forgiven them their sins, even for killing so many of Father Kino's saintly priests."

"They will probably kill me."

"No." The Jesuit removed his beloved crucifix. "Here."

Miguel recoiled. "I could not take it while you live! If I did that, I would always feel that I rushed your death."

Castillo surprised him by nodding with understanding. "Very well. After you are gone, if the fishing is not so good and I am about to die, I will do so at this spot in this river. But first, I will take this crucifix and place it here, like this."

Miguel watched, fascinated, as the Jesuit inserted the crucifix into the muddy bank beside the river, with the chain dangling in the current, dully gleaming through the water like a string of tiny gold nuggets.

"Father," he said, turning his eyes away, "could we talk about other things?"

"Such as?"

"Do you think my brother and his soldiers will ever find treasure?"

"You already know my answer."

"Then ... then do you think I will live to return to Casa Grande and then to Mexico City and one day to Spain?"

"No, Miguelito, I do not."

Miguel's heart sank and his voice betrayed his emotion when he choked, "Then I will die out there someplace?"

"Yes, but you will die well, and first you will live long."

"But I want to see my family in Cadiz!"

"I am sorry."

"I want—"

"Shhh," the padre gently scolded. "You should always ask what *God* wants."

"I know," Miguel replied. "I know, but—"

"You will be happy again," Father Castillo promised. "I feel sure of it. I have prayed very hard for you."

"And your prayers always come true?"

"Almost never," the priest admitted, "but this time, I think they will."

"I am afraid to die. That is why I could not find the courage to stay with you. When my brother touched the handle of his sword, my heart shrank to the size of a bean. I am ashamed."

"Do not be ashamed."

"I am a coward. If I live through this, I will not become a soldier like Hernando."

"You are not a coward, but I am glad that you will not become a soldier. Now, enough of this bad talk."

Miguel nodded, but an unbidden question came to his lips. "Padre?"

"Yes?"

"Do you believe that my own brother would have killed me for disobedience?"

The padre shook his head. "No, of course not."

Miguel sighed with relief. He believed Father Castillo and he was very glad. "I am going to take a nap now. Hernando says we will march all this night."

"Go to sleep, Miguelito."

"Only for a little while. Then I will make you some rabbit traps, just in case you tire of fish before I can return."

"Thank you," Father Castillo replied, leaning his head back against the mud beside the crucifix and closing his sunken, bloodshot eyes.

_____ Chapter _____

FOUR

M iguel stood among the soldiers in the fading light
of day. No one was talking and the air was op-
pressive and still very, very hot. In this country,
only the river breathed life into a man. A few hours before, there had been a very serious argument among the
soldiers about whether or not they should continue to wear
their heavy bullhide vests and other protection that cooked
their hearts like acorns in an oven.

Hernando had been insistent that his soldiers retain their
vests which he hoped would deflect Indian arrowheads, but
the old-style metal helmets had been replaced by all manner
of improvised head gear. Many of the soldiers had decided
to simply wrap their skulls in bandannas. Others more skill-
ful had fashioned crude leather hats that would also shield
their eyes and their faces. A few had taken the lead of Father Castillo and had woven hats made of leaves and
branches.

Muskets had been cleaned and reloaded. Swords and
daggers dulled by digging had been sharpened on river
stones. Now that it had been decided to follow the Gila
River, the value of the skin water bags was greatly dis-
counted, yet every man was warned to keep his bag full.

And now, as they huddled in the shadowed protection of Casa Grande, all eyes turned to follow the river marked by a thin, wavery line of cottonwoods and palo verde that meandered beyond sight into the desert. And far, far beyond the low, hot valley floated a lavender apparition of hostile mountains. It stretched the imagination that such mountains could ever be large-shouldered and tall enough to support lakes, grassy meadows, and pines.

Miguel stood apart, watching the others. When they had left Mexico City, he had yearned to be one of these brave and hardy soldiers. His heart had swelled with pride to see his own brother lead them north. He had dearly wished that he could describe to his parents how magnificent Hernando appeared at the head of their expedition. It would make them so proud. But now the mule was dead, the burros dead too. And the padre was dying and there was no wealth at Casa Grande. Now Miguel was thankful that his mother and father could not know how pathetic and desperate this expedition had become. Even more, how his heart had turned against his brother and the others who had disgraced themselves in their unbridled lust for buried treasure.

"Miguel?"

He turned to see his brother motioning him into the shadowed interior of Casa Grande. Miguel entered the ruins and followed Hernando, stepping around the gaping potholes ripped out of floor by the soldiers. The excavations defiled the ruins, made them seem less noble.

Hernando led the way far back into one of the small rooms and then he made sure that they could not be overheard before he said, "We must talk."

"Why?"

"Because there are things you must know," Hernando whispered, head swiveling back and forth, eyes darting about like nesting swallows just driven to flight.

For an unguarded moment Miguel saw his brother for the despairing and unsure man he had become. It was a shock. Hernando was still in his twenties, yet he seemed to have become old just in the last twenty-four hours. Or maybe his brother had become old soon after they had entered this desert, and he had not noticed.

"Listen to me," Hernando began, his voice betraying his desperation, "and listen well. It is more likely than not that there isn't any treasure or Lost Cities of Cibola, but I can't tell the soldiers that or they would kill us."

Miguel had been expecting a lecture, not an admission. Surprise, even shocked, he said, "But if you believe this, why did you agree to lead the party north in the first place?"

"Why not? I was offered a large sum of money by a rich and greedy Spanish official currying favor with our king. What was there to lose? Perhaps I would find Cibola and fame like Pizarro or Cortez. And if not, my payment still awaits my return in a Mexico City bank. The payment is in *both* our names."

"Both, but why?"

"Because my life is in greater danger than yours, Miguel. If something should happen to me, then you must return to Spain and provide for our mother and father. Promise me this!"

"I promise. But Father Castillo does not believe I will ever return."

Hernando scoffed. "Father Castillo is a dying priest. Pain clouds his thinking. He welcomes death and cannot understand why we do not."

Miguel wanted to argue, but his brother's words were true, so he kept his silence.

"The litter bearers have told me," Hernando began, "that Father Castillo is going to give you his crucifix when he dies."

Miguel's eyes widened. He took a step back, hoping that his first thought was to prove unworthy of Hernando.

Hernando grabbed his arm, fingers biting flesh. "Is that not true!"

"It is, but I do not want the cross!"

"Don't be a fool! Someone will take it for it is worth

a small fortune. Or would you rather some Indian dressed in a rabbitskin breechcloth use it to scrape his bloody pelts?"

"Of course not, but—"

"You must take it as the gift it was intended to be before we leave tonight," Hernando said forcefully.

"No!"

"Then I will take it for you. If we do not, one of the soldiers will kill the padre and take it for himself."

Miguel had started to say something in anger, but his brother's words stopped him cold. "They would *do* such a thing?" he breathed.

"What do you think?" Hernando said, folding his arms across his bare chest.

Miguel twisted away in shame because he knew that men like Captain Ortega and Pablo Escobar would kill the padre for the precious crucifix.

"It is only by taking it now that you can save Father Castillo's life and be sure to have the crucifix for yourself. It is what the priest wants, is it not?"

"It is, but—"

"In Spain, it will be worth ten times what it would bring in Mexico City. Then we would both have something out of this misery."

Miguel's mind reeled. How could he explain that the padre wanted him to have the crucifix, but only in order to first impress and then to convert the Pima Indians?

There was a long pause, and then Hernando said, "The priest will die before we return, Miguel. Better he gives the crucifix to you, as is his wish, than it be taken in a moment of unspeakable horror."

"You are right."

Hernando's voice softened. "Of course I am. Now go down to the river and accept the padre's precious family heirloom. While you are gone, I will tell the men that the Castillo family crucifix is in your hands and, if it is taken from you, I will not only kill but also torture the thief."

Miguel dipped his chin with understanding. He had

already said his good-byes to Father Castillo several hours earlier, but now he would say them again. He started to turn, but Hernando's words stopped him in his tracks. "If the men mutiny, you must not try to help me but must instead run for your life. You are quick and strong. It would be your only chance."

Miguel was appalled by this suggestion. He shook his head back and forth emphatically. "Hernando! How many times have you yourself told me that life is nothing without honor?"

"The words of an idle idealist. I was wrong, Miguel. There is no dishonor in saving your own life when to forfeit it would gain nothing. And if you cannot agree, then at least you would be saving the padre's precious gift fit for our king's crown."

Realizing that Hernando's words were true and from his heart, Miguel left his brother. When he passed outside, one of the soldiers started to follow him, but Hernando's sharp command brought the man back to the ruins. Miguel did not hear the resulting conversation, but he knew it would not be pleasant.

"Father?" he called into the darkness made almost black under the spreading limbs of the cottonwoods and the denser palo verde. "Father Castillo?"

He peered ahead through the pale moon and starlight until he thought he saw the place where he and the priest had prayed together before saying good-bye. A great horned owl floated silently from the dark canopy of a cottonwood to follow the Gila River west.

"Father? Father!"

The priest was gone.

Miguel rushed to the Jesuit's resting place and dropped to his knees in the soft, riverbank mud. He shook his head in confusion. Cupped his hands to his mouth, head swinging back and forth, eyes probing the dark shadows. "Father Castillo!"

There was no answer. Panic set in. Miguel ran his fingers over the mud, and then he found the square hole punched by the base of Castillo's beloved crucifix.

"Holy Mary, mother of God!" he breathed. "Did they already murder you!"

Miguel's first and overpowering impulse was to race back to Casa Grande and his brother. He started to rise, but froze in the grip of a terrible thought. What if . . . no! Hernando would not do such a thing, or be any part of . . . murder?

Miguel jumped up and ran a short way up the riverbank, softly calling for the priest. There was no answer except for the distant, mournful howl of a coyote. He ran back downriver, eyes straining to see a footprint in the mud that would tell him the priest might have suspected his life and the crucifix were in danger and had taken it upon himself to hide until the soldiers had marched away to find Cibola. But the light was poor, the damned moon just a yellow wedge in the sky. What could he do?

Miguel staggered back to the place he had said goodbye to the padre and collapsed to his knees. He buried his face in his hands and wept uncontrollably. He was sure that poor Father Castillo had met a terrible death and that the crucifix had been stolen.

Miguel did not know how long he cried, but only that it was Hernando who laid his hand on his shoulder and said, "So, the unspeakable has already been committed against our dying padre."

Miguel's head jerked up and he stared at his brother, not knowing or caring if Hernando could see the accusation in his face. He tried to speak, but could not.

"Miguel," Hernando said gently. "I was afraid this might happen."

"Maybe Father Castillo was afraid also," Miguel finally blurted, "and he decided to leave until we were gone so that no one could steal his crucifix and take his life."

"Maybe," Hernando said after a long hesitation. "But I don't think so. Not with that broken leg."

Miguel's mind raced. Hope bit into despair. "But if

poor Father Castillo dragged himself out into the current, it would carry him downriver a little ways."

"I don't believe that. Father Castillo would never slink away like a frightened dog. He did not fear death and would not have abandoned us to save himself."

Miguel's spirits shattered about his feet like pottery. "No," he said bitterly. "he would not."

Hernando pulled him to his feet. "We will search every soldier and find the padre's murderer when we find his cross."

It was all that Miguel could do to nod his head. He didn't care about the crucifix, but the thought of someone murdering a dying priest was so abhorrent that his mind burned for revenge.

"Come on!" Hernando ordered, grabbing him by the arm and propelling him back downriver. "We *will* find the murderer, and this night he will wish he had never been born!"

Miguel knew that Father Castillo would not have wanted revenge or torture, even to his own murderer. But there were some outrages so heinous that they demanded justice and defied the Bible's lesson of the infinite forgiveness.

And this, Lord help them, was exactly such an outrage.

"Hernando!" Miguel called, running after his brother. "How are you going to do this thing?"

"I am still the captain. I will just order them to line up, and then I will gather their muskets as if it is an inspection."

"At night?"

Hernando stopped. He frowned and shook his head. "You are right. They would be very suspicious."

"They would revolt and refuse."

"Never mind," Hernando said with a wave of casual dismissal. "I will think of something."

He started to turn, but then hesitated. "Miguel. If this is my time to die, then it is your time to run. Head downriver. They would not follow if they know you do not have the crucifix."

Miguel's throat swelled. "I couldn't just—"

"Do as I say," Hernando ordered, but there was no authority or heat in his words before he turned and trudged on toward Casa Grande.

"Why did you hit me in the face so hard yesterday?" Miguel called.

"Because," Hernando muttered, "you deserved it. And besides, it is better if the men think we do not like each other."

Miguel did not see why this was true, but realized that this was not the time to argue. He wished he had a musket or at least a sword like his brother, although he was unskilled in the use of either and would not have stood up well against a trained soldier like Sergeant Ortega or even a man like Pablo Escobar, who prided himself upon the mastery of weapons.

Miguel's heart was pounding, not from exertion, but from fear and worry. "Hernando, I want to do something to help."

Hernando stopped. He drew his sword with his right hand, then his dagger with his left. "Here," he said, extending the dagger to Miguel. "But put it under your waistband and don't use it except to save your life. Promise me this!"

Miguel nodded because he did not trust his voice.

"Just stay back," Hernando cautioned as they approached the ancient adobe ruins and the waiting soldiers.

Miguel did stay back, but not far. He was so scared that he could not have spit.

"Line up for arms inspection!" Hernando ordered, his sword still in his fist.

The men stared at him but no one moved to obey.

"You heard me!"

Sergeant Ortega stepped out of the shadows. His musket was resting in his hands. "Captain," he said, "we must have misunderstood the order. Surely you didn't mean—"

"I want an arms inspection formation!"

The musket shifted in Ortega's hands. "Captain," he grated, "be reasonable! You couldn't even see—"

Hernando's sword whistled through the air and Ortega cried out in pain as the musket and the tip of his thumb dropped to the dirt. He swore and dropped to one knee.

"Any more of you that want to question my authority!" Hernando challenged.

The soldiers formed a line.

Hernando visibly relaxed. "Miguel, collect the muskets for my inspection."

Miguel collected them. Only Pablo Escobar held his musket longer than was necessary, so that Miguel had to use force to wrestle it away.

When the order was carried out, Miguel stepped back. He could feel hatred radiate like heat from the suspicious soldiers. Sergeant Ortega was back on his feet, his left hand soaking a handkerchief with blood, his face twisted with pain.

"You have made a bad mistake, *Captain!*" he choked.

In reply, Hernando raised his sword in a threatening manner, but Ortega spat on the ground in contempt. The two men glared at each other, and it was Hernando's eyes that fell away.

He retreated a few steps and squared his shoulders. Miguel could scarcely breathe, and the night was filled with demons, real and imagined. "My soldiers," Hernando said in a calm voice, "there is among you the murderer of Father Castillo."

This statement visibly rocked the soldiers. Sergeant Ortega's jaw dropped. "Captain, how can this be!"

"That is my question," Hernando said. "I believe that the padre was murdered for his valuable crucifix. I will search every man until I find it."

Ortega ground his teeth with pain and was squeezing the bandage and his thumb so hard that the tendons in his neck stretched like the strings of a Gypsy's guitar. "I will help you, Captain. But if no crucifix is found, then—"

"Then it means that the murderer was smart enough to bury or hide it until it could be found later," Hernando snapped.

Ortega did not accept that and neither did the soldiers, who had begun to grumble, each trying to work the next into a rebellious action against the captain.

The inspection was tense and very thorough. One by one the soldiers were ordered to remove their uniforms, even down to their shoes and stockings. Every article they wore or carried was meticulously examined; even their bota bags were squeezed to ensure that the crucifix was not hidden in water. It was a long and grueling inspection and it lasted well past midnight. When it was finished, the men stood naked to the moonlight, fists knotted, eyes burning with outrage.

"Who would murder a priest?" Pablo Escobar demanded with fists knotted like Thor's mighty hammers. "There is no crucifix among us!"

"And no priest either," Hernando replied.

"And no *leader*, by God!"

At that moment Miguel knew that Escobar was going to try and end his brother's life. A shout of warning rose to his throat, but it was too late. Escobar was a treacherous and powerful man. His fist came up and his rigid fingers speared into Hernando's eyes. Hernando screamed and slashed blindly with his sword, but Escobar was already well inside the killing arc of the weapon and driving his captain to the earth.

Sergeant Ortega didn't move to interfere as the big man grabbed Hernando by the hair and bashed his skull against the rocky ground. Miguel began to move forward, and without thought a dagger filled his hand. He was young and very quick. The dagger's blade had been freshly sharpened. It slid very easily between Pablo

Escobar's ribs and did not come to rest until it was buried to the hilt.

Escobar's spine bent like a wishbone. He turned his face up to the moon as if to utter a prayer, but from his lips instead poured blood and a strangled curse. Then the soldier shivered and toppled forward.

"Hernando!" Miguel cried, shoving the body aside. He started to turn to see if Ortega was going to kill him, but someone struck him behind the ear and even the moonlight died.

When Miguel awoke, it was broad daylight and he was lying on his back squinting up at the flaming sun. He groaned because the pain was sharp in his head. He sat up and his vision whirled around in slow motion. He could hear the voices of the soldiers, and then he saw two pairs of boots.

He looked up to see his brother, and beside him, Sergeant Ortega. His brother's eyes were blindfolded. Hernando's hand rested on his sergeant's sleeve.

"Hernando!" Miguel cried, struggling to his feet.

"I'm all right," Hernando said, though his beaten voice mocked his words. "My eyes will clear soon."

Miguel looked to the sergeant. Ortega just shrugged his shoulders. "Time will tell. I am no doctor."

"Last night I could still see the moon," Hernando whispered. "But when the sun came out, it hurt my eyes so bad that I thought they were on fire. We will travel at night when I can see."

"But Hernando, we—"

"We will leave tonight," Ortega said. He took Hernando's hand from his own sleeve and roughly slapped it against Miguel's arm. "He is your brother."

"And your captain!"

"Yes, and that is why he still lives," Ortega said, before he turned and swaggered back into the shade of Casa Grande.

"Take me to the river," Hernando whispered.

Miguel was only too glad to follow that order. He was so thirsty that he could not even swallow, and only the Gila River—blessed by poor Father Castillo—yet had the power to ease the pain in his head. But as they walked, Miguel could not help but look at his brother, and tears filled his eyes.

"What will become of you?" he choked.

"I will regain my sight," Hernando promised, hand viselike upon Miguel's arm. "And then we will find Cibola."

"What of the crucifix?"

"It is lost. I would not be surprised if Ortega is behind all of this. I will find out later. But for now, we must just thank the Lord our God that we are still alive."

"Yes," Miguel said through teeth clenched against pain.

"You killed Pablo Escobar before he cracked my skull," Hernando said with grim satisfaction.

"I . . . I guess that I did."

"You make me proud!" Hernando said passionately a moment before his foot caught a rock that caused him to stumble so badly that he almost fell.

Miguel caught his brother and wrapped his arm around Hernando's waist. When he looked up at the bandanna, he could see that tears were also running down his brother's cheeks. Maybe they were the weeping of eyes poked blind. But then a small sob escaped from Hernando's throat and Miguel knew for sure that his brother was only crying.

Chapter
FIVE

With the sun low in the west, Sergeant Ortega led the men toward the Gila River, and then, because it was so choked with cottonwood, palo verde, and willows, they flanked it and marched east. Miguel kept turning his head back to stare at Casa Grande and the eroded remains of the other ancient ruins. The sun made them all glow like polished copper, and it struck Miguel very forcibly that this place had always witnessed men arriving with hope and leaving with disappointment. Why had the ancient peoples abandoned this place? Had they once planted fields of maize, beans, and corn where cactus and mesquite now grew? Miguel could see no signs of canals or dikes which would divert the Gila River to agriculture, and yet he knew there once must have been hundreds of acres of irrigated fields and pastures.

All gone. Like Father Castillo. At the thought of his dear friend, Miguel choked with pain. No doubt the padre would have died of his leg wound, and perhaps the quick strike of an assassin's knife would have seemed like a prayer answered in the last moment of his life. He had been in great pain, and yet . . . yet Miguel remembered how they had laughed and made their confessions to each other. The padre had been very lenient yesterday, almost as if he sensed that he was about to enter the Kingdom of God.

But still, to kill a priest was a terrible thing. Miguel stared at the line of soldiers up ahead, wondering if the assassin had been Pablo Escobar and if he had buried the crucifix someplace at Casa Grande. If so, it might be centuries—or an eternity—before that cross was found.

Beside him, Hernando grunted with pain as his leg brushed a cactus. "Forgive me," Miguel said, pulling his dark thoughts back to the care of his brother.

"You are very quiet," Hernando said. "Are you thinking of death?"

"Yes, but not of my own. Of the padre's."

"He is much happier now," Hernando said. "If anything, we should envy him."

"I know, but the idea of him being murdered fills me with more grief than I can bear."

"I worry about my eyes," Hernando confessed. "I *must* have my sight again, otherwise . . ."

Hernando did not finish the sentence, but Miguel knew what he had meant to say. As the sun dropped lower, Miguel could feel his brother's dark despair as they struggled to keep up with the soldiers. His brother's hand rested on his shoulder like a severed claw, a thing brittle and without life.

All day long, none of the soldiers spoke a word to them, but their eyes mirrored hatred. It was easy to see why. Captain Santana had humiliated them with his accusation about the priest and then had been proven a fool when no crucifix had been discovered. Moreover, Pablo Escobar, while a very cruel and brutish man, had been an exceptional fighter, one whose courage had great value, especially if they were attacked by Indians.

Miguel knew that stabbing Escobar to death had not impressed anyone. It had been, after all, an act of desperation and one requiring no skill. Anyone, even a woman, could have driven a sharp dagger into Escobar's back and lived to tell the story. So now the soldiers hated both the Santana brothers and considered them a liability. The wonder of it to Miguel was that Sergeant Ortega had not ordered both brothers to be put to the sword.

Hernando tripped over a young barrel cactus and swore in his helplessness. He pushed the bandanna up from his ruined eyes and tried to open them. Miguel bit back a gasp of shock to see that the eyes were bleeding and suppurating. He looked away quickly.

"It is that bad, huh?"

"Not so bad."

"You are a worse liar than Father Castillo," Hernando grunted. "But when night comes, I will wash these eyes in the Gila River. Then I will raise them to see the moon and stars again. Each day they will get better."

Miguel forced himself to look back into his brother's eyes. "Put the bandanna back down," he said. "You must be careful."

"They burn," Hernando said. "I can feel them leaking. I try to roll them in my head, but the pain—"

"Give them rest," Miguel said, helping his brother pull the bandanna down again. "At least until it is dark."

"Where is my map?"

"The sergeant has it."

"Good. At least he knows how to read a map, not that it is necessary if we are going to follow this river."

Miguel said nothing, but tromped on in the fading light. The soldiers were a good two hundred yards up ahead and steadily widening the gap. As darkness fell, the moonlit mountains became luminous.

"Miguel?" Hernando asked as the first star appeared. "Who do you think killed the priest for his crucifix?"

"I don't know." In truth, Miguel did not even want to think about it.

"I think it was Pablo Escobar," Hernando said. "I think he is the only man that evil. And I think that is why he tried to blind me, so that I could never find where he had hidden the crucifix."

"Maybe."

"If we return, we will search hard for it. First along the river and then in Casa Grande. He must have buried it there."

"I suppose."

"You don't sound very interested," Hernando said, turning his blindfolded face toward Miguel. "If you do not want the crucifix back, then I will gladly take it."

"I am only concerned with getting us both out of this desert hell alive," Miguel snapped. "I cannot think of money we might not live to spend."

A wry smile formed on Hernando's mouth. "You should not give up on us so easily. When I can see again, I will take command, and then things will be much better."

"Of course," Miguel said, trying to sound as if he believed this could happen.

"What do we have for food?"

"Dried fruit and beef. A sack of parched corn."

"You need to shoot a snake or a rabbit," Hernando said. "Do you have a musket?"

"No."

"You must get a musket. What about Pablo's musket?"

"One of the others, Mendez, I think, his musket was broken and he took Pablo's for himself."

Hernando swore in anger. His hand tightened on Miguel's shoulder. "Mendez only looks tough. I will order him to give you the musket."

"He won't do that," Miguel warned.

"He must!"

"Yes, Captain," Miguel muttered as he carefully guided his brother around the sharp fingers of a spreading ocotillo.

"Miguel, you worry me," Hernando said. "I must be able to count on you."

Miguel stopped, his face burning with anger. He threw his brother's hand off his shoulder. Watched as

Hernando took a faltering step and then tripped over mesquite and fell on his face.

"What the hell are you doing!" Hernando shouted at the earth.

"Damn you! You worry *me*! And what do you think I did last night before Pablo Escobar cracked your skull like a walnut!"

Hernando pushed his bandanna up from his eyes and blinked redly. His hand lifted in supplication. "Of course I know what you did."

"Say it!"

"Say what? Miguel, I—"

"Say . . . say thank you for saving my life, probably at the cost of your own."

"All right. Thank you!"

"Jesus," Miguel whispered, watching the shadowy silhouettes of vanishing soldiers. "Why are we torturing ourselves?"

Hernando's hand banged against Miguel's leg. He grabbed it like a rope and clung to it. "Miguel! I am the *captain*! I am the leader. And just as soon as I can see again—"

"And if you never see again?" Miguel asked, surprised by the cruelty of his question.

Hernando froze. His face wilted and he balled his fist and slammed it to the dirt and rocks. "If I cannot see again, then you leave me to die in this accursed desert and return to Casa Grande. Find the crucifix and then try to make it back to Mexico City where my money awaits. Then depart New Spain forever."

Miguel hated himself, but he nodded in agreement.

"Will you do that?"

"Yes, except that I would not leave you to die out here," Miguel said, helping his brother back to his feet. "Never!"

Hernando threw his arms out blindly and hugged Miguel with all his strength. He whispered, "It was a mistake for me to send for you from Mexico City. A tragic

mistake. I should never have been so foolish. If we both
die—"

"Come on," Miguel said roughly. "You still have
your sword and I have your dagger. We will see this thing
out. Who knows, maybe we will find so much gold in the
Gila River that the Seven Cities of Cibola will look like
poor Indian villages."

"Ha!" Hernando barked a laugh. "Maybe so!"

About midnight Sergeant Ortega gave in to the grum-
blings of his soldiers and they went to the river to rest and
refresh themselves.

"One hour," Ortega said. "If we are to find Cibola,
we must not delay."

The soldiers ran to the river, dark shadows vanishing
over the bank and throwing themselves headlong into the
blessed waters. It took Miguel and his brother almost another quarter of an hour to reach the water. The soldiers
were too tired to talk or joke. They just lay in the shallows
like beached porpoises and moaned with pleasure.

One, a man named Ruben Estrada, said, "If I could
stay right here—even without the promise of gold, wine,
or women—I would gladly do it. I hate the desert!"

Several men chuckled, others made coarse remarks
about Estrada coupling with river animals. Turning his
face from them all, Hernando silently removed his bandanna, then dipped his head underwater. Miguel watched
as starlight played across the rippling current. He could
see how his brother was gently scrubbing at his eyes,
washing them clean. He placed his hand on his brother's
leg and squeezed it to show that his prayers were with
Hernando. When his brother raised his head, the bandanna
was gone and water was streaming down his cheeks.

"Look," one of the soldiers said out of the corner of
his mouth, "our *captain* is trying to see again!"

The soldiers snorted and hooted with derision, but
Miguel paid them no attention. Every bit of his concentration was fixed on his brother, and when Hernando drew a
deep breath and opened his eyes, Miguel's breath stuck

like a bone in his throat. For a moment there was no sound; even the soldiers were fascinated with the drama.

Finally, it was Ortega himself who climbed to his feet and waded over to stand before Hernando. "Do you see me now, Captain?"

Hernando began to blink very rapidly. His face was strained and pale. His lips moved but made no sound.

"Captain! Do you see me?"

"Yes!" Hernando proclaimed, his voice rolling over the water. "Of course I see you."

Miguel grabbed and hugged his brother. "I *knew* you would see again!"

Hernando nodded rapidly. "Yes, but . . . but not clearly yet. It's just a little blurry still."

Ortega leaned forward and waved a hand back and forth just inches before Hernando's face. "How many fingers am I raising?"

Hernando lifted his whiskered chin and tried to smile. "Sergeant, I think we should rest here for another full day. And then—"

"How many!"

"Why . . . four."

Miguel shook his head. In the pale light of the moon and stars, anyone could see that the sergeant was holding up all five of his fingers.

"I don't think," Ortega said, unable to conceal his contempt, "that you should be making any decisions or be given a musket."

Hernando tried to bluster but failed. He dipped his head and drove his knuckles into the sockets of his eyes. His voice was a tortured curse against the calm water.

"We will leave soon," Ortega said to Miguel. "Try to stay up with my soldiers from now on."

"And if we cannot?"

Ortega's hand came to rest on his sword. He stared down at them and then waded back onto shore.

That night was one that Miguel would never forget, as he and his brother continued to struggle after the soldiers. They talked, really talked, as never before. Miguel was surprised to learn that his brother wished to retire from the king's service and return to Cadiz.

"I would marry a beautiful woman and raise horses and children," he said. "And goats. I like goats."

Miguel was amazed. "But I thought that you loved the danger and adventure found here in New Spain."

"So did I, until this past month. But now I understand why de Vaca finally became so bitter and disillusioned. I still long to be rich, but I don't care about this country or its Indians."

"Have you ever met one?"

"Not a Pima or Apache," Hernando admitted. "And if we don't see any on this expedition, so much the better."

"Father Castillo said the Pima were good people but that the Apache were devils."

"He said that?"

"Yes."

"He was right. Everything I have read about the Apache chills my blood. It is said that they can run a hundred miles in the hottest part of summer without water!"

"I don't believe that," Miguel said.

"I do. They are so tough that they prefer to walk instead of riding a horse. Did you know that they *eat* their horses?"

"Why?"

Hernando shrugged. "Maybe because horses starve in this hard country, and when they are too weak to be of use, the Apache eat them. It is a sad thing, no?"

"Very."

"Miguel?"

"Yes?"

"Father Castillo did not get you to make any foolish promises, did he?"

"Like what?"

"Like remaining in this hell and trying to convert the Indians."

Miguel frowned. "He asked me to use his cross to

show them the true way of the Lord. And yes, to stay and keep his crucifix so that its beauty might prove to the Indians that the Church is the only true teacher."

"That might be, but after hearing you, I am glad the crucifix was stolen and no longer binds you to that pledge."

Miguel frowned and thought on that one as they trudged along. He was not sure that he agreed. Losing a priest like Father Castillo, or such a beautiful crucifix, was serious indeed.

"Miguel, do you remember the money I have in the Mexico City bank?"

"Yes, and I know the bank because we went there several times, remember?"

"That's right. Well, you ask for the manager and he will have a letter from me. Open it up before him and—"

"Don't talk like this anymore," Miguel interrupted. "I don't like it."

"Like it or not," Hernando said quietly, "if my eyes do not clear, then I will never return to Mexico City or to Spain. I will die here in this wilderness."

"I will take care of you."

"You will run as I have ordered. One of us must return to let our parents know of our fates."

When Miguel said nothing, they fell into an uneasy silence. The desert stayed hot, and it was difficult to keep up with Ortega and the soldiers. Twice more they stopped to refresh themselves in the Gila River before continuing their march. Each time, Hernando washed his eyes and tried to see but failed.

When the sun lifted like a giant fire, the desert was washed in liquid gold and small creatures took to their burrows. Miguel squinted his eyes and felt the warmth of the sun on his cheeks. He looked sideways at his brother, who could not even see the sun.

As if reading his mind, Hernando said, "One, perhaps two more nights, Miguel. By then the river waters will have done their healing and I will see again. Just you wait."

"Yes," Miguel said with as much feeling as he could muster.

They marched until the heat and glare of the morning sun caused them to stagger with dizziness, and then Sergeant Ortega mercifully called a halt for the rest of the day. Miguel and Hernando were almost a mile behind and it took them a full hour to reach the others.

Sinking into the river and gasping with relief, Miguel pulled his brother into the shade of an overhanging cottonwood tree. The soles of his feet were on fire, and when he closed his eyes, white spots skittered back and forth behind his eyeballs like water bugs. He was famished, but so exhausted that he knew that he would not be able to move for at least an hour.

"Miguel."

Miguel opened his eyes to look up at Ortega. The sergeant's hands were on his hips and one hand was on his dagger. "Miguel, go set some rabbit snares."

"Why him?" Hernando shouted, struggling up to his feet and glaring slightly to one side of the sergeant. "I will order a few of the soldiers to set the snares."

"You will order nothing," Ortega hissed, throwing a leg and a stiff forearm at Hernando and spilling him back into the river.

Hernando cursed and tried to get up so that he could drag his sword from his scabbard. Miguel drew his dagger, but Ortega had anticipated that and the tip of his sword touched Miguel's gullet.

"The rabbit traps, eh?" Ortega said in a soft, deadly voice. "Now."

Hernando cursed again, but Miguel, his voice trembling, stammered, "Yes, sir!"

He was gone before Hernando could protest, and he did not look back until he was on the riverbank. Then, turning to catch a glimpse of Ortega humiliating his brother, Miguel desperately wished he had suffered the sergeant's sword and died honorably.

Chapter

SIX

The soldiers rested under the shade of the trees all that day while Miguel set rabbit snares—useless because even rabbits were too smart to move in the heat. But a few of the soldiers did catch fish. That, coupled with an abundance of fat frogs, made a good meal, and everyone felt much better by nightfall. Everyone, that is, except Hernando, who acted dazed and locked into a pit of despair.

"Miguel, check your rabbit snares," Sergeant Ortega ordered at sunset, "and then follow along with your *captain*."

The way the sergeant used the word "captain" was so contemptuous that it evoked hoots from the soldiers. Miguel's hand quivered to pull his dagger and plunge it into Ortega's chest. Ortega must have sensed it, because he beckoned Miguel to draw his weapon.

"Come on," he said to everyone's amusement. "Rabbit boy, if you can't snare rabbits, what good are you except to lead a blind man through the wilderness?"

"You will rot in Hell for this cruel treachery!" Hernando raged. "The king will—"

"Make me a nobleman if I bring him treasures from

Cibola," Ortega said airily. He reached out and jabbed Miguel in the chest with his thick forefinger. "Go check the snares, rabbit boy. Then bring your captain along, like a puppy on a leash. If you do not hurry, we will leave you for the Apache!"

Hernando's curse was buried by the soldiers' laughter. He grew old before Miguel's eyes. Miguel decided at that moment that Sergeant Ortega would never return to Mexico City a rich man, but would die out in this hard country—one way or the other. If necessary, he would kill the sergeant in his sleep to punish him for his betrayal and cruelty.

At sunset a rabbit chanced into one of Miguel's looped snares. Miguel killed the terrified creature and then skinned it with his brother's dagger. It was a messy, unpleasant job, and when he returned to the vacated camp, Miguel dropped the rabbit's carcass into the dying campfire and cooked it well. All the time, Hernando said nothing, but sat beside the river with his head resting on his knees.

"We will eat this rabbit later," Miguel said, fishing it out of the fire with sticks and wrapping it in a leather pouch. "Come, we must hurry or we will lose them."

"They will follow the Gila because they are unable to think of anything else to do," Hernando said, allowing himself to be pulled to his feet. "Help me into the river, Miguel. I want to wash my eyes again."

"You just washed them a short time ago. Maybe—"

"Please."

Miguel helped his brother to edge of the river and sat down to watch another brilliant sunset transform the sky into a multicolored veil of spun silk. The few stretched cirrus clouds that were floating over the high desert floor melted like butter into the fading light. The moment the sun plunged into the horizon, there came a gentle breeze to caress the river and cool Miguel's face so pleasantly that he sighed with gratitude.

"I am ready," Hernando said, squinting to the emerg-

ing silhouettes of the saguaro cactus that stood like senti-
nels on the black-rocked slopes. "And I think I am starting
to see things again."

He pointed up at the heavens. "There! Isn't that a
first star?"

"It is," Miguel said, even though none had appeared.
"You *are* getting better."

Hernando squared his fine shoulders and raised his
chin. His voice sounded hopeful again. "It is this Gila
River! I believe that God heard poor Father Castillo bless
its waters before he was murdered. These waters will re-
store my sight, Miguel."

"We'd better go, Captain. The soldiers are already a
long way ahead of us, and we will have to work hard to
keep them within calling distance."

"If it were not for the fact that I expect to find a city
of gold, I would not even bother to follow them."
Hernando grunted. "Also, I have vowed to kill Ortega
when I can see him."

Miguel started to say that he too had vowed to kill
the sergeant but changed his mind. Hernando would object
out of both a sense of his own duty and the belief that his
young brother would fail and then be slaughtered.

"Come," Miguel said impatiently. "We must not let
them find all the treasure, eh?"

Hernando managed a smile as he laid his hand on
Miguel's shoulder and followed along beside. As the darkness deepened, he began to turn his head this way and
that, squinting and trying to see again. When the moon
rose higher, Miguel could see how intense was his brother's struggle. But he could also see Hernando's red and
terrible eyes, which filled him with sadness.

All that night they climbed steadily out of the lower
desert, so the morning found the Spaniards on a high plain
where the creosote brush and mesquite were much taller,
with an aqua hue. Miguel could also see many places
where dried tufts of grass awaited the next rains. Along
the river he began to notice oak, hackberry, and even syc-

amore, new varieties of trees that the lower deserts could not support. On the hills, the saguaro and prickly pear cactus stood taller and thicker, and at dawn Miguel saw what he was sure was a small band of mountain goats. Truly, he thought, they were leaving the worst part of this desert. Had they been crossing it in the heat of the day, the changes would not have been so dramatic, but having walked all night and seeing this new, gentler land, Miguel felt encouraged.

The day was born hot, but all the Spaniards could see, way off in the hazy blue vistas to the east, the outlines of a high mountain range. And though it was as yet only a dark line, the promise of cool forest and meadow lifted everyone's spirits.

"The people who left Casa Grande will be somewhere up in those great mountains," Sergeant Ortega predicted with confidence. "Probably in the Lost Cities of Cibola, where we will at last have our fortunes."

"How many days' march?" a soldier asked.

"Three days, maybe four," Ortega answered. He looked to Hernando. "What do you think, Captain? How far are those mountains?"

It was another cruel joke enjoyed by the soldiers at Hernando's expense, and it made Miguel's blood sizzle. Miguel and Hernando said nothing, however, as it was clear that any outburst on their part would result in further punishment and humiliation.

"Rabbit boy, make snares," Ortega ordered with a tone of mockery as some of the men set about baiting fishing lines with bugs and worms. "And this time, I want meat!"

Miguel glanced sideways at Hernando, wanting to let him know that it was all right, that they could endure this for now. But one look at his brother's face told Miguel that these insults were killing Hernando, as surely as a knife cut away pieces of flesh. Hernando had always been older and stronger. He could not bear the inability to protect his only brother from harm. His immense pride refused any compromise, no matter what the true circumstances.

"I will bring you rabbit," Miguel said, wishing he had poison to add for seasoning.

"See that you do," Ortega came over to stand beside Hernando. "Tell me, Captain, how are your eyes tonight?"

"Better."

"How many fingers do you see?" Ortega asked, holding up one hand and two fingers.

"Three."

Everyone laughed, especially Ortega, who said, "At least you are getting closer, Captain Santana. Maybe tomorrow night you will guess correctly for a change."

Hernando stiffened and turned to step into the river where it dropped off quite sharply. He fell headlong into the water amid howls of laughter. Miguel rushed forward, intending to grab his brother, but Ortega's sword flashed before him, cutting edge to his belly.

"This is Spanish steel, rabbit boy! Oppose it and it will slit you open like a ripe melon."

Miguel could actually feel that he had been cut and that a trickle of blood was running down into his pants. His heart was racing and he was sure that Ortega was going to open his trembling belly and spill guts into his cupped hands. He almost fainted with fear. He gasped for a deep breath and tried to keep his senses.

"Rabbit meat," the sergeant said in a soft, deadly voice. "Don't come back until you have it."

"Yes, sir."

"Don't *ever* come back," Ortega said, his meaning chillingly clear.

Miguel glanced at his brother, who was righting himself, hands dripping mud and torn reeds. "I'll be back soon, Hernando. Just . . . just be still!"

Hernando tried to speak, but his chin quivered and he struggled to keep from breaking. Finally, he nodded, squatted in the shallow water, and bowed his face to the current to splash water into his eyes.

"Tsk, tsk," Ortega said with amusement. "The way those two say good-bye, you'd think that they were *lovers*, not brothers."

The men crowed with laughter. Several suggested that Hernando and Miguel were *both* lovers and brothers. It was all that Miguel could do not to throw himself at them and end this mortification. Instead, he stumbled through the trees that lined the river and headed for the brush, in the hope of snaring a rabbit so that he could return to camp and not be left to die alone in the wilderness of New Spain.

Miguel was successful in snaring three jackrabbits that day, but at great cost to his flagging energy. Ortega made him clean and roast the carcasses and then serve them to the soldiers.

"You and your brother can have the head, the tail, and the long ears," Ortega said, devouring the steaming flesh.

Unlike the day before, Hernando was again wearing his bandanna. He turned to Ortega's voice and said, "The moment is coming, Sergeant, when you will live to regret treating me and my brother so unkind."

"Unkind? Ha! The wonder is that I have spared you at all! What good are either of you to us if we are attacked by the Indians? All you do is eat our food and slow our travel. If I were the great Cortez or Pizarro—your heroes—I would have had your throat slit back at Casa Grande."

"The way that you slit Father Castillo's throat?" Miguel recklessly blurted.

Ortega dropped the greasy rabbit leg he had been gnawing on and sprang to his feet. He drew his sword and rushed at Miguel, who rolled sideways to avoid being skewered. Miguel yanked his dagger free and backed to the river's edge. His knees were knocking but he was ready to die if only he could take Ortega with him.

"I ought to kill you for saying that," Ortega hissed.

"Why? It is the truth. Admit it!"

"I admit nothing!" Ortega roared, backing Miguel knee deep into the water.

"Where is Father Castillo's crucifix? Did you hide it in one of the holes you dug at Casa Grande? I know which ones are yours. I can find it."

Ortega lunged with the sword and its edge caught Miguel across the ribs. He gasped with pain and felt blood wash down his tunic, but knew that he had only been scratched. He surprised himself by stepping in and slashing upward with his dagger, catching Ortega on the forearm. The sword dropped from the sergeant's hand. Ortega lashed out with his boot and caved in the side of Miguel's knee. The boy cried out with pain and fell backward into the river.

"Miguel!" Hernando screamed, stomping and waving his arms in helpless rage. "Miguel!"

Miguel righted himself in the swift current. Sergeant Ortega had retrieved his sword. His arm was flowing with blood and his face was ashen.

"Shall we kill them both now!" a soldier cried, drawing his own sword.

"No!" Ortega shouted.

"But—"

"I have a better end for them in mind," the sergeant choked, motioning for one of his men to bind the wound. "If we are found by the Apache, I will trade them for our lives. I am told that the Apache enjoy seeing their captives die. They like to spend hours making their victims scream. It brings them more pleasure than a great Spanish bullfight. They would consider a boy and a blind man a good prize."

The soldiers grinned. Mendez, however, said, "But what if we see no Apache?"

Ortega snickered. "Then we will use them to pack out our gold, like burros, eh?"

The soldiers were in full agreement. Ortega walked over to Hernando and kicked his legs out from under him. Hernando fell hard but immediately bounced back to his feet. Doubling up his fists and charging forward, he was beaten by the soldiers until he collapsed in a heap beside the Gila.

"Stop it!" Miguel cried, coming out of the river with his drawn knife.

Ortega brandished his gleaming sword. "Throw the dagger to me and come out, rabbit boy. Come out or I will let them kill him."

Miguel threw down his dagger and rushed back to the bank, one eye on his poor brother and the other on the sergeant who raised his sword and then brought it whistling downward. Miguel's life passed before his eyes, and he prayed that death would come instantaneously. Instead of merciful oblivion, however, he felt searing pain, and he must have passed out, for when he opened his eyes, he was lying on his belly in the mud with his hands tied behind his back. He saw the soldiers sleeping under the trees.

"Hernando!" Miguel whispered.

Hernando grunted, and Miguel rolled over to look the other way and see his brother had also been tied hand and foot, half in and half out of the water. Hernando was close, and Miguel rolled to his side. The shadows from the trees told Miguel that it was very late in the afternoon, and when he looked closely at his brother, he saw something besides the hideous bruises on Hernando's face and neck. The bandanna had slipped down onto the bridge of Hernando's nose to reveal his eyes.

"Your eyes!" Miguel breathed in wonder. "They are clear!"

Hernando squinted hard, blinking like a bird. "Yes," he said in a very low voice. "I can see again. If Ortega holds his fingers up to my face, I will count and then bite them off."

Miguel twisted around to watch the sleeping soldiers.

"The fool did not even leave a sentry," Hernando said with contempt. "The Apache could come and kill them all in their sleep."

"We can escape!"

"Not yet."

"But why!"

"Shhh!"

"But—"

"Two reasons," Hernando interrupted. "First is that I *must* at least try to find one of the cities of gold."

"But there aren't any!" Miguel whispered. "I told you what—"

"I have to try! Besides, I will not leave until I have killed Ortega with my own hands after he tells us where he hid Father Castillo's crucifix."

"Damn the crucifix! We must save our lives right now!"

"Miguel, I can see your face and even the camp, but my vision is as if I am looking through water. In a day, two days at most, maybe I can see clearly enough to kill Ortega and take back my command."

"Let Ortega lead them to Hell!"

Hernando closed his eyes. "These are Spaniards. Disloyal to me, that is true. But they do not deserve to die under such a man as Ortega. Perhaps they can even redeem their honor."

Miguel thought his brother was talking crazy, but there could be no doubt about his sincerity. Arguing solved nothing. "So what do we do?"

"I wear the blindfold in the daytime and we pretend that our spirits are broken until the time is right. And then we kill Ortega and I will take command."

"The soldiers might kill us both."

Hernando managed a slight shrug of his shoulders. "If so, we will tell God that we were good and true men, friends of Father Castillo, eh? That ought to get us into Heaven."

Despite everything, Miguel grinned and so did his brother. It was craziness, true, but now that Hernando could see again well enough to fight for his own life, at least there was still hope for a little gold and a little glory.

Chapter

SEVEN

Fearing that Miguel would run away, Ortega did not allow him to leave camp but instead sent other soldiers to set rabbit snares. Miguel was left untied so that he could work and cook, but he was guarded constantly for the next few days as the expedition moved ever higher into foothills thick with pinion and juniper pines.

Despite being weary and noting increasing signs of Indians, the party's spirits were as elevated as the land they now passed through. The Gila River seemed clearer and colder, and the nights were blissfully cool. Just ahead loomed a vast mountain range, and they could all see that it was forested with lofty pines.

"That is where we will find the Seven Lost Cities," Ortega promised as they followed the Gila by day and slept peacefully beside her at night. "Who in their right mind would stay down below in that hellish desert when they could live up in those mountains?"

It was a question that no one could answer, and even though the expedition was exhausted from steadily climbing, they demonstrated an excitement that Miguel had not felt since their approach to Casa Grande.

Hernando wore his bandanna every daylight hour to

convince Ortega and his soldiers that he was permanently
blind. In fact, Miguel knew that his brother's vision was
steadily improving. At night, while the others slept,
Hernando would remove the bandanna and gaze up at the
moon and stars. In low whispers he would describe the
constellations, and when an owl passed overhead, he could
see the bird nearly as well as Miguel. That gave Miguel a
great deal of hope. Over and over he and his brother made
plans for the death of Sergeant Ortega and what they
would do afterward. Miguel believed that the soldiers
would kill them before they gathered their senses.
Hernando was firm in his opinion that, once Ortega was
dead, the soldiers would realize that he was their true
leader and would yield to his commands. Miguel prayed
that his brother was correct, otherwise ... well, all this
talk would be for nothing.

One afternoon when Ortega had called a rest stop, the
soldiers went to drink and refresh themselves in the Gila.
While cupping his hands and drinking with head bent low,
one of the men suddenly cried, "Gold! Madre mia! Gold!"

A frenzy seized the expedition. The soldiers rushed to
the man's side and gaped longingly at his immense gold
nugget. It was long and wrinkled, like a fat catapillar, and
it possessed a dull gleam. The soldier bit into the nugget
and sighed with happiness to see his own teeth marks.
"Gold," the man whispered over and over. "Gold!"

One of the soldiers dove headlong into the shallows.
He began scooping up and hurling sand onto the riverbank, then spreading it with his fingers, eyes bugged and
burning with greed. The other soldiers quickly followed
suit, and in less than a minute everyone except Miguel and
Hernando were pitching handfuls of sand and gravel onto
shore, then frantically smearing the mix across the riverbank mud. This madness continued for at least a quarter of
an hour while Miguel and Hernando watched in detached
silence.

"Is there no more!" a soldier cried in desperation.
"Where did that nugget come from?"

The others kept working along a quarter-mile stretch of river. Another hour passed without any cry of gold, and the soldiers gave up, their faces bitter with disappointment. The man who had found the lone nugget now looked very apprehensive, and he shrank back from the others, the nugget clenched in his fist.

Ortega climbed out of the river, thin lips twisted downward at the corners. "Private Galindo," he said, "this expedition will share our wealth. I will take that nugget for safekeeping."

Galindo shook his head, eyes pleading. Ortega patted the hilt of his sword. "You know the penalty for disobedience."

Hernando shouted from behind his blindfold, "And you, *Sergeant*; will one day learn of it too!"

Ortega swung about, and Miguel had never seen such pure hatred. He drew his sword, and Miguel's heart leaped because he was sure that the sergeant was going to behead Hernando. But just then one of the soldiers attacked Galindo. In seconds Galindo was buried by other men, who clawed for the big nugget in his hand.

Ortega raced to the pile of grappling soldiers and began whipping them with the flat of his sword. It was a terrible beating, and now Miguel realized how his own head had been injured. Only a few blows fell, but those that landed were marked by bloody welts. The men crabbed off Galindo, who still held the nugget.

"Private," Ortega said, his voice shaking with fury. "Once more, give me the nugget for safekeeping."

This time Galindo practically threw the nugget to Ortega, who caught it and dropped it into his pocket. "Very smart decision," Ortega said before turning to address his men.

Ortega cleared his voice and raised his sword toward the sky. "Listen, you fools. If there is one nugget in this river, there will be others. Many, many more. Not here . . ." Ortega dramatically pointed his sword toward the tall green mountains, ". . . but higher."

The soldiers followed his gaze, and Miguel could see hope rekindled in their expressions.

"So," Ortega said, his eyes raking the men before he sheathed his sword, "let us march on to Cibola!"

He reached into his pocket and raised the nugget between thumb and forefinger. "But I will promise you this, we will make camp early this evening and again search for nuggets. And with God's grace, I am sure that we will find many, many more—perhaps baskets full!"

The soldiers grinned and nodded with vigorous approval. They collected their arms, sacks of food, and whatever armor they had not thrown into the brush on this long journey up from Casa Grande, and were soon prepared to continue on into the mountains.

"Get into your places," a soldier named Octavio Velasquez ordered, shoving Miguel away from the river.

Miguel batted the soldier's hand aside and grabbed his brother's sleeve. "This way, Hernando."

Hernando nodded and placed his hand on Miguel's shoulder before they continued along a riverside trail made by generations of Indians.

Late that day they came upon a huge beaver dam and marveled at the strange-looking creatures. The Spaniards made jokes about their queer appearance, especially their flat tails and long rodent's teeth which could fell the largest cottonwood and aspen trees. The beavers gazed myopically back at the soldiers, but when approached, they swatted the pond with their paddlelike tails and vanished with barely a ripple.

"Do you think they live underwater?" one soldier asked, musket raised in hopes of getting some fresh game.

"They must," another said. "They looked like big rats, but I guess they are really fat fish."

"Don't be stupid," Galindo snarled, still pouting from the loss of his nugget, "fish do not grow fur!"

"Maybe they do in New Spain," Velasquez offered.

This conversation continued for nearly an hour until

dusk, when the men gave up hope of shooting one of the beaver.

"They probably taste like shit anyway," Mendez growled. "We should have fished for our supper."

That night it was actually chill, and Miguel shivered constantly. He found sleep difficult and counted three shooting stars, which many thought was a sign of impending good luck. Miguel tried to dream about the ballerina girl, but she refused to appear when he wanted her most. She was fickle and vanished whenever he needed her sweet comfort to crowd away his nightly goblins of fear. He drifted off to sleep far, far after midnight, and awoke to the most bloodcurdling scream he had ever heard.

Dawn was sneaking over the high eastern mountains with a weak, ashamed light. Miguel sat bolt upright as the scream intensified until it sounded like a woman dying in childbirth. The scream ended with an abrupt thud and was followed by a strange whirring sound that Miguel thought might be an immense covey of quail taking wing. But then Hernando cried out, and through the gloom Miguel saw that his brother was staring at the shaft of an arrow buried in his belly. Before Miguel could react, he heard more screams and then grunts. Miguel rolled toward his brother, but some sixth sense made him flatten to the earth as a diving Indian struck him and somersaulted into the Gila. With the sound of death and dying all around, Miguel drew his dagger and jumped at the Indian. They were the same height, but the Apache was much more powerful. He gripped Miguel's wrist and began to turn the blade around so that it inched toward the boy's throat. Unable to match the Indian's strength, Miguel slammed his forehead into the Apache's face again and again until he felt the Indian's nose turn to mush. Miguel's fingers raked the riverbed and seized a smooth rock. He brought it up through the water in slow motion, but when it broke the surface, the rock battered the Indian squarely between the eyes. The eyes rolled upward and the Indian's grip faded. Miguel threw himself away from the man and crawled back onto shore.

The camp was an arena of death as Indians and Spaniards clawed and stabbed wildly, rolling on the ground.

"Hernando!" Miguel shouted, throwing himself at his brother.

"Go!" Hernando begged, his body bent over the arrow and his face waxen in the gray dawn. "Run for your life!"

Miguel's eyes lifted and he saw two Indians beating and stabbing a soldier in such gleeful frenzy that it made his blood freeze. One of the Indians looked up, saw him and charged. Miguel fell back and a shred of reason made him kick both feet upward. Miguel was very quick, and he jumped on the Apache's back. They rolled over and over, Miguel holding on for dear life. They rolled into the smoldering campfire, and only luck kept Miguel on top of the Apache, whose hair caught on fire. The man bucked like a horse and went insane. He threw Miguel off and crashed into a tree running full stride, yelling and slapping at his flaming hair.

Miguel grabbed up a fallen sword and raced back to Hernando. Grabbing his brother by the coat, he dragged him into the river and under the water. He felt the current spinning them around and dropped the sword in order to cling to Hernando as they bounced along the river bottom, striking submerged rocks. Lungs bursting, Miguel tried to drag his brother to the surface, but Hernando was a lifeless mass. Miguel screamed silently, unwilling to release his brother to the Gila and yet unable to summon the courage to die with Hernando. His mind exploded with colors, his lungs were on fire, and he kicked off the bottom of the river. A huge gasp broke from his throat as his head cleared the surface and he sucked for air.

"Hernando!"

But Hernando was gone. Miguel dove to the bottom but the light was so poor he could not see. He swam downriver, struck a boulder, and was almost knocked unconscious. He came clawing back to the surface, numb in mind and body. He submitted to the Gila and allowed its powerful current to carry him downriver.

"Hernando!" he repeated over and over.

When he looked back, he was already sweeping around a bend. He heard the soldiers shouting and screaming. There was a musket fire and wild Indian yells. Overhead, the sun grew bold and the river narrowed through a gorge. Miguel was thrown up into the air and then began to spin down through boiling white rapids.

He forgot everything except keeping his head above water. The blessed Gila had turned into a devil, and the devil wanted his soul. Miguel fought the Gila with every bit of his strength until at last he shot out of the canyon and the river flowed again, sparkling like champagne spilling from an oaken cask.

Miguel looked all around. "Hernando!"

There was no reply, only echoes that even his confused and traumatized mind understood would never again be heard by his brother, but which might very well be heard by the Apache.

Miguel let the Gila River carry him away, down, down toward the hell of the Sonoran desert.

Chapter

EIGHT

Miguel stayed in the Gila river as it moved off the pinion- and juniper-covered foothills and across the high desert. Every time the current churned a branch or mossy log to the surface, he thought it might be Hernando and he shuddered with fear. It made his flesh crawl to think that his brother's body might be chasing him downriver, his spirit calling for help.

Drowsing off with the sun burning neck and shoulders, Miguel had daytime nightmares. He began to remember glimpses of the morning his brother had died. Of Spaniards being hacked to pieces and of a headless Indian lying at the feet of a raging Sergeant Ortega. Miguel wondered if his life was over. After all, the Apache must have seen him drag Hernando into the Gila, and they would probably be hurrying downriver to kill him. And even if the soldiers had managed to defeat their attackers, their ranks would be decimated. Perhaps they would also take to the Gila in a daring bid to escape the Indians.

Either way, the expedition was finished. Father Castillo and Hernando were dead. Miguel's chances of crossing the Sonoran desert into Mexico without food, weapons, or a bota bag to carry water were nonexistent.

Miguel almost wished he had remained with the other Spaniards and fought to his death. It would have been far more merciful an ending than to waste away in this wilderness without hope.

That night, Miguel slept fitfully on a small island among reeds and willows. Just after dawn, he awoke feeling something slither across his arm. Startled, he threw the thing into the sky and saw a most beautiful snake twisting against the rising sun. The viper was small, only as long as his lower arm, and thin, the diameter of his thumb. It had alternating rings of red, cream, and black. When it landed on the gravel, it made an angry popping sound and its forked tongue flicked menacingly.

"I think," Miguel said, picking up a rock, taking aim and crushing its head, "you were a coral snake. Very poisonous."

The snake's body whipped back and forth in death, and Miguel stepped onto the rock and tore off the viper's head. He held the still writhing body up and admired its beautiful colors. The red and black bands were as vivid as oil on an artist's palette. The body was very hard and the scales felt waxy. With no dagger or weapon, Miguel had no choice but to bite into the beautiful skin, ripping with his teeth until he found the meat. He devoured the snake, regretting that he had to destroy something so beautiful. After all, the snake could have bit him while he'd slept, but the creature had merely wanted to pass unmolested.

"Out here," Miguel said, studying the hot, quiet land, "there is no justice. It is either kill or be killed."

Miguel removed the rock from the serpent's head. He picked the severed head up and used a fingernail to pry open the reptile's mouth. How poisonous was this little viper's venom? Still poisonous enough to take his life? A morbid curiosity compelled Miguel to place the tip of his finger against the point of one of the fangs. If he squeezed the jaws shut, surely the venom would—

"Aiieee!" he shouted, casting the head into the river. "I am going mad!"

Miguel dropped to his knees. He prayed the rosary even though he had no rosary. He prayed it three times and then he prostrated himself on the island and rolled upon his back. Raising his arms to the sun, he cried out, begging God for His forgiveness and protection.

"And if I am not to have Your protection, then a merciful end to my suffering," he begged. "Lord, I do not want to be caught by the Apache and tortured to death. I am not worthy of being a martyr. I might curse your name in the last moments of my life! If I do that, surely you will turn your back on me and I will go to an everlasting hell. Better, Lord, for you to take me now! I beg you, if I am never to see another white man again, kill me now!"

Miguel closed his eyes. He lay still, sure that, in this great wilderness, his lonely plea must be heard by God and answered. He lay for an entire hour with the sun frying his face and burning white heat through his eyelids. And finally, he rolled over onto his belly and sobbed with despair. Later, the heat drove him into the water like a turtle to float down the Gila into the searing desert.

Again the vegetation changed as Miguel was carried back into the Sonoran. Along the river itself, palo verde and mesquite crowded the banks, fighting each other for water. But farther out, the creosote brush and other vegetation became dull and stunted. Even the stately saguaro cactus was pinched with pain.

Miguel hunted frogs in the early morning and evening, but they were few and hard to catch. He grew weak and might have perished if he had not come across a landlocked lagoon beside the Gila River, teeming with stranded catfish and trout, all swimming aimlessly back and forth. He might have floated past the lagoon if he had not heard the big-bodied catfish splashing the water, frantically searching for a channel back into the deep, cool river. Miguel crawled across the body length of land that separated the fish trap from the Gila and stared at the stranded fish.

"So," he said, "like me, you are also about to die."

Many of the catfish were immense. They swam with such force in the evaporating water that their dorsal fins and the upper parts of their tails made the water's surface roil.

Miguel dragged his body across the narrow gauntlet of earth and slipped into the shallow lagoon as hungry and focused on his prey as an alligator. The lagoon was very, very warm. When his body entered the hot water, the fish went crazy. Sleek trout flashed away with the speed of dark arrows. The huge catfish whipped their tails so hard that the water clouded with mud. Miguel grinned wolfishly. At first he tried to grab the big catfish by their bodies, but they were too slick and muscular.

Overhead, the sun blazed, causing Miguel's head to feel light and dizzy. Under the surface of the lagoon, his hands darted like the trout, grabbing at the heavy catfish, feeling their slime glide through the palms of his hands as they escaped.

Miguel began to laugh. The water was hotter than a bath, and the fish were in a frenzy. Again and again he dragged himself up and down the lagoon attempting to snag a huge catfish. And finally he did. Quite by accident, he hooked the gills of one monster and instinctively bent his forefinger like a fishhook. He drove another finger into the opposite gills and operated his fingers like a pair of ice tongs.

"Got you!" he cried, ripping the catfish overhead to flap wildly. For a moment Miguel almost dropped the fish because he swore that he could see a pleading in its gelatinous, empty eyes. But then he struggled though deep mud and crawled out of the warm lagoon to pounce upon the catfish, pinning its tail with his knee while he ripped its belly open with his teeth and fingernails. He devoured the thrashing monster like a starving animal.

Miguel remained at the natural fish trap for three days. He ate catfish until he could not stand the sight or the taste of them, and then he ate more, until he retched and shuddered with revulsion. Knowing he had to go on or he would die, he tore his sleeves away and fashioned a long, braided cord which he used to thread through the gills of the remainder of the biggest catfish. Then he excavated a channel linking the lagoon to the Gila River. He opened a little earthen floodgate and clapped his hands with delight as the lagoon emptied through his channel, freeing the quick dark trout and the remaining catfish into deep water.

Miguel eased his heavy fishing line of big cats through the channel into the Gila and floated away with them swimming along behind. He felt good, very good, about saving the little fish, but worried that the importance he attached to this trivial act of mercy was an indication that he was becoming feebleminded. As senile as the shaky old men he had often seen wandering through the parks of Seville and Madrid giggling to themselves while completely oblivious to the affairs of the real world.

Casa Grande. Miguel saw her now. Saw her in her best light, with dazzling sunset a golden lacy crown laid soft upon her broken peaks and crumbling ridges. Casa Grande.

Miguel anchored his fishing string to the mossy root of a cottonwood tree and lay in the mud, staring at the now familiar ruins. For some reason, their presence filled him with inner peace. He laid his head upon the back of his hand and offered a prayer of thanksgiving to God for delivering him to this place. As least he would now die where the great Father Francisco Tomas Castillo had died. In the midst of his fervent prayers, Miguel heard soft padding sounds, and when he raised his eyes, he saw feet, many bare brown feet.

Apache!

He closed his eyes and held his breath, waiting for pain and eternal darkness. He waited until he could hold his breath no longer, and then he opened his eyes and saw even more brown feet. He lifted his chin and saw women and children staring at him with heads cocked a little sideways in curiosity. The Indians began to talk with great excitement and gestured toward Casa Grande. Miguel blinked with wonder and astonishment to see Father Castillo lying on a bed of animal skins in the shade of the towering adobe ruins. The priest was smiling. In his left hand he held his magnificent crucifix, while in his right he clutched his Bible. On both sides of him and the ruins, the desert shimmered with heat waves.

"A mirage!" Miguel whispered. "Or else a dream that will surely turn into a nightmare!"

But the dream did not turn into a nightmare. Miguel pounded his forehead twice against the hard earth, which caused a great stir among the women and children. Finally, he pushed himself to his hands and knees and began to crawl toward Father Castillo's beckoning vision. Miguel wondered if he was already entering the gates of Heaven. Maybe Heaven was Casa Grande, the home of God and Father Castillo.

"Miguelito!" the voice rang, high and sharp. "Miguelito!"

A sob exploded from Miguel's throat. He jumped up and ran to the wall of Casa Grande and collapsed beside the padre. "You live!"

Father Castillo hugged him and wept with joy. He could not speak for a long, long time, and then it was to praise God for His goodness. Only later, when he unfolded Miguel from his thin arms, did he say, "I asked the Lord to bring us together again so that you could have my crucifix and do my work. And the Lord heard my prayers and answered them. I can die in peace now."

"No! I will help you to live!"

In answer, the priest lifted his robe to show his black, rotten leg. "Miguelito," he said gently. "God wishes for me to come to Him now."

The stench of the leg was so overpowering that Miguel could not understand how it could have escaped his notice even from the banks of the river. It took all of his will to say, "But . . . maybe that is not what God wishes! Father, perhaps—"

"Listen to me, Miguelito, for this night I will tell you

all that I know and then I will make to you my last confession."

"But I cannot! I am not a priest!"

"I know," Father Castillo said, covering the ripe, offending leg. "We have had this conversation before. And again I tell you that confessing my sins makes me feel good. Besides, I have committed many since last we saw each other."

"Then I will listen. But first you must tell me what happened that night that you disappeared. Hernando . . ." Miguel choked with emotion when he told the priest how his brother had been slain by an Apache's arrow.

"We will pray for his soul, and those of the others who died."

"I cannot pray for Ortega's black soul," Miguel spat. "He treated my brother and I worse than dogs. I am *glad* he is dead!"

"Hatred poisons the soul, just as surely as this broken leg has finally poisoned my body."

"Father, what *did* happen to you that night?"

"I fell asleep and awoke feeling someone trying to steal my crucifix! I struck out and then rolled into the water. The thief tried to catch me, but he could not swim and I was in deep water. My robe was so heavy that I too thought I would drown. But instead, I was swept downriver and tossed upon a sandbar. These good Pima were camped only a few leagues distant and they found me. They brought me back to Casa Grande and have treated my leg with their native medicines. For a time, I thought their medicine would save me, but . . . well, God has other plans."

"Father, who was the thief?"

"It does not matter."

"It does to me! Was it Sergeant Ortega?"

"No."

"Then?"

"It was . . . Mendez."

"I will kill him!"

"No!" The priest lowered his voice. "Let God be his judge—and mine."

Miguel bit his lip. "I would do anything to save you, Father. I would give you my own leg if that would keep you here."

"You are kind and generous, Miguelito. I saw that you had a good heart from the very first. But it is my time. None of us can change, for an instant, his own time, my son."

"Yes, Father."

"And you must teach the word of God to these people, as I have tried to do these past few days."

"I will do my best."

"Good. And even though the soldiers turned on you and your brother, you must forgive them and help them all."

"Help them?"

"If they are dead, pray for them every day. If some have lived, do what you can to ease their hardships."

"I will try."

"Good."

The priest closed his shrunken, feverish eyes. When Miguel took his hand, it was on fire. The bones of Castillo's face seemed about to escape through the pale parchment of his flesh. Miguel knew that Father Castillo was indeed dying. The miracle was that the padre still had his beloved family crucifix and that they would be together when last he breathed.

That night was one that Miguel would remember all the rest of his days. It seemed as if Father Castillo had only clung to life, waiting until he could pass on his dying wishes and his beautiful crucifix.

Miguel took the crucifix and its gold chain and his eyes glistened in the moonlight. "I am so unworthy, Father."

"All men are unworthy. God forgives. He always forgives, Miguelito. He asks only that we do the best we can."

"I don't know very much about—"

"You will have my Bible," the padre said, "and the

great Father Kino's words and a few of my scribbled re-
flections. When in despair, read and pray, Miguelito!
Peace will never fail you if you listen and pray."

"Yes, Father."

"And one more thing, I want you to wear my black
robe."

"No! I . . . I couldn't! Everyone knows that it is the
mark of the Jesuit."

"Let the Indians think that. Father Kino says they are
simple, like trusting children. They call themselves the
River People. To them, this robe will set you apart from
all other Europeans. It will mark you as a man of God."

"But Father, you know that I am *not*!"

"No matter. Act as if you were among the chosen and
you will become saintly. All that is important is that they
believe in Him through you. Miguelito, all things will be
forgiven. Trust in Him."

"Yes, Father. But to take everything from you, I—"

"You take nothing that I need in Heaven, my son."

The priest closed his eyes. His thin chest rattled and
he labored for breath. Then he sighed and his frail body
went limp.

"Father?" No answer. "Father!"

Castillo's eyelids fluttered open. It was as if Miguel
had called him back from the dead.

"Father, I . . . I want to go home!" Miguel blurted.
"I'm sorry, but I don't want to stay in this awful country.
I want to see my mother and father. To marry a Spanish
woman and raise our children in—"

"Have . . . faith!"

"But I don't want to disappoint you or be sent to
Hell!"

The priest's lips rustled like dead leaves in the wind.
Miguel leaned close enough to feel Castillo's faint breath in
his ear. "What did you say? Father, I couldn't hear you!"

"All . . . things will be . . . forgiven, Miguelito. All
. . . things!"

Chapter

NINE

Miguel exchanged the priest's heavy black robe for his own clothes. Fortunately, they were both six-footers, but it was very difficult for Miguel to trade his ragged shirt and pants for a Jesuit's robe. Father Castillo had asked to be buried without clothing, but Miguel's mind and sensibilities had rebelled at the thought of the priest lying naked against the cold earth. And even if the padre had wished to depart this world without any worldly goods, Miguel's clothes were so threadbare that they would have repelled a Mexico City street beggar.

Under the spreading limbs of a beautiful cottonwood tree, Miguel and the Pima scooped a deep grave in the soft riverbank soil. After Father Castillo had been gently laid to rest, Miguel read the Lord's Prayer and other passages from the Holy Bible. He held up the magnificent crucifix while intoning the rosary, and the Pima appeared to be impressed. They seemed willing to believe that Miguel was himself a man of God.

"I am an unlikely impostor," he told the dead priest lying peacefully at the bottom of his grave. "And soon, the Pima will realize that I am not even a good Christian."

Miguel took a handful of the damp river bottom soil

and held it aloft. "Ashes to ashes and dust to dust," he said, allowing the earth to slip between his fingers. Then he began to fill the grave.

The River People helped, and when the burying was finished, Miguel borrowed one of their sharp stone knives to cut and shape a grave marker out of cottonwood. After is was placed, he sat grief-stricken and cross-legged at the foot of the grave. That afternoon, the Pima discovered his fishing string and were delighted by the huge catfish. They admired how he had kept the fish alive to eat whenever he was hungry.

"Cook them all," Miguel said miserably. "I don't care."

The Pima roasted the fish on willow branches and presented him with one, but Miguel barely nibbled at the sweet, white meat seasoned with desert herbs. That evening, he watched the sun glow like fire and then fade and die. Miguel thought about his poor brother, but mostly he thought about the priest. Father Castillo had hungered to resume Kino's missionary work but had lived among the Indians only a few precious days. In that time, he had probably learned less than a dozen of their words, in addition to the few that were mentioned in Kino's writings. No doubt he had baptized many and prayed for all, eternally grateful for their ministrations to his poisoned leg.

The River People had quickly put Father Castillo's death behind them. But for a time they had grieved his loss. Their sadness had not been faked or exaggerated; children had cried, women and men had gazed at the wasted body with genuine sorrow. It was a tribute to the padre that they should have mourned his passing after knowing him only a few days. Miguel meant to see that Castillo's life had not been forfeited in vain.

He remembered the padre telling him that the Pima and the Papago Indians of this country spoke a dialect that was not altogether unrelated to the Aztecs of Mexico. Father Kino had not been a linguist, but he and his fellow missionaries had considered the Pima language easy to master.

Miguel hoped that he did not have to remain in this desert wasteland long enough to learn their language. He had openly confessed to the padre that he wanted nothing more than to return to his parents in Cadiz to lead a normal life raising a family. Was that so much to ask? He would track down Father Castillo's Jesuit order and return the crucifix like a good Samaritan rather than sell it for personal gain. Beyond that . . . well, he had lost and suffered enough.

Miguel slept beside the priest's grave for three consecutive nights. The Pima had devoured the catfish on the first day, and afterward began to bring him food. They cornered and speared a javelina and roasted it until it was tender. They supplemented the pork with various small game as well as corn and beans which they transported in large woven baskets. Their food was well-prepared and well-seasoned, but Miguel had no appetite.

This concerned the Pima, and finally a half dozen of the tribe's head men came to sit beside him. They stared at Miguel so long and so intently that he began to feel uncomfortable.

"What do you want?"

The Indians smiled, and one indicated that he was to lift the crucifix up toward the sun. Miguel understood. He raised the crucifix so that it glinted this way then that, and the Indians were delighted. With fingers, they pointed here and there, following the refracted light which jumped all around. But after a while Miguel's arms became heavy and he lowered it, then fidgeted as the Pima resumed staring.

"All right," he said, taking up the chief's Bible. "I will see if reading makes you happy."

The Pima liked the reading very much. Of course, they understood nothing, but the soft cadence of Miguel's words pleased them. They gave Miguel the impression that they could listen to him all day and all night if he had the energy to read that long.

Finally, however, the Pima made it clear that it was time to depart from the ruins of Casa Grande. They took their places, women and children behind, men in front, and all started southwest along the Gila River. They indicated that Miguel was to join them.

"I can't," he confessed.

They heard resignation in his voice and understood. One Indian who appeared to be a leader actually came over and gently tugged on Miguel's arm. When Miguel resisted, the Indian sighed with disappointment and sat down to stare at him. The other Indians sat down too. They seemed to be waiting for the Spaniard to explain.

"Look, I know that you are kind, and I appreciate what you tried to do for Father Castillo and now for me. But if I leave Casa Grande to go with you, I ... I just don't think that I will ever find my way back to civilization. I will disappear out there in that terrible desert and no one will ever find me."

Tears made his eyes sting. "I will live the rest of my days in this hell and suffer every day the memory of life among my own people. I will fall into a mood of despair so deep that nothing will save me from misery. I will have no one that I can really talk to. Who among you could possibly understand the mind of a man from Spain? How could you possibly even care about my family or my boyhood dreams?"

The Indians nodded their heads as if they understood. They looked so wise and serious that it was laughable, and Miguel did chuckle. The Indians liked that! They laughed too. A little at first, then quite heartily. Soon they had Miguel laughing like a loon, until he realized that he was sitting next to the grave of his beloved Padre Castillo.

He was shocked at his irreverence, but after a moment said, "I shouldn't feel any guilt. The padre had a wonderful sense of humor. He loved to laugh. I will not feel guilty, because, if he is watching from Heaven, I think he would consider our laughter a very good thing."

Miguel nodded his chin up and down. "Don't you, my friends?"

The Indians, even the women and children, nodded their heads up and down.

Miguel laughed again.

At first light the following morning, the Indians indicated they must leave. And for some reason, Miguel decided that he had better go with them. Up to that moment, he had secretly harbored some faint hope that any surviving soldiers might return to this place and together they could all make their way back down to Mexico City. But now Miguel saw how futile that hope really was and how his only two choices were to go with the Pima and live or to remain here at Casa Grande and die.

"All right," he said, coming to his feet. "I come."

"I come," echoed a Pima who clapped him on the back and grinned.

Miguel paused to join the women and the children, but the Pima would have none of that. They insisted that he walk with the front men, and Miguel reluctantly obliged. As he had the last time he had left Casa Grande with his poor blind brother, Miguel often gazed back at the ancient adobe ruins, wondering about them and about his own fate. But soon the Pima came to a path beside the Gila River, and Casa Grande disappeared behind the water-loving trees and brush.

It was all that Miguel could do to keep pace with the Indians. He could not believe how quickly they traveled, even though slowed by their large families. Even more impressive was that the men helped the women and the women helped the children. Miguel was pleased to see that. He began to study these people for the first time.

They were short of stature, often bandy-legged, and quite dark complected. Their hair was long, shiny, and often tied with leather thongs and decorated with feathers. They wore very little, the men just skin or cotton breechclouts, and the women skirts that fell a few inches below the knees. Their children were naked, and everyone wore thonged sandals made of thick leather while on the march, but usually went barefoot when they were camped. Miguel was surprised by the love these Pima had for jewelry. Both men and women wore earrings made of shells, turquoise, and red coral. The shells gave Miguel hope because it meant that these Indians either traded with a seaside people or else journeyed to the coast. In either case, trade might bring them in contact with villages or an ocean, with its ships which could deliver him from this punishing desert.

What Miguel did find visually disturbing was that many of the women had blue tattoo lines etched from the corners of their mouths to their chins. He could not understand why they would do this to themselves, especially when it was obvious that the tattooing would be very painful. He guessed that these lines were considered decorous or perhaps were added to make the women's faces seem more interesting.

Two days of travel brought them to the Pima principal village alongside the Gila River. At the sight of Miguel, the village people fell silent, although their dogs barked and bared their teeth. Miguel halted and remained motionless, wondering what would happen next. It was possible that he had been duped and would be killed now that he was surrounded by the Pima and completely helpless to escape. He could see and feel the questioning of these people, and he estimated that their village numbered perhaps two hundred. Their houses were small domed affairs made of sticks and brush, with dirt packed over the top. They were windowless, and the doors were covered with skins. Baking in the heat, Miguel imagined the little huts were blessedly dark and cool inside.

A vicious-looking cur advanced, hackles raised and lips pulled back to expose its yellowed fangs. Miguel steeled himself for a bite, but one of the Pima lashed out with his sandaled foot and caught the dog in the side. Ducking its tail between its legs, the animal raced away, yipping with fright. The Pima exploded with laughter, and at that moment Miguel knew that he would not be made their victim of sacrifice. So relieved did he feel, that he reached under the black Jesuit's robe and found the Castillo crucifix, which he raised up before them. The Pima drew a deep collective breath. One old man even made the sign of the cross and fell to his knees, clasping his hands together in supplication. "Praizeez me to God!" he cried.

Miguel was stunned. So stunned he almost dropped the pouch of sacramentals. He ran over to the old man. "You speak Spanish?"

The old man beamed and squared his thin shoulders, aware that he alone had been singled out for special attention. "Si! Poco."

Miguel was astounded. The importance to him of this man was nearly impossible to comprehend. "Mother of God, how!"

In halting Spanish the old man explained that he had been taught the white man's language as a boy by one of Father Kino's disciples. "All forget but me," he said, eyes shining brightly. The old man turned and scuttled off, but not before yelling, "Wait!"

Miguel waited. He was so delighted to find a Pima whom he could communicate with that he smiled broadly. The Pima smiled back, and a few minutes later the old man returned with a very, very old scrap of what appeared to have once been a letter. Its edges were charred.

Turning the scrap this way and that, the old man's face wrinkled with concentration. He cleared his throat and then, without preamble, he began to read, "On the seventh day of July, we began to harvest the corn using the Indians. Ochoa is my constant companion and an especially good student."

The old man looked up at Miguel. He grinned, exposing mostly gums and very few teeth. "Me Ochoa," he said, prodding his bony chest with his forefinger.

"Yes."

The old man read the rest of the words, but because the scrap of paper was torn diagonally, the sentences became shorter and made no further sense to Miguel, except that it said something about irrigating the fields. No matter. This old Indian could speak, and that was enough.

"How old are you?"

Ochoa threw up his frail hands and dropped them to his side with a shake of his head.

"Never mind," Miguel said, "it is not important. We will be friends. And you will teach me the language of these people as I teach them the word of God."

"Good. Good! Amen!"

"Yes," Miguel laughed. "Amen."

Turning to the others, he began to speak, and Ochoa translated, slowly and with great difficulty at first, but gradually with remarkable fluidity. It occurred to Miguel that whatever priest had taught this old Indian Spanish had done well and had indeed found a remarkably bright student. Perhaps even a native genius. Ochoa might be fifty or he might be eighty, but while his body was failing, his mind was as bright as Spanish silver.

"I bring you the word of God," Miguel pronounced, reaching into the padre's leather pouch and sorting among the sacramental items until he found the Bible. "I bring to you the word of the Lord!"

The Pima looked at the old man, who began to rant and wave his arms, pointing to the sky. Miguel raised the Bible in one hand and the crucifix in the other, and like wheat falling before the scythe, the Pima dropped to the dirt.

Miguel threw his head back and shouted, "Praise to you, God!"

Ochoa cried out, and Miguel fell to his own knees and prayed. Perhaps he would find some rewards in this hell if he had faith and perseverance. Perhaps, like Moses, he was meant to wander in the wilderness for a time.

Miguel did not allow himself to think further along those lines. He would live, and with Ochoa's help, he would preach and he would learn how to survive among these good and gentle people. But come the first chance, he would return to Mexico City and then to his own beloved Spain, from which he would never again depart.

With Ochoa close as his shadow, Miguel was led into one of the larger houses, blessedly cool and dim. He was brought food, more than he could have eaten in a week. Mostly it was corn, beans, and squash with roasted chunks of meat, all excellent.

"Rabbit?" he asked.

Ochoa's brow wrinkled. "Uh?"

"Rabbit." Miguel repeated, picking out a chunk of the tasty meat. He popped it into his mouth, growled with satisfaction and then, to show the Indian, he used his hands to form long ears. Then he made a fist and used it to hop across the dirt between them.

The Pima laughed, but Ochoa snapped a harsh word at them and then turned back to Miguel. He pointed to the entrance of the hut where a dog was lying.

"This is dog?"

"Si! Dog. Woof. Woof! Dog!"

Miguel began to pick at other things from the bowls placed before him. There were roasted green roots and what appeared to be cactus buds, all of them delicious. There was also a big catfish cooked whole. Miguel avoided that along with the dog meat.

He and the other head men of the Pima tribe ate well and the meal lasted for over two hours. Miguel, using Ochoa as a translator, learned that this was only one of many Pima villages that formed a necklace of settlements along the Gila and another large river to the north.

"What about the Lost Cities of Cibola?" he asked.

Ochoa kept answering, "Eh? Eh?"

So Miguel tried something different. He pulled the crucifix, pointed to its golden tree and said, "Gold? You have gold?"

The Indians shook their heads and so admired the crucifix that Miguel let them all take a turn at holding it.

Later he learned that these people mostly subsisted by irrigating and farming in fields beside the Gila River. In the wintertime, however, their hunters also traveled to the distant eastern mountains in search of deer, sheep, and other larger game.

It was not until after dark that the Pima, through Ochoa, told him they were the adversaries of the hated and feared Apache, which in their language literally meant "the enemy." It was very clear, even had Ochoa not been translating, that the mere mention of the Apache brought a change upon these people. Their voices grew loud, strident, and thick with fear and anger. They became visibly upset.

"Apache kill many River People," Ochoa explained. "River People kill many Apache."

"They also killed *my* brother and people," Miguel confessed. With his own voice thick with emotion, Miguel went on to describe how the Apache had attacked the soldiers' camp in the high country along the Gila River.

The Pima grew very excited by this. They all talked so fast it was difficult even for Ochoa to sort out their questions.

"How many?"

"I don't know," Miguel answered. "They came at dawn."

"How many you?"

Miguel held up all of his fingers. Twice, then four more.

"All dead?"

"I don't know," he answered again. "Probably."

It took several minutes for him to convey the meaning of "probably" to Ochoa, but when he finally got the point, the Pima understood and looked very upset. They grew even more upset when Miguel said, "I must go back and find out if any of the soldiers survived. I cannot allow them to die. I promised to help them."

Ochoa and the head men of the Pima began to argue with such passion that Miguel could not break up their squabbling. After a half hour of listening to their angry words, Miguel could not stand it any longer and climbed to his feet. That stopped the arguing, but only as long as it took him to exit the hut and step outside to look at the stars and then to admire a beautiful young girl who rushed from the campfire to bring him a dish of steaming meat.

"More dog?" he asked, raising his eyebrows in question.

The girl shrugged her pretty bare shoulders. In the firelight her complexion was golden. Not yet tattooed on the face, she was taller than most Indian women, and slender, yet he had only to drop his eyes to her budding chest to see that she was indeed a woman. She pulled the reed bowl closer to her bosom and said something with a shy smile. Then she shook the dish of food. Miguel saw that she very much wanted him to take some of the meat and that she was nervous with the other women watching.

"All right," he said, "even if it is dog meat, how can I refuse such a beautiful one as you."

When he selected a morsel and chewed it, she smiled with perfect white teeth and urged him to eat even more. Miguel, who was already full, felt compelled to select more meat. In a gentle voice that only she could hear, he said, "I'd eat the whole dog to please you. What is your name?"

She shook her head.

"Your name." Miguel pointed to himself. "Miguel."

"Nanata," she said, raising her head with a half smile.

"You remind me of a dream that . . . never mind."

Nanata raised her woven plate of meat and Miguel selected another morsel and then, on impulse, he pressed it to her lips. She opened her mouth and her tongue flicked out and then the meat was gone. Miguel felt his passions stir, and he was about to say something when Ochoa rushed outside. The old man clutched and shook Miguel's arm.

"What?"

Ochoa was so excited that his Pima overwhelmed his

halting Spanish. Miguel had to calm and slow the old Indian down. "Tell me, what is it?"

"We go Apache too, eh, Miguel?"

"You mean to fight them?"

"Kill!"

Ochoa made a fist, turned it inward and pretended to stab himself in the chest. He even staggered, groaned, and rolled his eyes. The effect might have been comical under other circumstances. Now, however, Miguel found it chilling.

"I don't think you understand," Miguel tried to explain. "I just have to find out if any of the others are still alive and, if so, save them. If they are, they'd probably have reached Casa Grande. Maybe if we go there, we can—"

But Ochoa wasn't listening. The other Indians' headmen poured out of the hut and they too began to dance and gesture in a manner that left no doubt that they had decided to join Miguel and to go kill Apache.

Miguel drew a hand across his face. This was madness! Was there a full moon? No. He looked for Nanata, but she was back with the other women, head turned and big brown eyes round with fear.

"Tomorrow!" he yelled. "We'll talk about all this tomorrow!"

And then, because old Ochoa and the rest of the Pima were too stirred up by hatred to understand, Miguel walked back to the Gila River, laid down and tried to go to sleep. One thing he knew for sure, if Father Castillo was watching from Heaven, he would be displeased with the way things were now unfolding.

_____ Chapter _____

TEN

Miguel had been able to stall the Pima headmen for almost a week while he rested enough to regain some weight and strength. During that time, he found himself torn between his pledge to Father Castillo to help any soldiers who might have survived the Apache attack and his simple desire to avoid further bloodshed.

The heat remained intense but it did not appear to bother the Pima, who seemed perfectly well-adapted to temperatures that would have caused Europeans to swoon and even die. The Pima conducted most of their daily affairs during the very early morning or late in the evening. The women tended the fields while the men were constantly laboring over their complex system of canals, a marvel of ingenuity that kept the Pima fields of beans, squash, cotton, and corn well-irrigated. To Miguel's amazement, those crops not only seemed to grow in the desert soil, but actually seemed to thrive.

Having come from a family of prosperous Cadiz merchants, Miguel had never been attracted to farming. But in the evening when the women sang and harvested the earth's bounty, he felt an irresistible urge to join them on the wet, dark earth, picking weeds and vegetables. However, that would have been a severe breach of etiquette, one that he realized would have lost him face among these River People.

Even so, Miguel found it impossible not to watch for Nanata. Even in the twilight he could pick her out among the other women, because of her height and slender figure. And at night while he was beside the campfire reading from the Bible or learning from Ochoa the Pima words, Nanata drew his eyes to hers like a magnet. At such times Miguel would forget what Ochoa was teaching or lose his place in the reading. The old man would follow his gaze, then frown with disapproval.

Finally, one evening Ochoa said, right before all the others, "Holy man sleep with God, not Nanata. Uh?"

The question should have been one that Miguel had anticipated, but he had not. Now it rocked his head backward and he felt a rush of shame. Was his growing desire for Nanata so obvious? And what if he told Ochoa that he was not really a man of the cloth? Not a priest, but instead an inept pretender? What would happen to him after that? Would the Pima still respect and feed him?

Miguel thought they probably would, but there was still a nagging doubt in his mind. And with each passing day of this facade, he felt as if he were slipping deeper and deeper into a morass of deceit. This feeling was greatly intensified when Ochoa proudly escorted a young mother to him and made it clear that Miguel was to baptize her newborn child.

"Ochoa," he blurted, resolved to finally free himself of all deceit, "I must tell you something. I must tell all your people something which is very important. I am *not* a priest."

Ochoa just stared at him. Finally, he said, "You wash devil away."

"I can't. I'm sorry, but I don't have that grace."

The woman could hear the pleading in Miguel's voice and saw the shake of his head. Her smile died and she shrank back a step. The old man grabbed Miguel's arm with surprising strength. "What matter?"

"I am not a priest!"

"You take away sin!"

Miguel glanced at the young woman. He saw her eyes welling with tears of hurt and disappointment. He knew he could never make her understand. Her faith, if you could even call it that, was too simple to accept the complexity of a true Catholic ordination. At most, she believed that anyone wearing a black robe and having a Bible, crucifix, and articles of the sacraments was a holy man—a priest.

The woman would have turned and rushed away except the old man also grabbed her. Ochoa hung between them, eyes blazing with anger and confusion and he would not let go.

"All right!" Miguel cried, remembering Father Castillo's dying words that all things will be forgiven. "I will baptize the child."

The old man's faith was badly shaken as they proceeded to the Gila River. Miguel had seen baptisms before, and he tried his best to imitate them. With the entire village looking on, he thought about how the padre had blessed this entire river so that perhaps it really was holy water. He took the infant and cradled it in his arms while he stepped into the water. Then he eased the baby down into the warm Gila and heard it gurgle with pleasure as the current soothed its hot skin.

He stood up with the dripping, giggling child in one arm and the Castillo crucifix held out for all to see. With the base of the crucifix he made the sign of the cross and loudly proclaimed, "I hereby baptize you in the name of the Father, the Son, and the Holy Spirit."

He looked up at Ochoa, who was grinning, and then his eyes sought Nanata, who also looked very pleased. Miguel took heart. All was going just as Father Castillo had prophesied. Only what would these trusting Pima think if he ever lost control and took Nanata into his arms to kiss her lovely lips? No doubt Ochoa would be horrified and would denounce him. No doubt the Pima would feel betrayed and would kill or at least banish him from their village, an act tantamount to death.

Miguel looked quickly away from the girl. Perhaps it was best that he no longer stall; that he lead the Pima back upriver past Casa Grande into the hated Apache country. There, he would either be killed or else demonstrate once and for all that he really wasn't a man at peace with himself and with God—that he would and could take human life in defiance of the Bible's teachings.

That evening, without giving a damn what the Pima thought, Miguel walked past the irrigators and out into the largest field of beans. He stepped up to Nanata and took her muddy hands in his own.

"I know you don't understand any of this," he told her as she glanced nervously from side to side and all of the women stopped their harvesting to stare, "but I have fallen in love with you. I have not seen my dream balle-rina since coming here, and I never will again. You are real, you are even more beautiful than my lost dream dancer."

He moved closer to the girl. So close that her bare bosom was pressed to his rough black robe. Miguel felt giddy with passion. This was insane!

"Nanata," he choked, "if I removed this accursed robe, then I could feel our hearts beat together."

He looked down at her. Her face was oval and gilded by sunset, just as it had been the first moment he'd laid eyes upon her. "Before I leave at daybreak, you must know that I love you."

The girl tried to smile but failed. She did not under-stand. Confusion and concern dominated her expression. Miguel felt her begin to tremble and he stepped back.

"It's all right," he whispered. "If I live to return, it will be a clear sign from God above that my desire for you is not sinful. Can you understand that?"

She hung before him, waiting for what he did not

know. In his own confusion, Miguel spun away and hurried back to the village. When he reached it, he looked back, but the sun was down and it was too late now to pick her out among the many.

Casa Grande was a red blister floating in a sea of heat. The Pima war party did not even bother to visit her cool shadows, but pressed on up the Gila River despite the enervating afternoon temperature. There were sixty-seven Pima warriors including Ochoa, who would have died before leaving Miguel to journey off without him to fight the Apache. Some of the warriors were barely in their teens, but all were sinewy, determined, and well-armed with bows and dozens of stone-tipped arrows. The strongest warriors who desired to fight at close quarters carried small leather shields and wicked-looking clubs made of hard wood.

In addition to their weapons, the warriors had prepared themselves well with magical incantations. Every night that week they had danced and sung magic words, believing that they would give them overwhelming power against the fierce Apache. When Miguel asked Ochoa what their songs said, the old man told him that the songs recounted past victories against the Apache and told how these hated enemies would soon be vanquished. Some of the warriors used campfire char to blacken their faces and make their countenance terrifying.

As they followed the river northeast, Miguel's thoughts swirled with doubts and fears about how he would conduct himself in battle. He took some comfort in the fact that he was blooded now, for he had killed both Pablo Escobar and an Apache, but only the latter had really been a contest. He believed that even if they were overwhelmed by a superior force of Apache, his courage would not be found lacking. If necessary, he would fight to the death to avenge Hernando, and he would not die meekly like a priest, but like a warrior, a noble Spaniard. In fact, it was his intention to cast his Jesuit robe aside at the first opportunity, certainly no later than when the battle was imminent. He did not know what he would replace the black robe with, and modesty prevented him from throwing himself into a battle naked.

As they steadily tramped out of the accursed lower desert, Miguel wondered if all the Spaniards had been slaughtered during the same dawn of his brother's death, or if some had continued on, looking for the Lost Cities of Cibola. As much as anything, he did not want to be responsible for the deaths of these Pima men. They were good people, not really hunters or warriors by nature, but instead villagers and farmers. And if all of them should be slaughtered by the Apache, it would so weaken the strength of their Pima village that it would long be vulnerable to the marauding Apache.

When Miguel tried to voice this fear, Ochoa told him, in a fashion, that in that case the village would move and join another village where there were more young men to take in the widows. The children would have new fathers and would not starve, because the Pima knew that their only hope for survival against the enemy was in the force of their numbers.

"But surely this raid we are about to undertake will bring Apache retaliation," Miguel argued.

It took some time for Ochoa to understand the meaning of "retaliation," but when he did, he just shrugged. And in his broken Spanish, said, "Then we kill all, eh?"

"Yes," Miguel said, though he truly did not relish the idea of killing anyone. "But if we find the Spaniards alive, there is only one among them that I will kill, and then we will bring the rest back to the village."

"What man?"

"Ortega," Miguel gritted, as the hot memory of how the sergeant had humiliated both Hernando and him burned his cheeks.

"Ortega devil?"

"Yes," Miguel said. "Ortega devil."

"Devil die too."

Miguel nodded. Without weapons of his own, he scarcely knew how he would fight, until he remembered that he had relinquished a sword to the Gila River in a vain attempt to save Hernando. Could he find the weapon again? He was not sure. Everything had happened so fast and in the midst of such terror that he couldn't remember how deep he had been in the current. He knew that the sword was heavy enough to sink straight to the river's bottom. It might have been rolled downriver by the current, but Miguel thought that unlikely, given the river's rocky bottom.

What would the Pima think when he cast off his robe, dove into the deep water, and came up with a soldier's sword? No matter. He would face that problem later. One thing for sure, he had seen enough of the Apache to know that he was not going to go up against them bare-handed. His brother had taught him a few thrusts, parries, and moves with his sword, and Miguel meant to use them with all the skill and ferocity that he possessed.

The high desert was as he had remembered it, and when he looked back down on the vast, hazy sweep of the punished Sonoran desert, Miguel recalled how Ortega had declared that Cibola would be just ahead because no civilization would willingly live in the killing heat when they could enjoy the high mountains. Recalling that quote almost brought Miguel to ask Ochoa why his people did live in the desert instead of this cooler, higher country ringing with pines. But he knew the question was moot, at least until the outcome of this journey was decided. Besides, he suspected it was because the Apache, primarily being hunters rather than farmers, claimed this forested land for themselves.

One afternoon they rounded a bend and saw Hernando's decomposed body snagged among flotsam against a boulder about twenty feet out into a narrow, swift channel of the Gila River. Miguel fought his way past the Indians and out into the rapids, but the current knocked him over. Thrashing and choking, the nightmare of his earlier experience brought him to the edge of hysteria.

Using ropes made of woven cotton, the Indians tried to form a human chain and reach the body, but even that failed. In the end, after several hours of anguish and failed attempts, Miguel had to turn his back on his brother's corpse and continue upriver. His heart was broken and his step never heavier. He did not want to remember what Hernando's fate had been and what his remains looked like now after the fish, raptors, and the river had done their work. Instead he recalled Hernando's determination and the hope that had never deserted him, even in humiliation and blindness.

"If I find Ortega," he muttered to himself, "I swear I will kill him slowly!"

The next day, the Pima breached a beaver dam and then shot three while the creatures were frantically working to repair the damage. One of the beaver was swept through the breach and was lost downriver, but the other two were roasted and devoured, clearly preferable to the corn and beans that the Pima carried as their traveling rations.

When they finally arrived at the soldiers' death camp, nothing had prepared Miguel for the sight of the Spanish soldiers' blackened and charred bodies. This grisly spectacle hit him with even greater impact than the sight of poor Hernando's remains.

The Pima were also visibly shaken. After an initial glance at the twisted and grotesque remains, they averted their eyes and fanned out along the perimeter of the camp to read sign. Miguel was left with the old man, to stare at the unrecognizable bodies. He forced down his gorge and went to them one by one, searching for anything that might reveal their individual identities. He finally recognized a discolored sword buckle that had definitely belonged to the sergeant. It was melted into a hideous mound of charred humanity.

"Ortega," Miguel said in a voice that trembled.

Ochoa grinned. He lifted his breechclout, and before Miguel could recover from his own shock, the old man urinated on Ortega's hideous remains.

Miguel turned away, feeling gorge rise in his throat. He went to the river and knelt, retching silently until he remembered the lost sword. Taking deep breaths until his head cleared and the nausea passed, he removed the Jesuit's robe and dove cleanly into the Gila, feeling the river cleanse his mind as well as his body.

The current enfolded Miguel like a babe in the womb. It wrapped itself around him and spun him gently down, down. Miguel did not fight the river as before, but held his breath and swam with the river, his hands sweeping along its bottom, his eyes wide open until he felt a sharp pain across his palm and instinctively closed his hand on Spanish steel.

It was his! Miguel slid his hand along the blade, not caring about the pain. He found and gripped the handle and then pushed off the rocky river bottom and burst into the sunlight, sword waving at the sky.

"I found it!" he shouted.

The Pima gaped at him as he was propelled around a gentle river bend. Old Ochoa grabbed up his black robe and stumbled forward as the other Pima broke into a run down the riverside.

Miguel held the sword aloft. He felt both empowered and cleansed. If it had not been for the Pima running after him and calling his name with alarm, he would have let the Gila River carry him back down to his brother. He would have chopped poor Hernando's remains from the river's grasp and used Spanish steel to bury what was left of him beside the body of Father Castillo. And then he would have walked naked into the desert waving the sword until the sun and the heat drove him into sweet insanity.

Chapter

ELEVEN

Miguel wanted to return back down the Gila River. To stand as a common man instead of a priest before Nanata and proclaim his love. To bury his sword in the cornfields and perhaps find some happiness in the Sonoran desert. But the Pima made it clear that they had come too far and evoked too much magic not to attack their hated Apache enemies.

Ochoa was outraged when Miguel replaced the black Jesuit's robe with the Spanish sword. Over and over he held the robe up before Miguel, who stood naked beside the river. The old man pleaded, "Take God robe. Take God robe."

But Miguel remained steadfast in his refusal. He clutched the sword and shook his head. He was sorry that he could not follow Father Castillo's last wishes, but he could no longer impersonate a man of the cloth. Ochoa became so upset, he balled the heavy robe up and shoved it into Miguel's bare chest, pressing it hard against the Castillo crucifix. Miguel wadded up the robe and hurled it far out into the Gila River.

Ochoa almost went crazy. He dashed into the water and nearly drowned attempting to retrieve the Jesuit's robe, which fanned across the water like a jellyfish on the ocean and then sank. When two of the Pima dragged Ochoa back to shore, the old man was shaking with rage. Limping and spitting, the old man began to shout Pima curses at Miguel.

For as long as it took, Miguel quietly absorbed the old man's wrath, and finally he turned and walked back to the soldiers' desecrated camp. He squatted down against a cottonwood tree and closed his eyes, blocking out the angry words of the Pima, who had begun to argue among themselves. This place of death was evil. Miguel was not psychic or even particularly spiritual, but he swore he could feel the ghosts of the tortured Spaniards. Overhead, a faint breeze caused the leaves of the tall cottonwoods to chatter like ethereal voices. He listened with all his concentration and began to quake as he imagined a kaleidoscope of whirling death and savagery. He did not know how long he was gripped by this nightmare, but when he opened his eyes again, he was alone except for the old man.

Miguel came to his feet and then walked up to Ochoa, who said, "We go back."

Miguel looked past the wizened little Pima. "And your Pima warriors?"

"Kill Apache."

Miguel should have felt relief, but he didn't. He realized he was shaking his head. "If it had not been for me, they would not have come this far. I am responsible for their lives."

"We go back."

"No," Miguel said, "*you* go back if you want, but I'm going after them. Maybe I can convince them to turn around before it is too late."

Ochoa did not appear to understand, but when Miguel raised his sword and set off to follow the Pima tracks eastward, the old man grabbed his walking stick and fell in behind. He was frail but tireless, and could not have weighed more than ninety pounds. Ochoa was bent and he limped over his stick, but he had an iron will that carried him well beyond the limits of his physical abilities. Miguel hiked rapidly for almost an hour, but when he looked back, Ochoa was still coming, so he stopped and waited for the old Pima. Without a word, Ochoa passed him on the riverside trail, stick swinging back and forth like a pendulum, bony head and long silver hair swaying from side to side.

"I'm sorry," Miguel called. When Ochoa did not break his stride, Miguel added, "I ask your forgiveness. I am only a sinner."

Ochoa stopped. How much he understood of Miguel's confession was debatable, but it was clear that he comprehended its gist because he waited until Miguel came up to him and then he grabbed the crucifix in his clenched fist, shook it and shouted, "Jesus Christ!"

"Yes," Miguel said, sure that the old man was going to either break the heavy gold chain or his neck, whichever gave first.

"You wrong!"

"That is true."

Ochoa's body quivered and his eyes blazed. And despite his diminutive size, for an instant he was omnipotent. Their eyes locked as they stared into each other's souls, and then the old man shrank back into mortality.

"We kill Apache."

"I suppose we must," Miguel said, "or else they will find and kill us first."

Ochoa dipped his chin in agreement and hurried on after his tribesmen.

They overtook the Pima warriors at sundown and arose the next morning just before daybreak. Ochoa told Miguel what he had already suspected, that they were now deep into Apache country and the only chance they had of victory was to catch the Apache by surprise. Failing that, they would be annihilated to the last man. Miguel nodded with understanding. There would be no quarter asked and none given.

That afternoon, without any apparent reason, Miguel

noticed a change in his companions. They had been cautious but relaxed before. Now they were tense and no longer spoke. They moved in single file along the Gila, which now rushed through pine forests and between steep canyon walls. The Pima saw deer and elk and managed to kill one of the latter, which they quartered and ate raw, since a campfire would be courting disaster.

Miguel forced himself to eat the warm, raw meat because he knew he would need all the strength that he could muster against the Apache. He was given a breechclout and a tanned buckskin to wrap himself in for warmth. That night he prayed fervently for God to be with the River People and bring them victory.

He was awakened in the starlight, and Ochoa motioned for him not to say anything but to come along quickly. Miguel could not see the moon and he was not sure whether he had slept one hour or five, but he thought it must at least be past midnight. The Pima floated as swiftly and silently as wraiths up the forest trail. They crossed a meadow that shimmered with dew, their passing more hushed than the flight of the great horned owl. At the far end of the meadow, they circled a beaver pond so quietly they did not even disturb a flock of sleeping mallards.

They traveled for a long time. Just when Miguel sensed that dawn was about to grace the eastern mountaintops with a patina of gold, they came upon an Apache encampment. Miguel saw a few wickiups, dark inverted bows covered with leaves and branches. He counted five campfires, but the sleeping figures lying about were in shadow and their numbers remained a mystery.

What they could count was the size of the Apache remuda grazing in a second smaller meadow. They were black blots shifting against a backdrop of ebony forest. And yet, anyone could see that there were at least fifty horses, perhaps as many as a hundred.

The Pima numbered thirty-seven. They drew close together and whispered rapidly as they made their plan of attack. Miguel did not understand a word. He pulled Ochoa close and breathed, "We mustn't kill the women or the children. They wouldn't do that, would they?"

"Shhh!" Ochoa hissed.

"But they can't—"

One of the Pima warriors jumped forward and clamped his hand down on Miguel's throat. He squeezed powerfully and stared into Miguel's eyes with his knife raised.

Miguel broke away, struggling not to choke or cough, which would be fatal not only for himself but for all the Pima. He looked back at the Apache camp. Was this a hunting party? God, he hoped so, because if it was a permanent village with families . . .

Miguel passed his hand across his eyes. He could scarcely fill his lungs. He concentrated on his breathing. He prayed to God for forgiveness and knew that his soul was already lost if innocents were about to be slaughtered. He glanced sideways at Ochoa and was appalled to see that the old man wore a grin on his wasted face. How many of his family had this vengeance-minded old Pima lost to the enemy? It must have been many because Ochoa looked rejuvenated, as fierce and deadly as any of the young warriors.

Miguel studied the other Pima and noted cold anticipation in their gaunt faces. They aren't going to spare anyone, he cried silently within himself. They are going to slaughter every last one! My God, Miguel thought, fighting down an insane urge to shout a warning to the Apache women and children, forgive us!

The Pima formed a line and crawled out of the forest into the grassy meadow on their hands and knees. Ochoa nudged Miguel and they both began to move. The old man was too unsteady to shoot arrows, but there was a stone club in his fist. Miguel hurried after the Pima, his sword whispering through the wet meadow grass which chilled him to the bone.

Halfway across the meadow, three of the Pima came to their feet and silently herded the Apache remuda off into the trees. Miguel was a good horseman and vowed he would grab one of the animals and run if it appeared that there was no chance of victory over the sleeping Apache. He would ride back to Casa Grande and on to the Pima village and ... then what? He shook his head. He was thinking crazy thoughts. One minute he was going to shout a warning and save women and children, the next he was going to run for the horses and escape. In truth, his mind was winging like a bat, darting this way and that.

How many Apache were up ahead? It was impossible to tell. There might be seventy or eighty and there might be half that many. Miguel saw the three Pima fold back into the meadow grass and slither more rapidly than serpents toward the Apache camp.

The first Apache dog to sense their approach materialized out of the shadows and growled, hackles lifting as it marched to the perimeter of the camp. It was a large dog and its growl was a deep-throated rumble. It opened its mouth as if to bark, and Miguel was sure that it would signal the attack while the Pima were still much too far out to overrun the enemy camp. The beast sniffed suspiciously at the air, but he was upwind and after a few moments the growl died. Yawning, the dog trotted back into the shadows.

After several minutes the Pima moved again, and had closed the distance to half when a dog they could not even see began to bark.

A guttural command from the camp only made the dog bark louder, and it was soon joined by several other dogs. The silhouette of a confused, half-asleep Apache lifted from the earth, and Miguel heard the now familiar whir of arrows in deadly flight. In the next instant the night silence was shattered by terrible screams as the Pima launched themselves into a hard run at the Apache camp. Miguel did not even remember coming to his feet. Suddenly he was up and sprinting forward, leaving poor Ochoa behind. A swarm of arrows buzzed past his ears, and Miguel leaped across a campfire, slashing at a silhouette. He felt the shock of the blow radiate upward from his wrist and heard his victim sigh into the cradle of death.

Bodies were flying in all directions. Miguel tried to ignore the screams of women and children. Dawn was breaking across the meadow, but they were killing under the darkness of the forest and it was blind, bloody work. He stumbled forward, thrusting and slashing and praying that he was attacking warriors instead of women and children. Something knocked him down, and when he tried to come to his feet, Miguel realized that he was dazed and wobbly. An Apache warrior screamed in his face and grabbed his hair. Miguel felt a stone knife brush his throat as he was flung down on a cushion of pine needles. He rolled and stabbed upward, impaling the Apache in the groin.

The warrior howled and struggled to open Miguel's throat wide. His knife furrowed Miguel's chin. The Apache lost his footing on the slick pine needles and toppled forward, driving another four inches of Spanish steel into his body. Skewered, he danced on the sword and then collapsed. Miguel jumped up, tore his sword free and charged back into the fray, slashing like a man gone mad. His blade chopped into an Apache's thigh. The warrior went down, and Miguel shoved his sword through the Apache's chest. His sword bound in the man's rib cage and would not pull free. Miguel tugged frantically, and when another Apache jumped at him, he forgot the sword. They locked, bodies straining.

The Apache smelled of horse and smoke. Miguel twisted away and drove his knee into the warrior's crotch. When the Apache groaned, Miguel grabbed two fistfuls of dirt and hurled them into his eyes. The man batted at his face, and Miguel doubled up his fists and punched him hard in the mouth. The Apache staggered. He screeched like a lion and gathered himself to leap at Miguel, but took a Pima arrow in the neck. Choking, he crumpled to the ground and began to gag. Miguel fastened both hands on the hilt of his sword and wrenched it free. Then he waded back into the melee.

Each time he felt the shock of his sword radiate up his forearms, he cried, "Hernando Santana!"

His cry transcended the howling mass and it became the Pima mantra of death. They did not understand the words, but they took them up all the same and the Apache died by the score. Several tried to escape but were overtaken by Pima arrows that struck them down like dark messengers of death. Miguel killed only men. In fact, he did not even see the Apache women and children, and assumed that they had escaped deeper into the forest. But in truth, he was too blood-crazed to care.

When the first bright shafts of sunlight filtered through high leaves into what was left of the Apache camp, Miguel collapsed with exhaustion, struck nearly dumb by the full carnage. He was heartsick to see a few older Apache women who had apparently elected to remain and fight to the death with their men. No Apache moved except the dying, not even the enemy's dismembered camp dogs. There were no dead children, but that gave Miguel scant comfort.

The forest floor was littered with bodies, both Apache and Pima. Miguel's mind was too numb to count the losses. And then he saw an odd thing. At least twenty of the Pima had detached themselves from the others and had darkened their faces with charcoal.

"Ochoa!"

Out in the meadow the old man rose from the body of an enemy, Apache scalp in one hand and a dripping war club in the other. The rising sun bleached the mountain meadow and ringed Ochoa's grinning face in a golden halo. The old Pima looked euphoric, and when he came to stand before Miguel, he held out the scalp and said, "You kill, you take."

Miguel recoiled. "No."

"Take!"

Miguel shook his head. He saw that a few other Pima

already had scalps. He turned back to the group of silent men with the blackened faces. "What ... what are they doing?"

Ochoa dropped his club and scalp. He reached out and grabbed Miguel's hair.

"What ... let go of me!"

But Ochoa did not let go. Instead, he smeared charcoal on Miguel's face. Miguel still held his sword, and it was all he could do not to use it on this crazed old man. Reason told him that it would be unwise to oppose these men. He did not understand what was going on, and was just about to demand an explanation from Ochoa when, suddenly, a motion caught his attention. He turned to see an Apache girl stagger out of the forest, obviously hurt. She grabbed a pine tree, steadied herself, and stared at the camp.

For a moment no one moved, and then the girl screamed. Miguel jumped forward and raced ahead of the Pima. He had always been a swift runner, and he reached the girl first. She had a knife and used it to inflict a nasty gash across Miguel's shoulder. He yelped in pain and knocked her to the forest floor. She struggled, and he struck her in the head with the base of his sword. The Apache girl went limp. Then Miguel raised his bloodied sword. The Pima crowded around and waited anxiously for the sword to fall.

Instead, Miguel choked, "If anyone tries to kill this girl, I swear to God I will kill them first."

The Pima frowned with confusion.

"Get back!" Miguel cried, taking a menacing step forward and slashing at the Pima, who retreated. "Ochoa!"

The old man pushed through the ring of angry, confused warriors.

Miguel shouted, "Tell them I will not stand for any more killing! This girl will live!" When the old man said nothing, Miguel cried, "My God, she can't be more than nine or ten years old! Have mercy!"

Ochoa translated, shaking his head with disapproval all the while. The Pima grew angrier by the minute.

Finally, Ochoa turned back to Miguel and said, "They would kill you and the girl both."

Miguel's veins flooded with ice water. He looked at the impassive, unyielding faces of the Pima warriors. "Tell them I fought bravely at their side. Tell them I want this girl."

"As your woman? An Apache!"

"I ... I don't know! But we can't leave her and we can't kill her. Don't you understand?"

"No."

The girl moaned. Miguel pleaded, "Tell them that God will be pleased if they spare this child. Tell them that someday ... someday she will be a blessing to the Pima."

Ochoa didn't believe it but he faithfully made the translation. The Pima argued bitterly until Miguel picked up the dazed girl and carried her away. Then they contented themselves with stripping the dead of their weapons and belongings and rounding up their ponies. By midmorning the girl was stretched across the withers of a pony and Miguel was riding along behind the group of black-faced Pima on their return down the Gila River.

_____ Chapter _____

TWELVE

The Apache girl would not speak, but she could snarl like a cornered beast. Not that Miguel had expected her to be conversant or animated, and frankly, there had been little time to communicate with the she-wolf who had at first tried to put a blade into his heart and then attempted to bite off his fingers.

At Casa Grande the Pima stopped for a full night's rest. Now that they were out of the mountains, they grew more relaxed, although they still posted guards just in case the Apache were on their back trail. That, however, was extremely unlikely. The Apache also appreciated the element of surprise, and when they did attack, the River People knew it would come at a most unexpected moment—possibly sometime in the fall or winter when the Pima migrated out of the desert after their summer crops were harvested.

What Miguel noticed most was how the Apache ponies, accustomed to the coolness of the mountains and fattened on the lush meadow grass, suffered. By the time they reached Casa Grande, their ribs were already outlined and they had lost their feisty spirit. Heads down, tongues lolling, the ponies had difficulty adapting to the low desert. What feed they could locate was confined to the thin grass that trailed the Gila River, and the ponies did not seem to think that very appetizing.

"What will happen to them?" Miguel asked. "Surely they will die out here."

Ochoa said, "Papago. Navajo and Zuni. We trade."

"I see."

Miguel was relieved. He did not know where those tribes lived, but he could not imagine that it would be any harsher than this fierce desert country. Many times a day he glanced back toward the distant blue mountains and could not help but envy the hated Apache their cool hunting grounds. He theorized that the Indians operated on the same basic levels that had always characterized the rise and fall of European nations: the stronger civilizations drove out the weaker ones and claimed the better lands. That being the case, it was understandable why the Apache occupied the game-rich mountains and why the gentler Pima were forced to exist in the harsh desert, the lowest rung on the ladder of geographic desirability. But the Pima had managed to harness the life-giving power of the Gila River.

Ochoa motioned toward the Apache girl, who now rode her own pony, led by Miguel. "We trade Apache, eh?"

"Who would take such a girl?"

"Mexicans. Papago. Navajo and Zuni."

The idea of selling a girl, even one as vicious as this Apache, was appalling to Miguel. "No. If anything, I'll return upriver and release her back into the mountains."

Ochoa's expression made clear his disapproval. Nothing more was said on the subject until they rode into sight of the Pima riverside village. The victorious warriors began to yip like a pack of coyotes as they raced their Apache ponies swiftly downriver. It was a stampede, and Miguel was sure that some of the women and children who rushed to greet them would be trampled to death.

The Pima warriors galloped around and around their

village, waving Apache scalps and shouting at the tops of their lungs. They threw the scalps and their weapons to their excited wives and children, who picked them up and began to dance and holler. It was a moment that Miguel would always remember, but not without sorrow. The families of the warriors lost in the battle searched in vain for their men. Soon, however, they began to wail in anguish, falling to their knees and tearing at their hair.

Miguel glanced sideways at the Apache girl. He could read her fear and loathing. He wondered if she expected to be stoned, beaten, or worked to death by her people's enemies. She was so young and yet so proud. She visibly shook herself and raised her chin, dark eyes flashing with defiance.

"Don't worry," Miguel promised, knowing she could not understand. "I swear that these people will not harm you."

Two of the mourning women saw the Apache girl and began to shriek. They grabbed up sticks and came flying at the girl, shouting and cursing, faces contorted with hatred.

Miguel drove his horse between the captive child and the Pima woman. He drew his sword, slashed threateningly at the air, and bellowed at the hate-crazed and determined Pima women. For several moments it was touch and go, with Miguel doubting he could keep the Apache child from being torn off her pony and flogged, or worse. Finally, he managed to escape the enraged squaws who hurled rocks at the girl.

"I'm sorry," Miguel said, drawing their horses to a standstill, "I never imagined that they would blame a girl for the loss of their men."

The Apache girl calmly studied his face with a hint of curiosity but without any evident gratitude. And then she did something that Miguel would never forget. She reached out and grabbed the gold crucifix and chain dangling from his neck and attempted to rip it free.

"No!" he barked, roughly tearing her hand away.

The girl stared at the crucifix, then peered deep into his eyes. She said something that he would have given anything to understand. She raised her face to the sun and began to sing. Miguel was shocked to realize that her song was a prayer for death.

"My God," he whispered, "what have I done?"

At that moment, Nanata came running forward. Miguel leapt to the ground and scooped her up in his arms, and her lips were wine to be savored. His head swirled and he pressed her body closely to his own, feeling her heat burning his flesh.

"I'm going to take you to be my wife," he said. "I'm going to marry and protect you."

Nanata hugged him tightly, now fiercely possessive. Miguel was about to kiss her again when his Apache girl drove her heels into the flanks of her pony and sent it lunging forward. The lead rope tore out of Miguel's hand and the girl and her horse shot off back upriver, racing like the wind.

"Damn!" Miguel shouted, grabbing the mane of his pony and swinging onto its back.

Nanata called out to him, but Miguel's full concentration was on the Apache girl, who rode as if she was a part of her horse. Being light, her pony outdistanced Miguel's flagging mount, and after two miles of running, his horse gave out altogether.

Behind him came other Pima, and when their bowstrings began to hum and arrows fill the air, Miguel attempted to drive his exhausted pony into them so that they could not hold their aim.

"Stop!" he cried. "Please. Let her go!"

Two of the Pima lashed him with their bows and rode on after the Apache child. Miguel was helpless to stop them, and they were on fast horses. He watched as they closed on the girl. He saw her look over her shoulder, judge the outcome of the race, and then swerve her pony into the Gila River. For a moment her horse floundered as it struck a deep channel. Then it began to swim with all its strength. The Pima could not get their Apache ponies to enter the water. They whipped them savagely until they finally entered the swift current, but then they turned and swam back.

The warriors were furious, but Miguel didn't care. He saw the Apache girl's horse gain the far shore and saw her glance back. And he swore she waved and that he heard her mocking laughter float across the Gila. In an instant she vanished into the palo verde and cottonwoods, going home. Going back to the mountains and to her people.

Miguel could feel the Pima's hot anger. Like the Apache girl, he raised his head and suffered what he was sure were Pima curses. Then the Pima spun their ponies around and went galloping back to their village, with Miguel close behind. When he rejoined Nanata, he searched her beautiful face in vain for recrimination. He took her back into his arms and kissed her mouth.

"It was God's will that the girl escaped. I couldn't have protected her from those squaws. They would have killed her while I was making love to you."

In reply, Nanata took his hand and pressed it to her soft bosom. Then she led Miguel and his lathered Apache pony toward her lodge. That night there would be celebrating and dances in their honor, as well as in honor of the Pima warriors both returned and killed in the high Apache country. Afterward, Miguel knew he would be expected to spend four days and nights in the hut with Nanata's family. After that, he would build his own mud and stick house, and he and Nanata would be considered man and wife according to the customs of the River People.

What even Nanata did not know was that Miguel would bind them in holy matrimony using his Bible in a private Christian ceremony. And so he attempted to straddle both cultures. And in that simple way, perhaps he and Nanata would be blessed with children, a long life, and as much happiness as a Spaniard could expect after being cast into the wilderness.

That night the Pima did celebrate. Old women

marched around the campfires with the hated Apache's scalps impaled on long poles. One by one the warriors were called forward to tell their version of the battle, which they did with great animation, waving their arms, striking at the invisible enemy, even mimicking shrieks of dying Apache.

Miguel found the entire display troubling. However, Nanata had only to look at him and smile with loving pride before his dark thoughts evaporated like spilled water. And when she leaned close against him, Miguel felt her shiver and knew that while the war party had been gone, she had been thinking only of him.

At last, when it was Miguel's turn to relate his version of the killing, he tried to beg off, but that was impossible. The River People made it clear they had already forgiven him for allowing the Apache girl to escape. With everyone laughing, Miguel was dragged to his feet. He raised his hand and sword while the Pima village cheered and hooted with appreciation.

"Talk," Ochoa ordered with a grin.

Miguel really had no wish to talk about slaughter and death. However, when he gazed into Nanata's lovely eyes, he knew that he would shame not only himself but this young woman if he refused this moment of dubious glory.

"I went into the battle," he began slowly, so that Ochoa could translate his words with accuracy, "with the others, and killed at least two of the enemy, maybe many more with my sword. One of these enemy would probably have killed me except that he was shot in the throat with a Pima arrow."

This bit of information set the Pima to clapping and cheering with the unabashed glee of innocent children. Having seen the Apache die so horribly, Miguel could not share their jubilation, and yet when he looked at Nanata, he could see her glow with love and pride. For her alone he forced his reservations aside and pushed on. And like other warriors before him, he began to act out the fight, slashing this way and that with his Spanish sword.

The River People were overjoyed. Pride radiated from their faces. They stomped their feet in appreciation and hooted with approval as Ochoa continued to translate. Miguel was aware that the old Pima was having a wonderful time embellishing his story, and had him hacking to death at least a dozen Apache.

When Nanata squeezed him and squealed with delight over his killing of another mythical Apache, Miguel forced a grin. He knew that it would be wrong—and probably impossible—to try and correct Ochoa. And when he looked into Nanata's beaming face, it was easy to let Ochoa go on with his glorified account of his conquests over the defeated Apache.

Miguel silently asked God and the spirit of Father Castillo to forgive him. He reminded both that becoming a Pima was not a thing that he had chosen out of his free will, but out of absolute necessity. That being the case, he believed that he might as well be a man respected among men. A warrior. A fighter like his brother. A man who tried to uphold the spirit of Christianity, yet was prepared to use the edge of his Spanish sword to save his adopted people from their traditional enemies.

Was that possible? Miguel did not know. All he knew for sure was that he had saved the life of a brave Apache child, and that this night he was going to make love to a beautiful Pima woman and claim her as his wife. And for now and a good long while, the lovely Nanata would bring him more pleasure and happiness than if he had found all seven of the Lost Cities of Cibola.

_____ Book II _____

VITORIO—PIMA WARRIOR

Chapter

THIRTEEN

Vitorio Santana glanced back over his shoulder to see his father laboring up the steep mountain trail. Vitorio laughed and called in Spanish so that only his father could understand his good-natured taunt. "Old man, you should be making baskets with my mother. She would make sure that you had enough corn mush to strain through your missing teeth."

Miguel was breathing hard. He stopped and peered up the trail at his son, the leader of this adventurous Pima hunting party. Miguel's lungs were on fire and he was visibly shaking from the exertion of the climb. It took him a moment to form a suitably insulting reply. "Vitorio, like your mother and the other old women, you talk too damn much. How are we supposed to kill deer if you scare them all away, more clumsy than a sleepy brown bear?"

"Don't you worry," Vitorio said, shaking his bow and arrows. "I will shoot us a nice fat buck, tender enough even for you to eat."

Miguel chuckled, not doubting his son's pledge for even a moment. It was autumn and the aspen were ablaze with color. This was the twentieth year that he had brought his only son hunting into the Mogollon Mountains near the headwaters of the Gila River. For most of those years, Miguel himself had led the Pima, twice fighting the Apache and always escaping back down into the Sonoran desert to boast of his victories.

But now the Apache that had long ago slaughtered his brother and the Spanish soldiers were only part-time residents of this high country. Most often they were off raiding the Mexican or Papago villages far, far to the south. Sometimes they were to the northwest, where they attacked and looted the Hopi or Navajo. And once in a great while they followed the Gila River down into Pima country, where they attacked and killed River People.

Miguel bore numerous scars from his battles with the Apache. He had been wounded many, many times, and one arrow in the thigh had given him a permanent limp. But a scar that Miguel was most proud of and often recounted receiving was the one inflicted across his shoulder by the little Apache girl whom he had saved from slavery or death. That had been a long, long time ago, and the years since had been surprisingly good for Miguel. He had been blessed with Vitorio and two handsome daughters. Blanca had married well and had two daughters, while his youngest, Jacova, had yet to marry, despite her beauty and the attentions she received from the young men of her village. She was sixteen, and even Nanata complained it was time for Jacova to take a husband, but Miguel loved her too much to make marriage an issue. He was looking for someone special for her. Someone outside his poor village, who would bring many horses in trade and would give her a more privileged life.

"Come on, old man!" Vitorio called, laughter in his voice.

"If you do not be quiet," Miguel replied with scorn, "you will chase all the deer away and attract Apache."

"Let them come," Vitorio said boldly. "We will let them feel the taste of Pima arrows."

Miguel and the others laughed, but not too loud. And as they continued on up the steep game trail that skirted a narrow canyon pinching in on the Gila River, Miguel tried not to think about how Vitorio was inhibiting their pace just so that he could join the hunt once more.

If I had any pride, Miguel thought, I really would remain at the Pima village with the women and the children. It was all right for old men to go out in the desert in the cool of early morning or evening and hunt snakes and rabbits, but venturing into these big mountains still claimed by the Apache remained a young warrior's privilege.

The thing of it was, Miguel could not bear to miss the beauty of fall in the high mountains. These towering mountains had beckoned him into danger for all of his Pima years, and he would gladly die in them rather than remain always in the desert. The brilliant colors of autumn lifted Miguel's very soul and made him sing praises to God, Jesus, and even—during the last few years—to the Pima holy spirits.

Miguel had always been the first to be critical of his failures, and time had not softened his harsh self-judgments. In truth, he had not failed completely in his Christian work, but he had certainly not succeeded as Father Castillo would have wished. The Pima had long since tired of admiring his crucifix or listening to him read from the Bible. Asking for divine forgiveness, Miguel had found it necessary to meld his Christian views with the Pima native religion. This compromise had bought him many years of success, but gradually the River People had lost their passion for the word of God.

The Pima stubbornly believed that Earthmaker had created the world from a tiny ball of dirt. He had danced upon the dirt until it had spread so very thin it touched the very edges of the sky. At that moment there had been a loud banging sound and Itoi had jumped out of earth to form the world with its mountains, valleys, and deserts. Human people then came into the world, but they were disrespectful, so Itoi and Earthmaker destroyed them with a flood. Itoi became known as Elder Brother and he was given the task of creating new and better people out of clay, and also teaching them the right way to show respect. Elder Brother lived with these new people a long, long time, but they grew weary of listening to him and finally banished him to the underworld. These were not the Pima, but instead the ones who built Casa Grande.

Under the earth, Elder Brother at last found the Pima. He led them back up on top of the world, where they drove the bad people away from Casa Grande. Elder Brother was very happy with the Pima. He promised them that the Gila River would flow forever and showed them how to irrigate and farm in the desert so that they would never grow hungry. He told them that he would return someday, and then he vanished. The Pima were very grateful to Elder Brother and vowed to wait for him forever. And that was why they had no desire to leave the Sonoran desert and attempt to drive the Apache from the cool, green mountains.

Years before, Miguel had scoffed at this simple tale of creation, but the River People had remained steadfast believers. Frustrated, Miguel had at last been forced to raise Elder Brother to the level of his own Christian deities. In this way alone had the Pima accepted Jesus, God, and Mary.

Now, as headman, it would have been wrong to argue with the Pima about their version of creation. And if he allowed himself to think about it long enough, Miguel turned melancholy and guilt-ridden when he remembered Father Castillo. On such occasions he would journey upriver to sit beside the padre's unmarked resting place and confess his failures. Miguel would ask for forgiveness and try to explain how difficult it was for a man to be born and baptized into one religion, then expected to live and accept another.

Miguel only wore the Castillo crucifix on hunting trips such as this, where it gave him comfort and protection. However, even in the desert he would occasionally ask Nanata to unwrap it from a sheath of soft leather before he dutifully recited the rosary using the links of its golden chain for beads. Sadly, the Pima no longer listened or tried to learn the rosary, but that was just as well, because Miguel was sure that age had betrayed his mind and he was not saying it correctly.

"Father!" Vitorio hissed with some urgency. "Get down!"

Miguel was pulled to the earth by one of the warriors. He was furious with himself for allowing his mind to wander again. He saw that Vitorio and the other Pima hunters were staring down the canyon toward the Gila River, and he squinted his eyes through the rising mist to see what they found so important.

"Father, look!" Vitorio said, crawling back down to the trail to his side. "They are white, like you! Spaniards, eh?"

Miguel squinted harder. His eyes were failing but not so that he couldn't finally see the source of Vitorio's excitement. Yes, these men *were* white! But they were unlike any Spaniards that Miguel had seen. They wore skins for clothing. They carried muskets that bore no resemblance to the old Spanish muskets borne by his late brother and the soldiers. These men carried no lances or heavy bullhide vests, and they had no horses, only mules. And what were they doing wading about in that river above the beaver dam?

So many questions! And no answers. Miguel was aware that Vitorio and the Pima hunters were staring at him, anxious for an explanation.

"Father, who are they?" Vitorio breathed as he and the others slipped deeper into the aspen grove and watched with fascination.

"I . . . I don't know!" Miguel admitted.

"If not Spaniards, who else?"

Miguel's head swirled. He blurted. "Maybe English."

"English?" Vitorio frowned with confusion. "Who are English?"

Miguel had to reach back to his childhood. Dimly he remembered his father's passionate denunciations. "The

English are a bad people from across the sea. Or the French! Another bad people. The enemies of my forefathers."

"Then we shall kill them," Vitorio said, nocking an arrow onto his bowstring. "It will not be so hard. Are those the talking sticks that you warned us about?"

"Yes," Miguel said. "They make loud noises and they kill, but they are not very accurate. Not like the bow and arrow."

Vitorio was the Pima "bitter man," a term that meant war or hunting party chief. It was his job to lead the River People into battle.

"Wait!" Miguel whispered frantically as doubts began to assail him. "I can't be sure. They might seek only peace."

"What are they doing in the water?" a warrior asked, lifting up to get a better view downslope.

"Maybe they are looking for gold," Vitorio said. "Maybe they have given up looking for their Seven Lost Cities of Cibola and are trying to find gold in the streams."

"Maybe," Miguel said, doubting it. "But my eyes are not so good anymore. Look closer, Vitorio."

Vitorio frowned. "It looks as if . . . they are killing the flat-tailed creatures! See their iron jaws!"

Miguel could not see the iron jaws, and yet he knew at once what the white men were doing. "They must be very hungry."

"And poor shots," Vitorio said. "Otherwise, they would shoot elk and deer."

"That is true," Miguel said. "Who would eat such ugly things when they could have roasted venison?"

The Pima watched closely. There were exactly ten of the white men dressed in buckskins and carrying muskets. They dragged many beaver out of their ponds and then sat down and filled their pipes with tobacco. As they smoked, they laughed and skinned the beaver. Then, to the Pimas' astonishment, they cut off the beaver's tails but threw their bloody carcasses into the thickets.

"They eat only the tails?" Miguel asked with astonishment.

Vitorio shrugged. "We have heard that the Ute Indians eat the hump and the tongues of buffalo."

"I never believe that," Miguel said. "But now maybe I do."

"Who cares what they eat," a Pima growled. "Let's move in close and shoot them full of arrows. We can take their fire sticks, buckskins, and those long knives."

Most of the Pima were agreeable, but Miguel held strong reservations. "It would be better," he suggested, "if we talked with them first. Maybe they are good French or Englishmen."

"Maybe," Vitorio said, sounding doubtful. "But if we talk, then we lose the advantage of surprise."

The Pima began to argue the point back and forth. And despite all his years of living with Indians, Miguel still chaffed at this tedious and inept method of arriving at a group decision. In fact, as often as not, the Pima never did reach a consensus, and that meant that no action was taken.

The arguing went on for nearly an hour, and before they had taken the first vote of whether or not to attack, the white men moved downriver and out of sight beyond the cliffs.

"Now look what we have done!" Miguel stormed. "Talk is useless since we cannot see them anymore."

"Maybe it is just as well," Vitorio offered. "If we killed or even wounded just one, the others would be very angry. If they were friendly before, they would then become Pima enemies. They might even join the Apache and come to hunt for us."

"Perhaps they are friends of the Apache," a Pima said.

"No," Miguel replied, "the Apache do not make friends."

This logic was so irrefutable that it settled the issue.

The white men were not friends of the enemy. But who were they?

"There is only one way to find out," Miguel said, coming to his feet and starting down the trail. "I will ask them."

"No!" Vitorio protested, running after him. "I will not let you take such a risk."

"I am old," Miguel reminded his son. He brought out the crucifix. "I will show them this. If they are English or French, they will recognize it and, as Christians, not kill me. If they kill me, you will know that they have the black hearts of the Apache and deserve to die."

"I will go with you," Vitorio decided.

"I would rather go alone," Miguel said. "You have a wife and children."

"So do you!"

"But you are grown and Nanata is old."

"All the more reason why she needs you," Vitorio said firmly.

"All right," Miguel said, deciding that he had lost the argument. "Come, then. We will see if these are good men or bad."

Vitorio looked pleased. He was a tall, handsome man, now in his thirties. He had inherited Nanata's beauty and high cheekbones along with the characteristic broad chest and shoulders of the Pima. From Miguel he'd inherited height, insatiable curiosity, and a slightly hooked Spanish nose. Miguel had taught his only son how to hunt and fight, but also about Jesus the Christ and Padre Castillo, about the legend of the Seven Lost Cities of Cibola. Nanata had taught him the religion and customs of her River People. She had blessed Vitorio with her warm and generous nature.

The Pima warriors did not like the plan agreed upon by the Santanas, father and son. They argued loudly that they wanted to come and, if necessary, fight. The debate became heated and threatened to become so protracted that, in the end, Miguel and Vitorio agreed that everyone should come along.

"But you must wait in the trees and not show yourselves until Father and I are sure these whites mean us no harm."

"Obviously, they cannot shoot deer. How could they harm us when they are such poor shots they eat the flat tails?" one of the Pima asked in a voice that dripped with contempt.

It was a question that neither Miguel nor Vitorio could answer before they started down a narrow, winding game trail toward the river. Halfway down the side of the mountain into the river gorge, they could smell the flat tails roasting, and it made their stomachs growl with anticipation. They were all reminded that they had killed no deer or elk for several days and that they were very hungry.

"Maybe we should pick up the bodies of the flat tails and eat them before we go see the white faces," one of the Pima suggested.

It was a good idea, so they momentarily forgot about the white faces and collected the carcasses, then went downriver a little ways and started their own fire under the canyonside rocks. In a short while they were eating well and the sunlight was fading quickly. It would be dark very soon.

"Perhaps we should wait until morning to pay them a visit," Vitorio said. "It is not good to visit at sundown."

Miguel nodded. He tried to remember if his parents had visited their friends at sundown. Finally, he decided that they had not. "If we visit them at sundown, they might think we come wanting their evening meal and the use of their robes and blankets against the chill of the night."

"Yes," Vitorio said. "We will wait until tomorrow and go see if they have eaten all the flat tails. Maybe we will shoot deer at sunrise and bring them presents of venison.

Perhaps then they will see how much better it tastes than the flat tails."

Everyone agreed to this plan. The warriors found a pool of water and tried to spear and shoot trout with their arrows. But the shadows were upon the water and they only managed to kill a few. Fortunately, they had pouches of cornmeal and plenty of roasted pinion nuts. Their fire was very small and made carefully with very dry wood so as not to make smoke. After all, this was still Apache country.

Vitorio arose before dawn and awakened two of his best hunters, Mitra and Cosan. Together, they readied themselves to hunt and left the Pima camp. It was difficult hiking back up the mountainside, but they wanted to have a commanding view of the river gorge so that they could see deer coming down to water. In this way it was easy to sneak downhill and lay an ambush.

Only they did not see any deer or elk that morning, and the reason became very obvious just as the first rays of sunlight were struggling over the steep canyon walls.

"Apache!" Vitorio hissed.

There were eighteen Apache trotting in single file toward where the unsuspecting whites were camped. Vitorio quickly took command. To Mitra he said, "Go back and awaken the others. Tell them what we have seen and that we have gone ahead to warn the white people before they are caught sleeping and easily slaughtered."

The hunter nodded and vanished into the trees. Vitorio glanced up the mountainside. His companion followed his eyes and understood. To have any chance of reaching and warning the whites before they were surprised by the Apache, they would have to climb like mountain goats and cut straight across these cliff tops and then try to get back down into the canyon on time. It seemed like an impossible order, but there were no easy alternatives.

It struck Vitorio that he might be acting stupidly. That the whites might actually be friendly with the Apache and had intended all along to rendezvous with them along the Gila River. But if that were so, why were the Apache moving so quickly before the sun was even over the lip of this deep river canyon? Vitorio thought that there could be only one answer, that the Apache had murder in their hearts. And even though his father had said that the whites must be either French or English, enemies to his lost people across the great water, Vitorio would have sided with the devil himself rather than allow the Apache a bloody victory.

"Hurry!" he called, bounding up the mountainside while at the same time being careful not to dislodge any rocks or debris which might tumble down and warn the Apache of their presence.

When they finally clawed their way out of the canyon, they ran through heavy pine and cedar forest for nearly a mile. Then, ducking under a twisted limb, they shot down a steep mountain trail better suited to a goat than a man. Pebbles and small rocks skidded out from under their feet and rolled into the manzanita and heavy brush, but Vitorio could not help that. He was unsure how clear was the path along the river, but unless the Apache had to take some detours or even had to enter and swim around half-submerged boulders, the race would be lost and the whites annihilated.

They bounded from rock to rock, often flying downward at a breakneck speed and without control. Arms waving like wings, feet striking rock and shale, somehow they both stayed erect until they emerged from the trees and found their progress blocked by a sheer drop-off just seventy feet above the river.

"Where are they?" Cosan gasped.

"There!" Vitorio pointed, almost straight down and a little to the south. "By my father's Holy Christ! Look at the fools!"

The whites were wrapped in their robes and still sleeping peacefully. There was no sign yet of the Apache, but Vitorio knew that the enemy could emerge from upriver at almost any moment. There was not a heartbeat to waste. Not nearly enough time to find a way to circumvent the cliff that blocked access to the camp below.

Picking up a fist-sized rock, Vitorio aimed for the smoldering campfire around which the sleeping whites were scattered. As with all Pima boys, he had tested his arm thousands of times by hurling stones at rabbits, birds, lizards, and snakes. Vitorio had long since graduated to the bow and arrow, but he knew his aim was still good and his arm very strong. But throwing downward was tricky and called for adjustments. Vitorio made them, then hurled the rock with all his might. The rock sailed on him a little and instead of hitting the fire and its kettle, it struck one of the sleeping figures.

"Owww!" the man howled, bolting into a sitting position. "Gawddamn! What the—"

"Apache!" Vitorio cried, letting another rock fly and having the satisfaction of seeing the kettle explode with water and steam erupt from the dying coals. "Apache!"

They could see the shock and amazement on the faces of the whites as they jumped to their feet and grabbed their rifles. Two of them wasted not a moment and fired up at the Pima. Incredibly, one of the rifle balls plucked at Vitorio's leather hunting jacket and the second ball whanged meanly between his legs.

"They think *we* are the Apache!" Vitorio cried, dropping to the ground as another bullet whip-cracked across the cold morning light.

Vitorio's companion was just about to say something when the Apache war party burst into view. They shrieked like banshees and charged the whites, who whirled and opened fire on them with a devastating volley. Vitorio watched in awe and amazement as rifle balls felled almost half the attackers like his father's old Spanish sword. The first volley was so lethal that the surviving Apache lost their will to fight. Wounded and in shock, they managed to unleash a few arrows, but no whites were struck down.

Vitorio and Cosan unleashed their own arrows, but

missed because of the great downward distance. Reloading quickly, the white men took aim and fired their second round. Three more Apache died trying to turn and run. A few dove into the water, but the whites shot them the moment they surfaced for air. Facedown, their inert bodies spiraled away in the river's current. Unfortunately, two of the swiftest Apache managed to dodge the bullets and reach cover upriver. The whites went after them, but Miguel knew that they would never overtake the fleeing Apache.

With gun smoke hanging over the riverside camp, and the echo of rifle fire ricocheting down the canyon walls, the whites gazed back up at Vitorio and Cosan. They called out in a language that Vitorio did not understand, and then they called out in his father's old language. "Hola! Hello!"

Vitorio grinned. He alone besides his father knew well this language. It meant that these whites were Spanish invaders. Miguel would be amazed and very happy to meet such people after all these years. Vitorio raised his hand in salute and the men below returned his greeting. They grinned. He grinned.

"Cosan," Vitorio said, barely able to contain his excitement as he pounded his Pima friend's shoulder. "Me, Vitorio!"

The whites called out what Vitorio thought were probably their own names. They motioned for them to come down and join them, and Vitorio was more than eager to accept this invitation. Already he could see a few of the whites were drawing their skinning knives and beginning to scalp the dead Apache.

This was good. Now, if they could find something to eat besides flat tails, there would be a feast and a celebration between the Pima and these strange new friends. But if the two Apache who escaped did not run into his father and the other Pima who would kill them, then Vitorio knew that they had to leave this river before more Apache came seeking bloody revenge.

Chapter

FOURTEEN

Miguel's eyes snapped open. He sat up noting that the sky was turning salmon overhead but that it was still very dim in the Gila River canyon. Their campfire was dead, and Vitorio, Mitra, and Cosan were already off on an early morning hunt. Miguel hoped that they were successful because it would be good to bring the whites a gift of venison. Besides, his own warriors were hungry.

Miguel struggled to his feet, joints popping and back stiff from sleeping on the hard, cold ground. Maybe this really was his last year to join the fall mountain hunt. And yet, Miguel could not bear missing the beautiful Fall colors during this annual high mountain deer hunt.

A noise foreign to the mountains caused his chin to lift and his lungs to hold their breath. There! He heard it again! Miguel strained to hear through the river's roar. What was that faint, discordant sound? Mountain thunder? No. He cupped a hand to his ear but the sound was lost. He moved over to the river and squatted on his heels. He splashed the snow-fed water into his face. It helped to awaken him. He did not hear the thunderlike booms any-

138

more. Perhaps the whites were shooting beaver for breakfast.

Miguel went downriver to collect some wood to rekindle the fire. He hoped that Vitorio, Mitra, and Cosan would be successful in their early morning hunt. Otherwise they would have to shoot some trout and would have nothing to give the whites in greeting.

Who were these strange men with buckskins and bearded faces? Miguel really had no idea. They were dressed unlike anyone he had ever seen before. In all the years that he had lived with the Pima, he had seen no other whites. And after a long time, he no longer wished to see them. He was Pima now. Just an odd old Pima who spoke Spanish, wore a golden crucifix, and sometimes talked like a padre or read his worn Bible and muttered the rosary to remind himself that he was a Christian born and once baptized—in Spain—of good family. No one took him that seriously anymore, although Miguel knew that he was much loved and respected by the River People.

It was enough to have love and respect, a good wife and three healthy and handsome children. It was enough to have enough to eat and to be listened to. And to laugh often. Miguel wondered if he could have done even better had he been able to return to Spain. Probably not. So, this was God's will for him, and what else was there to think?

Miguel spotted some driftwood wedged into boulders just a few feet out in the river. The driftwood had been tossed up higher in the cracks during a spring flood, and so he knew it would be dry. It was bleached white. His step faltered because the driftwood reminded him of poor Hernando's bones, also washed and bleached by water and sun.

Miguel's hand brushed across his eyes, clearing them of that terrible memory. Why did he repeatedly flog his spirit over Hernando's death after so many happy years? Why did the perversity of his mind insist on flashing that vision when it only brought him fresh pain from an old wound? He did not know. Hernando was long dead, and it was wrong to be reminded of his decomposed corpse trapped by this Castillo-blessed river.

Miguel stepped into the water. It numbed his feet and ankles, and he waded toward the rocks and the driftwood which would fuel their campfire. The narrow channel he had to cross was deeper than expected, and Miguel grew cautious as the water lifted to his knees and then to his thighs. He could feel the sand shifting out from under his weight as he leaned forward to grab a heavy piece of driftwood. The wood was lodged tightly into the boulders and he had to work to get it free. But finally he slid it out of the rocks and started inching back toward shore. He was halfway across the channel when two Apache attacked with stone knives.

Miguel instinctively threw the big piece of driftwood up to parry their attack. He felt a knife bury itself into the driftwood. He heard an Apache curse as they swarmed over the top of him, driving him over backward and deeper into the Gila. Miguel kicked and tried to fight the Apache warriors, but he was unarmed and they were strong, youthful, and desperate. One grabbed his crucifix and began to strangle him with its golden chain. He tried to fight, but it was hopeless. He was an easy prey. Just an old man gathering firewood.

God and Father Castillo, please forgive me all my sins! he cried silently as an Apache knife ripped into his chest, filling his lungs with Gila water.

Miguel ceased to struggle. Cold terror fled and he felt warm and peaceful as his mind shimmered into absolute darkness like the blaze of a shooting star.

A half mile upriver, Vitorio and Cosan were greeted warmly by the whites, several of whom spoke excellent Spanish.

"My name is Ben Jury," the leader said, extending his hand and looking curiously at Vitorio. "I am leader of this trapping party. Who are you?"

Ben Jury was sunburned, with a peeling nose and

strange, sky-blue eyes. They were the same height, and both were square-jawed and big-shouldered. "My name is Vitorio Santana. This is Cosan."

"What tribe do you call yourselves?"

"We are the River People."

"This river?"

Vitorio dipped his chin in assent.

Jury turned and glanced at his men, who were displaying the scalps they'd taken and talking with excitement. He frowned and turned back to Miguel. "The Spanish at Socorro told us that all the Apache were off raiding villages far down in Mexico. Obviously, they didn't know what the hell they were talking about."

Vitorio had no comment. He had never heard of Socorro, but he knew that his father was going to be very excited about this Spanish settlement. It was even possible that this Socorro was only a few days' journey and they could visit the Spaniards. Vitorio was sure that would please his father beyond measure.

Jury folded his powerful arms across his chest. "Do you River People go by any other name?"

"Pima," Vitorio said. He pointed downriver. "Our land is seven days' long walk."

"Into the desert?" Jury's bushy eyebrows rose in a question.

Vitorio nodded. He wondered why Ben Jury's tone of voice indicated he found that so hard to believe. Vitorio also wondered if all whites asked so many blunt questions.

Ben Jury wore a full blond beard and looked to be Vitorio's age, give a few years. His buckskins were well-made but covered with grease. He smelled of fat and blood. The lower part of his right ear was missing, and his peeling nose was crooked and probably fist-busted. He looked amused at the inspection he was receiving not only from Miguel but also from Cosan.

"What is the name of your people?" Vitorio asked.

"We're Americans!"

"Hmmm," Vitorio mused, wondering if his father had

ever heard of these people and if they had also come from another part of the world.

Cosan nudged Vitorio. He wanted a translation, and when it was given, Cosan said, "Ask him if they eat anything besides the flat tails."

Vitorio asked, and his reply was Ben Jury's resounding belly laugh. Vitorio flushed with embarrassment. He thought it very rude behavior and wondered if he should strike the fool down.

Before he could decide, Jury said, "Excuse me for laughing. We kill the beaver for their pelts, not their meat. Their furs are worth big money to us."

"Hmmm," Vitorio said, wondering why these furs were valuable. Even the largest beaver would not make a robe or a shirt. But Vitorio knew that he could not waste time worrying about such things. There were the escaped Apache to think about. In a few words he told Ben Jury that other Apache would soon come to fight. Maybe hundreds more.

"Are you sure?"

Vitorio bristled. He was not accustomed to having anyone question his judgment. He turned and pointed upriver toward where his hunting party was camped less than a mile away and said that he needed to warn them. After that, the Pima could decide if they wanted to leave at once, or risk spending another couple of days hunting on one of the many branches that fed the Gila River. If that were their decision, they would hide their tracks and disappear into the mountains, staying one step ahead of the Apache.

Jury turned to his own men and translated to those who did not understand Spanish. They began to talk with angry and excited voices. Vitorio was losing respect for these Americans. First they did not even post a guard against the Apache and would have been slaughtered in their sleep if he and Cosan had not awakened them. Next their leader acted amazed that the Pima would live in the desert, and now . . . now they quarreled among themselves like children.

Vitorio turned without a word and started upriver. He suspected that Mitra had already warned the Pima and that he would meet them coming downriver. Vitorio was anxious that his father should meet these Americans and learn of this Spanish village called Socorro. "Hey!" Jury called, hurrying after Vitorio and Mitra. "Whoa up a minute."

Vitorio stopped and turned. He did not know what "whoa up a minute" meant, but he thought it was that he should halt. He waited for Jury to speak.

"Listen," Jury began, struggling for his words. "I wanted to say thank you for saving our lives. *Muchas gracias, amigo.*"

Vitorio relaxed. For a moment he had feared that this big white-face might try and detain him. That would have been unacceptable.

"You coming back?" Jury asked. "If you do, we can maybe work out a plan together to surprise any Apache who might be stupid enough to come looking for a fight."

Not wanting to waste any more time, Vitorio nodded, even though he was not certain he understood this American. But if he *did* understand him, Vitorio thought that Ben Jury must be even stupider than he'd first supposed. There was no telling how many Apache were in this country. Hundreds might even be camped within just a few miles, and when they learned of their people being slaughtered by the Americans, their blood would be up and they'd be wild for revenge.

"We'll see you!" Jury called out, waving. "We'll be right along!"

Vitorio was not sure that was such a good idea. The Americans were deadly fighters with their long rifles and much better shots than his father had remembered, but they weren't very smart. The fur of the beaver tails was not nearly as thick and warm as that of bear. What kind of men hunted only flat tails, anyway?

Vitorio was confounded by these questions and yet

filled with anticipation when he thought of his father's reaction.

Cosan had to run to keep up with him as he hurried
upriver, moving through brush and around huge, mossy
boulders.

"Be watchful!" Cosan shouted. "Those two Apache
might be waiting to shoot us the moment we step around
a boulder."

Vitorio knew that his friend was right. He nocked an
arrow into his bow and proceeded with more wariness.
And when Mitra suddenly appeared, Vitorio almost put an
arrow in the Pima.

"You should announce yourself!" Vitorio scolded.
"How was I—" Mitra's face was pale and streaked with
tears. Vitorio forgot what he was saying and blurted,
"What is wrong?"

"It's your father," Mitra said. "He was killed by the
Apache."

For an instant Vitorio's knees turned to hot grease,
and he might even have fallen if Cosan had not grabbed
and supported him. Then he found his strength and threw
himself past Mitra and raced on to the Pima camp. When
he arrived, Miguel was stretched out dead on the sandy
bank. He had been stabbed many times and his throat was
badly discolored. Vitorio could see the marks of the
golden chain that had bitten deep into his flesh, perhaps
even strangling him to death while he was being stabbed.
Vitorio's beloved crucifix was gone.

Vitorio collapsed at his father's side. He bowed his
head and wept bitterly. He rocked back and forth with despair. He beat his breast and raked his flesh with his fingernails until he was covered with blood. Nothing helped.
Nothing would help until he had revenge.

Vitorio looked up to see the Americans standing
around, some holding Apache scalps in their fists. The
Pima eyed them warily, bows nocked, hands close to
knives.

"I will go after the ones that did this," Vitorio announced.

Ben Jury stepped forward. There was no happiness on his face now. "If you had not warned us and saved our lives, this might not have happened to your father. We are responsible."

"The Apache will pay," Vitorio said, going over to gather his things and prepare to track the Apache down.

"I'm going with you," Jury said.

"No."

"I will give you a long rifle and show you how to shoot it. You saw its power."

"No."

Jury spoke in a hard voice. "Listen, I want to repay you in the only way I know how!"

"You could not move fast enough."

"I can run as fast as any man," Jury said. "And these mountains have toughened me for climbing. I'm coming."

"Take me instead," Cosan begged.

"Me too," Mitra pleaded. "I loved your father."

Vitorio looked down at his father's knife-torn body. "I hope he is finally in his Heaven. And I swore I would wear that crucifix in his and Father Castillo's name. So I will."

"What crucifix?" one of the whites dared to ask.

Vitorio did not favor the man with an answer. Instead, he used his knife to cut off his long, black hair as a sign of mourning. He tried hard to think what was the proper thing to do. His mother would want Miguel to be buried close to their village. His father would have probably wanted to be buried at Casa Grande next to Father Castillo. This dilemma was complicated even further because the River People believed that death was dangerous to the living because the dead became very lonely and would try to pull them along into the Spirit World. That was why the Pima buried their dead as quickly as possible and tried not to think of them even when their loss was freshest and most painful.

"Bury my father downriver," he heard himself tell the Pima. "Away from this death place where the sun touches a green meadow and the colored leaves from the trees sparkle in the sun like flecks of river gold. Hunt game for three days. If I am not back, hurry on to our village and make ready for war."

The Pima wasted no time asking idle questions like the Americans. They began to break camp and fashion a litter to carry Miguel's body downriver.

"What did you tell them?" Ben Jury asked quietly.

Vitorio explained. When he was finished, he said, "Now, we will go. But what about your American friends?"

"They came to trap beaver. I reckon that's what they'll want to keep doing."

Vitorio could not understand this great ignorance. "Ben Jury, if we don't find the Apache who did this to my father before they reach others of their tribe . . ."

Vitorio did not have to finish the sentence. Jury might not be the smartest of men or the most wary, but he understood. "I'll explain that to them, but I doubt it will make any difference. The trapping is good on this part of the river and damn sure worth the risk."

Vitorio did not think these Americans understood their real danger, but he had given them his warning and that was enough. He gathered his things and made ready to leave.

"You won't need that bow and all those arrows," Jury said, taking one of his companion's firearms and ignoring the man's cry of protest. "Not with *this* rifle."

Vitorio took the rifle, pouch of ball and powder, but he made no apologies for retaining his trusted bow and his flint-tipped arrows. Arrows might not shoot as far or as straight, but he could fire ten as fast as the white-face could fire one ball, reload, and fire another. And one other thing, arrows killed in silence. Given that they were going deeper than he'd ever been into this high Apache stronghold, silence might be their only salvation.

Chapter

FIFTEEN

Before leaving, Vitorio learned that the Apache, after murdering his father, had fled up the mountainside rather than risk entering the Pima camp. It was easy enough to see their trail, although it was extremely steep with very few footholds.

"They went up *that*?" Ben Jury exclaimed, craning his head back and staring up at the impossibly steep mountainside.

Vitorio kicked off his moccasins and stuffed them into his quiver. He focused on the mountain, retreating as far as possible into the river. Only then did he see a very faint game trail that traversed the mountainside far overhead. The Apache, in their desperate escape from this canyon, had not even chosen the best line upward. It was truly amazing that they had not slipped on the moss and mist-slickened rocks and tumbled to their deaths. But somehow they had crabbed up to the game trail and escaped.

"This way," Vitorio said, choosing a meandering cleft in the rock and jamming his toes into its hard wetness.

"Christ! You got to be crazy!"

Vitorio *was* crazy. Crazy for revenge.

"Christ almighty! Wait up! What am I going to do with my boots and these rifles?"

Vitorio did not care. He had wasted enough time. Give an Apache an hour's head start and you might chase him all the way to Mexico. The murderers of his father had at least an hour's head start. Vitorio thought it best if Jury stayed behind.

Hatred drove Vitorio up the cleft in the rocks. It drove away the pain he should have felt in his toes and in his fingers. It took him upward faster than seemed humanly possible. The rock face seeped water. The river mist made every hand- and toehold risky. Twice the rock pulled out from under his hands and feet, almost dropping him to the rocks far below. But finally Vitorio inched over the lip of the thin game trail and dragged himself to safety. Glancing back down, his eyes snapped to the prostrated body of his father and he began to shake with rage.

Ben Jury had slung both rifles across his broad back, and his boots were tied by their laces and draped over one shoulder. He was coming up. Slow, muttering curses, but coming none the less. Vitorio was neither pleased nor impressed. He was sure the fool would tumble to his death. He should have remained with the other American flat-tail eaters. In truth, Jury would be a liability in these high mountains. Even if he did climb this rock wall, his inexperience and lack of stealth would get them both captured by the Apache.

But the fool *was* still coming. Vitorio contented himself with the knowledge that if Jury didn't fall to the rocks below, his long rifles would ensure that the two Apache who had killed Miguel Diego would die. Vitorio did not allow himself to think about what would happen afterward. He would fight to the death rather than be captured and tortured by the Apache. After his death, Nanata as well as his children and friends would grieve. But they would survive, and soon, because they were more Indian than Christian, they would push him out of their minds and become another man's family. That was the way of the River People.

Vitorio reached the game trail and slipped on his moccasins. He traversed the narrow trail until he arrived at the place where the Apache left it to strike higher up the mountainside. From this point on over the crown of the mountain, the terrain was thick with brush and forest. Vitorio knelt to examine the Apache tracks in detail, and for the first time he saw the drops of blood. Vitorio's spirits soared like a hawk on the hot, updrafting desert winds. His fingers traced across the damp, dark earth and he found more blood. In the heat of the desert it would already have dried. In this cold, misty canyon, it remained sticky.

So, at least one of the Apache had been wounded. But how badly? Enough to slow him down? It didn't seem possible that a seriously wounded man could have scaled the mountainside, but these were Apache.

Vitorio stared up toward the top of this ram-headed slab of granite with its thick forest riding its sweaty crown. The sky overhead was very blue, and the sun welcomed and then burned away the rising river mist. Over the muted roar of the water below, he listened for the sounds of birds and heard nothing. The forest was very still and the Apache tracks were deep-set into the pine needles, so that even camp women could have followed them. Where were the Apache going? It was too early to tell, but probably northeast toward the higher snow-covered peaks. Peaks loftier than any Vitorio had yet climbed. Peaks ringed by mist and buffeted by blizzards alien to a desert Pima.

"Hey!" Ben Jury shouted, his voice banging back and forth across the narrow defile of rocks. "I'm stuck! I can't go up and I can't go down. Dammit, Vitorio, you'd better not leave me hanging on the side of this slippery mountain!"

The American's words were hard and edged with desperation. Vitorio saw him clinging like a bug to the bark of a tall tree. Jury was stuck. Vitorio decided to leave him hanging. Better that than to allow him to come along and get them both killed.

"Hey!" the white man bellowed. "I'm going to fall and kill myself if you don't lower me a damned limb and pull me up! Do you want my death on your conscience! God will punish you, Vitorio! I swear by all that is holy!"

Vitorio did not know the word "conscience," but he did understand that Jury was calling God into this affair. That stopped him in his tracks. If God were truly angry at him, he would not allow him the pleasure of revenge. And Jury was right, it was not good to be responsible for the death of an innocent man, even if he was an American fool.

Vitorio found a long branch and returned to the game trail. He bent low and extended the branch down to the American, who grabbed it with both hands and gave a powerful yank. He almost sent Vitorio hurling over the cliff to his death. Only Vitorio's desire for revenge gave him enough strength to brace his legs wide and plant his moccasins on the faint, rocky trail. Jury possessed the dead weight of a brown bear. Grunting and straining, Vitorio bent his back to the mountainside and his lips drew away from his teeth in a grimace as the American scrambled up the last few handholds and grabbed his ankle.

"Don't move," Jury grunted, ripping Vitorio's foot from the trail. "I said, don't move!"

Vitorio tottered on the trail, every muscle in his body fighting gravity and the American's weight. And just when Vitorio was sure that he was about to be torn from the mountain, Jury threw a leg up onto the game trail and slithered over the lip of rock. He clung to the trail, his shoulders far broader than its width. He was breathing like a man who had run for hours.

"Jeezus!" Jury groaned, twisting around to stare at the men and the water far below. "We'd sure better get those Apache after surviving that!"

Despite himself and the empty, bleeding hole in his

heart due to the loss of his father, Vitorio made a wry smile. This white man, this American, he did not know the first thing about the forest or about Apache, but at least he was brave. Well, now he would see if the American really was strong enough to keep up with a pace that would overtake the Apache. Vitorio very much doubted it. And if it were not for the fact that one of the Apache was wounded, there would be no hope of catching and killing them at all.

"Hang on while I pull on my damned boots!" Jury swore, edging into a sitting position. His rifles, pouches, and blankets were tangled up together around his shoulders. Vitorio thought it a miracle that one of the rifles did not explode and kill the man outright. He waited with stoic impatience. He glanced up at the soft azure sky. No storm clouds on the horizon. That was good.

"All right," Jury grunted, pushing to his feet and balancing on the trail. "Whew! Long first step down, I tell ya!"

Vitorio turned and started after the Apache. Behind him he could hear Jury kicking loose rocks, sticks, and pebbles off the trail, which then cascaded down on the people below. He knew that, somehow, he was going to have to teach this big American how to walk softer. Maybe his heavy boots were partly to blame. If he had thought of it, he would have asked one of his hunters to trade the American's boots for a pair of leather moccasins. Too late now. But when they began to close on the Apache, Ben Jury was either going to have to learn to walk softly in his boots or else he was going to walk barefoot.

They traveled all that morning in hushed silence, constantly moving higher into the mountains. Vitorio was not the finest tracker among his people, but the two Apache were not expecting to be pursued and made no attempt to hide signs of their passing. Furthermore, one of them being wounded, they were slowed, and wherever they crossed rocks, there were drops of dark blood. The blood was exposed to the sun now, but it remained sticky to the touch. Vitorio knew that the Apache were less than a mile ahead.

"How far?" Jury asked.

Vitorio stood and wiped the blood on the bark of a Douglas fir. When he spoke, his voice was soft. "Between us and that bare ridge," he said, pointing to a rocky spine less than two miles distant.

Jury unslung both of his rifles and handed one to Vitorio. "Maybe it's time you put that bow and arrow away and I taught you how to shoot a *real* weapon."

"No," Vitorio said, gripping his bow tighter. "I keep my weapons."

"You want me to kill both 'Pache?" Jury asked. "One with each rifle?"

Vitorio almost scoffed at the suggestion. This American had a very high opinion of himself.

"Listen," Jury said, "I'm telling you that I'll put a bullet into each one of 'em before you can even fit an arrow to your bowstring."

Despite himself, Vitorio reached out and took the rifle. He was surprised at its weight. No wonder the American had been so hard to drag up the face of that rock wall. Why, those two rifles alone would weigh more than a fat beaver.

"Here, I'll show you how to cock, aim, and fire," Jury said, leaning his weapon against a tree. "I'll get 'er all loaded and ready."

Vitorio scowled. While they were talking, the Apache were moving. Still, he well remembered overseeing the devastation that the long rifles had dealt the Apache war party. Furthermore, since childhood he had been fascinated by the stories his father had told about the soldiers' old Spanish muskets.

"Now look," Jury said patiently. "These are both primed and ready to fire, so—"

"Shhh!" Vitorio commanded.

"What is it?"

Vitorio grabbed and yanked Jury off the game trail

into the surrounding forest. He leaned forward and held his breath. There, he heard it again! The call of excited voices flowing down from the higher mountains.

Apache voices.

Vitorio swore in anger. If he and the noisy American had run a little faster instead of talking, they would have overtaken the two murdering Apache before they reached their camp. Now Vitorio was sure that they had lost that opportunity.

"What are we going to do?"

"Kill them."

"But if they've reached their village . . . hell, Vitorio! We don't even know which ones put their knives in your pa!"

Vitorio had heard enough talk. Angry and determined, he shoved the rifle back into Jury's chest and took off at a run through the forest. When he looked back, Jury wasn't to be seen. Just as well. Vitorio was certain that if he had any chance of getting to the Apache camp and avenging his father's death, he needed to do it alone.

Ten minutes of hard running brought him to the crest of the barren ridge. Vitorio's lungs were on fire. A thousand feet above, the timberline glistened with snow and its lofty peaks swam in a sea of pale blue sky. Vitorio fought for breath. He had never been in such thin air. It robbed his legs of their speed and power. Vitorio lowered himself against the ridge and squirmed up to the crown of the ridge to peer down into a saddleback where snow melt had formed an alpine lake so deep it was almost violet. The lake was ringed by meadow.

He watched as his father's killers staggered down into the saddleback to join what was obviously an Apache hunting party. There were a half-dozen Apache camped beside the alpine lake, and perhaps a dozen ponies grazing on the meadow grass.

Vitorio saw the badly limping Apache fall. The man was helped up by his stumbling companion and then joined by the other members of the hunting party. Even from a distance of nearly a quarter of a mile, Vitorio could see his father's murderers pointing to the southwest where the Gila River churned through deep canyons flowing down the western slope of the Mogollon Mountains.

The Apache were very excited. They began to shout and beat their breasts, probably at the news that so many of their number had been slain by the American rifles. Vitorio hugged the ridge line. He focused on his father's assassins, and his mind held but a single purpose—kill them to the last man. No matter what, at least get the pair who'd murdered Miguel.

If the Apache chose to return to the Gila, that would play in his favor. He could locate a good shooting position, then ambush his father's murderers and try to escape with his life after having satisfied his revenge. But if the Apache chose to unite with others of their people to attack in greater numbers, then Miguel would have to intercept them first and take his chances.

It was a waiting game. The air was crisp and the sun felt good on his back as Vitorio watched the Apache attend to the wounded man who had taken a rifle ball in the thigh. The leg-shot Apache was very weak, and Vitorio had to give the young man credit for traveling this far in hard country with such a bad wound. Miguel Santana's other assassin was a tall warrior with a yellow headband. He was very angry and kept shouting and exhorting his companions to join him in returning to kill all the Americans and Pima.

"Hey!" a voice whispered.

Vitorio twisted around, his hand streaking to his knife. He relaxed to see Ben Jury drop to his hands and knees and crawl up the ridge to join him.

"Thought you got rid of me, didn't you," Jury said with a loose grin. "Thought I'd turned tail and headed back to the Hee-lay like a cowardly coyote."

"Shut up," Vitorio ordered, returning his attention to the saddleback.

Jury did keep quiet, for about two minutes. Then he

said, "I reckon I can figure out that the one with the bad leg has your evil eye. Who's the other 'Pache you're so determined to kill?"

"The one with the yellow headband."

"He seems real upset," Jury said, dragging his rifles up beside him. "You want me to calm him down permanent?"

Vitorio stared. "You can do that from this great distance?"

Ben Jury wet his finger and held it up. "Not even the slightest riffle of a breeze. Distance about three hundred yards, maybe a shade more. Yep. If I can get him to stand still, I can put a ball in his brisket."

Vitorio reached for the rifle. "I'll do it."

"Oh no!" Jury hissed, pulling away. "This kind of shootin' would have tested even old Daniel Boone. You may not appreciate my runnin' or climbin' ability, but I expect you'll soon appreciate my marksmanship. And I hope to hell you realize that we are about to start one hell of a fight. Those 'Paches down there are going to be madder than a teased weasel."

"No more talk."

Jury edged back down the slope a few yards and admired his rifles as if they were young women or fast horses.

"These are both Kentucky rifles," he explained, "but neither one was made in Kentucky. Mine comes from the finest gunsmith in Pennsylvania. I ordered it special. Now this other rifle, the one I was going to teach you how to fire, it comes from a gunsmith down in Chattanooga, Tennessee. It's a little heavier and shoots a .40-caliber ball a wee bit farther than mine, but I don't know her as well and she ain't as pretty. You can see that the craftsmanship isn't—"

Vitorio had heard enough of this nonsensical prattle. He grabbed Jury by his buckskin sleeve and hissed, "No more talk!"

Something like a cold wind passed across Jury's eyes and they grew as hard as blue ice. "If you'll let loose of my arm, Vitorio, I'll get your killin' done."

Vitorio released the man. He watched as Jury took his

Pennsylvania rifle and slithered back up to the crown of the ridge. "All right," Jury said, "you, bein' an Injun, know those Apache better than me. After I shoot the one with the yellow headband, what's going to happen?"

"They'll attack."

"On horses or afoot?"

Vitorio considered the question. From past encounters with the enemy, he knew they were skilled riders, but in a hard fight they much preferred to fight from the ground. "On foot."

"Good!"

Jury stretched the long rifle across the backbone of the ridge. He cocked the hammer and laid his cheek to the polished wooden stock. Vitorio watched with fascination as the muzzle of the rifle shifted to bear on the tall Apache.

Only instead of killing him, Jury said, "As soon as I fire, hand me the other rifle and I'll try and finish off the one with the bloody leg."

"No," Vitorio said. "I kill him."

"Fine," Jury breathed, closing one eye as he took aim. "God knows I'll still have plenty more targets. I hope you can use that bow and arrows. They'll be on us before I can load twice more."

"Shoot, you American!"

Jury took a deep breath and held it for a moment as his finger slowly squeezed the trigger. The Kentucky rifle's retort shattered the high alpine stillness. Smoke belched from its muzzle and Vitorio stared. For what seemed like forever, the Apache in the yellow headband stood rooted in place, and then, as if touched by a bolt of lightning from the heavens, he lifted onto his toes and his hands fluttered to his chest.

Vitorio watched a small crimson rose soak into the Apache's buckskin shirt. Despite the distance, he witnessed the Apache's bewildered expression as the enemy stared down at the wound before he toppled face first into the short meadow grass.

Jury dropped the first rifle, snatched up the second one

and fired in a single, fluid motion. The Apache below were stunned. They gazed up at the cloud of rifle smoke even as Jury's second rifle ball whistled through the lean mountain air and embedded itself in another warrior's stomach. The man threw back his head, grabbed his belly and folded to his knees, howling at the sun. His companions scattered for their weapons and then they came boiling up the slope.

Vitorio jumped to his feet. He cursed the charging Apache and danced to mock the enemy until they were within the killing distance of his arrows. Displaying even greater Pima disdain, he turned his back on the screaming Apache and calmly watched Jury reload.

Jury's movements were precise and well-rehearsed. He dropped the butt of his rifle on the ground and used his powder horn to measure and pour a quantity of coarse black powder down the barrel. Next, he placed a ball wrapped in a greased linen patch over the barrel and held it with his thumb before ramming it home with a smooth stick. He slipped a little metal percussion cap over a nipple and tossed the rifle to Vitorio, yelling, "Hold it ready for me while I load the other!"

Vitorio held the rifle. He turned to watch the pack of shrieking Apache as they struggled up out of the steep saddleback even as they fitted their arrows on their bowstrings. Had they been attacking across flat ground, the Apache would have already been firing. As it was, they still had another fifty yards to climb.

Vitorio cursed them. He bumped the rifle to his shoulder and laughed with scorn as the Apache threw themselves on the ground, expecting the rifle to belch fire, smoke, and death. It cost the Apache three or four seconds before they realized that Vitorio was only mocking them with the threat of the American's rifle. By then Jury had the second weapon loaded.

Again the rifle boomed and an Apache was kicked over backward to tumble down the slope. Vitorio handed the American the remaining loaded weapon. The Apache kept coming, although there were now only four—then suddenly three as the second rifle reached downslope like a finger of death to touch another warrior.

"That's it," Jury said.

Vitorio spread his feet and drew back his bowstring. A Pima arrow whispered downslope and found the heart of an Apache. The last two warriors halted and unleashed arrows. But they were firing uphill and their shots were much too hurried. Vitorio dropped one Apache and then sprang forward drawing his knife. He had the downhill momentum and the revenge. His knife found and penetrated the enemy's rib cage.

Vitorio shouted in victory and went racing downslope toward the last Apache, the one with the hole in his leg who had killed his father. As Vitorio attacked, the wounded Apache pushed himself to his feet, leg still bleeding. He was thin and very pale. He swayed on one leg and drew the knife that had taken Miguel Santana's life down in the Gila River.

Vitorio skidded to a halt, crouched and extended his own knife. He wished to see the wounded Apache's fear. To watch him panic like a rabbit caught in a noose as the hunter approached to end his worthless life. Instead the Apache took a faltering step forward and snarled without a hint of fear.

Vitorio straightened from his crouch. He studied the Apache, realizing that he was little more than a boy. The boy took another step forward, yelling in a pathetic attempt to unnerve him. Vitorio lowered his knife, with admiration enough to outweigh his hatred and revenge.

He walked over to the dead Apache with the yellow headband and stared at the crimson hole dead center in the front of the buckskin jacket. Ben Jury was truly a man to be feared with that long rifle, but Vitorio did not feel good about this death. There was no honor in killing a man from such great distance.

He reached down and his blade flashed, cutting the dead Apache's jacket away to reveal the Castillo crucifix mired in jelling blood. Salty tears filled Vitorio's eyes as he grabbed the warrior by the hair and cut a scalp lock. Shaking it at the boy, he again looked for fear but found none. Vitorio removed the crucifix, wiped it clean on the dead warrior's ruined jacket, then placed it around his own neck.

"Vitorio Santana!" he shouted at the youth. "Pima!"

Instead of recoiling in fear, the Apache took another hobbling step forward, his own knife whipping the air between them. He reminded Vitorio of a young eaglet he had once found abandoned in its nest. The eaglet had died of hunger rather than allow itself to be fed by a man. Its obsidian eyes had burned with defiance to the last moment of its proud life.

Vitorio studied the Apache's mangled leg and he heard himself say, "There is no glory in this. My father's death has been avenged."

Vitorio turned his back on the Apache and went to gather the ponies. Behind him the youth kept shouting his feeble challenges, swaying around in circles, hot eyes revolving between Vitorio and the big American who came striding down through the Apache bodies to help gather the ponies.

The Apache boy began to stagger up the slope in a desperate attempt to reach the weapons of his dead companions. But by then Vitorio had the ponies gathered and was leaping onto one's back. "Vitorio, are you just going to leave him?" Jury asked, slinging the rifles over his own back before he climbed onto a pony.

"Yes."

"Better I should shoot him and end it quick. With a leg torn up like that, and out here alone in these high mountains, he's sure to die."

"No," Vitorio said, watching the youth fall and begin to drag himself up to his dead friends and their weapons. "He is Apache."

"If he lives, he will tell his people what you have done and there might be trouble."

Vitorio had thought of that, but the idea of Apache attacking his people was nothing new. Better, in fact, that they would expect an attack and be ready to defend themselves and gain a great victory.

"What will you do now?" Vitorio asked the American.

Jury shrugged. "Trap beaver. Maybe go along with you people out of these Apache mountains and see what the lower country has to offer. I don't know. Why do you ask?"

"Apache come soon. Better we fight together."

Jury barked a laugh. "Oh, I see how it is! Now that you've a taste of what a Kentucky rifle can do, you're more of a mind to tolerate us Americans, isn't that the way of it?"

"You talk too much," Vitorio said, reining away.

"Yeah," Jury called, "but I back up my talk with my shootin'. Even a Pima like you can see that by now!"

Vitorio had to admit that he had greatly underestimated Ben Jury. He'd never expected the white-face to climb the rock cliff out of the Gila River gorge, and he'd been sure that Jury would quit on the trail of the Apache. He'd been wrong on both counts and impressed beyond words by the American's marksmanship.

But one thing he was *not* wrong about. Ben Jury *did* talk too much.

Vitorio and Jury herded the captured Apache ponies out of the saddleback toward the distant Gila River. At the crest of the ridge, Vitorio reined in his pony. He gazed down at the Apache and again shouted, "Vitorio Santana!"

His voice echoed and rolled around in the saddleback. The last Apache looked up and screeched like an attacking eagle as he pushed himself to his feet and tried to fit an arrow onto bowstring.

"Yahnosa!" the youth cried, banging his thin chest.

Ben Jury frowned. "Is that his name, Yahnosa?"

"Yes."

"We'd both better hope that he never comes up on us from the backside."

"Maybe we will meet again some day when he is a man and have a good fight," Vitorio said as he reined his pony away, smiling to hear the Apache scream in helpless fury.

Chapter

SIXTEEN

It felt good to ride Apache ponies back toward the Gila River. All afternoon Ben Jury talked about Socorro, Santa Fe, and the United States of America. He spoke of iron horses made of steel that belched smoke and could run great distances without ever getting tired. He told about huge cities in the East where there were houses taller than trees. Of magnificent southern tobacco and cotton plantations and a river so wide that nothing could swim it. Of buffalo and Sam Houston, who was his personal hero, and of a fight for independence that was brewing in a place called Texas between the Americans and the Mexicans.

"I mean your people no disrespect," Jury said with a tone of warning, "but all the Indian Nations back East are no more. I expect there were once millions of Indians along the East Coast, but they've either been killed or driven away. Vitorio, if I were you, I'd consider making a quick peace with the American government. It's your only chance."

"Chance for what?"

"Chance for keeping your people from being killed or driven off their lands."

"Who would want our desert lands?"

"From what I've heard, you have a good point," Jury agreed. "But you never know. And comes a time when you have to chose between helping Americans and helping Mexicans, you'd be wise to chose us over them back-stabbin' greasers."

"You Americans can hunt our beaver. You can swim, fish, and drink our water. The harvest of our fields is life to us, but we will share what we can."

"You are a good and a generous people." Jury looked at him closely. "Let me ask you this. Have you ever found gold in the Hee-lay River?"

"No," Vitorio said, deciding not to tell the American that once, long ago, a conquistador had found a golden nugget in the foothill country.

"That's probably a good thing," Jury said, but with an unmistakable note of disappointment in his voice. "It means that the only thing you have to offer is a few short-haired beaver, and I mean to trap them out before next spring."

Vitorio objected to this plan. It seemed foolish to kill all of anything, for then it could never replenish itself. Later, if the Americans really came with their traps to catch the flat tails, he would speak to them about such a foolish practice and make them see the wisdom of leaving some of the creatures to propagate.

"The thing of it is," Jury said with a thoughtful frown, "you being able to speak Spanish, you can generally find someone who will listen. But you also need to speak English. When I come down to your village, I'll teach it to you."

Vitorio was not at all sure that he wished to learn English. The fact that he spoke Pima and Spanish and was conversant with the Yuma, Navajo, Apache, and Papago seemed plenty good enough. And yet, if the Americans spoke English and they were in the habit of killing the Indian, then perhaps it would be wise to learn English.

"If the Mexicans come marching to your village, you

had better fight them," Jury solemnly warned. "They're as double-dealing as the Apache. You can't trust them."

"The Pima do not want to fight anyone, not even Apache. But against Apache, we either fight, be killed, or be enslaved."

"Them Chiricahua Apache were the first I'd ever shot," Jury confessed. "Killin' 'em gave me no satisfaction. Indians or not, they're still people."

Vitorio stared through the white man. "You talk too damned much."

Jury flushed, realizing what he'd said. Then, to hide his embarrassment, he began to talk about a girl he knew in a place called Tennessee.

"She cried when I left her, of course, but I had to go. Her father owned a general store and he tried to put the yoke around my waist while she tried to put the noose around my neck. 'Course, I ran like I'd seen a ghost. Rode all the way to Santa Fe and worked as a teamster for two years, watchin' the trappers come in to trade their plews. That's beaver pelts."

"Oh."

"Decided to start up my own little fur-trappin' expedition. Saved up some money, borrowed a whole lot more for provisions, traps, and such. That's why I can't exactly up and leave the rest of the boys. Half what they wear, shoot, trap, and eat belongs to me and my Santa Fe partners."

"I see," Vitorio said, not sure if he saw at all. But he enjoyed learning about the Americans and about the exciting things that were happening on the eastern side of the great mountains. It made him wonder if his own life among the River People was as fulfilling as he had always supposed.

Oncoming darkness forced them to make camp before they were reunited with their friends. Vitorio and Jury found a box canyon with good grass and water. They drove the ponies into it for the night and made their camp beside the entrance.

At dusk Vitorio hiked up toward a stand of aspen where a small mountain spring fed the canyon. As expected, just at twilight, several deer came out of the woods to drink. Vitorio's bowstring hummed and his arrow flew long and straight. He returned in darkness with fresh venison.

"Nice work," Jury said, cutting up some fresh steaks and skewering them on willows over his fire.

"There are times," Vitorio pointed out, "when the silent death is better than the noisy one."

"I suppose you're talking about not rousing any Apache who might still be in these parts."

Vitorio nodded. He was famished and the meat sizzled, causing his stomach to growl like a mean dog.

"You reckon there are more Apache hereabouts?" the American asked.

Again Vitorio nodded.

"You sure?"

Vitorio gazed across the fire at the white man. It seemed like a stupid question since no one except the Apache could predict where they might be or what they might do next. "No," he said, "I am not sure. But it is my guess they are close."

Jury sighed. "That's bad news for me and the boys. We came over from Socorro expectin' to have these mountains to ourselves, and now you're tellin' us we might have to leave 'em or lose our scalps."

"There are beaver down in the lower country," Vitorio said, describing how several rivers and streams joined the Gila in the foothills and desert. In these places the beaver were plentiful.

"Well, that's nice to know," Jury said, looking happier. "But the thickest and most valuable pelts are in these high mountains where the nights get real cold. Still, it'll be snowin' here in a few weeks, and might be that we'd come out just as well takin' more beaver down in your hot country, even if they aren't top quality."

Victoria finally asked what "quality" meant and what

was so special about the beaver. At this, Jury chuckled and turned his venison steak to burn the red side. "Aw hell, of course you wouldn't know! Beaver pelts are used to make fancy high hats for the eastern gentlemens!"

Jury then used his hands to indicate how tall the hats were and describe their shape. Vitorio was not impressed. Why would anyone want to wear such a ridiculously shaped hat? If he understood the American correctly, these beaver hats had almost no brim to ward off the hot sun, and their height would most certainly cause them to blow away in a stiff breeze.

Jury thought his reservations very amusing. "Well, Vitorio," he said, "as you can see, I ain't wearin' a hat at all. But when I do, it's one with a low crown and a big brim to keep the sun off'n my face and neck."

The venison steaks were ready, and for the next half hour Vitorio and Jury ate greedily. When finally satisfied, they carried the rest of the unquartered deer up into the rocks so that if any hungry grizzly bears scented the kill and came to eat, they would not suffer an attack.

"One thing I would like to know," Jury said, producing a corncob pipe and tobacco. "I saw that there crucifix you took off'n the dead Apache. Prettiest thing I ever laid eyes on."

"It was my father's," Miguel said, lifting it out from his collar and holding it up to gleam in the firelight.

"Your father's?"

Vitorio nodded, and when Jury raised his eyes in question, Vitorio felt he had no choice but to explain. "My father arrived in New Spain with his brother, who was a captain of the conquistadors. On that same expedition, there was also a saintly old priest named Father Francisco Tomas Castillo, whom my father loved."

"Your father was a Spaniard? Figures, you both being so tall and light-skinned."

"He was of high birth from a city called Cadiz. Have you heard of this place?"

"Nope. Don't even know where Spain is, exactly."

"Well," Vitorio said, "no matter. My father told me many, many times that the priest was seeking to baptize and save Indian souls. My uncle, Hernando Diego Santana, and his conquistadors were seeking the Seven Lost Cities of Cibola."

"Even I have heard that men once believed in them fabled cities. Amazin' anyone could think that there were cities of gold in this wilderness."

"Such places have been discovered before," Vitorio reminded the American. "In Mexico and in Peru."

"I wouldn't know about that," Jury confessed. "I only got a couple years of schoolin' back in Virginia. I can read, write, and count, but I'm ignorant of history."

Vitorio admitted that he could not even read and write and that all he knew of history was what his father had told him about Spain and her enemies, the English and the French. He confessed that he had never even heard of Americans before now, and asked Ben Jury to tell him about his own people.

"Americans are a rough and rebellious bunch," Jury announced, looking very pleased by his own definition. "Like the Spanish and the French, we also hate the English. We booted 'em out of our country before I was born and founded a republic that became these United States. We're expansionists, Vitorio."

"What does this mean?"

"It means we intend to go to war with Mexico, who threw your father's Spaniards out of California not long ago. We'll kick Mexico out of Texas *and* California one day, unless I'm badly mistaken. After that, we'll seize by force all this North American continent from the Atlantic to the great Pacific Ocean."

Vitorio had no idea where either California or Texas was located, although he had heard those names spoken when other tribes had traded with the Pima. But the notion that his father's Spanish people had been defeated by Mexico caused him considerable discomfort. He was glad that Miguel had not known of the Spanish defeat, although he might not have greatly cared after living so many years as a Pima.

They talked very, very late that night, eating venison and tossing sticks onto their fire to keep away bears or other wild animals. Ben Jury was interested in conquistadors as well as the Castillo crucifix. He asked if there was any other beautiful legacies of the Spanish priest.

"Only a chalice, a Bible, and a few other things not of great value," Vitorio assured him.

"You got any Spanish armor?" Jury asked. "Didn't them conquistadors have helmets, breastplates, and swords?"

Vitorio had to smile at the question. "It seems that you *do* know a little history. Yes, all these years we have kept a few pieces of armor. But now they are rusted and worthless. My father said that they were always worthless and that the Spanish soldiers hated to wear them in the Sonoran desert."

"Have you got a wife and children?"

"Yes," Vitorio said, telling him of them.

"And what about brothers and sisters?"

"Those too." Vitorio told him about Blanca and Jacova.

"Are you happy living as a Pima?"

"I am," Vitorio said, feeling a little insulted that the American would ask such a question.

"I'm glad," Jury said. "Now me, I'm a restless man that couldn't be happy settling down in one place for very long. If you had the same itchy feet, I could take you to Socorro and even on over to Santa Fe when our trapping is done. Might be real valuable for you to see the white man's settlements."

Vitorio allowed that it might in fact be. However, despite being half Spanish, he told Jury, he was at heart and by nature a Pima Indian.

"Who wears a golden crucifix," the American said with a half smile. "And who speaks Castillian Spanish and is about a foot taller and three shades whiter than his fellow Indian warriors."

Vitorio did not like being the object of another man's amusement. "You talk too much, American."

"But I shoot straight," Jury said, finally closing his eyes beside the fire. " 'Night, Vitorio."

Vitorio studied the man. He had never met anyone so stupid at one moment and so knowledgeable the next. Jury was an enigma, and Vitorio supposed that the other Americans were too.

When the white man began to snore, Vitorio laid down and tried to go to sleep. He thought about the Apache and especially Yahnosa. He was glad that he did not kill the Apache boy. Someday soon, this decision might prove his as well as the River People's undoing. But at the moment of decision, when he'd taken back the crucifix and placed it around his neck and then shook a bloody scalp, Vitorio had felt it very wrong in his heart to kill the wounded eaglet boy. It would have been dishonorable. And besides, a long, long time ago, his father had bestowed the gift of life on an Apache girl taken captive by the River People.

Miguel had always related this story with great pride and had never stopped wondering what had become of the Apache girl. She would, of course, be a woman now. Probably with many children, if she was not already dead or enslaved by the Mexicans or another Indian tribe. Vitorio thought it worth remembering that to his father's dying day, he had believed that single act of mercy would be his most powerful argument for gaining the joys of Heaven, where he would once more stand beside his beloved Father Castillo. And perhaps, Vitorio mused as the stars twinkled overhead, that was why I also spared an Apache who would not hesitate to return the favor by cutting my throat.

When they arrived back at the Gila River the next day, their friends rejoiced at the sight of the Apache ponies. Vitorio and Ben Jury explained to both the Pima and the American trappers what had happened. Upon learning that Yahnosa had been spared, Vitorio's hunting party prepared to flee back into the desert. The Americans, however, began to argue among themselves.

"The trappin' is good here, and I'll be damned if I'm leavin' these mountains!" one of the trappers declared. "We was told that the Apache was mostly down in Mexico."

"Well obviously," Jury said biting back his exasperation, "that isn't the case. Me and Vitorio just killed six more up in the high country in addition to the ones we shot attacking our river camp."

"Then we've probably killed off the red bastards that stayed behind," another trapper said. "They were probably just a bunch that splintered off and decided to stay here while the others went raiding in Mexico."

"We can't afford to bet on that," Jury argued. "If we're wrong, we'll be attacked by more than we can whip."

"But if we're right, then we can trap here through the fall and get rich! The colder weather will bring us longer fur. Hell, Ben, this is virgin river and the best time of the year!"

The arguments went on and on until finally Vitorio and his hunters grew disgusted. They bid the Americans good-bye and then took their share of the ponies and rode away quickly.

But at the last minute Vitorio reined back to speak in private with Jury. "The Apache will come," he predicted. "They will come from all sides, and even your long rifles will not shoot fast or straight enough to kill them. They will kill *you*, Ben Jury."

"I can't leave these men," he said. "We all made a vow when we started out that we'd stick together come hell or high water. If we do that, we've got a chance. Besides, I still got those Santa Fe partners to think about."

Vitorio shook his head. "Against the Apache you'll

have no chance. These 'partners' will not be able to protect you from Apache arrows."

Jury scowled. He leaned closer to Vitorio's pony. "I'll keep a sharp eye," he said. "Every night and every day. If they come, we won't let them catch us by surprise."

"You won't see them until you feel their arrows in your bellies," Vitorio argued with mounting exasperation. "And then it will be too late."

Jury's characteristic good humor was not in evidence when he said, "Well, I made a vow to stick with 'em and protect the interest of my partners, so I guess I'm bound by it. Adios, Vitorio."

"Adios," he said, genuinely disappointed. He had grown to like this American who talked too much and even occasionally said stupid, hurting things, but who had a good and brave heart.

In the days after leaving the Americans, Vitorio and the Pima managed to kill several more deer and then an elk before they left the mountains. The elk was big and fat, and the Pima were well-satisfied. In addition to the elk, they could trade the Apache ponies or even eat them if they grew hungry during the winter and their rations of corn, squash, and beans began to dwindle to a dangerous low point.

But even after they arrived back at their winter village in the pinion and juniper foothill country, Vitorio could not shake a sense of foreboding. He was almost sure that the Americans would be wiped out to the last man, and he prayed that they were all shot dead rather than captured and tortured to death.

His wife, Eutia, noticed his preoccupation and was concerned. "Are you feeling well?"

"Yes."

"Then why is there no joy in you?"

"I miss my father and the beauty of the mountains," he said vaguely.

Vitorio thought it would sound unmanly to tell his

wife that he was worried about the Americans' fate. And even more troubling was his daily preoccupation with the settlements that Jury had described. How many days' journey was Socorro or even the great Santa Fe? Vitorio could not remember. Perhaps ten days' walk. Ten days through the high mountains plagued by Apache.

Vitorio went about his life and tried hard to be happy, but as autumn chilled into winter and the leaves on the cottonwood trees decorated the Gila River, his curiosity about the fate of the Americans became obsessive. One night he even had a vision that his father's spirit told him to go back to the mountains. The next day, he went to his aged mother and his sister. "I must find the Americans."

"Why?" Jacova demanded to know.

"I need to learn to speak English and bring them out of the high mountains. If the Apache have not already killed them, the snows will."

"You should stay with the People," Nanata said, looking particularly frail since the death of her husband. "You have a wife and two children."

"I know, but there is plenty of meat, corn, and beans for winter. If I can save the Americans, maybe they will not all come and take our lands."

Jacova had already heard this many times since Vitorio's return. As before, she shook her head with doubt. "To go into the mountains is not good for a Pima."

"The spirit of our father tells me to do this." The two women were silent for a long time before Nanata said, "Then go."

It was what Vitorio had yearned most to hear. He spent the entire next day hunting, and shot two fine bucks which he dressed and gave to his wife for winter meat. He received promises that his family would be well cared for in his absence. Hawitsa, his brother-in-law, would make sure that if anything happened to him, his wife and children would not starve or go unprotected. Vitorio's children cried, and on the last day in the village, he and his wife made love three times and twice more in the stillness of night. It made Vitorio sad to leave.

"I am going with you," Jacova announced early the next morning as Vitorio stepped out of his winter hut in his heavy leather robe, leggings, and moccasins.

"No!"

"He was my father too. I will follow no matter where you go."

Jacova's iron will was renowned among the Pima. As a small child, she had demonstrated a fierce independence and a willfulness that had baffled Nanata and Miguel Diego Santana. Once she had even attacked a wild boar who had killed her puppy. She had whipped it across the snout with the spine of an ocotillo cactus, not even aware of the damage to her own small hands. Upon becoming a strikingly handsome young maiden, she had lashed a too ardent suitor with her grandfather's old Spanish sword. Quite by accident—it was hoped—she had cut the young man's breechclout away and then chased him into a stand of prickly pear cactus.

After that, no more suitors came to see Jacova, and the fiery-tempered, half-breed maiden seemed happier taking care of her mother and even hunting small desert game. It was said that Jacova was a better hunter than many of the Pima warriors, another fact that discouraged any other suitors from calling.

Vitorio had never understood his sister, but had always admired her spirit and courage. Jacova was good to everyone, although—with the exception of her immediate family—she seemed to prefer the company of animals to Indians. Vitorio knew with certainty that his sister was an extraordinary tracker of small game, and he supposed that this talent might serve them both well in Apache country.

"All right!" he blustered. "But if you cannot keep up, I will leave you behind."

"I will walk you into the ground, Vitorio," she pledged with a snort of derision.

Vitorio bristled, and yet he was too excited by the

journey to become angry. And when Jacova returned with a bow and arrows, a heavy horsehair robe, and a big leather pouch of dried meat, Vitorio realized that she had always intended to journey with him into the mountains. He set off at a very hard pace that carried them rapidly up the Gila River, past the final big stands of saguaro cactus and into spruce and pine forest.

They hiked in silence each day, but at night they talked of many things. Jacova, also being half Spanish, was fascinated by Ben Jury's tales of great cities and of conflicts between peoples that she had never imagined even to exist. Over and over she asked Vitorio to recount his battle with the Apache. When Vitorio told her of the great killing range of the Kentucky rifles, she would nod with understanding but her dark eyes reflected disbelief. And like Vitorio, she did not understand why anyone would want to wear tall hats with little brims made out of flat tails.

A week passed until they stood in light snow beside their father's grave and chanted Pima songs of death and honor. Again Jacova asked to hear the story of how their father had died, and then every detail of how Vitorio and Jury had exacted a bloody retribution.

"You should have killed the boy Apache named Yahnosa," she declared when her brother was finished.

"No," Vitorio said with conviction. "Better he lives like the Apache girl saved by our father."

"She is no girl now. I think she is long dead."

Vitorio wished to avoid an argument. "It does not matter."

They listened to the wind sing through the tall, water-carved canyons. As yet, they had seen no sign of either Apache or American. Not in this place nor lower along the Gila.

Jacova made a campfire in a bowl carved by high water under the face of the same cliff that Vitorio had scaled with Ben Jury. When he pointed out to her their incredibly difficult climb, Jacova made the sound of passing wind and then laughed in his face.

That night the Mogollon Mountains were battered by a fierce snowstorm that continued through the following morning. There was nothing to do but to wait and hope that the storm would pass quickly and then the sun would come out to melt the snow. This did not happen for two more days, and when they finally emerged from their shelter, Jacova was filled with wonder.

"This country is more beautiful than even our own," she said.

"Without question."

"Where do we begin to seek your stupid American friends who talk too much?"

The phrasing of the question annoyed Vitorio despite its merit. Not wanting to appear indecisive, he said, "We follow the river."

"To where?"

"To where the mountain peaks touch the sky," he grandly proclaimed.

Jacova sighed. "You mean to where the snow is deeper and colder."

"But no Apache," he reminded.

"And no Americans. They were probably all scalped before the last leaves fell into this river." Jacova's arms swept out to encompass the canyon and all it contained. "For all we know, their frozen bones are scattered all around us."

"I do not believe this to be so. We will follow this river to a place called Socorro," Vitorio said rashly. "It is there that I will find Ben Jury, and he will show us the ways of Americans and teach us to speak English in behalf of our River People."

Jacova surprised Vitorio by nodding in agreement before giving him a gentle push up the trail that followed the Gila River.

SEVENTEEN

The warm weather held for the next two days, and the snow-fed Gila River boiled down the mountain slopes under a bright mantle of sunshine. Vitorio and Jacova struggled upriver, often having to climb out of the flooded river canyons. Each morning, Vitorio climbed a vantage point, hoping to see that they had finally reached the summit of this rugged mountain range; each morning, he returned to camp reporting to Jacova that ahead of them lay yet another even higher ridge of mountains.

For one entire day they were forced to leave the Gila in order to progress. But the next morning, after a long, steep hike over a series of pine-forested ridges, they crested a pinnacle and gazed down upon a lush mountain valley.

"Look!" Vitorio shouted. "See how three forks feed into the Gila River. Surely this must be the union of this river's headwaters."

Jacova brushed back her long black hair and nodded with agreement. "This is the river's womb," she said, eyes lifting to the soaring, snow-crowned peaks and divides. In every direction she turned there were ruggedly beautiful mountain ranges, all dotted with Douglas fir, ponderosa, and pinion pine, all fed by bubbling streams rushing down to join the three forks of the Gila.

"I can feel the heat lifting off that valley," she told her brother. "I see hawks riding the warm air into the clouds."

"It looks like beaver country to me," Vitorio said. "If I were the Americans, that is where I would set my iron jaws to catch the flat tails."

"Which way is Socorro and Santa Fe?"

Vitorio really did not know. All he could think to do was to point to the east and mumble, "That way is the United States of America."

When Jacova looked at him a little funny, Vitorio felt compelled to pivot south and add, "That way is Mexico."

"Of course it is," she said. "Where is Texas?"

Not wanting to appear ignorant, Vitorio pointed southeast between the United States and Mexico. "That direction."

"I don't think you know what you are talking about," Jacova bluntly told him. "Even if you are my brother."

Vitorio shrugged his shoulders. "I know that we should not be standing outlined on this ridge. This is the home of the Chiricahua Apache."

"We have seen no tracks or smoke from campfires."

"The Apache are never seen until it is too late. But this is their home. I can feel their evil presence."

Jacova's lips turned down at the corners. The air felt chill and she drew her horsehair robe closer to her body. "Let us go down to the warmer valley," she said, "before those dark clouds come bearing more snow."

Vitorio had also noted the approaching storm on the northern horizon. It was a wall of darkness stretching from mountaintops to heavens, pushing the heated valley air toward them.

They hurried down into the valley toward the west and the middle forks of the Gila for almost three hours while the temperature plummeted. To the north, Vitorio could feel the approach of an icy blast, and the mountains were already obliterated by towering thunderheads.

"We'd better find shelter up in one of those canyons," he warned, striking upriver at a trot, knowing his sister would not lag behind. They crossed over a beaver dam fed by a stream that poured out of a narrow canyon. Vitorio was so intent on his footing that he did not see the carefully placed stick jutting out behind the dam.

"Vitorio, what is that?" Jacova cried, pointing.

Vitorio had observed the white men set their beaver traps, so he recognized at once what had caught his sharp-eyed sister's attention. Hope soared. Perhaps his friend Ben Jury was still alive and camped nearby. "It means that this place was visited by the Americans."

"But we've seen no sign of them. Not one."

Vitorio removed his dry moccasins and leggings, then waded out into the pond. He found the chain attached to the stick and pulled at a heavy weight. Drawing up the chain hand over hand, he raised a dead beaver. It was bloated, eyes gray and distended. The creature had been caught by its hind leg and had half gnawed it off before he'd apparently drowned.

"Drop it!" Jacova said, turning away with a pained expression. "Is that what these Americans do?"

Vitorio waded out of the pond. He dried his lower legs and feet quickly with sand and then he pulled back on his moccasins and leggings. The storm was almost upon them, and his eyes followed the beaver stream up into the mouth of a deep canyon. Perhaps the Americans had also taken refuge from winter storms up there, in a place where shelter could be found.

"Ugh!" Jacova said with disgust, still looking at the bloated beaver. "I do not like this, Vitorio. To kill quickly for food or clothing is necessary, but to kill that way is wrong."

"They would not freely abandon their traps," Vitorio said, his mind racing as he recalled that each trap was prized. "Hurry, let us go into that canyon before the storm!"

The snow was whirling around them when they hurried up the stream into the narrow canyon. The moment they entered the narrow defile, the air felt hushed and stilled. Snowflakes swirled high overhead and the light became dim and shadowy. There was enough illumination, however, for Vitorio to note that the cliffs were layered. The top layer was tan, successively lower ones deep browns, ochres, and reds. Besides the usual fir and pine, there were also walnut and oak trees, tangles of canyon grape, and even occasional patches of yucca and prickly pear cactus, indicating to Vitorio that this valley and especially this canyon was a haven from even the fiercest storms.

He heard a distant roar which he thought was the crash of lightning. A split second later he felt a terrible pain in his leg. Crying out, he was knocked spinning into the creek.

"Get down!" he shouted at Jacova, who rushed to his side and dragged him out of the water and behind the trunk of an oak tree.

Jacova drew his knife and cut a strip of horsehide from her robe. She swore in fury as she bound the wound, grunting along with Vitorio as he rode waves of pain. He ground his teeth together, watching his sister tie the binding and staunch the flow of blood. He had never realized she had such strong and capable hands. He saw those hands reach over her shoulder to pluck an arrow from her quiver.

"No," he grated. "It might be the Americans!"

"I think it is Apache. They have killed the Americans and taken their weapons," Jacova said angrily. "If it were your stupid American friends, they wouldn't have shot you or left that beaver to rot in the stream!"

Vitorio realized this was true. His spirits plummeted. If indeed an Apache had shot him, they were doomed.

Jacova would not abandon him, and it would be useless to try and make her do so now.

"Stay down," Jacova ordered, nocking an arrow on her bowstring before disappearing into the thickets.

Jacova moved light on her feet and soft as a breeze. She tracked up the stream, staying low, eyes probing the high canyon walls for the enemy. She believed that she would be dead in a few moments and that her brother would quickly follow her into the Spirit World. But she was also determined to die in a hard fight and hopefully kill an Apache or two. After all, Vitorio had already savored the sweetness of revenge against their father's killers; Jacova wanted the same in the final moments of her life.

She knelt behind a rock, eyes straining to penetrate the gathering gloom. The snow swirled thicker, and in the last light of this day, Jacova watched it weave like a pale dust devil swaying to the music of the universe.

Where were the Apache?

Jacova realized that her breath was coming quickly and she was damp with sweat, though the air was cold. She had never killed anything except out of need, certainly never a human. But she was more than prepared to kill Apache, whom she did not consider human. And although she had never suffered personally from their attacks, she knew that many of the smaller villages along the Gila had been wiped out entirely by the enemy.

Where were they?

A cast of moving darkness attracted her eye, and Jacova threw her bow up and unleashed an arrow. It disappeared, but she heard it strike a rock and clatter back down the cliff. She tried to swallow, but her throat was parched by fear. Since childhood she had been told that the Apache were able to sneak up on their enemies like wraiths. That they could camouflage themselves to appear as bushes and even rocks. Jacova did not see how this could be, but as she waited for an attack, she believed.

A dislodged rock tumbled down through the swirling

snow. She could wait no longer. Sprinting from tree to tree, she sought the higher ground. If she could get directly under the canyon's wall, perhaps . . .

A faint shaft of sunlight lanced through the whirling snow, and Jacova blinked to see six huge, oval-shaped caves sculpted into the cliff about two hundred feet overhead. She stared with disbelief, and before the snowflakes obscured her view, she realized she was beholding ancient cliff dwellings. Was this canyon the actual womb of the mountain Apache civilization?

Jacova was so astonished by her discovery that she forgot the enemy until another shot blasted through the deepening growl of the high winds. Jacova felt death whisper in her ear. She flattened on rock and drew another arrow. Her fingers shook so badly that her arrow clattered and clicked against her bow and she did not believe she could have hit even a horse at close range.

Jacova could see nothing through the thickening swirl of snow until, like an apparition, a tall man dressed in buckskins jumped out at her with a drawn knife. Instinctively, she drew her bowstring and fired. Her arrow clipped the man's shoulder and he bellowed, more in rage than pain. He crashed into her and they went tumbling down into the stream, Jacova fighting and scratching his eyes and yelling, "Pima! Pima! Amigo!"

Ben Jury recoiled with shock. He stared at her face and said in Spanish, "You are Pima?"

"Si, you stupid American fool! I am Jacova, Vitorio's sister. You have shot him by mistake!"

"Good Lord!" Jury cried, coming to his feet and dragging her erect. "I've shot poor Vitorio?"

"Si!"

"Damn!" Jury swore, pivoting and charging out of the water.

When they reached Vitorio, Jury knelt beside his friend and studied the nasty leg wound. "I thought you were Apache."

"Do we *look* like Apache?" Jacova challenged.

Jury ignored her. He reached down and helped Vitorio to his feet. Guilt-stricken and filled with remorse, there seemed to be a need in him to offer his Pima friend a measure of hope.

"We aren't finished yet, Vitorio. The Apache won't come up to these cliff houses, which they believe are haunted by ancient spirits. But one by one they've picked my trappers off when we've had to go out and hunt for food. I'm the last, and that's only because I been able to shoot across this canyon and kill game on the far canyon wall. Get 'em after dark, when the Apache leave this canyon for fear of the spirits."

"Where are the enemy now?"

"Takin' cover from this approachin' blizzard," Jury said. "Same as we'd best do in a hurry. Here, lean on me."

"Where are we going?" Jacova demanded.

"Up to the cliff houses, of course. Where else is there in these bloody mountains that the Apache won't sneak up and murder us?"

Jacova tipped her head back and stared, but the snow was a shimmering, impenetrable veil.

"We'll have to take it slow," Jury warned. "This trail was made for goats, and being icy and all, it's going to be a bitch fer certain."

Jacova didn't know what "bitch" meant, but it sounded bad. She took Vitorio's other arm and they began to ascend, slipping and grasping for handholds as they inched their way up the impossibly steep canyon walls. Obviously, these great cliff dwellings were not the enemy's womb. And just as obviously, one cliff dweller, armed with a rifle or bow and arrows, could kill many enemies along this treacherous trail which could only be navigated very slowly and in single file.

"Almost there!" Jury grunted as they scrambled up the last few yards. The footing was perilous, and Jacova did not know how they made it up through the mountain fury of the blizzard into the large cave.

"I've got a fire going over here," Jury said as they eased around an impressive wall built of mud and stone.

The moment they passed around the wall, Jacova felt the strong presence of old spirits. Light splashed over the wall to reveal a cavern packed with rock houses. Each was constructed with beamed roofs and T-shaped doorways. She closed her eyes, breath catching in her throat. She felt no death or sorrow in this ancient spirit world, only a pervasive sadness due to their departing these lovingly constructed houses and ceremonial kivas.

"Jacova?" It was the American, and he looked impatient but also concerned. "Are you all right?"

Spell broken, spirit whisperings stilled, Jacova managed to nod her head before she pressed onward, stepping over a shard of red pottery. Her feet fell silent on the powdered floor, and when she glanced up at the domed ceiling of the cavern, she saw that it was coated with the centuries' soot of the ancients' campfires.

"Here," Jury said, easing Vitorio down on the floor beside the campfire. His hand involuntarily reached out toward the leg wound, but he caught himself in time and pulled it back. "Damn, I'm sorry this happened. I was planning to make a run for Socorro during this blizzard. Thought I might be able to slip past the Apache and get out of these mountains. Take as many furs as I could pack and leave the rest here to come back for next spring."

Jacova was not sympathetic. "You shoot my brother by accident and then tell us that we have ruined your chances to leave? What kind of men are you Americans?"

"Jacova!" Vitorio gritted. "Be still. We are dressed like Apache, not Pima. How was he to know?"

"He should have made sure!"

"Hell, woman!" Jury swore, fists knotted in anger. "Who in their right mind would ever have expected a couple of crazy half-breeds to come into these high Apache mountains smack center in the dead of winter!"

He glared at Jacova and then at Vitorio. "Why the

hell did you bring your sister up here? You realize what the 'Pache will do if they get her in their bloody grasp?"

Vitorio did. Only right now, his leg was throbbing so painfully that it was all he could do to grit his teeth and keep from howling.

"If that ball of mine is still in the leg, it'll have to come out," Jury said, taking his knife and cutting away the horsehair tourniquet that Jacova had fashioned.

The moment the pressure was loosened, the leg began to bleed heavily again, but not before Jury had a good, close look at it in the firelight. "Can you wiggle your toes?"

"Yes."

"I don't think it's broke," Jury said. "Looks nasty, but I think we got lucky. Have to dig that ball out, though. That is, unless you want the leg to turn black and poison you."

"Take it out," Vitorio said, remembering his father's stories about how a broken leg had once claimed the revered Padre Castillo.

Jury nodded. He looked at Jacova and said, "You up to helping me save your brother's life?"

"Yes." Her voice held a note of accusation. "But you're no medicine man."

"That's true, pretty woman, but I have had some experience digging out rifle balls. Going to need some hot water. Maybe you could take that tin cup of mine, fill it with snow and get it to steamin' over the fire."

Jacova did not appreciate directions from an American fool, but she knew little about surgery. She had never seen such a wound where the object that entered the body disappeared entirely in the flesh. With an arrow or lance, you pulled the point out and concocted herbal poultices to heal the wound. But things were much more difficult with a rifle ball. Jacova guessed she had better do this American's bidding or her brother really would die.

When she carried the tin cup outside, the snow was coming down so thick that Jacova could not see the opposite side of the canyon, only two stone throws distant. The narrow footpath they'd climbed was obliterated, and Jacova tried to take some comfort in the knowledge that no one could possibly sneak up on them. She scooped up a cupful of the fresh snow, packed it down tightly, and then scooped up more. The cup was a wonder to her, much lighter and thinner than pottery. For a moment she stared out at the driving snow, watching it dust the tops of the tall ponderosa pines below and whitewash the canyon. She shivered with cold and fear and the incredible majesty of these mountains. Now she understood why Vitorio had to return. These mountains held their own spiritual beauty.

Turning, Jacova paused to consider these ancient cliff dwellings. It humbled her to think that an entire civilization had lived and then vanished without record or ancestors to honor their passing. What had they looked like? Had they been a fierce, warlike people like the Apache, or gentle farmers perhaps taken away as slaves? Did the seed of their culture now flourish somewhere far, far away— perhaps deep in Mexico? And if it did, was there yet anyone who remembered the love and the promise that had empowered them to build these magnificent ruins?

For reasons Jacova did not even try to comprehend, she sincerely hoped that someone, somewhere, remembered, and that their souls were in harmony with the ancient and kind spirits that she now felt flowing through these caverns. It pleased Jacova to think that, like her, the ancient women had gathered snow to be boiled in pots and then had prayed to their gods that one of their own family would not die from a lance or arrow wound. She closed her eyes and prayed that they would help her brother recover from his terrible leg wound.

"Hurry up!" Ben Jury shouted, suddenly appearing from around a wall. "Why in the hell are you just standing here when your brother is bleeding to death!"

Hot, angry words formed in her throat, but Jacova ground her teeth and swallowed them. Later, when the white man had practiced his medicine, then she would give him a piece of her mind for shooting at them in the first place. But right now, Jacova knew that she had better be silent and compliant.

Jury swished his knife blade around in the steaming tin cup. He cut strips of cloth from a blanket and used one to wash the leg as clean as possible. "Vitorio, this here is a Bowie knife," he explained, holding up a huge blade. "I know that doesn't mean a damn thing to you, but Jim Bowie is a famous fella and he invented this knife. It ain't exactly designed to save a man's life, but we're going to put 'er to the test right now. So grab ahold of something, and if you feel like hollerin', then go right ahead. But you got to stay still, Vitorio. I can't be probin' and proddin' with this blade and have you jumpin' one way then the other."

"You talk too damn much," Vitorio whispered.

"Yeah, well, here goes."

When the knife blade cut into the heavy muscle in his thigh, a scream was torn from Vitorio's lips and he fainted. Jacova tried to tear the fearsome-looking knife from the American. She had not imagine that he would inflict such a deep wound.

"Stay back!" Jury shouted. "If you can't be a help, then git!"

Jacova had no intention of leaving. She made herself be still and watch as the American cut even deeper into her brother's leg. Finally, retracting the heavy blade, he said, "I'm all thumbs and my fingers are mighty thick. You've got long, slender fingers, see if you can pull-pinch the ball and dig it out with your fingertips before your brother bleeds to death."

Jacova started to protest, but he grabbed her wrist and squeezed it hard, saying, "Do it now!"

Her protest fell silent. Steeling herself, she slipped her fingers into Vitorio's leg and was greatly relieved to feel the sharp and irregular edges of the misshapen lead ball. With a pounding heart, Jacova hooked the lead with her fingernail and teased it out. The lead was flattened and about the size of her thumbnail.

"That's it!" Jury cried. "By damned, Jacova, you did it! Nice work!"

Detesting herself for loving the man's flattery, Jacova helped Jury rebind the wound. Later, when the storm passed, she would venture back down the trail and pick some mountain plants to make Pima medicine for her brother. She would also pray to the ancient cavern spirits, the white man's Jesus, and finally her own Pima gods, to save Vitorio and then somehow get them safely out of these high mountains past the terrible Apache.

Book III

JACOVA—PIMA
WOMAN

EIGHTEEN

Jacova left the campfire and went exploring through the cliff dwellings. She had closely examined the work of the ancient peoples at Casa Grande, but these old ruins were far more ambitious and extensive. This cave's many storage rooms and dwellings extended from the soot-blackened ceiling to the irregular floor upon which huge slabs of the roof had collapsed. Jacova walked over to a fire pit and knelt to examine its contents. She stirred through the broken pottery and discovered bones, charred hooves, and corn cobs.

"They probably did a lot of farming, like your own people," Ben Jury said, coming up behind her. "To your right is a storage room and it's filled with corn cobs whose kernels are as hard as golden nuggets. Besides the corn, I've found beans and squash in almost every home. My guess is that whoever lived here farmed the valley down where the Gila forks."

Jacova turned to look at the American. "They were more than farmers. These are charred bones."

"Oh sure," he said offhandedly. "This country is too damned high and cool to have a proper growing season. They probably hunted this country out and then maybe had a few short summers and lost their crops to the freeze. That'd be my guess why they left."

Despite herself, Jacova found this theory very interesting. But it was her nature to challenge men who seemed too overconfident of themselves, especially one who had stupidly wounded her brother.

Besides, Jacova had her own carefully considered theory, which she was not afraid to voice. "I think the Apache must have driven them away. The people who built all this would not have done so if they were not sure they could raise crops every year and that the land would always replenish itself with deer and other wild game."

"Don't be too sure of that," Jury argued. "I suspect people are like animals—when they've plenty of food, they start to overpopulate until the land can't support 'em. So then there's a famine, so they hunt for richer land and more plentiful game. Besides, if you look around, you'll see no signs of battle."

"Time erases all things."

"Maybe," he said, "but all the corpses I've found have gray hair and seem to have died of old age."

"You found the dead?" Jacova whispered in horror.

"Sure! That's why the Apache won't come up here. They're afraid of spirits. Are you?"

"No."

"Well then, come along and I'll show you the other caves. I've had plenty of time to look them all over, and I like this one the best. When the weather is good, the sun pours in and warms things up. Right now, though, the air is damned chilly."

"What does 'chilly' mean?"

Jury rubbed his hands together. "Cold."

"Oh."

"Come along and I'll point you out a few interesting things."

"I had better not," Jacova hedged, not trusting the American.

He misunderstood her reservations. "Oh, hell, Vitorio

will sleep for at least a couple more hours. Besides, being part Indian, maybe you can solve a few riddles."

"Riddles?"

"Questions I can't answer," he explained. "For instance, why are the doors so small and T-shaped?"

"The ancient ones were small."

"I know that from looking at their skeletons," he said. "But they'd still have had to duck to get into their houses, and that don't explain the T-shapes."

"The doors are low so that an enemy would have to stoop to get inside and make him easier to kill. They are T-shaped because that allows you to stoop and yet carry things inside."

To illustrate her point, Jacova demonstrated. She shaped her hands around an imaginary pot and then lifted her elbows wide as she ducked under a make-believe doorway.

"Well I'll be! Sure, that makes sense. Huh! I knew that a smart and pretty Indian woman like yourself would know the answer."

Jacova's cheeks warmed to the compliment. Jury grinned so broadly that she was sure that he sensed her embarrassment. Pima men were not in the habit of being complimentary. Compliments between River People were neither given nor expected.

"Come along," Jury urged with a faintly challenging smile. "I want to show you the rest of this cave and then the next one, which is so huge I'll bet it housed a couple hundred people. And wait until you see the mummies and the pottery!"

"No bodies," Jacova said quickly. "But I will let you show me the pottery."

"Fair enough," Jury said, angling away between a two-story dwelling and a high rock wall. "I didn't think about it at first, Jacova, but it must have taken a powerful lot of time and work to build these ruins. Why, most of the year they'd have had to haul every drop of water to mix an ocean of mortar up from that stream way down in the canyon, using pots or animal skins."

Jacova realized that Ben had a good point. All the structures were made of rock, but the rocks were held together by smooth mortar. Even the floors, though covered with the dust of centuries, were plastered smooth, as were the insides of all the houses. She knew that generations had labored their entire lives building these ruins. And what a terrible heartache it must have been for them to abandon this beautiful city of stone and then to venture out into the wilderness where they would never again know such lofty protection from man and nature.

"This one I call the 'castle,' " he said, stepping aside so that Jacova could drink in the full impact of the enormous cavern. "Ain't she somethin'!"

Jacova drew a sharp breath and gazed at the immense cavern with a sense of wonderment. The Castle was indeed spectacular. It was a complex maze of architecture soaring from floor to ceiling. Some buildings were three stories high, and there were old ladders and narrow walkways linking walls and structures of every description. It was a village in and of itself, and it would have been home to hundreds of the ancient people. When Jacova closed her eyes for a moment, she could almost visualize entire families working and playing in this city of pale, silent stone.

As a child Jacova had spent thousands of hours playing on the bank of the Gila River, building houses of rocks and mud, but never had she created anything to match these intricately designed ruins. Whoever the people had been, however long ago they had come and gone, it was easy to see that they had been as industrious and hardworking as ants.

Later, Jacova knew she would meander through this maze of silent houses and again listen to the spirits of those who had come long before her. When you entered Casa Grande all alone, you could hear the spirits whispering through the towers and the cornices. Mostly, you heard

the voices of women at work. You could imagine them
talking about crops, the hunting, and their husbands and
children. You might hear the rippling laughter of the children as they played, running after balls or playing tag or
tickle.

"Jacova?"

"Yes?" she asked, snapping out of her reverie.

He leaned close. "What were you thinking just now?"

"My thoughts are my own." She retreated a half step.

He actually looked hurt. "I didn't mean to pry or anything. It was just that I got to know your brother pretty
well one night up in these mountains. And I discovered
that although you were raised as a Pima and your father
was a Spaniard, we had a lot of things in common."

"Such as?"

"We all speak fluent Spanish."

"And?"

Jury toed the ground and expelled a deep breath.
"You're pretty rough on a man, aren't you?"

"I think that I had better go back and stay with my
brother."

"Suit yourself, but I thought that you might enjoy
seeing all the beautiful pots I found in the next cavern."

Jacova's curiosity would not allow her to just turn
away without seeing if the pots really were beautiful. "All
right, let's see them."

"Good! Won't take but an hour or so."

Feeling as if she were compromising her dignity,
Jacova dutifully followed the American up a wooden ladder onto a second-story terrace that faced out into the canyon. She saw that the snow was still falling so hard that it
obscured the opposite canyon wall.

"Watch your footing," he warned, taking her hand
and holding it tightly. "You fall from here and it's adios
forever."

She saw that he was not jesting. There was a narrow
outdoor path connecting the caverns, and it was slick with
ice and sloped downward. She held Ben Jury's hand

tightly and hugged the cliff as they made the precarious crossing. By the time they were back out of the wind and the snow, she was freezing and her teeth rattled.

"I guess I should have waited to show the pottery to you," he said, wiping snow from her hair and shoulders. "Now you're half frozen again."

Jacova shivered, and he stepped in, pressing his body to hers. She wanted to recoil, but she *was* shivering. He rubbed her shoulders and back, drawing circulation and warmth to her body in a rush.

"We'd better see that pottery," she managed to say. "I don't want to be away from Vitorio so long."

"Sure," he said, his voice husky. "Follow me."

Jury walked into the cavern and followed a winding path up into the ruins. They were magnificent and seemed to Jacova to be in perfect condition except for a few roofs that had collapsed over the centuries. She saw a broken pot and stopped to pick it up, but he laughed and said, "That's nothing. Wait until I show you the real treasures."

Jacova followed him until they climbed up onto a third-story rooftop. From this lofty vantage point, the curved overhang of the cliff left only a narrow moon of light to shine across the many balconies and terraces, most of which had smoke holes from lower rooms.

"Follow me," he said, grabbing a ladder and descending through a ceiling.

"Where are we going?" Jacova called down into the dim recesses of the building.

"To see the pottery. Don't worry, the ladder might be a thousand years old, but if it will hold my weight, it will hold yours."

It wasn't the ladder breaking that concerned Jacova. However, pride demanded that she follow Jury into the place where he had found the pottery. The room into which they descended had two windows facing out toward the canyon, and illumination was poor except for two squared shafts that penetrated the gloom. But these shafts fell upon a row of bowls and pots that were so exquisite they caused Jacova to clap her hands together with delight. The bowls were of all shapes and sizes, and made of clay. Most of them were a pale salmon color, but some were a deep crimson with black designs. There were at least a half-dozen huge water jugs and many, many cooking pots, which were easily identifiable because their bottoms were blackened by fire.

Jacova went over to a particularly beautiful pot and cradled it in her hands, then inspected it from all angles. Her own people were not as gifted in pottery as the Hopi or the Navajo, but she had seen enough of their work to recognize the extraordinary skill and beauty of this ancient creation. The pot was perfectly symmetrical, with a rounded bottom and a wide mouth, lipped downward for easy pouring. Whoever had made this pot would have taken enormous pride in their artistry.

"This one was for heating water," she said.

"For what purpose?"

"To make herbal tea, medicines or to heat poultices," she replied. "I don't know for sure. But look at the wonderful designs!"

He reached out and cupped his hands under hers. "Beautiful," he said, gazing into her eyes and ignoring the pottery.

Jacova shivered, but not from the cold. She could hear her heart begin to pound and she felt humiliated, certain that he could hear it pound too. What was wrong with her? She was twenty-two seasons old. No little girl to be acting giddy at the touch of a boy. And especially not this strange but handsome American who had, indirectly, gotten her father killed and then had shot her brother.

True, he had not consciously wished to bring her family harm—but he had, and if she did not keep him at a distance, Ben Jury would break her heart. Against all reason, Jacova felt irresistibly drawn and yet repulsed by this American. These confusing and opposing emotions crashed like storm-tossed waves against her crumbling bastions of self-defense.

"Jacova," he whispered passionately, "I am twenty-eight years old and own nothing of value. The Apache have wiped me out of everything except a few beaver traps, my rifle, and the clothes I'm wearing. But someday, if I can recoup my losses, then—"

She struggled free, unwilling to believe what she was hearing. It was a shock to realize that she feared herself more than the man. She grabbed for the ladder, but the desperation in his voice caused her to freeze with indecision.

"Please don't go," he said. "I've never been any good with women. I've always either ran from the good ones or used up the bad. I never saw anyone like you until now, Jacova. You're not Indian and you're not . . . I . . . I don't know what you are except that you've gotten into my head, filled it to exploding and left no room for me to think."

"Shhh!"

"Yeah, yeah," he said, shaking his head, eyes spilling desolation. "I know that I talk too damn much. And I guess it'd be easy for you to think that I'm hopin' to take advantage of you, but look at my damn hands, Jacova!"

He held them out between them, and she could see them tremble like autumn leaves over the Gila. "Isn't that crazy?" he shouted, voice booming around in the cavern. "What the devil have you done to my mind?"

She didn't have an answer. All her adult life, she had been fighting men and fighting herself. She didn't know why she had always been at war and why she had no faith in men. She had loved her father and she loved her brother. But young men had always been attracted to her, and very early on it was clear what they wanted most. She had never dared any man would want more than her body or that she could make them tremble for any reason other than desire.

And yet . . . yet this American's trembling convinced her that he felt love in his heart. This jarring revelation awakened things inside Jacova that left her dizzy with elation and sick with fear. If this was what happened between a man and a woman in love, she wanted no part of it, not today—not ever.

She hurried up the ladder.

"There is another room with more pots next door," he desperately called after her as she vanished up through the roof.

"Oh well, maybe next time," Jacova heard him say as she hurried out into the blowing snow, to the safe security of her poor brother.

The storm had lasted almost a week, and by the time it blew away, the canyon was buried with snow so deep that it was impossible to return to the valley and hunt, much less flee the Apache, even if Vitorio had been healthy. Jacova stayed close to her brother while Ben hiked down into the canyon to gather armloads of firewood. It was hard and dangerous work, but he did it without complaint, hauling branches up the treacherous trail and piling them beside the fire pit. His eyes looked haunted, his step was heavy. He gazed at Jacova constantly, but she was too embarrassed to return his fevered staring.

Each time he brought firewood, Jacova could only nod her head with approval and whisper, "More."

He finally exploded one wintry afternoon. "Dammit! We aren't going to be boiling a bear in those pots!"

"More," she insisted.

So he brought more and more firewood, until it was stacked higher than his head, while Jacova filled her water pots with snow and boiled water. Into the water went the centuries-old corn cobs. The boiled corn disintegrated into corn mush. It wasn't as bad-tasting as Jacova had expected, and it seemed to sustain their strength. And seeing how depressed Ben appeared, she began to talk to him again as if nothing had happened between them. As if they were just two people caught in a strange and isolated world which they hoped to escape at the earliest possible moment.

While they waited for warm weather to melt the deep snow down in the canyon, Ben began to give them English lessons.

"Amigo is friend," he began, "and if you know that word, you can get along pretty good. Say it—*friend*."

"Friend."

"Friend."

They said it over and over, adding many new words each day. The lessons were fun and they began to consume all their spare time. Jury had a fine sense of humor, and soon they were laughing as he made funny sounds and faces to convey his meaning of strange English words.

Jacova was amazed at how quickly she and her brother picked up the language. There were, she decided, quite a few similarities between Spanish and English. *Acto*—act. *Familia*—family. *Mapa*—map. *Rapido*—rapid.

"You are both very *inteligente*—intelligent," he liked to say.

So are you, Jacova thought, for she no longer had any illusions that the American was stupid, and his declaration of love now seemed something that she must have conjured up in her mind. Jacova allowed herself to be trusting again. And after a month she began to go alone with Ben Jury to explore the other caves and their fascinating cliff dwellings. Once, in a moment of bravado, she even asked to see the ancient corpses, but Ben had declined to show them to her, and later she was grateful.

Their conversations became English lessons. Jacova found herself striving to please him with her quick grasp of the English vocabulary. One warm afternoon while exploring the caves during a chinook, Jury stood in the sunshine and regarded the distant valley. "Jacova," he said, "I have to go hunting. We can't keep boiling centuries-old corn cobs."

"But why? And what about the Apache?"

"I don't think we should worry much about them," he

said. "No doubt they've returned to winter in the lower country. They aren't any more interested than we are in freezing or starving."

"But what if they left a few warriors to guard against our escape?"

"If they did, then I'll try and kill them before they kill me. And then we can think about leaving these mountains before the main body of 'em returns in the spring. They're a murderin' bunch, Jacova. They killed off my boys one by one. Almost killed me a time or two. I don't know why I'm the last, but they know I'm here and they figure to get me. I might just as well settle the issue now as later."

"I think you ought to wait," she heard herself say as her heart began to beat with fear. "I think that going out alone is too dangerous."

He grinned and shrugged his broad shoulders. "Dangerous or not, Jacova, my backbone is wrapped around my stomach and about to choke it to death. I've got to have some meat before I'm starved down to a nubbin and haven't the strength to hunt or fight."

"I will come with you," she blurted.

"Not a chance."

"I *will* go. I do not need your permiso—permission."

He studied her face, then laughed and took her hand. Drawing her close, Jacova felt powerless to resist when he bent and his lips touched her own. She wrapped her arms around his neck and kissed his mouth hard.

Jacova wanted this man, and she knew that he wanted her. Probably not for any longer than it took for them to leave these Apache mountains, but that did not matter anymore. And so, when he scooped her up in his arms and held her before the sun-drenched canyon and then whirled to carry her into one of the ancient ruins, she did not resist.

She burned to his touch.

He swept her into the largest house and lowered her to the soft, powdery dust of the floor. He ripped off his buckskins, and Jacova reached for him, opening herself wide. She moaned with pain and pleasure as he fell upon her like a starving animal and they became one. For Jacova, it was a wonderful experience. Frightening and beautiful. She felt an immense sense of joy and happiness. She wished to die in this state of bliss.

"More," she breathed, when he was finally spent and lay panting beside her.

He chuckled. "Soon, darlin'. Soon."

A short time later they walked hand in hand back to the mouth of the cavern and lay down on smooth, warm stone, where he took her much more slowly, with the sun warming their flesh and with the smell of wet pines heavy in their nostrils. And when the sun began to slip below the rim and the shadows raced across the canyon, the big American said, "I don't want you to go with me into the valley. There is too much chance of death."

"Without you I will die anyway," she argued softly. "Better that we die together."

"And Vitorio?"

She thought about her brother for a moment and then said, "He will die as well, with us or alone."

Jury rolled away from her and sat up. He pulled on his buckskins, muscles rippling like water dancing over river stones. He ran his thick fingers through his long, black hair, laying it straight back. He was smiling, but when Jacova looked deep into his eyes, she saw that he was sad.

"Don't worry," she told him. "We have made love. If we die together, it will be as intended."

" 'As intended'?"

"Yes."

"Intended by who?"

"By your Christian god or our Pima spirits. It does not matter."

He barked a laugh without humor. "Well, it might not matter to you, but it sure as hell does to me! I don't want to die. I want to make love with you a hundred times a day."

"Impossible," she said with a smile, knowing she was blushing like a young maiden.

He took her hands. "I only have one rifle and very little ammunition."

"I have a bow and many arrows. If there are Apache waiting for us at the mouth of this canyon, you will need me to kill them quickly and in silence."

He looked away, his eyes taking in the sunset colors reflecting on the opposite canyon wall. A soft magenta color had infused the light, and the sky was aglow.

"Ben," she said, using his given name. "Now I *must* go with you."

After a long moment he looked back at her and slowly dipped his chin. "All right," he said with a sigh of resignation. "We'll leave tomorrow at daybreak."

"Good," she said. "I will tell my brother that I have taken a man and you have taken a woman."

"I'd like to be there when you tell him that I mean to take you not only as my woman, but also as—"

"Ssssh," she breathed, "you talk too much."

He just stared at her, and then he laughed, because they both knew that Vitorio held the same steadfast opinion of the big American.

Chapter

NINETEEN

T hat winter, she and Ben had gone hunting twice in the valley without seeing the Apache. On each occasion, her tall American had shot an elk, and so they had survived on meat and ancient corn. Now, with winter finally passing, Jacova marveled at the first Canadian geese that sailed like a gray wedge across the glistening mountaintops. Spring wildflowers poked out of every nook and cranny in the rocks, while down in the canyon the stream had become a frothy torrent.

Vitorio's leg had almost mended, and the snow was now melted enough to try and escape their cliff dwellings before the return of the Apache. Jacova was ready. They had decided to return westward to the Pima village rather than northeast to Socorro. To do otherwise would have forced them to traverse even higher mountains, and they feared that the passes would be blocked for at least another two months. By then the Apache would be certain to have returned to the upper forks of the Gila River.

"We'll follow the river down just as we did coming up," Vitorio said, limping back and forth across the cavern floor.

Vitorio was upset with the condition of his leg. The

damned thing persisted in stiffening every night, which required a vigorous early morning massage and exercise before it would limber up so that Vitorio could walk without a pronounced limp.

"You going to be able to hobble on home?" Ben asked with a mischievous wink. "You look pretty rough to me."

"I'll make it to my village," Vitorio promised, sick and tired of being caved like an animal, and badly missing his wife and children. "I'll make it if I have to build a raft and float down to the desert."

"You might have to with that limp," Ben said, clucking his tongue with sincere regret because it was his bullet that had caused Vitorio such discomfort. Had he been fit, they'd have attempted to fight their way out of the Mogollon Mountains weeks earlier.

"We'll make it," Jacova vowed, now speaking as fluently in English as in Spanish. "But don't worry about Vitorio, he'll keep up."

"That's right," Vitorio said, "but we'll have slow, hard going because the canyons will be flooded in many places. That means we will have to skirt the river where it flows high through the narrow canyons."

"Then let's get started," Ben urged. "Time is wasting, and those Apache know we'll try and escape as soon as the snow begins to melt."

Jacova looked around their cliff dwelling one last time, feeling the same hesitation to leave as the ancient ones must have felt. And although these caverns were bone-chilling in the wintertime, they were also dry and safe. Jacova had never been happier than she was this winter. She and the American had become man and wife and had shared their robes, their lives, and their bodies. They had lived every moment to the fullest, knowing that somewhere outside, the enemy waited, ready and eager to capture, torture, and then kill them.

It still amazed Jacova how she and Ben had forced the Apache out of their minds, except during the two hunting trips which Jacova had found dangerous but thrilling. Looking back, she knew she had lived more intensely these last three months than she had lived her entire life before meeting Ben. She had never felt better, stronger, and more alive than while in Ben's arms or just walking at his side, gathering wood, cooking elk meat or sitting together at the mouth of the cliff, gazing down at the canyon and watching spring burst across these high mountains.

"I am not sure if I will ever be happy again in the desert," she commented one dazzlingly bright afternoon as an eagle soared over their canyon.

"I want to see your people and meet your mother," Ben said. "After that, we'll be coming back to the mountains."

"These mountains?"

"I don't think so." Ben squinted with pain at the memory of his dead companions. "Maybe we'll find some mountains where the Indians are a little friendlier. Maybe we'll prospect gold and I won't have to trap beaver anymore. I know how much you dislike that idea."

"I think I know where there is gold," she said, quite innocently.

From that day until this, gold had often been on the American's mind, and that was another reason they were following the Gila River back into the Sonoran desert.

"Ready?" Ben asked, shouldering the heaviest pack, which was stuffed with corn, jerked elk meat, and the few beaver traps that he had been able to retrieve from the ice-coated streams. He also carried his Kentucky long rifle, though he was nearly out of ball and powder.

Jacova worried about her brother. While she and Ben had flourished this winter on love and a sense of excitement, poor Vitorio had suffered pain and loneliness for his wife and children. They had tried to cheer him, but the long, cold winter had taken its toll, and he did not look strong enough for what would be an extremely difficult journey through deep snows. And yet to wait any longer would increase their chances of meeting Apache. In fact, and although no one had said so, they had already waited too long and the danger was now great.

Vitorio nodded to indicate that he was ready. He tried to hide his limp as he shouldered a much lighter pack, a bow and quiver of arrows. During his convalescence he had insisted on doing women's work, and Jacova had patiently shown him how to tan the elk hides in order to make them all new moccasins, leggings, and pants which badly needed replacement.

"Just promise me one thing," Vitorio said with a wry grin, "and that's never to tell my wife that I can tan hides and sew."

They had all laughed at this little joke at the time, but Jacova knew that Vitorio's pride was at stake and that she would never reveal how her beloved brother had passed his lonely, painful winter.

After their steep and slippery descent into the canyon, they all paused to stare back up at the cliffs. It was the first time that Vitorio had seen them from a distance in good weather, and he was deeply affected by their silent, haunting beauty. Jacova could see the emotions play across his dark eyes, and she knew that he would always remember this winter.

"And so," Vitorio said, speaking only in English now, for he believed that the Americans would one day rule this land where the Spaniards had been dispossessed by the Mexicans, "the valley below is where the danger starts."

"And also the Gila River," Ben told him with a wink. "Don't worry, we'll get past the Apache and you'll be hugging your wife and children in a few weeks. And once back into your hot desert country, that stiff leg of yours will work better than a boy's."

Vitorio just smiled. He raised his face to the warm sun and took a deep breath. Casting one last glance upward at the ancient cliff dwellings, he turned his back on them and limped down the canyon toward the valley which was patched with melting snow. In many places the ground was boggy, and although the sun was shining, the air was cold and cutting. On the upper peaks the snow-capped mountains sweated like the breasts of fat women. They had to wade through icy streams, and several times the wet meadow was so soft that they sank to their knees and had to backtrack to solid ground.

"Right about here," Ben said, "we was caught by the Apache last fall. Right out in the open. There were four of us, all carrying traps and beaver pelts. The Apache attacked us from that stand of pine trees just yonder and they didn't make a sound. First thing I heard was one of the men—I think it was Ike Childress—he screamed and dropped to his knees with an arrow in his gut. Before I could drop my beaver and traps and throw this rifle to my shoulder, the Apache were swarming over us. There must have been two dozen."

Jacova stared at the trees. She could almost visualize the attack and hear the Apache shouting as the Americans began to fire but also fall like stalks of corn at harvest time.

"I shot one and drew my knife," Ben remembered, halting to gaze at the trees without really seeing them. "I whirled around and around and hit another with my beaver and traps. Knocked him flat, I did. But then I could see that I had to run for my life. So I dropped the beaver and traps and took off for the canyon. I heard the Apache howling like demons and my own men screaming like—"

"No more," Jacova pleaded softly as she took Ben's arm and laid her head against his shoulder. "You must not think about this again."

"Yeah," he said, stroking her face, "you're right, pretty woman. What is done, is done. And my trappers knew the risks as well as the rewards of coming into these mountains. But the way it worked out, there wasn't any rewards—only death."

"You couldn't have known that. Let's go," Jacova said, pulling him past the place of death that caused his face to turn old and gray.

That first day, they traveled less than five miles because of having to double back so often around deep patches of snow. The days were still short, and they made camp beside the Gila in late afternoon, hoping a weak sun would dry out their moccasins and leggings. As darkness approached and they were shivering in their wet buckskins, they decided to risk a fire. But the wood was wet and the fire boiled smoke.

"Let's dry our clothes as fast as we can," Vitorio said, "and put the fire out before it is seen by Apache."

"I don't think we need to do that," Ben argued. "This is still mighty early in the spring and the Apache wouldn't—"

"You have no idea what the enemy will do or not do," Vitorio snapped. "In this matter, *I* will decide—not you."

"Now wait just a minute," Ben said, cheeks darkening with anger. "I realize that you know more about Apache than I do, but I'm telling you that we haven't seen any signs of them heathen buggers, and I say they're probably a couple hundred miles south down in Mexico."

"I don't care what you say," Vitorio insisted. "If we were in Socorro or Santa Fe or any of your American settlements, I would listen and accept your advice. But we're not. We're in the mountains where I've hunted since boyhood, and I *know* Apache better than you. And I say we kill this smoky fire."

Ben came to his feet. "Listen," he growled, "we're all wet and chilled to the core. I say we need the heat of this fire tonight or we're likely to be half sick from pneumonia by tomorrow morning. What do you say, Jacova?"

She swallowed. Never one to be shy about expressing her opinions, Jacova did not wish to come between these two men. However, she knew that her brother was right about the Apache. The enemy always appeared when least expected. And while it was miserable to suffer from cold and wet clothing, Jacova knew they would survive the hardship. If the Apache smelled their campfire smoke, there would be no escape.

"Ben," she said, softly, "I will kill the fire."

His jaw dropped, then clamped shut like one of his beaver traps. "You're sidin' with Vitorio!"

"Maybe tomorrow night, if we get down lower, we can light a fire. But we are still—"

Jacova did not have a chance to finish explaining. With an angry curse, Ben kicked snow onto the fire until it sputtered into darkness. The chill of the night rushed in almost as soon as the darkness. A faint slice of white moon overhead gave them scant comfort, and when Jacova went to her man's side, Ben roughly pushed her away.

"I should have known that you would take your brother's side when it came down between us," he complained. "I guess Indians always side with Indians."

Jacova's hand streaked out and her palm smacked Ben across the face so hard she broke his lips. Even in the pale moonlight, she saw the blood trickle down his chin. In a fit of remorse, Jacova threw her arms around his neck and hugged him tightly.

For a moment Ben's body was hard as stone, but then he relaxed, wiped away the blood with his sleeve and rolled back, pulling her down with him.

"Pull your robe over us so we can get warm together," he urged in a voice hoarse with desire.

"No, not with Vitorio so close." Always before they had gone to another cavern to make love.

"All right," he said, jumping up and pulling her with him. "Let's find us some privacy."

Jacova was propelled off her feet as the American dragged her into the woods. He spread their robe and pushed her down upon it. Without preliminaries, Ben yanked up her buckskin skirt and roughly mounted her. While she clung to him, he took her with a bone-jarring fierceness, and when he roared with pleasure, Jacova felt his hot seed flood into her body. She locked her legs around his waist and held him so tightly she ached, clasping his head to her bosom until he finally stilled, breathing raggedly.

Later she felt him lift from her body and roll off to the side. "Why did you take me that way?" she asked.

For a long time he was as silent as the stars that glittered in the heavens above. Then he said, "You need to remember one thing, pretty woman. Ben won't play second fiddle to anyone in your heart—not to any kids we might someday have, and damn sure not to Vitorio."

Jacova climbed on top of him. "It is not a matter of concern," she said gently. "You are my man. It is just that you were wrong and my brother was right."

"Is that so?" he challenged.

"Yes," she said, kissing and stroking his beard, feeling his powerful body, hard and uncompromising, under her own. "I swear on Vitorio's golden crucifix that is true."

After a long time she felt him relax. Jacova kissed his mouth, feeling her own heat rising. She kissed him over and over until he held no anger whatsoever. And somehow, he grew strong again with his manhood and she knew that everything would be all right between them as long as they both lived.

In the morning they awoke to the ominous howl of a cold wind in the pines. It wasn't snowing and the corridor of sky over their river-cut canyon was indigo blue, but the signs of an approaching storm were evident.

"Damn!" Ben swore, stomping and slapping some feeling into his powerful limbs. "We're in for it now unless we can get down off this mountain in a hurry. Vitorio, how are you feeling?"

Vitorio tried to walk but his injured leg was throbbing with cold and stiff as a bow. "I'll be all right," he said, peg-legging back and forth and continually glancing up at the sky. "I'll walk it out, let's gather up our things and leave."

And that's what they did. They left without eating and hurried along the angry Gila River, whose roar filled the canyon and made conversation almost impossible.

They hiked all morning and twice had to skirt around places where the river was too engorged with snowmelt to allow passage along its banks. Their progress was slow. Their breath burned and steamed in the cold air, and when at last they came to the hallowed ground where Miguel Santana was buried, Vitorio and his sister were appalled to see that it was covered by the surging river.

"I remember," Vitorio said to his sister, who could not hide her tears, "that our father believed that the Gila River was blessed. He said it was blessed by the old priest who gave him this crucifix."

Jacova just nodded and watched as her brother's hand retrieved the crucifix from under his buckskin jacket. She seemed mesmerized as Vitorio held the crucifix out before him and rocked it back and forth like a pendulum. The weak sunlight made it shine, and the crucifix's ruby gleamed like the eye of a feral night animal.

"Do you think that Father Castillo held the crucifix like that when he blessed this river?" Jacova asked.

"Yes," Vitorio said. "I believe that he did. Only then, it was down by Casa Grande, and the river was warm and lazy. Not like this."

"Rivers are like people," Jacova said, tearing her eyes away from the swinging crucifix and looking to her husband, "they change sometimes even as they stay the same."

Ben looked uncomfortable. "I'm sorry that your father is resting underwater, but I guess he don't care much anymore. I think we'd best climb out of this canyon again and make some time."

While Ben started to climb, Jacova went to Vitorio and touched his cheek. "I know this is hard," she said, "but think about your wife and your children instead of about the death of our father. Remember, he believed in the Christian god, and to them it does not make any difference where our bones turn to dust."

"You are right," Vitorio said, "but I cannot help but

think of how the river claimed both him and his brother Hernando so long ago."

"It will not claim us," Jacova vowed, taking her brother's hand and leading him to a steep path that would deliver them up, up to the high ground overlooking the Gila.

Ben was already climbing into trees a good distance above them. "Hurry!" she whispered.

But just as Jacova began to climb, she heard a terrible cry from above and, as if in a nightmare, she saw her American lean back from the mountainside, grab an arrow jutting from his throat and then slowly pitch out into space and hurtle downward, long rifle still clenched in his fist.

Jacova screamed. When Ben struck the rocks beside her, his eyes bugged and blood gushed from his ears. She heard the breath whoosh from his lungs and knew her husband was dead.

"Ben!" Jacova cried, throwing herself across his lifeless body. "Ben!"

Vitorio reeled back from the steep mountainside. He looked up to the place where the American had died, and now he saw the Apache appear ghostlike from the forest and rocks. Ten, no twenty and then thirty! Short, squat men with flat brown faces and merciless eyes.

Vitorio snatched up the Kentucky rifle, took aim on one of the braves and fired. The rifle's hammer snapped with a metallic sound but its percussion cap had been lost in the fall. The weapon was useless.

Vitorio reached for Jacova's bow and took an arrow in the back. He stiffened and grunted with pain, hearing Jacova's wail swirl skyward to greet the gathering storm.

——————— Chapter ———————

TWENTY

J acova drew her bowstring and shot at the onrushing Apache. She struck one in the hip and he grunted with pain, lost his balance and came tumbling down the mountainside. She drew another arrow, nocked it on her bowstring and shot it too, hitting a second Apache moments before he launched himself off the mountainside, intending to bury his knife in her chest. As Jacova retreated, Vitorio was overwhelmed by knife-wielding Apache. Horrified, she tried to save him, but a sudden and searing pain exploded between her eyes.

Jacova awakened in pain and darkness. All her bones felt broken. She heard the voices of Apache surrounding her, and when she tried to move, she could not budge. She felt as if her head were ready to explode, and knew that she had suffered a terrible blow across the back of her skull. Her hands and feet were bound so tightly that they were numb, and she was terrified.

Once, as a child, Jacova had fallen from a cotton-wood tree twenty feet to the earth. It had been a hot summer day and she had lain stunned and unable to move for nearly an hour while the sun baked her face. It had been the only helpless experience of her life, until now, and Jacova still had nightmares about being paralyzed.

But this was worse, a thousand times worse. Jacova was an Apache captive, perhaps soon to be tortured in unspeakable ways before being killed. She feigned unconsciousness while her frenzied thoughts detonated like kernels of corn tossed into a campfire.

She could understand more than a smattering of the Apache language, for the Papago, Hopi, and many other tribes spoke a similar dialect. The Apache, however, spoke faster than the River People and their words had an unpleasant guttural sound. They weren't easy to understand, but Jacova could track the thread of their excited conversation. The Apache warriors were angry—very angry. The pair she had wounded were arguing for revenge, while the others tried to remove her arrows. There were many words that meant nothing to a Pima Indian, but Jacova gathered that the Apache's conversation was centered around whether or not Ben's prized Kentucky long rifle was beyond repair. The enemy were in sharp disagreement about if it had been permanently damaged during its long fall down the mountainside.

Jacova involuntarily sobbed when she remembered the death of her strong American husband. In horror, she saw a vision of his dead face with eyes glazed and protruding. She also remembered the Apache arrow in Ben's throat and how he looked like a poor fish hooked through the gills. Tears rolled down her cheeks as she also recalled the astonishment on Vitorio's face when he had taken the Apache arrow in his back. And then how astonishment had changed to sadness before he'd pitched to the earth and been repeatedly stabbed by the frenzied Apache warriors. Jacova willed away the terrible visions of her dying husband and brother. She focused on her pain while tears rolled freely down her cheeks.

"Open your eyes, Pima woman!"

Jacova realized that she had been betrayed by her tears. She took a deep breath, and when her eyes opened, the face that stared down at her belonged to a young Apache warrior. He was tall but slightly built. Despite his youth, there was steel in his voice and he possessed a formal dignity. He wore a headband and his black hair was straight and fell almost to his waist. His shirt was deerskin, and like the others, he wore a breechclout that fell to his knees in front and lower in the back. He favored buckskin pants and moccasins that reached above his knees. A big knife was sheathed at his side, and around his open neck rested a magnificent turquoise necklace. Jacova saw at a glance that he wore beautiful silver rings on most of his fingers, and realized the tall Apache had already gained wealth and respect among his people. She had expected to see a lusting or hate-filled warrior instead of a proud young man who regarded her with something like sympathy.

"Who are you?" she whispered.

"I am Yahnosa."

"Yahnosa," she whispered. And then she remembered! "Vitorio spoke of you. My brother told me that he once spared your life."

Yahnosa nodded his head. He extended his hand and showed her the Castillo crucifix and gold chain. Jacova stared at the prize bequeathed by the old Jesuit priest to her father and then to Vitorio. Once again her eyes stung with tears.

"Why didn't you save *him*!" she recklessly demanded. "You owed my brother his life."

Yahnosa knelt beside her, his young face sad and troubled. "He had killed many Apache. It was not in my power to save his life. It was all that I could do to save yours. I thought you were his woman."

Before Jacova could comprehend what he was telling her, Yahnosa laid the magnificent crucifix and chain on her chest. "This is yours, in exchange for your brother's courage—and my life."

"You do this after your warriors killed my brother!" Jacova choked in anger.

"I did not know that your brother was the man who spared my life until after he was dead and I discovered that treasure under his buckskin jacket. By then it was too late."

Jacova tasted bile. She squeezed the Spanish crucifix until it bit into her flesh. "Will I be allowed to return to my people?"

"No," he said, raising his chin. "You will become like Apache."

"Your people killed my father, my husband, and my brother," Jacova hissed. "I will *never* become Apache! Kill me now!"

Her outburst brought several Apache rushing over with drawn knives, and Jacova's eyes dared them to end her misery. But Yahnosa, despite his youth, stood up to the warriors and began to shout. A fierce-looking Apache jumped to stand by his side, knife also drawn. For a tense moment Jacova thought—even hoped—that these people were going to kill each other. But then, as quickly as it had begun, the confrontation ended.

Yahnosa turned his back on the others and again squatted down beside her. "It has been decided. I will take you as my wife."

"What!"

"You will be my woman."

Jacova's head rocked back and forth. "Never! Kill me now, Yahnosa! Give me the same merciful gift of death that your people gave the only three men I will ever love!"

His dark eyes burned with anger. "You will bear me a son. What is your name?"

Jacova had difficulty telling him. Yahnosa thought about that for a long minute, and then he pulled her buckskin dress down over her knees and said, "I will bring you food and water this one time. From now until you die, you will bring *me* food."

"I will bring you nothing but sadness and anger," she vowed. "So kill me now, Yahnosa."

His hand actually shifted to the hilt of his knife, and

Jacova saw his internal struggle. Torn between the knowledge that she would bring him sorrow, and some code of honor that he felt due the sister of Vitorio, Yahnosa was trapped in a terrible dilemma.

"Please," she begged. "Kill me."

After a moment he stood up. "You will eat and drink well. Soon it will snow again and we will move under the rocks. You will stay close to me, and if any of my people touch you, then I will kill them."

"You're a fool," she told him sadly. "And I am the living dead."

Jacova lost track of the next three days as she endured a sea of pain and an overwhelming sense of loss. She was violently ill each morning and exhausted. That first day, a snowstorm struck the mountains and the Apache huddled under the bluffs that flanked the Gila River. When the storm passed, the sun appeared and Jacova was forced to shoulder Ben's pack. One of the Apache brought along the damaged Kentucky rifle, and Jacova, often catching him watching her with his black eyes, realized that he desired her body. She vowed to kill him or herself rather than allow that to happen.

It was not until the next day that Jacova even realized that the Apache were journeying down to the warmer foothills. They left the Gila and found another, smaller river but it was also gorged with water, and in one day alone they crisscrossed the river more than thirty times. There were occasions where they hugged the surrounding canyonsides and struggled into the icy water up to their waists in order to get past a narrow place.

The Apache had no dogs, horses or other women. Each day, several of the warriors went off to hunt, and they always returned with fresh game. If Yahnosa had left her, she would have thrown herself into the river in the hope of being swept to her death.

One morning when Jacova was sick to her stomach, stumbling with exhaustion and scratched bloody by thickets, the Apache came upon a series of boiling hot springs. Here they were greeted by women and children, perhaps thirty or more. The reunion was happy until the Apache women saw her and snatched up willow switches. Five of them advanced, cursing and yelling. Jacova shrank back and they attacked.

"Yahnosa!" she cried. "If I am your woman, help me!"

But Yahnosa folded his arms and shook his head as the women began to beat her worse than any dog. Jacova covered her face, and when the pain became unbearable, she tore off Ben's pack and hurled it at one old woman, knocking her flat. Emboldened by this small success, she threw herself at the Apache women, shrieking even louder than they. Her muscles were very hard from work and she was much taller than her opponents. She drove them back, knuckles marking their hating faces. She cursed them and spat at them, taking their blows and giving harder ones in return. When one of the women dropped her willow switch and fled, Jacova snatched it up and lit into the other women like a cat cornered by dogs. She was wild and profane. Lashes marked her cheeks and forehead, but Jacova scarcely felt them, for her blood was up and she reveled in seeing the Apache women cringe and then scatter like quail.

Jacova's lips drew back from her teeth and she shrieked mockery and triumph. She would have gone after the women, chased them right into their wickiups, except that Yahnosa pinned her arms to her sides. He lifted her from the ground as she howled at the Apache women.

"It is done!" he shouted in her ear.

Jacova finally quit struggling. She bowed her head and began to cry, which made Yahnosa angry. He scooped her up and carried her to a hot spring behind some trees, where they could not be seen by the village. Then he eased her into the warm, soothing water and used his knife to cut off her soiled buckskins.

While Jacova sniffled, Yahnosa cut a square from her

dress and used it to wash her bruised body. He washed her long black hair, and there was a mixture of pride and concern when he dabbed at the fresh welts on her face, arms, and body.

"I like you," he said, pushing her down into the shallow water and himself undressing. For a moment he fingered the crucifix she wore, and then he said, "Jacova, you *are* my woman and will give me a tall, fine son."

"As I said before, Yahnosa, I will give you only sorrow and heartache," she breathed, too empty to fight him the way she had the women.

Yahnosa took her in the pool of warm water, and Jacova wept because she felt broken in spirit and could not even summon the strength to fight the Apache. Also, because Yahnosa was gentle and had tried to help ease her burden on the Apache trail. And finally, because he had given her the Castillo crucifix, the precious last link to her father and her brother.

They soaked in the warm springs all the rest of that day. Yahnosa talked about his life and the proud ways of the Apache. That night they did not return to the village but instead remained apart from the others. Yahnosa was an ardent lover, very different from the only other man Jacova had known. Unlike the American, the slender young Apache was surprisingly gentle in lovemaking, and each time they were finished, he asked her if she thought she might now have conceived their son.

"Yes," she finally told him as they lay back and watched the steam rise to tickle the stars. "Now I carry your son."

He laughed with joy. He clapped his hands and jumped to his feet to dance with happiness. Jacova realized that she was smiling. And despite hating all Apache, she also knew that she did not nor could not hate this one. He was a boy, really, childish in the understanding of women and naive beyond imagination. She might have held him in contempt except that he had displayed the courage to stand between her and the other Apache warriors.

"Why didn't you stop those old women from beating me?" she asked that night.

"Because they would have beat you when I was hunting or raiding. This way, they will leave you alone. They know you are brave now, like your brother, and that you are my woman bearing my son."

Jacova saw a shooting star streak through the steamy mist. It occurred to her that she might already be with Ben Jury's child. It was possible, for she was sick in the mornings and always so exhausted. She prayed that she did carry Ben's son. But then she realized that her child might be killed if it were believed to be spawned from the seed of a white man.

That very instant, with the shooting star blazing out into the heavens, Jacova told herself that if she were with the American's child, she would never, never reveal that secret to these Apache. To do so would be madness. To deceive Yahnosa would be to give Ben's child the gift of life and maybe even a chance for escape and freedom. Yes, and it would be her own form of revenge against the enemy.

TWENTY-ONE

Jacova was heavy with child, Ben Jury's child. The morning sickness was gone, but now there was perpetual weariness and unending nights when sleep was impossible. She reeled with dizziness when the Apache broke camp and she was forced to walk all day under the hot sun, ever fearful of a surprise attack. Unlike her Pima, these Chiricahua Apache were constantly relocating to hide their women and the children while the men went off for weeks at a time and raided farms, ranches, and villages.

A flood of American fur trappers had entered the Mogollon Mountains with the coming of spring, and the Apache blamed themselves, because one of Ben Jury's trappers had escaped to inflame the Americans' greed with stories of rivers teeming with beaver. Upon the arrival of so many well-armed American trappers, the Apache had been pushed south. Unlike the River People, the Chiricahua Apache were hunters and raiders. They stole horses, mules, and burros from other Indians, Mexicans, and an increasing number of scrappy Americans. Jacova had never gotten over the revulsion of eating horseflesh but eat it she did in order to save her unborn child.

Now, the Apache medicine woman, Kiati, who sat across from Jacova on the huge boulder and slowly worked a stone pestle into a bowl in the rock while grinding nuts and seeds, began to retell her favorite story. It was of the time that Jacova's father had spared Kiati's life and taken her as a slave to the Pima village. Kiati grew animated as she described her bold escape on an Apache pony across the Gila River. She showed how she had mocked her Pima pursuers, and then told how she had ridden for ten days back into the Mogollon to be reunited with her own Apache people.

"When I saw that cross," Kiati explained, "I knew your father was a Spanish priest, for I had been told of such people and that they were good. I could see kindness in his eyes, but the River People were angry and I knew that he could not stop them from killing me."

"They would not have killed you," Jacova repeated as always. "The Pima do not kill children. They would have taken you into their village and treated you well. Maybe, if you had stayed, you would still have a Pima husband and children."

At this, Kiati snickered. She had already lost two Apache husbands and a son, all killed raiding in Mexico. Kiati would have been taken by her last husband's brother as his wife, but she had chosen to support herself as a medicine woman. "I will mourn no longer for husbands or sons," Kiati muttered with a trace of bitterness.

"My son will be a great warrior," Jacova said, more to herself than to her older friend and protector.

Kiati made a face. She was as brown and wrinkled as wet leather and just as tough. Without her patronage, Jacova did not think she would have survived in the Apache camps. The younger women had never forgiven her for being chosen by Yahnosa to be his wife. Even worse, that Jacova had whipped and driven their mothers away with their own willow switches, like so many cowardly bitches. Jacova knew that she would never be accepted by the Apache women, and it did not matter. Kiati was strong medicine and both respected and feared. Even more important, Kiati was hinting that, in exchange for the Castillo crucifix, she would be willing to teach Jacova all her powers so that she too could someday become an Apache medicine woman. Jacova was careful to keep the crucifix out where Kiati could admire it whenever they were alone together.

"Is it only because of my father's mercy that you have become my friend?" Jacova asked. "Or is it because you want his golden treasure?"

"Both," Kiati said. "And also because you carry my cousin's son. Yahnosa is very proud. I think he is more anxious for the child than you, eh, Jacova?"

She looked away for a moment, lest her belief that she carried Ben Jury's son be revealed to this mystic old Apache woman. When Jacova turned back, she smiled guilelessly. "I think Yahnosa will be very proud of his first child."

"I will help you at the birth," Kiati said. "The first one is difficult, after that they are as slippery as fish in the hand."

To demonstrate, Kiati slid the heavy pestle across the callused palm of her hand. Then she cackled, her laughter reaching down into the Apache camp, where the women and the children were in hiding. Jacova smiled despite her weariness. She remembered how her father had also taken great pride in telling the story of how he had saved the life of an Apache child, only to have her escape on a pony soon after arriving at the Pima village. The story had obviously brought him a great sense of pride and satisfaction, and it was remarkable that Jacova would now find herself hearing it again from the Apache point of view.

A circle, Jacova thought. Good returns good, evil begets evil. And so it shall always be, and these Apache are mostly evil. But not all. Her husband Yahnosa was a very brave and honorable warrior. He treated her with kindness and respect, and Jacova knew that it had taken great courage to protect her from the other warriors. But with child, she had gained her own measure of respect.

Jacova prayed that the child would not have Ben Jury's blue eyes or his light brown hair. If it did, she was not sure what would become of them, and it was something that she was afraid to even consider. And while she knew that Yahnosa would feel betrayed and dishonored, Jacova did not actually think her Apache husband would kill her and the infant. More likely, Yahnosa would turn his back and abandon them both to a very uncertain fate.

"Kiati," she asked suddenly, "if I were in great trouble, would you help me?"

The Apache woman looked up from her metate filled with meal and stared at Jacova. "What do you mean?"

"I mean—" Jacova felt her chest constrict. She knew that she might be making a terrible mistake in confiding her darkest secret to this Apache woman, and yet ... yet the idea of having a blue-eyed son and facing her husband's wrath and possible banishment filled her with a sense of impending desolation. After childbirth she would be weak and defenseless. Without support ... Jacova was sure that she and her son would die.

Kiati frowned, then cocked her brow upward in question. She was missing her two upper front teeth, and there were streaks of gray like veins of Mexican silver running through her black hair. Her face was flat and square-shaped. Her nose was hooked, and the whites of her eyes were webbed with tiny blood vessels. Kiati was not an attractive woman even by Apache standards, and yet there was an indefinable strength and dignity about her that many of these people shared. Kiati looked strong even for Apache. Jacova desperately wanted her support.

"Speak plain," Kiati demanded.

Jacova had been leaning back on the flat grinding-stone rock, enjoying the late afternoon sun which filtered through an overhang of oak leaves. Now, however, she leaned forward and decided to confide in Kiati. She had

to. The burden of worry was too great, and she was afraid
that it would affect her ability to bear Ben Jury's son.

"The American that was killed along with my
brother," she began. "He was my husband."

Kiati made a face as if she had bitten into something
that tasted bitter. She began to grind the meal again.

"Kiati," Jacova said, "we are friends. My father
saved your life."

"And I have saved yours," the Apache woman said
without looking up from her work.

"Yes. But I want you to swear that you will not let
them kill my baby."

Now the stone pestle stopped grinding. Kiati's chin
lifted and her dark eyes burned. "Speak everything."

"I . . . I think this child I carry is not Yahnosa's son,
but instead the American's."

Pestle crashed against the metate, scattering meal,
seed, and nuts. Kiati stared at the scattered meal, and after
a long moment she began to sweep it back into the metate.

"Did you hear me?" Jacova asked. "Kiati, I think I
am carrying the white man's son!"

The woman's jaw muscles corded and framed her flat
face. Then she carefully collected her meal into a leather
pouch and left Jacova. And despite the lingering warmth
of the afternoon sun, Jacova felt a chill pass through her
swollen body. She guessed that Kiati had given a very
clear answer in response to her question. If the child was
unmistakably American, then Kiati would not help her at
all. No matter that Miguel Santana had once spared her
life. No matter that Jacova was her new friend and the
wife of her favorite cousin.

No matter.

Jacova buried her face in her hands and wept bitterly.
At first after the death of Vitorio and Ben, she had clung
to life with one thought in mind—she *must* survive in order to bring to life a child conceived in love rather than
Apache lust. But now . . . now she was no longer sure of

anything save she would be an outcast if she had not been impregnated by an Apache's seed.

The pains came late in the night, while Yahnosa was still away raiding in Mexico. They came softly at first, little more painful than a pinch. They woke Jacova from her troubled sleep, and she lay for hours, feeling them grow stronger and more frequent.

Jacova did not know what to do. She was deathly afraid for the first time in her life. She had not been afraid to fight and die when the Apache had taken her beside the Gila River, but now she suddenly felt very old, weak and vulnerable.

And indecisive. Back and forth she went, deciding to go to Kiati for help, then deciding that she would be better off stumbling going out into the night and having her son alone beside the canyon stream. At dawn, if it had light hair and blue eyes, she would know that her only hope was in escape. Perhaps steal a horse from the Apache, take her son and flee north, throwing herself upon the mercy of Americans.

Was that possible? Would she have renewed strength when the birthing was done or would it instead leave her weak and helpless? Jacova did not know for sure. All she did know was that the child she carried and which was now ready to be born deserved life. Kiati would not give it a chance if it were Apache, while Yahnosa would be shamed and embittered.

Jacova pushed herself up and staggered out of her wickiup. She was halfway across the sleeping camp when a contraction more powerful by far than the last drove her to her knees. Biting her lower lip until it bled to keep from crying out, she leaned forward on her elbows, rocking back and forth until the pain subsided. She struggled back to her feet and tried to run for the stream near the horses. She almost made it before another powerful contraction sent her sprawling across the warm earth. This caused her to groan and roll onto her back. The contraction lasted forever, and then Jacova felt something burst inside. Warm water or blood flooded between her legs.

"I am dying," she whispered. "Kiati!"

Her cry was weak and stricken with terror. When the contraction passed, Jacova rolled onto her hands and knees and began to crawl toward the stream. She crawled onto the damp sand and rolled over on her back, feeling a great pressure mount between her legs. Pain and pressure caused her to push downward. Her bloodied lips drew back from her teeth and she pushed until another cry was torn from her throat.

The terrible pain and pressure alternating with moments of total relaxation reoccurred with increasing frequency. Jacova lost her senses and began to sob like a child. Dimly, she heard Kiati's voice, and felt the surprisingly gentle touch of her rough old hands. Soon, blessedly soon, the pain vanished and Jacova settled into the wetness of the riverbank and closed her eyes and slept.

When she awoke, the sun was several inches above the eastern wall of their hidden Apache canyon. Startled, she threw her head wildly about and saw Kiati. The woman was sitting cross-legged on a rock close by, her feet dangling in the cool stream. She was chanting a song.

A death song.

Jacova covered her face from the rising sun and wept so hard her bloated, pain-racked body shook like a skin bag of water. At last, she sleeved her eyes dry and looked toward Kiati, who regarded her without expression.

"It was ugly girl born dead," the Apache medicine woman said.

"A girl?" Jacova whispered. "I don't believe you! You're lying! It was Ben Jury's son!"

Kiati never argued. She did shake her head.

Jacova struggled to sit up. "Where is he? I want to see him!"

Kiati stood up and then she disappeared. A few moments later she returned with the dead infant. It had been washed and wrapped in a blanket. The blanket was covered with dirt, and Jacova knew that it had been buried.

Kiati knelt and extended the blanket, which Jacova held in arms that trembled. She looked into the Apache's bloodshot eyes, and then she drew a deep breath and unfolded the blanket.

It *was* a girl. Jacova stared, and then without conscious thought thumbed back one of the little corpse's eyelids. It was coated with slime and dull in death, but it was unmistakably blue.

A cry exploded from Jacova's throat and she squeezed the infant and began to rock back and forth. Grief made her wail and shake uncontrollably. Jacova felt Kiati try to pull the infant away, and she screamed like a wild beast, curses boiling from her mouth until she felt something crash into the side of her head.

When Jacova awoke hours later, she was back in camp and Kiati was applying a poultice to her lacerated scalp. Jacova tried to claw the Apache woman's eyes, but she was too weak.

"White-eyed baby girl dead," Kiati said, clucking her tongue. "Poor Jacova. Poor Yahnosa. Maybe next one be Apache boy. Eh?"

Jacova shuddered, squeezed her eyes shut and welcomed the narcotic of sleep.

Chapter

TWENTY-TWO

"**K**iati?" Jacova whispered across the windy mountain darkness. "Are you awake?"

"No," the old woman muttered.

Jacova struggled to sit up and throw a couple of branches on their campfire. Embers twisted away into the wind. Overhead, the diamond blanket of stars was beginning to fade, and soon there would be a faint gray line across the eastern horizon of these hard Mexican mountains.

"Kiati. I want to talk."

The Apache medicine woman grumbled and pulled her blankets closer about herself. Kiati did not want to awaken, much less talk yet. Jacova knew she was going to catch hell for waking the old woman, but she didn't care. Kiati would forgive her anything. Now seven months pregnant, Jacova turned her face south and listened to the sound of the hot gulf wind. She did not move for long moments, and then she slowly relaxed and eased onto her back. She kept thinking that the camp was in danger, that perhaps the Mexican army was waiting to open fire upon them at dawn. Or that a party of American scalp hunters were sneaking up and preparing to attack their camp of women and children.

Jacova breathed deeply of the sage, and her hand snaked out to touch the Apache woman's blanket. Kiati, despite being very old and ill-tempered, was her only friend and her greatest comfort whenever Yahnosa was away on one of these long, dangerous raids.

It seemed impossible to Jacova that she was pregnant again after all these years, that this time she would have Yahnosa's child. So many years of disappointments, and now, at over forty winters of age, she was pregnant. Yahnosa was wild with joy, and Jacova desperately wanted her husband's son. Not for herself, but for Yahnosa, who had waited so many years for a man-child.

And wasn't *that* strange, Jacova thought. Strange because she was sure that the Chiricahua Apache were a doomed people.

Jacova placed both of her hands upon her distended abdomen. She could feel life, and wondered if it was wrong to bring a child into such a cruel and unforgiving world. A world that seemed to be closing in on the Apache as inexorably as the sun would rise and burn these cactus-studded mountains. As sure as her husband would return from their last raid with fewer Mexican horses, bags of grain, rifles, and silver bounty. And fewer Apache warriors. As sure as Apache squaws would wail and Apache boys would stoically mourn the loss of their fathers. As sure as next winter would be hungrier and more desperate.

"Kiati!" Jacova sat up again, hugging her belly.

The old woman snarled like a prodded dog. She pushed herself up on one elbow and glared, the light of the campfire playing across the deep wrinkles of her leathery face.

"Why don't the Chiricahua Apache become farmers and live in peace?" Jacova asked.

"Stupido!" the old woman cried and lay down again.

"Stupido?" Jacova whispered, rubbing her belly, feeling the life within. "What is stupid about a woman wanting the child she brings into this world to live to old age?

What is stupid about harvesting corn and not being afraid
each night that enemies will attack at dawn?"

Kiati did not reply, but then she might not have heard
because she was growing deaf in her old age. Her medicine was not so strong anymore. She had the Castillo crucifix, but it was Jacova who now had the power and
knowledge of healing.

The baby inside of Jacova kicked hard and she
winced. Yes, this one *was* a boy child. A child of three
bloods—Spanish, Pima, and Apache. Surely he would be
extraordinary. Perhaps as tall and strong as the great
Mangas Coloradas himself.

With the approach of dawn, the stars winked good-
bye one by one and the other squaws began to arise from
their blankets. It was cold, and more wood was heaped
upon the fires as a meal of rabbit meat and corn tortillas
was prepared.

Jacova pushed herself to her feet and waddled off into
the rocks to relieve herself. She leaned heavily against a
boulder and admired the way that the sunrise fired the
mountaintops.

"If you stand so long staring at the color of the sky,"
Kiati growled, coming to relieve herself too, "then the
baby will drop and land on its head and be crazy."

"Then maybe it would not someday be shot while
raiding as a boy chief," Jacova countered.

Kiati said something uncomplimentary under her
breath. She finished her business and turned toward camp.

"One thing I always wanted to know from you,"
Jacova called after her old friend. "Did my blue-eyed baby
girl really die in birth, or did you put your hand over its
nose and mouth?"

Kiati turned and stared at her. "Puta," she said, before
wheeling around and shuffling back into the camp.

Jacova bit her knuckle. It was useless to ask such a
question. It was not the first time she'd asked, though.
And every time, the old woman cursed her and walked
away. What did it matter after so many years if her daugh-

ter had died of birth or been suffocated? It mattered, Jacova told herself again, because Ben Jury had been her husband and they'd been in love. She wished that she could have watched his blue-eyed daughter grow tall and strong.

Hearing Kiati call her name, Jacova pushed the dark considerations from her mind and waddled back to the camp. The day warmed quickly in these barren mountains. By noon the temperature would be comfortable and there would be no need for her to wear her coarse Mexican serape. She went to the campfire and tried to help prepare the meal, but the other Apache squaws squeezed her outside their circle. Jacova did not take offense. She had long since given up the idea that she would ever be accepted. No matter. This business of trying to take her place at the fire was all ritual, and now that it was completed, Jacova knew that she would receive as much food as any of the others. More, in fact, now that she was with Yahnosa's child.

All that day, as they had the entire past two, hard weeks, the Apache women used stone axes to cut away the long, sharp leaves from around the edible root ball or heart of mescal plants. The mescal hearts were the size of small, round melons. It took long, difficult hours to chop them loose and pack them to the camp. While the toughest women hacked at the leaves, other women and children dug a pit about a yard deep and fifteen feet across that would hold several dozen hearts. This pit was located in the center of the harvest area. Jacova could do little more than collect wood which was thrown into the pit, covered with flat rocks, and set afire with prayers. After the fire burned down, a thick layer of wet grass was added. Then the mescal hearts were put in and covered with another layer of grass. A foot of dirt was heaped on top and a fire that would be kept burning for as long as it took the mescal to bake. After the mescal heads were thoroughly baked, they were excavated. The outer charred layers would be peeled and cut away, with the inner cores prepared as food. Jacova had never acquired a taste for them like the other Apache, but they were filling and could even be cut up, dried, and cached underground for winter. Most of this harvest would be transported during the band's frequent relocations.

"If we ever stayed long enough in one place," she told Kiati once again, "we could farm corn, beans, and squash."

"Why should we plant them?" the old woman asked. "They would need watering, no? And if we planted crops, how could we raid and escape Mexican soldiers? We would become like their peons, and other Indians would then come and take *our* food." The old woman grinned. "Much better that we steal food than have it stolen from us, eh?"

Jacova could see the logic but not the wisdom. The Apache were being killed faster than they could reproduce. Each year, the number of warriors who were shot, captured or hanged, outnumbered the babies born. Jacova knew that was why the squaws were treating her as an equal now, because she was carrying an Apache child.

At sundown Yahnosa and the Apache warriors galloped into camp, causing a stir. They had stolen rifles, food, and a herd of Mexican goats, burros, and horses. They had also returned with six Apache women who had undoubtedly been used by the Mexican officials or patrons as prostitutes and slaves. Jacova did not ask, but she thought these freed Apache women looked dead in the eyes and were probably Mescalero Apache. From every indication, it had been a successful trip, except that three of Yahnosa's warriors were badly wounded and two others had been killed.

"Yahnosa!" Jacova cried, hurrying to her husband and trying to look pleased with the captured bounty.

Yahnosa slid from his horse. He was still in his prime, but Jacova saw the tremor in his legs and knew that he and his warriors had been in hard fights and had probably been chased for hundreds of miles before either ambushing or outrunning their Mexican pursuers.

Yahnosa reached out and enfolded Jacova in his arms, and she held him tight, hearing the wails of the squaws who now had no men to hold or to hunt for them. "I missed you," Jacova whispered. "Can you stay until after our child is born?"

"How long?"

"Kiati says two full moons. I think sooner."

"We must move this camp," Yahnosa said, studying the smoke that lifted from the mescal pit. "At sunrise."

Jacova knew better than to protest. And despite Yahnosa's words, she knew that they would have to wait until the mescal were finished baking. That would happen by late morning, and then the squaws would break camp and this band would hurry off again.

"Where to this time?"

Yahnosa glanced northward, and Jacova could read the concern in his eyes, and understood that he was afraid of crossing into the United States because of the trouble that they might have with the Americans. There could only be one reason why they were returning north so soon after crossing the border south less than a month before. The Mexican army.

"I will be ready," Jacova said. "Now I will wait for you in the wickiup and prepare food."

"No. You must help Kiati with the wounded soldiers. It is your medicine that is now strong."

Jacova nodded because this was true. The Apache warriors would have deep wounds, perhaps even bullets to be removed from their sinewy bodies. She knew how to do this because she had been taught by Ben Jury, her first husband. Not that she would have related this fact to Yahnosa, but it was true. Jacova would never forget the first time she had extracted a flattened lead ball from her own poor brother up in the ancient cliff dwellings near the headwaters of the Gila River.

Returning to her wickiup, she joined old Kiati and

they quickly prepared their medicines. Jacova brought a small but very sharp knife and a Yucca splinter with a thread of fiber still attached.

"We will need canaigre root, sage, sangre de drago, and yerba mansa powders," Jacova said.

Yahnosa turned and went to help prepare the camp for moving the next day. He did not have to tell the People that they were again in great danger. The People knew and set about making hurried preparations. They understood that their hands would be burned raw digging out the steamy mescal heads, with no time for them to cool before they were peeled, cut, and packed for transport on the Mexican ponies.

When Jacova and Kiati went to attend the wounded warriors, they found the three in bad shape. A man named Taska would certainly die, for he had a ball in the lung and was spitting up blood. The other pair had also suffered very bad wounds, but Jacova and Kiati were able to cleanse, then use their medicines to great advantage. Powdered canaigre root was very good to pack in wounds. Mixed with water, it made a healing solution. Sage was used by the Apache to induce sweating out a fever. Kiati much preferred the scarlet-flowered sage, although it was Jacova's experience that the more common purple-flowered sage when mixed in with willow bark to make a strong tea had a more immediate fever-reducing effect.

Sangre de drago, or blood of the dragon, was very effective for cooling and eliminating inflammation and infections. When used as a poultice, as Jacova most often prescribed, sangre de drago was also very useful to stop bleeding and reduce the redness around wounds. The herb could also be chewed to eliminate gum or mouth sores. Yerba mansa, also called lizard tail or swamp root, was a pretty, low-growing plant which turned brick-red in the fall. Highly popular even among her ancestral Pima, this herb was used for wounds that resisted almost every other form of medicine.

Kiati always prescribed yerba mansa as a last resort,

but Jacova used it as a first line of defense against infection and to promote rapid healing. It could be swabbed on the gums to rid infections from broken or rotting teeth. The herb was also used as a diuretic, which eliminated poisons from the body by encouraging the passing of water. Yerba mansa was also a great benefit to the older people who suffered the pain of sore joints. Jacova had found that mixing it with agave and applying it as a poultice almost guaranteed a reduction of pain and swelling.

Jacova removed one bullet but did not even consider attempting to remove the one in the lung. She used the yucca fiber to sew up the sword slash, and when she and the old woman had done all they could, they gave the dying warrior a warm cup of mescal and passion flower. The latter would slow the pulse and quiet the heart so that the dying man could spend his last hours in greater comfort while speaking to his family and preparing for his death.

It was late evening before Jacova was able to join her husband beside their campfire. For a good long while they sat close together without speaking. They could hear the wailing of the women and children, the sobs of the dying man's family and the death songs being sung from the nearby canyons and hills.

Yahnosa looked so discouraged that Jacova reached out and took his hand. Placing it on her abdomen, she said, "Feel your son move with life, my husband. There is also reason for joy."

His long brown fingers curled and stroked. The worry lines smoothed across his handsome face. Turning his head to look at her, he said, "Yes, maybe a son."

"I am sure a son."

"But if it is a daughter," Yahnosa said, "maybe it will be as beautiful as you and live longer."

A shadow passed across Jacova's dark eyes. Rather than speak to her husband in Apache, which might be overheard by others, she chose to talk in Spanish, with which they were both comfortable. "I have been thinking," Jacova began, "of teaching our child English."

He raised his eyebrows. "It is spoken by our enemies."

"I know. But that might change. If the child knows Apache, Spanish, and English, it will have a better chance of long life."

Yahnosa turned back to study the flames of their campfire. Jacova watched as her husband considered this suggestion. Usually, Yahnosa's decisions were quick, and once made, ironclad and unchanging.

"It is very important that I do this," Jacova dared to add. "We cannot look into the future, but I think it is bad for all the People, especially Chiricahua."

"And this English I have heard but a few times from your lips, it will help?"

"It will help," Jacova promised. "Our child will someday be a great leader. If he speaks English, he will work to make peace with the Americans."

"This is true," Yahnosa finally said. "If we are not all already dead."

Jacova felt her husband's hand tighten against her. She could see the pain in his expression, and knew that he was also thinking what a bad thing it was to bring an Apache child into the world when it had so little hope for survival.

"The Apache," Jacova said, "must one day stop the raiding. They must learn to plant crops and—"

"No!" Yahnosa lowered his voice and retracted his hand. "We will never be like Mexican peons tending their fields. Never!"

"Then we are doomed."

"Then so be it," Yahnosa said angrily before he climbed to his feet.

Jacova thought her husband was angry with her words and was going to stalk off to brood along with his dark thoughts of death. But instead Yahnosa reached out and drew her to her feet. "Come," he said, leading her into their wickiup.

Jacova knew that her husband would not try to make love to her until after the birth of their child. Yahnosa was so afraid that he would cause her injury that, when he was in camp, he treated her like a feeble old woman. If he discovered that she had spent the day collecting firewood for the mescal pit, Yahnosa would be very angry with the other squaws, and especially old Kiati. Jacova decided that she would tell him that she had been pampered by the other woman, even if it was untrue.

"What would we name this boy child?" he asked when she was almost asleep.

Jacova opened her eyes and stared up at the brush and dirt domed roof of their wickiup. "We have not decided."

"I would like *you* to decide."

Jacova was silent a moment, deeply touched by this great honor. She said, "There was a Spaniard once, a very good priest, and his name was Francisco."

"No priests!" Yahnosa lowered his voice. "Besides, you do not even have his crucifix anymore. It belongs to Kiati."

"I know, but she has told everyone that it will be mine again when she dies."

Yahnosa rolled over to stare at her in the darkness. "This is true?"

"Si. Kiati has become not only my teacher, but like my mother."

"Good," Yahnosa said, reaching out for her.

Jacova pressed as closely to her husband as she could, given her great belly. She lay her head against his chest and listened to the slow thump-thump of his heart. "Where will we run to now?" she asked.

He was quick to answer. "To the tall mountains that feed the Gila."

"And the Americans?"

"If they come for us while we seek only peace, we will kill them," Yahnosa vowed.

Jacova nodded. She knew that the Americans would come for them sooner or later. It was their way to want everything for themselves. There were no beaver left along the Gila after the whites had trapped them into extinction. But there was gold, and some of it had been found along the lower reaches of the river. It brought to mind a story her father had often told her and Vitorio. About how, long, long ago, a Spanish soldier had discovered a very large nugget and then had been forced to relinquish it to his evil superior, a man named, if she remembered correctly, Sergeant Ortega.

"What will happen to the Mescalero women?"

Yahnosa shrugged. "We take them back to their own people and they will reward us, maybe with guns, maybe with horses or mules. It does not matter."

"What if . . ." Jacova paused. "What if you talked to Mangas Coloradas or Cochise, and all the Apache became united. The Kiowa Apache, the Jicarilla, Mescalero, and Chiricahua. We would be strong in numbers. Perhaps we—"

"No," he said flatly. "That is not the Apache way. We will always be hunters and raiders. This land will not feed us all together."

"But the Mexicans have bad lands too! And they have an army. Why couldn't we have an Apache army, Yahnosa?"

"Don't talk stupido!"

Jacova's cheeks burned and she closed her mouth. She would never understand these people, except to know that they were prideful and fatally independent among each other. And that, Jacova was very sure, would one day prove to be their downfall.

Jacova awoke just before dawn. A hot, humid wind spawned in the warm Gulf of California was blowing across the Apache camp, whipping smoke and tiny embers toward the now starless night. Far, far to the east a faint, pale line was etching the mountains, and the tethered Mex-

ican goats were bleating in the scrub pinion and juniper
pine.

Jacova turned to her husband, who was snoring softly.
She rolled heavily to her hands and knees, then crawled
out of their wickiup and tasted the smoke from the mescal
pit. Pushing her hair back from her eyes, she slowly
gained her feet. She was thirsty, and went over to a skin
water bag hanging from one of the poles of a brush ra-
mada, of which there were many about the camp. Each
was made of cottonwood or mesquite poles covered with
a thatch of bear grass which provided the relief of shade
during the hottest part of the days.

The water was tepid and stale, but Jacova drank anyway. She listened to the goats. Most likely they had eaten
all the shrubbery within reach and were both hungry and
thirsty. Jacova felt sorry for the goats. They would be
trailed along with the band and slaughtered as needed.
Their eyes were large, brown, and trusting; she always felt
they were intelligent animals keenly aware that they were
about to be terribly betrayed.

Jacova's lower back ached from the strain of carrying
child, and she arched it and used her hands to massage
those muscles into submission. She knew that this would
be a long, hard day. First there was the very bad work of
digging up the steaming mescal heads, then the peeling
and cutting, then packing, and finally the loading of their
camp onto horses, mules, and burros. There would be no
time to feed the goats, perhaps not even enough time to
water them properly.

Jacova knew that it was impossible to go back to
sleep. She wanted to at least water the poor goats. It would
not be hard, for there was a small spring nearby. Picketing
the goats in new places would give them hours of feed. It
was such a small but important and kind thing to do. As
she neared the goats, they began to bleat all the louder.
They were probably used to the attentions of the Mexican
children who had raised and then milked them.

"I know," she said, reaching a nanny and stroking its

muzzle while its great brown eyes gazed up at her with ex-
pectation. "You are frightened, hungry, and thirsty. Perhaps you even need to be milked and your teats bring you
pain. Poor goat."

She pulled the picket stake up and led the goat across
the lightening desert landscape toward the spring. "How
many of you are there?" she asked. "A dozen? Maybe
more? You will have to drink quickly, dear thing."

At the spring the goat lowered its head to drink, when
something caught its keen eye. Its head jerked upward.
"Bbaaa!"

Jacova's eyes followed the goat's south, to see Mexican soldiers come boiling out of a nearby draw with sunrise framing them in bold relief. They possessed no color,
but were as black as death and even more frightening.

She dropped the picket line and pivoted on her feet,
clumsy and almost falling. "Soldiers! Attack! Attack!"

She followed her scream toward camp, trying to run
fast. But her stomach was like a great water bag strapped
across her belly. She could no more run than a mustang
could run after filling its paunch after a long drought.
"Soldiers!" she gasped as the Apache camp galvanized
into action.

Jacova twisted her head around, feeling the earth
shake as horsemen overtook her. She raised her arm and
saw the uplifted saber of a Mexican cavalryman. Her eyes
widened with fear as the man's face gleamed with hatred
in the strengthening sunlight, and his sword began its
downward arc.

Jacova staggered, and the cavalryman's horse struck
her with its shoulder. She felt herself lift from the earth.
Instinctively, she twisted, putting her back downward to
protect the life she carried. A wave of agony passed over
her like the charging cavalry horses, and a hoof struck her
in the face. After that, Jacova felt nothing until she opened
her eyes and found herself on horseback, clutched in the
arms of her stone-faced husband, riding through darkness.

She grabbed at her belly with a cry of alarm.

"It still moves," Yahnosa urgently whispered in her ear.

Jacova tried to clear her senses. "What—"

"We killed every one," Yahnosa spat with fierce pleasure. "You gave us warning enough to grab bows and rifles."

Jacova felt nauseous and even dizzy. Her lips were thick and she knew that her face was badly cut and swollen. That meant nothing to her. All that mattered was Yahnosa and the child of three bloods resting in her womb.

"Jacova? Are you shot!"

"No."

Her husband relaxed. "Kiati is dead. The old woman tried to reach you, but she ran into the Mexican soldiers' charge and was lanced."

Jacova bent forward and vomited. Retching and weeping, she would have collapsed again except for Yahnosa's strong arms, which pinned her against his bare chest. It was then that Jacova felt a wetness on the back of her neck and knew that her husband, despite being Apache, wept too.

___Book IV___

SANTANA—APACHE OF THREE BLOODS

Chapter

TWENTY-THREE

Santana, Apache youth of three bloods, reined his mount closer to his mother's grulla and said, "Your pony will soon die."

"I know," Jacova replied, reaching down in the pale moonlight to scratch the animal's drooping neck. "We must try and find him more food at our next camp."

"It will not matter."

Jacova's dark eyes flashed. "Suffering always matters. Kindness to animals is pleasing to God and the Great Spirit."

"Yes, Mother," the youth said quietly, so that the others would not hear, "and most pleasing to you, savior of the poor beasts."

Jacova gave him a questioning sideways glance, but Santana knew that his mother was pleased by his words rather than offended. Even so, her pony really would die soon, despite the fact that at each camp they took pains to find whatever extra grass there was available. Jacova said that it was because the animal was old and its teeth were ground down to nubs, making it difficult for the grulla to chew its food before swallowing.

Santana thought this sad and knew that tomorrow or the day after, the Apache would probably be feasting on the grulla. It was also true that, sooner or later, almost all the Apache horses, goats, and burros seemed to end up being quartered and roasted over the campfire. Santana would never have confessed that he too became attached to beasts of burden who labored so faithfully for the Apache. To do so would not seem manly among the People.

"Santana?"

He looked sideways at his mother and beyond to the moonlit sage and chaparral-covered plateau which rested between two southern Arizona mountain ranges, both strongholds of the Apache. "Yes?"

"You should ride up front instead of back here with the women and the children."

"This is my place," he said, speaking in English because it pleased his mother, who struggled to retain a working vocabulary of the language taught to her many years before by an American trapper. "If enemies were to attack, then I would be close enough to defend you."

To demonstrate his resolve, Santana drew from his waistband the old Navy Colt given to him by his father. The .36-caliber's wooden grips were broken, but Yahnosa had carved new ones with SAN cut into one side and TANA chiseled out of the other.

"Put the revolver away," Jacova ordered. "Before it kills one of us by accident."

"I have no caps yet," Santana admitted. "It is useless."

"Put it away," she repeated. "Besides, there will be no fighting this day. We have crossed the border and the Mexican army is far south."

"They would also cross the border if they thought they could catch us with so few warriors and so many women and children."

Jacova said nothing because this was true. There was a bounty paid for Apache scalps by the Mexican government, and plenty of men ruthless and bold enough to attack the Apache when they discovered weakness instead of strength. That was why they were traveling at night, even though this was offensive to Apache.

"I promised my father that no harm would come to you," Santana told his mother. "And I would rather die than fail my promise."

Jacova straightened and her weariness melted away to hear this naive but heartfelt declaration of love. This son that she and Yahnosa had received as a gift from the Holy Spirit was her salvation. No matter how desperate things became, and they had often been desperate since that terrible night many years ago when the Mexican cavalrymen had surprised and attacked their camp, Jacova knew that she had lived a blessed life to have such a strong and loyal son.

Jacova had already decided that if Santana were slain in battle, she would rather have died first and never known of his passing. For her heart had been broken long ago when Vitorio and Ben Jury had died, and she did not think that she had the strength to endure another great loss. Better, much better, that her own life should suddenly, even violently, end.

With daybreak edging over the rugged Peloncillo Mountains, their little Chiricahua band rode west into a beautiful canyon protected by red and rough-shouldered cliffs, spires, and domes. This was one of their favorite camping places because there was grass for the livestock as well as a fine trout stream surrounded by hills teeming with wild game.

One of Yahnosa's men, Nacienta, galloped on alone while the rest of the band waited for a signal that the canyon was unoccupied and safe. A short time later they heard the single retort of the hunter's rifle, and when it was not followed by more shooting, the Chiricahua smiled, knowing they'd have venison instead of the Jacova's grulla pony for breakfast.

As soon as they made camp, the women and children began to picket the horses and prepare roasting fires. Santana was expected to help gather firewood. Jacova no longer even pretended to want to join them, but instead rode higher up the canyon in search of a place where the grass was deep and summer-sweet. A half mile up the canyon she found just such a tiny meadow and hobbled the grulla. She was about to return to camp when Nacienta came leading his mount back with a three-point buck draped across his saddle. Blood dripped from the buck's nostrils, drawing many biting horseflies which terrified Nacienta's mount and caused it to rapidly swish its tail and nip at its chest and shoulders. The horse's behavior caused the buck to fall to the ground.

The Apache hunter dismounted, swearing in anger. He grabbed a big switch and began to lash the horse, but Jacova grabbed his arm. "It is the blood that draws the flies!" she shouted angrily. "Carry the buck yourself."

"Get away from me!" Nacienta warned, knocking her aside while trying to hang on to his fractious horse. "Stupid Pima puta!"

Jacova doubled up her fists and stuck the Apache hunter in the side of the jaw. Her blow was so hard and unexpected that Nacienta actually staggered and released his horse, which bolted downstream toward their camp.

Nacienta cursed and raised his switch. It whistled downward and caught Jacova on the side of the face, raising a terrible welt. Jacova threw herself at the Apache, but he easily sidestepped and tripped her to the ground. Then he began to whip her like a dog. Each time Jacova tried to stand, she was beaten down, and the stinging blows welted her upraised arms, scalp, back, and shoulders.

Suddenly, a cry and then the sound of racing hoofbeats reverberated off the canyon's walls. Jacova lifted her head to watch Santana drive his pony into Nacienta, knocking him for a complete somersault and sending both his switch and his rifle flying. Before the Apache hunter could recover, Santana reined his horse around and charged again. The horse leapt over the warrior and one of its hooves struck Nacienta on the side of the head. He writhed with pain, clutching his skull. Again Santana wheeled his mount and charged as Nacienta doubled up in a ball.

Jacova found a branch and attacked the prostrated warrior. She opened a deep gash across the bridge of Nacienta's nose and would have whipped his eyes out if the hunter hadn't jumped to his feet and blindly raced toward camp.

Santana chased the man down and kicked him in the back of the head, sending him sprawling across dead leaves. Jacova called out to her son, "Enough! Enough!"

Santana yelled something at the cowering warrior and then he spun his horse around and galloped back to his mother. He dismounted and ran to her side. "Mother, are you all right?"

Jacova hugged her tall, angry son. Proud tears streamed from her eyes. "I am all right," she pledged before reaching over to pick up Nacienta's fallen rifle. "Here, now this belongs to you!"

"To me?" Santana blinked with confusion. His hand, however, did not hesitate to accept the weapon.

"Yes. Nacienta will never speak of this, for it would shame him greatly. So now the rifle belongs to you."

Ignoring her painful welts, Jacova drew a skinning knife from her pack and knelt beside the buck. Once gutted, they would be able to lift the carcass onto her little grulla pony and deliver it to camp. The Chiricahua would not dare to shame Nacienta further by asking questions and Jacova would say nothing to ease their great curiosity. Better by far that this fight be a secret between them, or else Yahnosa would fly into a rage and challenge Nacienta. Not that Jacova cared if the hunter died or not, except that he was a good fighter and there was always the chance that he might get lucky and kill her husband.

When the work was finished and the buck loaded onto her pony, Jacova ordered her son to return to the Apache camp.

"But what will I say to them—and to Nacienta?"

"Say nothing. Do not worry about Nacienta. He will not show his face this day."

"But what about your face and arms?"

"Go," she ordered. "Remember I have strong medicine and will be along before sundown."

Santana did not want to go but knew better than to argue. Besides, he realized the honor that he was about to inherit and could not wait to declare the rifle as his prize.

When her son was gone, Jacova rummaged in her medicine pack for a small leather pouch containing powdered sumac leaves. Working quickly, she removed her buckskin blouse and knelt beside the clear canyon stream. She mixed the powdered sumac leaves with a little water to form a paste which she smeared across the angry welts. The sumac would soon reduce the swelling and redness. She would apply it all through the day, and that evening, under the cover of darkness, she would return to the Apache camp. By the next morning the sumac powder would have worked its magic and the whipping marks would no longer be visible.

Bent over a small pool of water, Jacova studied the many cross hatches of angry welts across her upper body and face as she applied the paste. Thank God that Yahnosa was gone off someplace with Cochise! And thank God that Santana's horse had not stepped on Nacienta and fatally injured the fool.

No, Jacova thought, everything had worked out very well. Especially for her son, and that was all that really mattered.

Two days later Yahnosa rode into the canyon, and Jacova had only to catch a glimpse of her husband's face to know that something was terribly wrong. Quickly, she counted the number of her husband's warriors and expelled a sigh of relief because none were missing. And yet . . . yet her husband's expression reflected intense bitterness.

Jacova and Santana hurried to Yahnosa's side, and after assuring them that he was all right, he climbed up on a fallen tree to address his small but determined band. Jacova held her breath, anticipating that her grim-faced husband was about to give them very bad news.

The Chiricahua took seats on the leafy mattress beneath the tall canyon trees. Women hushed and held their babies. Children pursed their lips, sensing trouble, and the old people fretted with worry.

"My people," Yahnosa began, looking bleak. "There

is great sadness in me, for a terrible injustice has been done by the Army of the United States against the great Cochise, who will soon join us."

This came as a shock to everyone for, among the People, each of the many bands of Chiricahua was autonomous. And while they might trade and visit together, and their children intermarry, they did not join forces except against a far more powerful enemy. Cochise was the leader of one large faction of the Central Band of Chiricahua, while his friend, the famed Mangas Coloradas, was a chief of the Red Paint People, or Eastern Chiricahua. Geronimo, another respected leader, belonged to the southernmost band of Chiricahua called the Nde'indai. All bands operated independently, and this had always been so, before even the elders could remember.

Of even greater concern to Yahnosa's people was the sudden realization that Cochise, being the most prominent Apache chief, would now make all their decisions, while their own chosen Yahnosa would become a mere subchief. This was indeed very troubling. For while Cochise was admired by all Apache, he was much more warlike than Yahnosa.

Santana glanced at his mother and noted sharp concern reflected in her dark eyes. Jacova had always been so proud that her husband was this band's respected leader and that he had kept his people out of bad fights. While he and his men sometimes were forced to kill, they did not ever do so without good reason or provocation.

Santana reached out and touched his mother's arm. Jacova smiled faintly, but leaned forward to better hear Yahnosa speak.

Her husband began by saying, "I was with the great Cochise when word came that a Lieutenant Bascom of the United States Army wanted to see him at the mail station near Apache Pass. Cochise said that we should all go there. Having no fear, he also took his wife, two children, his father, and two nephews. Our people camped nearby, expecting to sell Mexican horses to the Butterfield Stage Company."

Yahnosa shook his head as if what he was about to say

remained puzzling even to himself. "Soon we heard gunfire and much shouting. We grabbed our weapons and then Cochise and a few of his men came running over the hill to our ponies. Cochise had been tricked! The soldiers tried to capture him, but Cochise cut his way through their tent and escaped. He was very angry. Bascom had taken his family by force. But Cochise had also taken captives. Six whites. He swore to kill them all if Bascom did not release his family."

Several of the Apache murmured aloud.

"Yes," Yahnosa continued, "it was a bad thing. We could all see that nothing good would come of this deceit. After much talk and many days, Bascom released Cochise's wife and the children but hanged the others. In vengeance, Cochise dragged one white to death and tortured the others to death. It was a hard thing to watch. Better he had slit their throats like sheep."

Yahnosa fell silent and allowed this terrible news to sink in for a few minutes before he added darkly, "There will be much trouble with the whites now and no hope for peace."

"There never was peace with the whites," a warrior said angrily. "They come, they chop down our trees, dig at the heart of Mother Earth and kill our game. We should kill them all!"

"I agree," an old man named Kanseah said. "But why did this Bascom try to take the great Cochise as his prisoner? The Apache have never killed American soldiers."

"There was a coyote," Yahnosa explained, meaning a half-breed child, "that was stolen by Indians from a man named John Ward and his Mexican woman."

"I know that man," Kanseah said. "He drinks too much mescal and sometimes goes crazy."

Yahnosa nodded and continued. "Ward said that Cochise took his coyote son. He lied, but the lieutenant believed him. He ordered Cochise to return the coyote. Cochise said that he did not have the coyote but would help find and return him. But Bascom and the others would not listen. Cochise had to use his knife to cut his way out of the officer's tent and escape. The coyote was the cause of all the trouble."

"I have seen that coyote," the old man grumbled. "He is a worthless pup. Not worth a drop of Apache blood."

"True. But blood has been spilled and more will flow before this bad trouble passes. That is why we must join Cochise against the American soldiers."

While the People digested this news with stoic acceptance, Santana felt a growing sense of impending doom. From the time he was old enough to understand such matters, both his mother and father had impressed upon him that peace with the Americans was vital to the Apache, that the whites were too many to ever be defeated. Jacova in particular had argued this point while explaining that when an Apache warrior fell in battle or during a raid, there was no one to take his place. However, when a white man or soldier fell, others appeared more plentiful than the leaves of an oak tree.

"When will Cochise arrive?" a woman asked.

"Soon. This very day he attacks the stage line, seeking gold and revenge."

The People cast their eyes downward. Because there was nothing left to say, Yahnosa climbed down from the fallen tree and went to join his wife and son. "Your face," he said, looking closely at Jacova. "What is wrong?"

"It is nothing," she answered with a forced smile. "Come, and I will prepare you some venison. You are hungry!"

Yahnosa nodded, and Santana went to care for his father's weary horse. His mind swirled. It was exciting to realize that he would finally come to know the great Cochise and perhaps someday even ride with him, but Santana was deeply troubled by the prospect of war against the Americans. Over and over Yahnosa had preached that the Apache were doomed if they fought the white-eyes. And now . . . now Santana understood that he was about to learn if this were really the truth.

_____ Chapter _____

TWENTY-FOUR

C ochise and his band of Central Chiricahua, along
with Mangas Coloradas, arrived when Yahnosa and
Santana were high up in the mountains hunting
deer. The air was cool, the pines tasted sweet, and there
were clean grassy meadows with wildflowers blooming in
bright profusion. The hunting was good. When they returned to their camp, the women of Cochise's and Mangas's bands were already erecting their wickiups. There
were more Chiricahua in this lush canyon than Santana
had ever seen gathered in one place.

Santana looked at his father, searching for any trace
of resentment about his reduced status to a subchief.
Santana found none.

"So," Yahnosa said, "both Cochise and his father-in-
law, Mangas Coloradas, have arrived. We are very strong
now."

"We were strong before under your leadership," one
of their hunters replied.

Yahnosa did not try to belittle the compliment, but accepted it with grace. "We were strong enough to raid in
Mexico and keep a little ahead of their army, but we were
not strong enough to fight the Americans."

254

When the warrior did not dispute this fact, Yahnosa clapped his hand on Santana's shoulder and said, "Come, I want you to meet these great chiefs."

Santana drew a deep breath and trailed along beside his father. Yahnosa's band had visited the followers of old Mangas Coloradas many times. Mangas, which meant "Roan Sleeves" in Apache, was the chief of the Red Paint or Eastern Chiricahua Apache. Even though he was now very old, he was still a huge man, the tallest and largest that Santana had ever seen, dwarfing most of his people. Like Cochise, Mangas Coloradas had a reputation of being very fierce against the Mexican people but a friend of the whites. In fact, Santana knew that he had even offered his assistance to the white stage tenders and had often camped in peace near Apache Pass. But of course old Mangas would not be able to ignore the terrible wrong that had been committed against Cochise.

"Mind your manners," Yahnosa warned. "You are honored to be in the company of such great chiefs."

"Which is the greater?"

Yahnosa shrugged his shoulders. "One is very old, the other yet in his prime. It cannot be said."

"I think you are greater than both."

Yahnosa answered with a soft but appreciative laugh. As they walked, Santana reviewed what he knew about Cochise. Very little, actually, and much of Cochise's legend was confusing and contradictory. For example, even the name Cochise, formed from the Apache word *cheis*, was subject to different interpretations. To most Apache it meant "oak." But as Yahnosa had once explained, it was necessary to understand that the name referred more to the quality and strength of the wood than to the type of wood itself.

"Why is Cochise so feared?" Santana asked as they neared the camp. "How many Mexicans has he killed?"

"Many," Yahnosa replied. "Beyond count. He was elected chief by his people when he was a young man because of his wisdom and bravery. He is terrible in battle and very cunning. He does not lead his warriors into a fight that he cannot win. It is the responsibility of a leader to rule wisely and fairly. He must not allow dissension or jealousy to take root among his band. He is responsible for the safety of his people, but also for food, clothing, weapons, horses, and ammunition. All of these things, Cochise has well provided."

"As you have."

Yahnosa was pleased by this simple but heartfelt compliment, but he stopped, wanting to make a point. "I am a good chief, but not a great chief, my son. To be a great chief, you must hunger for a good fight. You must welcome death in battle and have no mercy on your enemies."

"And you do not hunger to fight?" Santana was surprised to hear this frank admission.

"I have no taste for blood," Yahnosa confessed. "Your mother loves all animals, but me . . . well, I do not like to kill the weak villagers of Mexico or take all of their corn, horses, and cattle."

A faraway look invaded Yahnosa's eyes as he lifted his head toward the mountaintops. "Do not tell anyone this, but sometimes in the night, when the wind blows from the south, I can hear the wails of hungry Mexican women and children. This causes me much unhappiness."

Santana wanted to share his own admission. "The other women think that Mother is stupid to feel sad over the animals, but I think they are wrong."

"The other women are *right*! After all, Santana, animals are animals. But women and children? There is a difference, eh?"

The way his father said this told Santana that even his father did not altogether believe his own words. Rather, he was arguing for the sake of argument.

"Come," Yahnosa said, leading his son past the Apache ponies of many colors.

As the only son of an Apache chief—even a subchief—Santana felt very proud as they weaved their way through the camps of Cochise and Mangas Coloradas. He saw warriors who fairly bristled with weapons of every description. He saw old and young people, but they stared at him sullenly and without greeting. One warrior was missing an arm below the elbow, and another had half his jaw blown away by a Mexican soldier's ball.

Santana observed that these people were traveling light and that their horses were very impressive. As he and his father passed into the camp, Santana felt the hard and defiant eyes of youth his own age. They were very different from the young men of his father's band and made Santana feel uneasy.

Yahnosa must have also sensed the antagonism directed at his son because he stopped, leaned close, and whispered, "Cochise's young men will challenge you. Do not be afraid, Santana. No harm will come except if your courage is found wanting."

"It will not be," Santana pledged, glaring back at a young man who eyed him with unconcealed dislike.

When they reached the center of the camp, marked by a huge oak tree, Santana recognized Mangas Coloradas. The old giant was already napping, head resting on a pair of battered saddlebags. One of his wives sat beside him with a horsehair switch to keep flies from landing on his face.

But Cochise was awake. When he saw Yahnosa, he came to his feet in a sign of respect. They exchanged greetings and Yahnosa turned to say, "This is my son."

It took all of Santana's effort not to squirm. Finally, the great chief said, "You are Three Bloods. I know of you and your Pima mother. It is said she wears a golden cross given to her by her Spanish father."

Santana was astonished. No one had ever called him Three Bloods before, and he could not understand how such a great chief could know the history of someone as insignificant as himself.

"This is true," Yahnosa said when it became clear his son was too shocked to answer.

Cochise seemed to look right through Santana into the very darkest corners of his spirit. The man finally said, "I think you will someday be a great leader, Three Bloods."

Cochise turned and pointed to a young man of about twenty, with his own strong features and height. "This is Taza, my oldest son. He too will become a leader of the Chiricahua."

Taza raised his chin with pride and a trace of arrogance. He wore turquoise jewelry and had inherited his father's broad shoulders. Taza proudly wore a beautifully tooled leather belt and holster with a pearl-handled Colt. Santana dipped his chin in greeting, but Taza dismissed him as a boy and looked away. Santana burned with humiliation. He hoped that his father had not noticed the embarrassing exchange.

Cochise began to speak with Yahnosa. Santana pushed Taza from his mind and seized the opportunity to study the famous chieftain. Cochise was a solid six-footer. It was true that he was not as physically impressive as Mangas Coloradas, the sleeping giant who even now began to snore, but Cochise was still large and exceptionally well-muscled. He was also extremely handsome, a fact that Santana had never been told. It was Cochise's eyes, however, that really commanded attention. They held a special luminance, like fire agate. Cochise possessed the eyes of a wild animal, one cornered and prepared to do anything in order to survive.

Santana stayed with his father and Cochise for the next few hours while Mangas Coloradas slept. During that time, the two chiefs discussed the bad situation with the soldiers.

"This Lieutenant Bascom," Yahnosa said, "perhaps he is just foolish and we should not declare war on all the Americans."

"No," Cochise said abruptly. "This man called me a liar when I told him I did not steal the coyote. Because of this treachery, I have lost my brother, Naretena, and two nephews. From now until my death I will be at war with the whites."

"What would you have us do? Fight the soldiers?"

"No," Cochise said. "We will attack the Butterfield Stage stations and coaches. Wagon trains will taste our fury, as will the miners who enter the land of the Apache. We will strike the ranches and leave a trail of blood and ashes. We will even wage war on the white settlements. Nothing will be safe. A hundred whites will die for every Apache."

Yahnosa looked to his son and then he turned back to Cochise and nodded with agreement. Cochise measured Yahnosa and then he glanced at Santana.

"Taza is a warrior. He will ride with us. Will Three Bloods?"

Santana sucked in his breath and held it while his father considered this question. Finally, Yahnosa replied, "This will be decided. Perhaps he will stay to protect his mother and the other women and children."

Cochise scowled. "Let the old men protect your women and children. A son should be taught to be a warrior. Taza has been well taught in the ways of the Apache. He can shoot a rifle well and knows how to kill."

"I am glad to hear that," Yahnosa said, trying to keep an edge from creeping into his voice, "but Three Bloods is still young. It is not yet time for him to follow the warrior's trail."

Cochise's lower lip curled down. "Three Bloods is old enough to ride and fight. Does he not yet know these things?"

Yahnosa jumped to his feet and Santana followed. He had never seen his father so angry. Yahnosa breathed, "You do not speak well or wisely, Cochise."

"This is for you and Three Bloods to decide."

The chief beckoned Taza and began to talk about his plans to strike the Butterfield Stage line the following week.

"We will kill the driver, the guard, and every man," Cochise declared.

Taza's eyes mirrored his excitement. "And the women?"

Santana heard Cochise answer, "We will take the young ones as slaves."

Santana did not have to use his imagination to realize what would become of the older women captives. And he did not need to look at his father to know that Yahnosa was humiliated and stung by his encounter with Cochise.

"Come," Yahnosa said, stalking away.

When they arrived back at the camp, Yahnosa was very upset. He beckoned his wife and son to follow him off from the others. When they were alone beside the stream, Yahnosa turned and began to pace back and forth with agitation.

"I do not like this," he said, shaking his head from side to side. "I share Cochise's anger against this Lieutenant Bascom, but I do not think that all whites are bad and should die."

"We must remain friends with the whites," Jacova said. "This is what we have always believed."

"Cochise has declared war on them! I am supposed to ride with my warriors under his leadership. He is poisoned with hatred and revenge. So much so that he expects our son to spill American blood."

Jacova's eyes dilated with shock. "Our son is not of age!"

"I *am* of age," Santana said, interrupting his mother. "I can fight."

"No! You are too young." Jacova rushed over to him. She touched his cheeks with her fingertips. "You are still part boy."

"I am a man," Santana told her. "I see many younger than myself among Cochise's band who are blooded warriors."

Jacova looked to her husband, eyes silently pleading while Santana's heart beat like a drum in his chest.

Finally, Yahnosa said in a trembling voice, "This boy is my life, you know this, Jacova. But he is also Apache. Not Pima and not Spanish. But *Chiricahua Apache!*"

"Then you will let him fight under Cochise?" she whispered.

"I will let *him* decide. Like a man."

Santana looked from his father to his mother. All his life he had been trained to make his own decisions. He had been raised by his mother to also accept that he was different because of her mixed blood. Unlike the others, Santana spoke halting English and fluent Spanish in addition to Pima and Apache. He had heard the stories of Jesus Christ and understood the meaning of the crucifixion told by the old Spanish padre of long, long ago. He knew the tale of Pima creation and understood that far down the Gila River, in the heat of the Sonoran desert, was the place where his mother's family still lived and farmed.

One of his great heroes was Vitorio, the half-Pima, half-Spanish uncle he had never known. And the memory of a half-white sister who had not lived beyond birth was so strong within Santana that he had even visited her burial place that he might listen for the cry of her kindred spirit.

All this knowledge of his unusual ancestry had been given to Santana in addition to the ways and beliefs of the Apache people. Rather than fragmenting his sense of being, he had been strengthened by the blood of so many brave ancestors, both red man and white. But nothing had prepared him for this moment of decision when he was torn between his mother, who wished him to remain by her side and apart from the bloodshed, and his father, who would ride with Cochise despite being insulted.

"Santana," his mother said as he wavered between going and staying, "you cannot decide now."

"She is right," Yahnosa said quickly. "The answer must come to you. Perhaps in a vision or a sign. You must watch and wait for the answer."

"And if you ride off to fight with Cochise before my answer?"

"Then stay," his father commanded. "Stay with your mother."

Santana looked to Jacova. Her eyes glistened with tears. He turned and started to walk away just as Taza galloped through their camp on his flashy bay gelding. Taza, eldest son of Cochise, at most three years older than Santana but already a blooded warrior.

For reasons he did not understand, Santana went to claim his own fine horse and follow the son of Cochise. Maybe to fight or to race horses or just to discover a measure of truth and understanding. Because something told Santana that if he understood the arrogant son of Cochise, he would have the answer to his own confusing destiny.

Chapter

TWENTY-FIVE

Santana's horse was a tall and tough strawberry roan gelding with a blaze face. He was lazy by nature, but if you whipped him into a run, his stride was long and swift. Santana had never won a short race on the gelding, and he'd never lost a long one. He didn't know why he wanted to challenge Taza to anything, except that the son of Cochise had snubbed him in the presence of their fathers, and Santana felt the need to redeem himself. In order to look more respectable, Santana shoved his Navy Colt into his waistband, loaded and capped.

The roan was not pleased about being singled out of the remuda. It laid its ears back flat and bared its yellow teeth, but Santana ignored the roan's bluff. In earlier days, most Indians had used mouth ropes pulled up behind a horse's back teeth to control their mounts, but now the Apache favored the more effective Spanish bit. The roan's headstall was fashioned from a dead Mexican's leather belt, with the cheap tin buckle blackened in the fire to keep it from reflecting sunlight to a distant soldier or scout.

When Santana grabbed a fistful of mane and vaulted onto the roan's back, it tried to bite him, but he kept the offside rein hitched up short. It took only a moment before he was mounted, and then he lifted his braided horsehair reins and kicked the roan into a reluctant trot up the canyon. There was a good trail that led all the way into the high mountain meadows, but Santana was sure that he would not have to ride very far in order to overtake Taza.

Santana was right. Taza was less than a mile upstream on the trail leading to the high country. He was waiting just around a sharp bend in the mountain trail with his rifle laid across the withers of his pony. Santana's roan almost collided with Taza's handsome bay.

"What do you want?" Taza demanded.

Santana did not know. Like a fool, he'd not even considered what he would say to this arrogant son of Cochise. Taza's eyes were hard and suspicious, and as the moments ticked by, Santana found he could think of no reasonable answer.

"Go back to your mother," Taza ordered, reining his gelding on up the trail.

"I . . . I know where there are beaver!" Santana called. "They are still worth much to the white-eyes."

"I *kill* white-eyes, I do not trade with them!"

Santana kicked his roan up the trail after Taza. "I do not like you!"

But Taza only laughed, like a man would at a boy. It made Santana so furious that he shouted, "My father is also a great warrior!"

"He is a woman compared to the mighty Cochise," Taza said with mockery, not even turning to look around. "Three Bloods, you are nothing."

Santana had heard more than enough. With a cry of anger, he drove his heels into the roan's ribs and the animal jumped forward. In two long strides it overtook the bay and Santana threw himself off his horse with a strangled oath, outstretched arms reaching for Taza's neck.

But the Apache leaned forward across the bay's withers and, in the same motion, drove his rifle butt backward into the top of Santana's skull. Santana saw an explosion matching the color of sunset and then he felt himself strike the earth. He rolled over and over, not stopping until he came to rest in the canyon stream.

"Go back to camp and nurse on your mother," Taza called down with scorn before he rode away.

Santana groaned. He felt as if the top of his head had burst like a gourd. For long minutes it was all that Santana could do just to keep from succumbing to darkness. Finally, however, he crawled out of the stream and lay panting and staring up at the trees.

Perhaps an hour passed before he was able to stumble and walk to the roan, which was greedily consuming a small patch of lush meadow grass. Santana collected his reins and led the horse over to a log, then managed to climb onto the roan's back. The animal automatically started to turn downstream, where it knew the other Apache ponies were gathered, but Santana sawed its head around and continued up the canyon. After a few miles, threading his way up along the trail, Santana checked to make sure that his old Navy Colt was still in good working order. To his shock, he discovered that it was missing, and because he had not yet found ammunition for his new rifle, he had left that prized weapon back at camp.

Santana ranted at himself for being so careless. It made sense to turn the roan about and ride back to where he'd been knocked from his horse and retrieve his gun before the afternoon shadows lengthened. But sense wasn't driving Santana now. He burned for revenge against the son of Cochise. To slink back down the canyon now would be to betray not only his own pride, but that of his father.

Shaking his head, he rode on, listening to the sounds of the canyon telling him that all was well. Overhead, a hawk soared on the warm, funneling air. The rugged stone canyons sides shimmered like gold in the intense afternoon sunlight.

Santana knew this trail very well, and when he arrived at the first big mountain meadow, he slid from the back of his horse and dropped to his knees beside the stream. He dunked his entire head in the water and felt refreshed. The sun was beginning to sink behind the most distant peaks, but the hoofprints of Taza's bay horse still led higher. How far was the son of Cochise going?

Santana knew that he had to find out. Climbing back onto the roan, he continued on, his head feeling much better. But at dusk he could ride no farther. Since he was unarmed and had brought no food, Santana spent the last precious moments of daylight gathering pinion nuts and grapes, which were stunted but tasty. He untied one of his reins and used it to hobble his roan before he went to sleep on a bed of leaves.

It was just after dawn when Santana heard a quick volley of distant gunfire. The shots were no louder than the snap of a child's fingers, but there was no doubt that they were caused by a pistol, perhaps even one like the Navy Colt lying somewhere back along the stream. Santana jumped for his horse, hoping that Taza had found it necessary to use his pistol to down a wounded buck or even a great bear. Far worse would be if Taza had come across a party of trappers or prospectors, who occasionally found their way into these rugged Chiricahua mountains. The beaver were still plentiful on the far slope, and there were men bold or foolish enough to risk their lives to take a few prime pelts.

Santana mounted the roan in a flash. He swung onto its back and sent the gelding charging up the trail following the tracks of Taza's pony. There were no more gunshots all that morning, and if it had not been for the fresh tracks he was following, Santana would not have believed that he was on Taza's trail.

Shortly after high noon Santana topped the last mountain ridge and dismounted. Shading his eyes from the sun, he could see where the tracks led down toward a clearing and then . . .

"Taza!"

Santana saw the son of Cochise trying to climb, bent

and dragging one leg. There was no sign of his horse, but he was carrying two rifles and a heavy sack was slung over his shoulders.

"Hi-yahhh!" Santana cried, drumming his heels into the roan's flanks and driving the animal down the mountainside in a cloud of loose shale and tumbling rocks.

Taza heard his approach and threw a rifle to his shoulder, but recognized the strawberry roan and lowered the rifle. When Santana reached the Apache, he jumped from his horse.

"What happened?" he asked, eyes dropping to a pair of bloody scalps dangling from Taza's fancy leather gun belt.

Taza was pale and his eyes were glazed with pain. He was out of breath and it was all that he could do to turn and point down the mountainside. "Go—".

"Go where?"

"Gold," Taza choked. "They found gold!"

"Gold is nothing to Apache." Santana knelt to examine Taza's leg wound. "And you know our people think it bad to take scalps!"

But Taza wasn't listening. Instead he grabbed Santana by the hair and jerked his head up. "Gold will buy guns and ammunition. Bring it now!"

Santana surged to his feet. He lashed out and knocked Taza's hand away and would have smashed him in the face except that Taza already looked to be in great pain.

"Let's get you on my horse."

But Taza shook his head stubbornly.

"You need a medicine man!" Santana said angrily. "My mother—"

"Three Bloods, listen! There are three bags of gold down there but they were too heavy for me to carry."

Santana did not care about gold. "They can wait until your father sends some warriors over here after them."

"No. Others might come."

Santana glanced back down the mountainside.

"You're as stubborn as a mule! Is anyone left alive down there?"

Taza shrugged his shoulders and thrust a rifle and pistol at Santana. The challenge was clear, and this time Santana did not hesitate. He shoved the pistol into his waistband and took the rifle before vaulting onto his roan.

"You find a tree and wait under it for me," he ordered. "I'll be back with the gold."

Taza nodded, and Santana rode quickly down the steep trail. He had never been on this side of the mountains and was not sure what he would find. This country seemed drier and lacked a single deep, verdant canyon. Instead it was covered with pinion and juniper, although a line of oak and cottonwoods trailed along the bottom, marking a waterway.

The prospectors' camp would have been easy to miss if it had not been for Taza's fine bay gelding, now lying in a pool of congealing blood. Only a few feet away a dead miner lay sprawled across a rock. Santana could not see his face, only the black patch of shiny bone and meat where his scalp had been removed.

Santana dismounted. The roan smelled death and it snorted with eye-rolling fear.

"Be still!" Santana ordered, tying the horse securely before following a trail that wound down toward the river below.

When he came to the river, Santana discovered the camp. It wasn't much. Just a few blankets scattered about in addition to another dead prospector. There were many flies buzzing in the camp. They swarmed back and forth between the prospector and a hanging quarter of venison.

Santana made a quick survey of the camp. He was looking for the three bags of gold. He couldn't find them. Angry and impatient to return and help Taza, he almost missed seeing the fresh tracks of a man leading downriver. Santana was caught in a moment of indecision. If there had been a third man who had hidden from Taza and was now escaping with the gold, then it would be wiser just to let him get away. Both Cochise and his own father would not fault him for returning to bring Taza back over the mountains. They would say it was the right thing to do.

Ahhh, but Taza would hold him in scorn for not following and trying to kill and recapture the gold. Santana knew this as sure as he knew the sun would rise.

Santana returned to his roan. He mounted, checked his weapons, and started after the third prospector. If the man were carrying three heavy bags of gold, it did not seem possible that he could have gone very far.

Twenty minutes later Santana saw the prospector. Smallish and Mexican, he cradled heavy bags of ore as if he were a woman rocking a baby. Santana shouted at him, and the Mexican stopped running. When he saw Santana bearing down on him, he let out a cry of fear and stumbled on. He tripped and the three heavy bags of ore spilled from his arms. He rolled over onto his back, dragging out a revolver. Santana leaped from his horse and struck the ground rolling. He came up with the rifle and snapped it to his shoulder.

They both fired—and missed. The Mexican cried out for the Lord to save him and began to fire wildly.

Santana dropped the rifle and drew his pistol as the brush popped all around him and a bullet creased his shoulder. He raised his pistol and fired wide again. Without thinking, he grabbed a rock and heaved it at the man, causing him to duck. The prospector was terrified. He emptied his gun and then tried to scoop up the sacks of gold, but a second rock whistled from Santana's hand. This time his aim was true and the rock struck the man in the back of the head and knocked him senseless.

"Yiii!" Santana screeched, snatching up his pistol and racing forward to kill the stunned Mexican.

Santana landed on the man's back and jammed the revolver to the bloody place where the rock had smashed his skull. He blinked sweat from his eyes and could feel the pounding of his heart.

"Yiiii!"

The Mexican was wearing a small silver chain and cross. It had slipped out of his open-fronted shirt. Santana's gaze fixed on the cross even as his finger eased up against the trigger. The gun shook in his hand, and if the prospector had moved, Santana would have blown the back of his already bloody head off. But the man was out cold, and Santana simply could not kill an enemy who posed no danger or could offer no resistance. Besides, the sun caused the silver to sparkle and carry Santana's mind back to an old Jesuit padre. He knew the padre and his faithful Spanish compadre, Miguel Diego Santana, would never have executed this hapless prospector.

After trying but failing to pull the trigger, Santana gave up the effort. He took consolation because the Mexican owned a good Bowie knife. Santana drew it from its sheath, tested its edge for sharpness against his thumb. He tore the man's worn-out boots from his feet, then his pants. Righting the boots and placing them neatly by the man's face, he tied the Mexican's pants legs at the bottoms and then he filled them with the bags of gold. From the last one he opened he removed a big handful of nuggets which he dribbled into the Mexican's boots. Pleased with himself for showing mercy, Santana hoped that the ancient spirits of Miguel and the Spanish padre were pleased by this act. In a hurry now, he cinched the pants up using the Mexican's belt like a drawstring.

"Adios," he said to the unconscious figure. "I hope God or Jesus is watching."

He threw one bulging pants leg over the roan's withers and balanced it with the other. Because he did not want trouble with the roan, he led the animal back toward the prospectors' camp. Santana did not look at the dead men killed by Taza again, but led the roan up the steep trail until he found the son of Cochise.

When Taza saw the horse and bulging bags of gold, his eyes widened and he exclaimed. "Three Bloods! You are a true warrior now! One fit to ride with the great Cochise!"

Santana pretended to look pleased even as he wondered if the Mexican prospector would live or die. He knew that it was a matter beyond his control and that he would let the Apache assume that he had killed the Mexican. And if the man survived, so much the better. He had won great respect this day, and if Cochise needed gold to buy guns and ammunition, then here was much gold.

Taza reached up for help, and when their grips locked, it was strength matching strength as Santana pulled the young warrior to his feet.

"You will ride this horse and I will walk," Santana decided.

Taza did not argue.

Chapter

TWENTY-SIX

The trip back over the mountain was long and difficult. Santana declined to ride double on the roan, and Taza had no choice but to swallow his immense pride and accept the arrangement. Because the roan was weary, it frequently stumbled and almost went to its knees. Each time, Taza turned pale because of his wounded leg.

"This horse is ready for us to roast," Taza gritted through the pain. "What you say we shoot him tonight and feast?"

"If we do that, I'm going to have to leave you on the mountain and go on foot for help."

Taza shrugged his shoulders as if that were not a problem.

"There are grizzly bear in these mountains," Santana reminded. "If I were wounded, I'd not want to be camped overnight beside a dead horse."

"Then we eat this one *after* he carries me to camp."

"Eat one of your father's horses."

Taza actually smiled. "I do not understand why you like this tall, skinny roan."

"He is a very good horse."

"If we eat him, my father will give you a better one."

"No."

Taza's smile died. "Three Bloods, *you* are the stubborn mule."

Santana didn't bother to reply. He was weary and troubled by the death that was being left behind. The two men that Taza had slain reminded him that the Apache were now at war with both the Mexicans and the whites. Always before, the whites had been left mostly in peace. But this thing with Cochise had changed all of that, and Santana knew how much this new and unfortunate turn of events worried both his parents.

"Tell me about the one that you killed," Taza demanded. "I did not see a third white man."

"He wasn't white. He was Mexican. I guess he was probably upstream looking for gold when you killed his friends."

"It is good that you found and killed him," Taza said. "Otherwise, he would have taken all this gold and escaped."

"The gold means nothing to me or my father."

In saying this, Santana was merely stating the traditional feeling of the Apache. Since the first Spaniards had sought the golden metal, the Apache had known that the white men lusted for gold. But to the Apache, gold was nothing. As a metal it was not hard enough to be used for arrowheads, utensils, or weapons. And as for jewelry, the Apache, like all southwestern tribes, much preferred turquoise and silver.

"We can use the gold to buy many weapons and much ammunition," Taza said with grim satisfaction.

"From who? Our new enemies the white-eyes . . . or our old enemies the Mexicans? Either would be fools to sell us weapons."

"There are many greedy fools among the white-eyes and Mexicans. They would sell or trade anything for gold—even their mothers."

Santana did not doubt the truth of Taza's words, for

he remembered the old stories of the Spanish invaders and how greed had led them north to suffering and death.

They talked about gold no more, but concentrated on making as much distance as they could before darkness fell. Just before sunset, they crested the mountains and made a quick descent to a mountain meadow where Santana shot a young buck. Using the Mexican's Bowie knife, he quickly gutted the animal, and before long juicy venison steaks sizzled over their campfire.

Both he and Taza ate ravenously, and later that evening, as they prepared to sleep beside the fire, Santana inspected the Apache's leg wound.

"The bullet did not shatter bone," Santana informed his companion. "You are very fortunate."

"Not fortunate. I have my father's great power," Taza corrected. "I have strong medicine of my own."

"That scalp," Santana said, "is it the first you have taken?"

"No," Taza admitted. "I have others."

"Why? Don't you know that if an enemy is scalped, he will wander through the spirit world without a scalp? This is bad because his spirit will cause us misfortune."

Taza's dark eyes flashed. "I do not believe that. The spirit of a white man has no power."

"We cannot know if that is true," Santana argued. "Why take such a bad risk?"

Taza glared at him with anger and disapproval. "The Apache did not take scalps until the governors of Sonora and Chihuahua offered bounties for *our* scalps. One hundred pesos for yours or mine, Santana! And fifty for our women and ten for our children!"

Santana knew that this was true, but two wrongs did not make a right. His lips formed a hard line, and he secretly hoped that the Mexican prospector was alive and getting help.

"Listen to me," Taza said. "Geronimo only began to take scalps after his family was slaughtered by the Mexicans."

"Did you see this?"

"No, but I have seen Geronimo, and know that he has taken Mexican scalps. What the Mexicans did to Geronimo at Janos was dishonorable. Already they have paid with much blood."

Santana knew the tragic story of Geronimo or, as the Apache called him, Goyakla, "One Who Yawns." Only a few years earlier, General José Maria Carrasco, a Mexican military governor, had invited Geronimo and his band south to the small town of Janos under the pretense of forging a lasting peace. The Apache, fearing deception, had camped well outside of town. However, when Geronimo and a few headmen left their families under heavy guard and rode into Janos, they were feted by Carrasco and his officers with tequila and presents of blankets, bright cloth, and food. That night there was feasting and dancing in their honor. The second day was much the same, and the warriors lowered their guard. Those who were asked to stay at the Apache camp to protect the families were given strong drink to drown their disappointment. On the third day, while Geronimo and most of his headmen and warriors were back in Janos being toasted by the Mexicans, General Carrasco's cavalry surrounded the almost unprotected Apache camp. When they were sure that escape was impossible, they opened fire and then charged with sabers and bayonets. The few hung-over Apache guards were cut down in the first volley. The women and children who were not riddled with bullets were hacked to pieces. No one, not even the babies, were spared. That day, over one hundred thirty of Geronimo's band died, and very few survivors were taken captive. That day, Geronimo lost his mother, his beloved wife Alope, and his three children. And that day, he swore eternal vengeance against the Mexicans.

It was said that Geronimo had been a happy Chiricahua before the murder of his family and people at Janos. As happy as an Apache could be with a good woman and three healthy children. But after their death, Geronimo became obsessed by the need for revenge. Even Santana had heard that the man was now a devil who lusted for Mexican blood. He was subject to almost insane outbursts of fury, and even his own people were afraid of him when his blood was running hot. It was said that many of the People followed Geronimo more out of fear than respect since Janos. And now Taza himself was saying that Geronimo took scalps, and Santana knew this had never been the Apache way.

In the morning, they were up and on the trail early, and the sun was barely over the eastern mountains when they were met by Cochise and Yahnosa along with a half dozen of their warriors.

Cochise listened as Taza explained how he had seen a plume of campfire smoke over the mountains and gone to investigate and found the prospectors' camp.

"Look!" he said happily. "See how much gold!"

Cochise dismounted, and when he opened the bags of gold, his eyes lit up with pleasure. He studied the scalps hanging from his son's belt, then distributed the bags of gold to his warriors and said, "This will buy many rifles! Food, blankets, and ammunition. Taza, you have done well."

"Three Bloods killed a Mexican. If he had not come to help me, there would be no gold."

Cochise placed his hand on Santana's shoulder. "Three Bloods, you are Apache!"

Santana's heart swelled, and when he glanced at his father and their own warriors, he could see the pride etched into their faces. Unsure of his voice, Santana just nodded, and when Yahnosa reached down, Santana took his father's hand and swung up behind his saddle, knowing that this was the proudest day of his life.

"We go to kill the whites now!" Cochise called to his excited warriors. Santana took a deep breath and wished he could hug his father.

The mining camp nestled in a deep Gila River canyon was named Edna and boasted a population of about fifty whites, a few Mexicans and Chinese. From a high vantage point on the north rim of the canyon, one of Cochise's warriors used a piece of tin to flash a message to Yahnosa's band of warriors on the south rim.

Santana drew in a deep breath when he saw the single flash of light. He hurried to his father and sat cross-legged under a brush remuda. The day was very warm and they were nearly out of water. The bright ribbon of the Gila River far below made Santana hunger for a drink.

"We attack at dawn," he told his father.

Yahnosa nodded. All summer long he and his warriors had ridden with Cochise's band of avenging Chiricahua, and the constant raiding and killing had taken a heavy personal toll. Yahnosa was in his sixties, yet remained every ounce a warrior and a fighter. Many times, Santana had seen his father shoot straight and kill a white or a Mexican. Twice, Yahnosa had been wounded and carried to Jacova, who had nursed her husband back to health. Those were bad times, with Jacova's pleas that her husband and son quit Cochise and seek peace with the whites no matter how severe their terms.

Yahnosa, however, could not quit. Unlike his wife, he was a full-blooded Apache and a sense of honor ran thick in his veins. "It is too late to stop the fighting now," he had tried to explain to Jacova each time. "It is too late for anything except to kill and to die."

Santana had watched his mother age at the same rate as his father. It had been as if the sun and moon had whirled through the sky in an accelerated cycle of light and darkness. It was as if there was no peace and no spirit left among the People, only an unquenchable thirst for vengeance. Cochise and Geronimo were waging a war, and there was no time for a Chiricahua Apache warrior to think and to pray to his ancestors and his Spirits. There was no time for a young warrior to dream of taking a wife and having children. There was only time for him to ride, hunt, and to attack—or flee in the face of greater strength than his own.

"There will be much bloodshed tomorrow," Yahnosa said in a tired voice. "As soon as it is dark, we will go take our position."

The Apache understood. They would spend the better part of the night riding and leading their ponies off these cliffs to take their attack positions just west of Edna. At the same time, Cochise, Taza, and the other Apache would descend and hide at the opposite end of the riverfront mining settlement. At dawn, even before the earliest white men started their cooking fires, the attack would be launched. And like a windswept wildfire, it would scorch the life from Edna and leave its canvas tents burning like pitch torches. Every last inhabitant would become as dead as the nearby lightning-charred tree that poked skyward like a black, accusing finger.

When Yahnosa's warriors went to their own hastily constructed remudas, Santana remained with his father. He stretched out on his horse blanket and closed his eyes, hoping for a few hours of sleep that he knew were impossible.

"Santana. Have you heard about this great war between the whites of the South and those of the North?" his father asked quietly.

"No."

"Cochise is very interested in this war. He says that maybe it will take the blue coats away. Perhaps they will all be killed and not return."

Santana had no comment.

"What do you think?"

"I do not know, Father."

"Cochise wants to know. He asked you to find out."

Santana sat up quickly. He was not sure that he had heard correctly. "Me?"

Yahnosa nodded. "Because you do not look Apache and you speak both Spanish and English. Cochise says that you could ride over to the town named Pinos. If you cut your hair and wore sandals, everyone would think you were a Mexican."

Santana was stunned. "But I've never even seen a white man's town! I would not know what to do."

"I know. I would not know either."

A silence fell between them as Santana's mind spun around and around like a silver coin. The idea of visiting the white-eyes and pretending to be a Mexican was the most exciting thing imaginable. And Santana clearly understood the importance of learning about this war between the north and the south. If such news were true, perhaps Cochise and Geronimo would stop the raiding and the killing and instead wait to see the outcome. ·And if the soldiers all shot each other in this great war, then the prayers of the People would come true. Once again Apache lands would belong to Apache.

"Maybe I will tell Cochise no," Yahnosa said.

But Santana shook his head. "I will think on this. If I am not killed at dawn, then maybe it is because I am meant to do this thing."

"Your mother would wail in anger."

"I could do this before she knows."

"Cochise says that if you will do this, we must capture a Mexican. We will kill him, but only after we have taken his clothes."

Santana was silent for a long time before he said, "I think I will do this thing."

"You could pass as a Mexican, but not a white-eyes," Yahnosa felt the need to add just as the sun was going down. "You are not ugly enough."

The attack at dawn was swift and bloody. Because Cochise was the head chief, Yahnosa held his impatient warriors in check until he heard the first shot fired by the Apache. By then the sun was a bronze river leaking through the eastern mountain passes.

The Apache struck with such suddenness that the gold seekers had no more chance than had Geronimo's band of slaughtered women and children during the attack at Janos. Santana galloped stirrup to stirrup beside his fa-

ther, both firing Navy Colt revolvers. When these weapons
were empty, rather than reload, they rode down the scattering whites, smashing the back of their heads with rifle
butts.

Santana saw a naked young woman race out of a
burning tent, and before he could protect her, she was shot
three times. She fell facedown. Santana was glad that she
had died so suddenly, for Cochise's warriors were savage
with captured white and Mexican women.

The light was poor in the canyon, and when Santana
saw two sobbing miners collapse to their knees and die
begging for mercy, he lost the will to fight. Pulling his
horse up beside a tent, he ran inside and began to rum-
mage for weapons or things of value until a burning arrow
struck the canvas top and set it to flame.

Rushing outside, Santana could see Apache racing up
and down the street killing the last whites. One of Cochise's men was standing over a little Chinaman. While
the Chinaman screamed with a high-pitched voice, the
Apache scalped him and then slit his throat from ear to
ear. Raising the Chinaman's scalp with its long, braided
queue as his prize, the Apache howled in celebration
and ran over to another miner, whose leg was shattered by
a ball and who was dragging himself toward the trees. A
moment later the warrior had a second scalp.

Taza drove a war lance through the lower back of a
fat miner and rode him to earth. When the miner kept trying to crawl toward the Gila River, Taza threw his weight
onto the lance, pinning the miner. Taza tore his knife from
his belt, and Santana looked away, lips curling down at the
corners. He entered another tent to see a miner attempting
to hide in a large trunk. The miner saw Santana watching
him and screamed.

Santana turned on his heel and left the tent. In a few
minutes it would be ablaze and the poor cowardly fool
would be baked to ashes in his trunk without having even
tried to defend himself.

When the fighting ended, a lone Mexican was

brought to Santana on the end of a noose so tight that his face was bluish. As Santana watched, the Mexican was stripped. He was so terrified that Santana could not understand his pleas, but he did accept the captive Mexican's entire outfit of clothing—from sombrero to sandals. The Mexican prayed for a merciful death, rolling upward to the heavens. He was still praying as excited warriors began to use their knives to strip away his quivering flesh.

The Mexican shrieked over and over. He tried to break free and run but was yanked over backward at the end of his rope, gagging and howling. The Apache went at him again with the knives.

Santana could not stand this torture. With a Spanish oath, he dropped the Mexican's clothing and tore a rifle from an Apache's hands. Before anyone could stop him, Santana ran over, placed the muzzle to the Mexican's ear and pulled the trigger, spraying blood, brains, and bone across the hard-packed earth.

Santana's eyes defied Taza and then even Cochise before he turned and walked back through this burning death camp to his roan. Numb in heart and spirit, Santana concentrated on the simple things that he would do next. And as he jammed his foot into his stirrup and reined his horse off to follow the Gila, he decided that he would bathe himself and the Mexican's clothes before he rode into the white man's settlement called Pinos.

Chapter

TWENTY-SEVEN

A s Santana trotted his roan to the outskirts of Pinos, he knew that he looked as Mexican as any Mexican. His sombrero was old and battered, his white linen trousers were baggy and stained, his sandals were torn and his serape thin and bleached by sun and rain. Santana's hair, a source of his Apache pride, had been cropped short in the style of a peon, and Cochise himself had given Santana a scarred old Mexican saddle.

Santana knew that if he were to attract any attention, it would be because of his unusual height for a Mexican. But there was no help for that, and so as he rode, Santana practiced both his Spanish and his English. His Spanish was *muy bueno*, his English only fair. On the outskirts of Pinos he had the good fortune to meet a pair of Mexicans, each leading a burro carrying firewood.

"Buenos dias, señor," one called.

"Buenos dias!" he called back with a smile, even as his heart pounded and his hand shifted to feel the solid confidence of the Navy Colt hidden under his serape.

But the two Mexican wood gatherers were friendly and in good spirits. They asked Santana what he thought of the terrible news of the Apache attack on Edna the previous week. Santana replied that it was indeed terrible news and that they should all fear for their lives. The Mexicans agreed, and each lifted their serape to show him that they were armed. Santana boldly displayed his own Colt, and that caused a good laugh and a chance to excuse himself and be on his way.

"Adios!" they called, and, with a sigh of relief and much more confidence than he had felt before, Santana returned that greeting.

Pinos was a mining town of about a thousand anxious souls. Anxious because of Cochise's rampage and the attack on Edna, less than fifty miles to the west. But the population was easily large enough to repel a direct attack or withstand a siege by the Apache, and the hard-rock mining was still good. There were jobs in Pinos and enough saloons for a miner to squander all his wages on whiskey, women, or the gambling tables.

Santana had been warned by both his father and Cochise to avoid the cantinas, or saloons, as they were called by the Americans. Instead he was advised to hang around the livery and the street and listen for news of the great eastern war. If eavesdropping proved to be of no value, then Santana was to seek out a drunken miner and offer to buy him a bottle if he would tell him of the war.

When Santana had received these instructions from Cochise and Jacova, they had seemed practical. But now, as he tied his roan to the hitching post, Santana felt as if every eye in Pinos was boring into his back and that someone would immediately realize that he was Apache and kill him on the spot.

For long moments he stood frozen with fear and fatalism, but at last, when no bullet ended his life, he dared to gaze up and down the street. Pinos seemed immense. Its row of main-street buildings made him feel pinched and small. The rough miners on the boardwalks seemed to stare at him, and it was all he could do to keep from vaulting back onto his horse and racing off into the wilderness. From inside the saloons came raucous laughter and the sound of strange musical noises which assaulted his ears. He could hear a woman singing in a loud, brazen voice. Smoke drifted over the bat-wing doors, and the unfamiliar smells were repugnant to the Apache.

Aware that he could not cling to the security of his horse indefinitely, Santana tied the animal with a single wrap of his reins so that he could, if necessary, make a very fast departure from this awful place. Mustering all his courage, he stepped up on the boardwalk and, feeling a hundred eyes watching him, went to a big store window and gazed at a remarkable selection of goods, ranging from blankets to barrels of flour. There were a few women inside the store, but most of the customers were men. The proprietor smiled to see Santana staring, and motioned him inside.

A sudden attack of panic caused Santana to retreat to the security of his roan, hand pressed hard against his hidden gun.

"Mighty nervous, ain't ya, Mex? What'd you do, stick a man with that big knife and steal that roan horse?"

Santana turned to see a pair of white men eyeing him suspiciously as they shared a bottle. He did not know the word "nervous," so he forced a smile, untied his horse and swung up into his saddle. It was his full intention to race out of Pinos and never look back. He would tell Cochise that the whites knew he was Apache and that they were about to kill him. Or else he would just say that these people did not know anything about the great war. Cochise would not be pleased, but he would have no choice but to accept this news.

"Well now, you don't have to run away just because we was joshin' ya!" one of the men called.

Santana did not know what "joshin'" meant either, so he sent his horse galloping down the street, hearing the white men laugh at him. He would have kept running except that a towering ore wagon pulled out of a side street into the roan's path. Santana had to rein the horse hard to his right, and it skidded up before a livery, almost running down a boy. He was pushing a thing that had one wheel and it was full of manure which tipped over as the boy jumped aside to avoid being trampled.

"Slow down, mister, or you'll run someone down on that horse! And look what you did!"

Santana had no idea why the boy was upset over spilled horse manure. However, he realized he was clearly at fault and had given the boy a real scare. "I sorry," he said in English.

"Well, you ought to be," the boy replied, going over to the livery and grabbing a strange-looking tool with a row of sharp daggers. Santana watched while the boy righted the one-wheeled, wooden-handled pushcart and quickly began to reload it with the manure, for what purpose, he could not even begin to imagine.

Santana glanced back up the street. The two men who'd accused him of stealing the roan were swaying off up the street. And now, feeling as if he should rectify this mistake, Santana climbed down from the roan and walked over to the manure spill. Without saying a word, he cupped his hands and began to scoop the manure up and toss it into the one-wheeled pushcart.

"Hell," the boy exclaimed with disgust, "don't use your damned hands! I got a pitchfork to clean it up."

Santana backed away and watched as the boy grabbed a pitchfork and quickly reloaded the cart. The boy was white-haired with freckles, shoeless and shirtless. Aware that Santana was watching him, the boy said, "You ought to feed that roan a whole lot better, señor. He's got the makin's of a good animal, but he's about two hundred pounds underweight. Looks like he could stand some grain. We could fatten him up quick and he'd be worth twice what he's worth now."

"Si." Santana nodded his head rapidly. Then, as an afterthought, he said, "Yes."

The boy cocked his head sideways like an owl and said, "You got dollars or pesos?"

Santana had been given pesos. He showed them to the boy.

"My pa would rather have dollars, but he'll take Mex money. This horse of yours is skinnier than a gart'ner snake. Damn feet are cracked and chipped all to hell too. You sure don't take good care of him.

Santana was insulted. The roan was in wonderful condition, and fat by Apache standards. Furthermore, he couldn't imagine a mere boy so ill-mannered as to chastise a grown man. Did these white-eyes have no respect for their elders?

Swallowing his anger and putting the purpose of his visit ahead of his own injured feelings, Santana blurted, "What do you know of the war?"

"You mean the Civil War between the North and the South?"

The boy had heard of the war. "Yes!"

"Well, I don't know all that much about it 'cept the soldiers are leavin' Fort Buchanan. I hear that they are callin' for recruits over in Tucson. Goin' to be a heller of a war, I'd expect. Won't take boys or Mexicans, so I guess we'll both have to just sit this one out. Fine with me."

Santana tried to understand what he'd just heard. Half of it made no sense. He wished the boy would talk slower.

"Be fifty pesos to put up this roan horse and grain him like a butcher hog, señor." The boy measured Santana, noting his poor clothes and battered saddle. "You want to sleep tonight in a stall, cost you only twenty more. But you can't smoke no cigars or cigarettes. My pa won't abide smokin' in the barn. No sir! You do that and he catches you, he'll skin us both!"

Apache did smoke, but because tobacco was an expensive luxury difficult to obtain, they saved it for special occasions and ceremonies. "No smoke."

"Good. You want me to put up your horse or not?"

Santana considered this and decided that fifty pesos was a small price to pay for the information demanded by the great Cochise. The boy was talkative and perhaps knew a great deal more about this war. And even if he did not, maybe there were other horsemen who would visit this livery and be willing to talk. Anything seemed better than returning to the confusion and chaos of the main street.

"Yes."

"Fifty pesos, señor. And what about sleeping in an empty stall? Only twenty pesos more. A tent cot up the street will cost you twice that much and you'll hardly get any sleep because of the drunks stumblin' around and throwin' up on ya."

Santana was not exactly sure what a "drunk" was, but he suspected it was a white man gone sick or crazy. "Yes, I take."

"Good!" The boy dropped his wicked-looking tool and stuck out his hand.

Santana shook it, for he had seen the whites do this before when parting at the Butterfield Stage station which Cochise kept under constant surveillance.

"No," the boy said, wrenching his hand free. "The *money*."

Santana paid him the seventy pesos. He had plenty more in his saddlebags and was thinking that he might even pay the boy extra to go back into town and get him something to eat. He was thinking hard on this when a pretty, dark-skinned girl about his own age swung a fancy one-horse buggy into view. Her fearful expression rather than her dark, innocent beauty grabbed Santana's attention.

"Uh-oh," the boy said. "Here comes big trouble."

Santana did not know why this lovely girl should bring trouble, but a moment later that too became clear. The girl was being pursued by three riders, and when she slewed the buggy up before the stable, the riders reined up too.

"Hey, Señorita Avila!" one yelled boisterously as he dismounted. "Come give me a little kiss! Give me more than a kiss and maybe I will marry you!"

"No!" another chortled. "I want to marry her and inherit her papa's gold mine. I can learn how to strut around in fancy clothes and look down my nose at the working folks same as her pa does."

"Go away!" the girl shouted, rushing up to the boy. "George, where is your father?"

"He went to look at some horses."

The señorita fumbled in her purse, trying to ignore the insults of her tormentors. "Please, take care of my horse and buggy. I've got some business in town and—"

Santana had been standing to one side, but one of the men roughly pushed him out of his path as he grabbed the girl by the arm and tried to give her a kiss.

Señorita Avila struggled. She managed to slap the man, but that only made him more excited.

"Hey!" George cried, grabbing up his pitchfork and waving it at the man. "Get away from her!"

One of the men kicked out and sent the pitchfork flying. When the boy jumped to pick it up, the third man slammed his foot down on the tool, pinning George's fingers under the handle.

"Owww!" the boy cried. "Please, mister, you're crushing my damned fingers! Please, get off it!"

Santana reacted instinctively. His sandaled foot moved in a swift arc that terminated in the man's belly. The man choked in agony and doubled up with pain. Santana's fist smashed into the side of his head and he dropped as if he'd been shot.

The other two men were much heavier and no doubt stronger than Santana, but they were not armed with guns, and Santana's Colt was still hidden under his serape. He'd use it only as a last resort, but use it he would before he'd allow himself to be beaten by these vicious white-eyes.

"You Mex whelp!" one of the men bellowed. "I'll teach you to kick a white man!"

He charged with both fists windmilling. He was powerful but slow. Santana easily ducked his blows and slammed a right hook under his ribs. The man grunted with pain, wobbled, but kept his footing and came back swinging. Santana knew better than to try to stand and fight. Badly outweighed, there was little doubt that the man would quickly knock him down and then finish him with his boots.

Santana dodged a looping right, pivoted cleanly and shot his fist to the man's throat. The fool didn't even lower his chin. Santana's knuckles sank into the man's neck at the same instant their heads cracked together, opening a deep gash across Santana's forehead. The man howled with pain, and Santana drove a knee into his groin. He started to leap back when the third man tackled him from behind and rode him to the dirt.

"I'll beat your head into mush!" the man cried, grabbing Santana by the hair and smashing his face into the rock-hard street.

Santana tried to buck and roll but the white-eyes was too heavy. Santana's head was bounced twice against the street. Somehow he managed to turn his face aside and avoid having the bones of his nose hammered into his skull. He was helpless. His gun was pinned below his body and impossible to reach. Santana was sure that in a few more seconds his skull would crack like the shell of an egg.

But suddenly the man riding him began to scream over and over. Santana felt the man's weight lift. Only half conscious, he rolled and looked up to see the girl driving the pitchfork into the man's back and sides. His entire upper body was streaming with little rivers of blood where the tines, longer and sharper than the spines of any cactus, were gouging holes.

The man rolled off Santana and threw himself at the girl, but George tripped him, and the girl stabbed the pitchfork into the seat of his pants.

"Ahhh! No more!" the man pleaded. "I quit! No more!"

"Get your friends and go away from here!" the señorita cried, lifting the tool with both hands and shivering with fury as she held it over the man's face.

"No, please!" he screamed, covering his eyes with his hands.

"Go!"

The man rolled onto his belly and slithered away faster than a sidewinder. The girl dropped the pitchfork and hurried to Santana. His vision was blurred. His mouth was filled with blood and he could barely move his broken lips. Little pieces of gravel were embedded into his forehead, and the world spun crazily as he looked up at the señorita.

"I've got to get you to a doctor!"

Santana did not know what a doctor was, but he was in no shape to ask. He felt himself being drawn to his feet by the boy and the girl, then led over to the buggy and helped up to the seat. A moment later the girl was whipping her horse down the street and Santana was hanging on to anything he could grab.

No words were said as he was pulled out of the buggy and rushed into a white man's wooden wickiup. He was in too much pain to be afraid, and when the doctor indicated that he was to lay down on a table, Santana meekly complied.

"What the hell happened to this boy!" the doctor demanded.

"Three wagon guards that my father fired last week were tormenting me. This man and little George tried to help. There was a terrible fight."

"And this Mexican got his head kicked in," the doctor said.

"How bad is it?"

Santana felt cool water on his face. He looked up at the doctor and saw double. The world continued to spin. The doctor pinched his nose and said, "Well, Maria, at least his nose isn't broken. Amazing."

"He is very brave," the girl said. "He beat two grown men before the last one jumped him from behind and started to bash his face into the dirt."

"Did a pretty good job of it," the doctor said. "But

I'm beginning to think it looks a lot worse than it is. Señor?"

"Yes?" Santana mumbled thickly.

"You speak English? Good. My Spanish is terrible. You've taken a serious beating and are bleeding from both ears. Are you seeing straight?"

Santana shook his head.

"Double vision?"

"Eh?" Santana did not understand the word "vision."

"*Uno*, uh . . . *dos medicos*?" the man said, first holding up one finger, then two as he pointed to himself.

"Two."

The doctor leaned back. "He's got a bad concussion, Maria."

"What does that mean?"

"It's a bruise of the brain."

"His brain is damaged!"

"Not permanently. If he's lucky and there is no serious internal bleeding, he'll have a complete recovery. If not . . . well, why don't we just wait and see."

Santana saw Maria's faces—both of them. Were those tears . . . or water . . . that the doctor used to cleanse the blood from his face? Santana did not know. The only thing that was certain was that his true Apache identity would certainly be revealed and that he had failed the Chiricahua. When these people discovered he was an Apache, they would probably hang him from the nearest tree and he would go to his Spirit World still seeing double.

TWENTY-EIGHT

S antana knew that he had lapsed in and out of consciousness since being transported by Maria's buggy to her father's immense stone house. It was not until several days later that he fully regained his senses and his vision began to return to normal.

"You have given us quite a scare, young man," a tall, elegant old man said. "My daughter says that you speak English. Is that true?"

"Poco. A little," Santana amended, feeling as if his head was a too-ripe gourd about to split in the noonday sun.

"My name is Baltazar Avila, and I am a Spaniard. At one time, I had possession of one of the finest ranchos in California. But the Mexicans overthrew our government and confiscated everything. Missions, ranchos—all the wealth that it cost us a century of blood and toil to accumulate. So now, I own a silver mine and try to live at peace as an American."

"An American?"

"Yes." Avila was a slender, dark-complected man well into his seventies. His suit was white with gold embroidery, and his thick mane was the color of silver. He wore a handlebar mustache and stood beside Santana's bed with his arms clasped behind the small of his back. His posture was ramrod straight and his manner quite formal.

"And your name?"

"Santana."

The man waited, and when no other name was given, he smiled and said, "Señor Santana, I welcome you to my house. You have nothing to fear in this place because I have armed guards and for seven years have been an American citizen."

When Santana said nothing, the mine owner continued. "Señor Santana, my wife was born in Mexico City but we met and were married at the mission in Monterey. The señora was a lovely and gracious woman. She died six years ago, when Maria was attending a finishing school in Boston. I lost a son for Texas independence, and now Maria is my only joy. I tell you this so that you will understand how extremely grateful I am that you had the courage and chivalry to intercede in my daughter's behalf."

"*Por nada.* It was nothing," Santana said, in the way of Mexicans.

Avila's silver eyebrows arched in disagreement. "Oh yes it was! Those three guards I fired were perfectly capable of doing my daughter grievous harm. I have taken the trouble to have them ... *removed* from this part of the country."

Santana had thought he knew the meaning of "removed," but now he was not so sure. How could you "remove" someone?

"Your roan is now in my stable." Avila smiled and added, "However, I forbid you to ride him until you are completely recovered."

Santana drew a hand across his eyes. This room though filled with treasures and things he had never imagined, was stuffy. He felt claustrophobic, and the mat he was lying upon was mushy and very uncomfortable. Furthermore, he was not even wearing his Mexican clothes but instead a soft cotton shirt that smelled of soap and desert lavender blossoms.

"Where is my gun?"

Avila moved over to a big piece of carved wood and, to Santana's utter amazement, drew out a hollow piece of it and showed him the gun and holster. "They are safe right here, but you will not need them. I assure you, those three bullies will never return to Pinos."

Santana nodded. A movement out of the corner of his eye caused him to roll his head sideways and see Maria appear in the doorway. When she realized that Santana was alert, she brightened and exclaimed, "So, you have finally rejoined us! Excellent!"

The girl marched right over to the bed and sat down upon it, acting as if she were Santana's woman. "Now, you must tell us all about yourself. Who are you? Where are you from? How did you learn to fight so well at your age? And how old—"

"Maria!" her father protested. "You will make his head hurt even worse than it already must by asking so many questions. Contain yourself."

She fluttered her eyelashes at Santana. "I am sorry, señor. It is just that in these times, there are so few men who would have risked their lives to help a lady. That makes you very special in my eyes . . . and those of my father."

Santana squirmed with embarrassment even as he recalled his mission. "What do you know about the great war? The one between the North and the South?"

There was a sudden and confusing silence broken only when Maria replied, "Why do you ask? Of what importance is that to you now?"

She glanced at her father, who shrugged his shoulders, indicating he too was at loss for an explanation.

Santana realized that he should have waited a bit before asking this question. He racked his throbbing brain trying to think of some other question to ask but drew a complete mental blank. He felt warm. The walls seemed to press in on him and he wondered if that great overhead wheel with candles would tear free of the ceiling, fall on his legs, and break them to pieces so that he would never walk again.

"Mr. Santana," the Spaniard said. "You were delirious for a full day, and during that time you spoke Apache."

His mouth went dry. Santana tried to jump from the bed but a spear of pain lanced his skull and he collapsed back onto his pillow. He felt sick and was panicked to realize he was about to vomit. He grabbed his stomach and blew out his cheeks, eyes pleading for help.

"Here!" Maria said, handing him a pottery basin.

Santana tried to empty his stomach but there was nothing to bring up. He gulped for air like a sick dog, and sweat beaded across his forehead. He felt weak, and when he stopped gasping, he closed his eyes, breathing hard. Never had he felt so terrible. If only Jacova were here! She would give him some vervain tea, perhaps mixed with a little mint and honey, which would settle his stomach and ease the pain in his head. Either that or a nice hot tea brewed from the puffed, cottony flowers of the buckwheat bush which had always—

"The doctor told us that your stomach would be upset for some time," Avila was saying. "But this will pass and then you will feel much better."

"Good," Santana breathed, certain that his true identity had been revealed and that these people would betray him.

"When you are feeling well again," the Spaniard said, "Maria and I would be honored to have you remain here as long as you wish as our guest."

"I . . . I can't."

"Oh?" Avila raised his eyebrows in question, then smiled. "But of course! You probably have a wife, perhaps already even a family!"

Santana began to squirm.

"No family?" Maria asked.

Santana did not know how to answer. Apache did not lie, and yet it was not possible to tell these people the truth. How could he admit to his *real* Apache family or that he had been sent by Cochise and had, in fact, even been among the Apache who had wiped out nearby Edna? Caught in this dilemma, Santana pressed his fingers to his temples to keep them from hurting.

"Oh dear!" Maria exclaimed. "Your poor head! You've forgotten!"

"Yes," her father said, brows knitted with concern. "But I'm sure that his full memory will return. Such things take time. Now, we must leave you to rest."

Baltazar Avila took his daughter's arm and led her out the door. "Rest," he said with a gentle smile. "You are very important to us, Señor Santana."

When the door closed, Santana took a series of deep breaths to clear his head and then he rolled off the elevated mat and searched for his clothing. Not finding any, he attempted to reach the big wood thing that hid his gun and cartridge belt. He made it just halfway across the room before his stomach cramped violently again and he staggered back to the bed, grabbing for the pottery water basin. For long moments he sucked for breath, body swimming in perspiration, hands trembling, breath rapid and shallow.

Santana thought of his beloved mother. He wished more than anything that she were here now. Jacova would know what to give him to settle his stomach and focus his senses. But Jacova was somewhere far away, possibly even in Mexico and worrying herself into a different kind of sickness over his fate among the Americans.

"I *must* leave this place," he said, taking a few more deep breaths and trying again to reach the place where his gun waited.

But the sickness gripped him again, and this time Santana fell heavily. From far, far away, he thought he heard a cry. Maybe it was Jacova, whose spirit searched for his spirit. But as he lapsed into unconsciousness, he realized it was the beautiful Maria Avila.

*   *   *

The Spaniard handed Santana his gun belt and then stepped back as Maria rose on her tiptoes and kissed Santana's cheek. There were tears of farewell in Maria's eyes, and Santana shared her parting sorrow. Even so, he knew that he had remained too long at Pinos living as if he were a rich gentleman and shamelessly taking all that was offered by the Spaniard.

It was still hard for Santana to believe that last winter, when the snow had fallen, he had finally confessed his mixed blood and that he rode for the great Cochise. The Avilas had been shocked but they had not found fault with him. To the contrary.

"So, you have a Spaniard's blood and a warrior's heart!" Baltazar had said, eyes wide with astonishment. "And your mother's gentle Pima spirit," Maria added, her voice soft with love and affection.

Now, six months later, Santana was still amazed at his candid confession. And also that, instead of a hanging noose, the Avilas had given him understanding. He had spent long hours with this pair talking about Geronimo, Cochise, Mangas Coloradas, and the injustices each had suffered. And later they had drawn from Santana his unusual ancestry. As best he could recall from his mother, he told the Avilas about the old Spanish priest named Francisco Tomas Castillo and the soldiers, one of whom was his grandfather, Miguel Santana, and his uncle Vitorio, a leader of the Pima Indians.

Santana told them how these men had all lived and violently died. And about his mother's Spanish crucifix that had been handed down from priest to Pima to Apache. And about a beaver trapper who had first stolen his mother's heart in the ancient mountain caves less than a hundred miles from Pinos. And through it all, the old man and his daughter had been spellbound.

Santana had been equally fascinated with Baltazar Avila and his highly adventurous life. He had been a poor Spaniard when arriving in California, but had won a land grant and eventually had become very wealthy. After the Mexicans had taken California from Spain and he had lost everything, he brought his family back to this country and turned to prospecting. Ignoring the overworked streams and the Gila River, Baltazar had arrived at Pinos and began to dig for gold in the high rocky places. And as if God were repaying him for past injustices suffered in California, the Spaniard had hit a rich vein of pure gold. Quickly claiming not only his own land, but buying all that surrounded it, Baltazar had founded Pinos, and the rest was history. Now, rich beyond his needs, he encouraged and supported dreamers and men of vision.

Santana had seen his world expand during his brief stay with the Avilas in ways that he could not have imagined. However, with knowledge had come many questions, and everything that Santana had been taught about the white people had been turned upside down, mixed and melded. He no longer even knew what was real and what was imagined. This confusion between fact and fiction regarding Americans had never been more pronounced than when he had accompanied the Avilas to Santa Fe, where they had been hosted by no less than the territorial governor. This important official had been extremely interested in Santana's unique upbringing and insights regarding the Chiricahua Apache. Having such an audience to plead a case for Apache justice had been a heady and unforgettable experience.

Always mindful of the reason he had left Cochise and entered the white man's world, Santana had also listened and learned much about the fundamental reasons for the Civil War, and tried to understand how it would affect the fate of the Apache and Pima people. His conclusion was that the North would probably win the war but that the South would treat the Indians with greater compassion and fairness. Santana knew it was going to be very difficult to speak to the Apache leaders about a war and a nation so badly divided. Such destruction and division among a single people was inconceivable to the Apache.

"Will you return?" Maria asked, taking his hand, her lips forming a silent promise.

Santana felt as if his heart were crumbling like sandstone. When he looked at Maria, he felt as stupid as an ox and as brave as a mountain lion. He could lose himself forever in this woman. Become whatever she wanted—do whatever her father wanted. Become a Spaniard . . . even an American. It was time to hurry back to his own people.

"Santana," the old Spaniard said. "You *must* return."

"Why?"

"I want you to be more."

"I am Apache."

"Then become a savior of the Apache," the Spaniard urged. "I have spoken to you about the school in Santa Fe. And then another in the East. I have the money. Honor me by becoming like a son and accepting my gift of opportunity."

"I am Apache. Among my people, there are some that call me Three Bloods."

"Of course! You are Apache. Pima. Spaniard. But someday, I think we will all be called Americans."

Santana felt his resolve crumbling. Other than his own father, he had never admired a man more than this wise old Spaniard. To ignore this rich and powerful man who had been blessed with the strength to overcome adversity was to turn his ear to truth.

"Santana, my son wished to become a doctor. Maybe you could be a doctor or a great healer for your people—like your mother."

"No."

"Then an attorney!" Avila clenched his fists. "Santana, you could master the law and use it to protect and help your own people. You could become a *different* kind of Apache leader. One that would not lead the Chiricahua to a military destruction, but instead would win them back their lands in the courts of law where the real battles will next be won . . . or lost."

Santana lifted his reins, but Avila grabbed them for a

moment. "You are a man of *three* bloods! Those are the very words that Cochise himself used to describe you. Then *be* of three bloods—only one of which is Apache!"

"Adios," Santana whispered, looking down at Maria and trying to fix her lovely face forever in his mind.

"You can do *more* than fight and die with the Apache!" Avila shouted with exasperation. "You have *more* than that to give!"

Maria reached up and her fingers clasped Santana's new white silk shirt. She pulled him down to her and their lips burned and melted together.

When Santana drew away, she said, "I *will* wait for you."

Santana touched his big-rowled silver spurs to the roan and rode away dressed like a man of wealth and importance. But once he was back into the wild country, he would bury this fancy dress and retrieve his Apache breechclout from his saddlebags. And his headband and knee-length leggings and Apache moccasins.

The only thing was, Santana was unsure if he would ever again be a true Apache warrior and manage to forget the rare prize and the promise he had just declined.

Chapter

TWENTY-NINE

The desert spring at the base of Apache Pass was considered by both Apache and white man to be the deadliest watering hole in the entire Southwest. And now Cochise had learned that a company of soldiers was advancing eastward from Tucson, probably to join the white man's civil war. It was time, the great Chiricahua chief proclaimed, to destroy the enemy once and for all. Mangas Coloradas, older even than Yahnosa, had also rallied his band to fight, as had the great war chiefs Victorio and Nana. There were over five hundred warriors gathered, more than had ever joined for a single fight.

Cochise knew that the soldiers would have to enter a narrow defile between two steep rocky hillsides in order to reach the precious desert springs. With this in mind, he had ordered the Chiricahua to do something unheard of by his people, which was to construct rock breastworks from which the Apache could unleash a murderous volley down upon the soldiers. The July weather was brutally hot, even for Apache, but they went about their preparations certain that they could finally deal the United States army a death blow.

Only Jacova, the woman of Pima blood, felt a premonition of disaster.

"You will die," she warned her husband and son before she and the other women and children were led to safety in the nearby mountains. "This will be the last time I will see either of you on this earth."

Santana held his mother and tried to hide his own grim thoughts of the impending battle. He could see that Yahnosa also shared his concerns. His face was deeply wrinkled, big blue veins stood out on the backs of his hands, and his eyes were shrunken into their sockets. He was, Santana thought, much too old to fight, but there was no more peace for an aged Chiricahua warrior. In these bloody times, every Apache was expected to fight until he was killed, and Yahnosa had proven himself a very difficult old man to kill.

Jacova was taken away with the other women, and the last of the breastworks were completed. Now, with the sun going down, Taza and another Apache scout arrived in camp with information that the soldiers would be arriving tomorrow.

"How many?"

"More than one hundred and twenty," Taza replied, his dark eyes glinting with anticipation.

This was encouraging to the Apache, who had expected a much larger force. That night, Cochise gave the order that no fires were to be lit and that everyone should ready themselves for battle. Santana could not help but also feel the excitement, despite his mother's dire predictions. He stood for a long time beside the breastworks, and when Taza came by, they greeted each other as brothers.

"I have heard that you wintered with the whites in Pinos," Taza said. "And that you learned that the big war between the North and the South will draw the soldiers from our lands."

"Yes," Santana told the young chief. "I am sure that is why these soldiers are riding east."

Taza smiled grimly. "They will die on *our* battlefield tomorrow."

When Santana said nothing, Taza studied him closely

in the bright starlight. "Tell me of this big village called Santa Fe."

"You heard?"

Taza nodded. Even in the starlight, his eyes were piercing, like those of his father. And despite their friendship, Santana chose his words carefully.

"Santa Fe is strong in numbers," he said. "The People cannot conquer it as we did the village called Edna."

"Not even when all the soldiers are gone?"

Santana shook his head.

Taza's face mirrored scorn and disbelief. "When the soldiers go east, we will forever sweep the white-eyes from our lands!"

Santana knew better than to argue. Wanting only to pacify the son of Cochise, he said, "And tomorrow, we will begin with the soldiers, eh?"

"Tomorrow will be a great day for the Apache."

After Taza left him, Santana stared down at the trail, attempting to imagine the impending battle. He was sure that the soldiers would be killed to the very last man. Not only would they be greatly outnumbered, they would be caught by surprise and forced to defend themselves behind what little cover they could find in the rocks and brush. What worried Santana more than the approaching soldiers was what would happen to his people when news of this slaughter reached Santa Fe and beyond. He was afraid that the whites would become so angry they would halt their own civil war and decide to kill every last Apache.

Santana went to rest beside his father. Yahnosa was very quiet and lay with his head on his saddle, gazing up at the stars. "What are you thinking, Father?"

"Of tomorrow. And of death."

Santana had been about to lay his own head down, but now he sat up and peered intently at Yahnosa. "When this is over, maybe it is time to lead our band north to the headwaters of Gila River. Near the caves of the lost ancient people."

"It has been long since I smelled the high mountain pines and meadows. Or fished for the speckled trout and

saw the swift white waters. It would be good to go home
to the mountains."

"You have only to ask and it will be done."

But Yahnosa shook his head. "Now Cochise decides
everything."

"No," Santana argued. "We have fought enough. It is
time to seek a peace with the whites. They are too strong."

"Even with their soldiers all going to war?"

"Yes," Santana answered without hesitation. "We are
few now. Each year fewer still. We must forge a peace."

"Cochise does not agree."

Santana opened his mouth to speak, then changed his
mind. After a moment he said, "Perhaps tomorrow will
satisfy even Cochise's lust for revenge."

Yahnosa said nothing—which said everything. He
laid his head upon his saddle and soon he began to snore.

When the Apache rifles opened fire and their arrows
filled the narrow canyon like fingers of death, soldiers toppled from their horses. Those that survived the first volley
took cover and managed to return fire.

"They cannot last!" Santana swore as he knelt beside
his father and fired down at the hapless cavalrymen. "We
must keep them from the spring!"

Yahnosa's eyes were dimming, and Santana knew that
his father could not clearly see the blue coats, but that was
unimportant. The scene below was chaos. It was just as
Cochise had promised, and when Santana dropped behind
cover to reload his Navy Colt, he could look both up and
down the ridge along the breastworks and see that the
Apache were feverish with anticipation and excitement.

"Look!" Yahnosa shouted.

Still in the process of reloading his Colt, Santana
dared to glance over the rocks and saw the muzzles of two
huge cannon being elevated toward their ridge. Santana resumed his reloading, for he was not concerned. The Mexican army had cannon and they misfired as often as they
fired. Besides, a cannonball could not penetrate rock.

When the first mountain howitzer roared, Santana stared with morbid fascination at the belching fire and smoke. He expected some round, fat ball to strike the mountain or perhaps to sail completely over the ridge. Instead, a strange object sailed over their heads and exploded. An instant later death rained down upon the astonished Apache. Santana heard Apache scream and saw Apache bodies being ripped apart. He whirled to stare at his father just as the second howitzer boomed.

At the same instant Santana felt shrapnel rip into his knee and saw his father's head turn to red grape jelly. Yahnosa's body jerked spasmodically. His pistol rattled against the breastwork rocks.

"Father!" Santana cried, throwing himself over Yahnosa's body.

The next few moments were lost to Santana. He felt the earth shake as the great howitzers tossed their exploding messengers of death upward to rain upon the Apache. All around him cactus and plants were shredded as if by invisible knives. Rocks burst like Mexican firecrackers and warriors were torn to pieces. Santana hugged his father, knowing Yahnosa was dead, and when another piece of shrapnel tore across his ribs, Santana knew that he had to take cover or his Pima mother would be left alone and unprotected.

Pressing himself tightly against the rock breastworks, he cursed in helpless fury until the howitzers fell silent. Rising up, he watched as the soldiers charged up the canyon floor to reach the safety of heavy cover and the gift of precious springwater. There were a few scattered shots, but the soldiers had escaped while all around him there were dead and wounded Apache.

Cochise and Taza were spared, but Mangas Coloradas was not so lucky. The old chief was badly wounded, though no one knew if it had been from a soldier's bullet or from the strange and terrible cannon which fired not heavy balls, but canisters of shrapnel.

Cochise galloped up and down the ridge, exhorting the warriors to attack again, but too many were dead. Perhaps, under the cover of night, the Apache could over-power the soldiers and kill them in hand-to-hand fighting.

Santana did not know. And as he held the riddled body of his father, he did not care. Ignoring the blood that ran freely from his own knee, he lifted Yahnosa and limped to his roan. This night, he would grieve with his mother, and tomorrow they would bury this beloved man.

Santana and his mother chose a lonely burial place high up in the Chiricahua mountains. It was on a moun-tainside overlooking a vast open tableland. Yahnosa was laid to rest in his finest clothes, along with his most prized possessions. The wickiup that Jacova had last shared with her husband was burned along with her household utensils, clothing, and blankets. Nothing was left to remind her of the young Apache who had captured and taken her to wife so many years ago despite her warning that she would only bring him heartache.

"He never believed me," Jacova whispered as they rode away from the burial place. "He *never* believed me."

Santana nodded, face taut with pain. A few hours earlier, Jacova had extracted a piece of metal from his knee and then applied her best healing medicine to keep his blood from being poisoned. The knee seemed to be healing, but it was stiff. It was an agony to ride this high, rugged mountain country.

The Battle of Apache Pass had been a disaster. A badly wounded Mangas Coloradas had been rushed to Janos, Mexico, where a frightened doctor had been warned his entire village would be slaughtered if the old chief did not survive. Mangas Coloradas survived.

"I am returning to my own Pima people," Jacova an-nounced as they rode down the mountainside. "Will you take me there?"

Santana was not surprised by this request. After all these years, Jacova was still by nature Pima. Only the love and devotion to her husband had kept her among the enemy.

"I will take you," he said, reining his horse toward

the vast, searing Sonoran desert and the slow, silver thread of the Gila River.

"You will meet your other blood ancestors," Jacova told him. "You will find peace at last."

Santana said nothing. His mother's people were not his people and they never would be. The Pima were farmers, while he had always strived to be like his father, an Apache warrior.

"Santana, you must find peace."

"How?"

Jacova reached into her shirt and dragged out the old Castillo crucifix and chain. "Maybe this," she said, extending it toward him.

But Santana shook his head. "No. It is yours until death."

"I will die with my own people."

Tears misted Santana's eyes. "I have no people," he said, the realization hitting him like a fist in the stomach. "I have never been a true Apache warrior. Not in spirit."

"Maybe, in spirit, you are Pima."

Santana wondered. Right now he ached for the loss of Yahnosa. Being alive could be far worse than death. His only hope was in the promise of that Spanish girl, Maria Avila. Even now, as Santana clung to his roan and the sweat poured from his face, he could envision Maria dancing on the hot desert winds. Like a mirage, she swayed and beckoned him toward Pinos, high in the Mogollon Mountains.

Jacova reached out and touched his cheek. Santana thought his mother was feeling to see if he had the fever. Instead Jacova whispered, "I can tell that the Spanish girl calls you, just as my people call to me."

Santana nodded, remembering Baltazar Avila's answer for a new and lasting way to help the Indian people. And, in remembering, Santana realized this was to be his destiny.

"From this day forward, I will fight with words, not guns," Santana told his mother as they rode straight into the heat of the desert.

EPILOGUE

Miguel Diego Santana was the full name he had finally chosen to grace their marriage certificate. And later it was how he wanted his name inscribed on his law school diploma. After all, this had been the name of Santana's Spanish grandfather, the one who had loved the dying priest and whose magnificent crucifix he now clutched in his fist.

Maria placed her hand on her kneeling husband's shoulder. "How old was Jacova?"

Santana stared at the fresh grave resting beside the Gila River. The dying sun was exploding across the western mountaintops, and behind him the ancient ruins of Casa Grande glowed like a shrine. "I don't know," he admitted. "Very, very old."

"Your mother outlived two husbands."

"Three," Santana gently corrected. "Jacova always considered herself married to that American fur trapper whose name I cannot even remember."

"Three, then," Maria said. "And is this really the place where the priest and your Spanish grandfather were buried?"

Santana filled his lungs with the desert sage. "It must be very close."

"I wish that I could have known Jacova," Maria said.

"She was magnificent," Santana whispered, absently brushing the crucifix back and forth across the grave. "Jacova had vision and strength."

Over near the ancient ruins, their buggy horse whinnied with impatience. "We can return as often as you want," Maria said. "As often as the tribal council and your law practice allows."

Santana's gaze lifted to the smooth, rolling surface of the Gila River. Just the trace of a smile tugged at the corners of his mouth. "The legend says that the old priest blessed this water . . . this whole river. Father Castillo must have believed he had great power with God."

Santana arose to his full height, a tall, dark man who wore a black suit, white starched collar, and, under his creased pants, Apache leggings and moccasins which supported and eased the pain in his stiff knee. The crucifix slipped from his hand to dangle from its golden chain. Santana raised it in tribute to the Gila River, then slipped it over his shoulder-length hair.

In Spanish and then Apache, Santana offered prayers for the soul and spirits of his ancestors buried beside this great river. Satisfied at last, he took Maria's hand and limped away.

ABOUT THE AUTHOR

GARY McCARTHY grew up in California and spent his boyhood around horses and horsemen. His graduate education took him to Nevada, where he spent many years living and working. A prolific novelist of the American West, Mr. McCarthy is the author of the popular "Derby Man" series, and has written several historical novels including *The Colorado, The Russian River,* and *The American River,* all in the "Rivers West" series. Before writing this historical novel, Mr. McCarthy and his son, Glendon, explored the Gila River from its headwaters in southwestern New Mexico's Gila National Forest to its joining with the great Colorado River near Yuma, Arizona. He makes his home in Ojai, California, with his wife and family.

If you enjoyed Gary McCarthy's epic tale, *The Gila River*, be sure to look for the next installment of the Rivers West saga at your local bookstore. Each new volume takes you on a voyage of exploration along one of the great rivers of North America with the courageous pioneers who challenged the unknown.

Turn the page for an exciting preview of the next book in Bantam's unique historical series

Rivers West

THE HIGH MISSOURI
by Win Blevins

(On sale in Spring 1994 wherever Bantam Books are sold.)

D ylan Elfed Davis Campbell looked at the lists of figures on the piece of paper. They squiggled. They dashed around like little black ants, racing here and there and everywhere. One thing they didn't do was sit still. The other was add up. If he had to look at them any longer, he would scream.

He told himself to take a deep breath.

If he did, he would choke—he was sure of that. Choke on air, on life itself. He clenched his fists and his teeth so hard he thought his entire body must be shaking.

Don't worry, he raged at himself, you can't die. You're already dead. Just past your twenty-second birthday in the first month of spring, you're dead. Call the embalmer.

It was Friday afternoon at the Bank of Montreal, and Dylan was proving that the amount in the cash drawers at the start of the day plus the amount deposited today added up to the amount of cash now in the cash drawers less the amount taken out in cash. He did this every day in the late afternoon. The figures never added up—they were too busy anting around. And when they didn't add up, he had to stay late and make them do it, without pay.

"Mr. Campbell," called the nasal voice of the bastard MacDonald. They called him that jokingly, half with malice, because Dugald MacDonald was his rich father's son via a French mistress. Mr. MacDonald now said, in his snotty way, "Mr. Campbell, *will* you complete that posting, *please*?"

Naturally, he called across the entire bank from the door of his own office, so everyone would know the poor dumb Welshman was late again. One of Mr. MacDonald's office jokes was that the bloody Welsh were always bloody, being by nature bloody poets and no men of business. Which irked Dylan, because he had as much Scots blood as Mr. MacDonald; half.

Dylan stood up. He gasped for breath. It came, and something changed—a door closed or opened, or a breeze moved him as it moves the first leaves in a tree—he couldn't have said what it was. It was as though he heard music inside his head, and the music was revelation. For a moment he was giddy.

Go, he ordered himself.

He stepped away from his desk, leaving the long columns of ants racing wherever they wanted. He crossed the room toward Mr. MacDonald, who stood there, transfixed, or stupefied—was the Welshman actually approaching the boss without the figures? Dylan enjoyed watching him stand there, dumbstruck.

Suddenly, halfway to Mr. MacDonald, Dylan stopped. No need to get in his face, he thought, where his gross pores and long nasal hairs will be offensive. I may as well call across the whole bloody room, as he does.

He called, "Mr. MacDonald, take this job and stuff it up your arse."

Dylan could see everything as he would remember it for eternity, fixed in its tiny place, mouths open, eyes gaping, nostrils flared in astonishment. Everything was rigid, all eyes fixed immovably on ledgers they weren't seeing.

Mr. MacDonald just stood there. Struck speechless, Dylan thought with satisfaction.

Dylan had had no idea he was going to say that. Delicious. Sublime. Heavenly. He wanted to dance.

He stepped back to his desk, moving through a room fixed forever motionless, as behind a glass display case. He gathered his few things, put on his coat, and went out into the late afternoon of the last day of winter in Montreal, 1820.

Let someone else catch the ants.

Oh Daddy Ni, ain't it grand?

In front of the great plate of glass bearing the distinguished firm's name, his bottom began to twitch. He wiggled it. His knees wobbled. He let them do it. His hands went akimbo. He danced a jig.

He knew immediately where, in his heart of hearts, he wanted to go. Not to his lodgings, and not to his father's house; no, neither. But he didn't want to go there immediately. He wanted to walk, and vigorously.

He hurried along the old wall of the city on Place Viger Station. He walked all the way to the hill called the Citadel. Montreal boasted that it was one of the oldest settlements in North America, founded by the French in 1642. Though the English had taken over sixty years ago, the city was divided. The commercial and professional people were Britons and Scots, the working people French. It was built on the St. Lawrence River, at the confluence of great rivers that led into the heart of the continent. Yet the huge ships of the sea sailed all the way to these wharves and dispersed to the far corners of the earth.

He turned toward the river. It wasn't yet clear of ice. Soon the spring day when the rivers were clear, usually late in April, would become a key day in his life. He would be traveling the waterways as his predecessors had, using the powerful currents of the earth to carry him forth on God's mission.

He felt light, gay, *free*. He hummed a little tune, and then, feeling foolish, began to sing it.

> *C'est le vent, c'est le vent frivolant,*
> *C'est le vent, c'est le vent frivolant.*

So went the chorus: "It's the wind, it's the frivolous wind." It was a song of the *voyageurs,* the canoemen, about the frivolous wind bringing a sad and unjust death to a white duck. He'd never known why he liked such a sentimental lamentation, and he didn't care. He was feeling absurd and wonderful.

He looked around and chuckled to himself. It was not a day to feel grand, not a bit of a fine spring day, but wintry, drizzly, as Montreal often was, gray, the light fading, the western clouds mottled gray and purple and mustard color, like bruises. And a wind, a gusty wind. Only a romantic would call it frivolous. Today Dylan was a romantic.

He hurried around the seminary and rectory to the face of his one true home in Montreal, his soul's home, the church Notre Dame at Place d'Armes.

He passed out of the blustery day and into its haven, a passage that always seemed to him from one world to another, from the physical to the spiritual, from the mundane to the ethereal.

He stood at the back of the nave, taking it all in, the arcade where worshipers sat, above them the ceiling divided into conical sections by gilt moldings. In the center of the ceiling arched a circular painting of the Ascension itself, in heroic-sized figures. Beyond this end of the nave was the transept, its cruciform arms reaching north and south, and in its center, the area called the crossing, the region of the approach to the altar, where communicants crossed from the earthly to the heavenly and at the altar partook of wonder and mystery, the body and the blood of Jesus Christ.

Above the altar, like a canopy, was an open crown,

supported by gilt pillars. Behind the crown, a full-sized statue of the Virgin Mary cut in white marble. On either side of the altar, paintings on Scriptural subjects. For Dylan the center of all was the rick ornaments on the altar, whence came divine communion, the miracle of the divine service, the locus where ordinary life entered its spiritual dimension.

He slipped into a back pew and knelt.

Dylan had always been impatient of ordinary life. He didn't see the point of the business his father spent his life on, trading furs. It honored the temporal, not the eternal. He knew that business itself was a low undertaking. In the end, that was why he had quit his job today, and not the affronts given by Mr. MacDonald. He could not bear the ignobility of commerce.

So he came here this afternoon to dedicate himself to his heart's adventure, his soul's quest. Now he would give his life to the Church.

He let his eyes roam the great church, the side chapels, the statuary, the ten stations of the Cross, the piers lifting to heaven. This was his home. It had always been his home.

Today, now, here, he began his great enterprise.

He felt given this enterprise personally, in a laying on of hands. His particular mentor was his father's best friend, Father Quesnel, a priest here. There lay a story. Auguste Quesnel had had great ambitions for God and the Church. In his heart burned an intense desire, a holy calling. He wanted to revive one of the greatest churchly traditions in Canada. He wanted to take the Gospel to the benighted of this vast continent, the Indians.

Starting two centuries ago, that had been the particular calling of the Jesuits of North America. They had walked boldly into the darkness bearing the light. It had been a terrible responsibility, and many had paid with their mortal lives. But surely they had burnished their souls to a holy brightness and had brought heathen souls to salvation.

About forty years ago Father Quesnel had been ready to enter the Jesuit order. He had gone to the city of Québec, there to receive his training and prepare for the calling he had dedicated his life to, carrying the word of God to the Indians of Canada. When he got off the stage in Québec, he was greeted by his mentor-to-be with dire news. All Jesuits were former Jesuits, said the priest. The Pope had abolished the order.

Abolished!

Not only was the order abolished, as it turned out, the missionary effort in Canada dwindled to nothing.

When Father Quesnel told the story in the Campbell parlor decades later, Dylan felt the devastation of that moment. To have a calling, a life, wiped out by the word of one man. Centuries of resentment of Jesuits all over the world had come to a head, said Quesnel, and the Pope gave in to pressure.

Father Quesnel attached himself to the single Catholic church in Montreal and spent his life administering the sacraments, counseling, preaching, administering the church's business—doing the ordinary tasks of any priest. He sometimes said he had discovered that such was the heart of the work of the clergy.

A decade ago, when the Canadian Church's missionary zeal was partly revived, and the St. Boniface mission was founded on Red River, wherever in the interior that was, Father Quesnel said he was far too old to set out on a new venture.

Dylan picked up his mentor's torch. He wanted to be a priest, and not a mundane servant of the people, but like the priest of St. Boniface—a torch bearer, a missionary to the Indians.

That was the biggest conflict he ever had with his father. Ian Hugh Campbell would not tolerate his youngest son's taking orders. Together, Campbell and Quesnel prevailed on the youngster to wait until the age of his majority, at least twenty-one, to make such a fateful decision. In the meantime he would learn banking.

Well, hadn't that come up fine? As shown by this afternoon's events. Dylan got restless on his knees, shifted his weight about. Now he was twenty-two. Now he was done with banking forever, with commerce forever. Now he would devote his life to his heart's desire.

He rose, slipped out of the pew and walked toward the altar. When he came to the crossing, he stopped in the light. On each end of the transept, north and south, light streamed in from the huge windows of stained glass. Doubtless the light outside, on this rainy day, was pale, gray, drab. But in this house of God it was transformed by the stained glass. Here it prismed into every color, rich gold, royal blue, glowing rose, vivid scarlet, every hue.

Dylan walked to the center of the crossing and stood in that light, like a rainbow, a promise by God. He knelt, facing the altar. To him the crossing was a special place. Father Quesnel said that, literally, it meant where the east-west reach of the nave intersected the north-south line of the transept. But it also meant where the laity crossed to the place of the clergy, where the world crossed to seek spirit. Thus it was a region of miracle.

Dylan knelt in the center of the crossing and faced the altar. He did not need to pray in words. His gesture was prayer, his being was prayer. He murmured a thanksgiving for his liberation, and promised his energy, his zeal, his love, his life to the mission task.

Tomorrow morning he would tell Father Quesnel his decision. It was wonderful. Now he would go to his father, who would rail against it.

Ian Hugh Campbell had lived among the dregs of the earth, the *voyageurs* and *coureurs de bois*, white men who penetrated the wilderness to trade for furs with the Indians. Campbell was fond of saying, "In the early days, the Frenchman didn't convert the Indians. The Indians converted them."

Campbell made sure his son heard the stories. In the wilderness men took on Indian dress, manners, ways, he explained. They drank, stole, rampaged, raped, murdered—as

Indians did. The ultimate signs of corruption: they took Indian wives, learned Indian languages, lived as Indians, mere beasts roaming the face of the earth, hunting, scavenging, rutting. Their very children were Indian. They permitted the light in their souls to be put out, and lived in utter darkness.

So Dylan Elfed Davis Campbell did not know how he would tell his ambition to his father now, to walk into this utter darkness.

The spot in the crossing where he knelt seemed momentarily to glow. He looked at his arms, trunk, legs. He thought the sun was striking him a little. He looked up at the stained-glass window in the south transept. Perhaps it was a little brighter. Perhaps the late afternoon sun was beaming at him through the drizzle. He thought of his father's cold rages. "If this is a miracle," he murmured, smiling, "I accept."

TWO

Dylan hung up his coat, mopped his wet head, and looked at himself in a hall mirror.

No, lad, he said to himself in his father's voice, you'll not do. Again in his father's voice, You ought to wear a hat in this weather. A thousand similar thoughts murmured in the back of his head.

Dylan drew a deep breath. His father's house had a distinctive smell—not strong, but sly—a smell covered by years of fastidious scrubbing and cleaning, one strangers might not even notice. It was the smell of illness. Ian Campbell had taken sick three years ago, which now seemed to Dylan the man's whole life. The young doctor who listened to his chest with a new invention called a stethoscope said he had a combination of heart ailment and rheumatism. When Campbell confessed to an unexplained fever in the wilderness a year before, the diagnosis was confirmed. And somehow, ever since, the house smelled like decay to Dylan, decay both physical and moral.

It also smelled like fear. Like not saying what you mean, like smiling because you're supposed to, and feeling rivalrous with your father and keeping it quiet, and loneliness. Especially loneliness.

The house didn't change, except to get grayer and more worn. It was empty and lonely. Dylan was gone. Only his little sister (well, half sister) Amalie was still at home, and she was only waiting for the first proposal of marriage. Dylan thought she would take the very first, regardless.

Lonely. Because it was motherless. Two children by two mothers, both dead now, and Dylan remembered neither of them alive. His own mother, who was Welsh and insisted on his Welsh names, died a week after he was born. He couldn't even remember his father's last wife, Amalie's mother, a Frenchwoman. She died when he was three. Since no one in the family was permitted to mention her, Dylan didn't even know what she died of.

Two wives dead. As a schoolboy Dylan often imagined his father as some sort of evil wizard. He brushed women with his secret wand in their secret places, and they died of his touch.

He pushed his hair back. It was wet from the drizzle on this wintry day, and falling in his eyes. In the mirror he saw what his father called a likely enough twenty-two-year-old. His father often remarked that Dylan was good-looking, then followed with, "Why don't you make more of yourself, laddie?"

One more glance at his reflection. Aye, boyo, it's well you don't look as scared as you feel.

This house and this life were like seeds chewed to pulp. Perhaps once they'd provided taste and nourishment. Now he needed to spit them out.

Thus resolved, he stepped into the double door of the parlor. He tried softly, "Father?"

"Yes, Dylan," boomed the voice.

Dylan looked at the great chair by the French windows where Ian Hugh Campbell would be sitting, snuff box nearby, snifter in his hand. The snuff would be cheap, and the snifter full of Burton's Ale instead of brandy. Dylan was well aware of his father's small pretensions: the house, struggling to be grand outside, much worn inside.

The furniture, nicked and kept presentable only by much rubbing with oil. The housekeeper, whom his father could ill afford but couldn't let go. The closets of his father's clothes, mended and mended until to a sharp eye they resembled patchwork quilts. Since his illness, he wore only a dressing gown anyway.

There was nothing for Dylan here, nothing at all, and never had been. Except Amalie, poor thing. But she was beautiful, and had beaux. Soon she would be married and gone.

Dylan supposed his father's life would be over then.

A harrumph. "*Yes*, Dylan."

He stepped near the great chair and looked down at his father. Ian Campbell was sizable, imposing, with huge, menacing eyebrows, both eyes too wide open, like a bird's, and opaque, unreadable features. With his stocky body, big head, and no neck, he looked like an irascible owl. The man was forty-eight, but no longer full of piss and vinegar. Forty-eight, and his life was already over. Just empty motions for a few more years, empty gestures of acquisition, and empty ragings.

Step forth and disappoint your father, Dylan told himself ironically.

He stepped close enough to shake hands.

"Pour yourself a glass, lad."

Ian Campbell watched Dylan get a beer glass from the side table, pour his own drink, and then fill his father's brandy snifter up to the rim, all without looking into his father's face. Yes, beer glass—it seemed important to the lad to say, This is ale, not brandy. Not that the lad's palate cared. Or that he cared at all. His son didn't know what it meant to be well-off, even to have riches within your grasp and see it all slip away. Because your heart betrayed you.

Ian Campbell snorted. His heart wasn't something he used a lot in this life. When he did, for two wives and this single son, it betrayed him. Suitable that this organ of so much trouble would bring him down.

Something else the lad didn't know. What it meant to love your son and for your trouble get his contempt dashed in your face.

Dylan lifted his beer glass in a salute and sipped, and set the glass on the little side table with his father's snifter and snuff.

"What's wrong now?" asked his father.

"Why should anything be wrong, Daddy Ni?"

Ian snorted at that language. When Dylan was a baby, Ian Campbell had revered the memory of his mother, and brought in the boy's maternal aunt, Meredith Davis, to take care of him and teach the boy a few words of the Welsh language and other things Welsh. Now the lad used these childhood indulgences to manipulate him.

"You've been skulking out there in the hall, afraid to tell me something."

Ian regretted the words immediately. Maybe he was a little drunk. He often was these days. When he drank too much, he stated the truth of life with a matter-of-fact bitterness the young were not prepared for. He felt more and more bitter these days, and cynical. Since his illness, he never went down to the office of Campbell Trading Company, which now looked derelict. A man who had roamed the vast interior of Canada, he was housebound, almost bedridden. If he could only get well! The doctor said he might. Dylan would never think so, but he himself did. He was only forty-eight!

"What happened, did you get discharged?"

Why did he speak so harshly to the lad? Since Dylan had moved out a month ago, he had asked him that question on every visit. Dylan didn't know how it felt to try to give your son a better start in life than you had, and worry that you'd failed. You trekked the wilderness, paddled those bloody canoes upstream and down, endured hunger and freezing, looked red niggers in the eye and stared them down, and endangered your very soul—for what? So your son wouldn't have to. And now the sod didn't notice.

"Why do you say that, Father?"

"Claude MacDonald sent your trunk around a few minutes ago."

His father handed him a note, the envelope opened, the paper rumpled. So his father intercepted his mail and read it.

Dear Dylan,

Uncle Dugald was just here in a frightful temper—said you'd insulted him publicly and all that. Whatever you did, old chap, you did it all the way. He's livid.

He made me pack your things while he watched, got a carter, and sent your trunk to your father's place. Can't do aught about it, the family owning the hotel, you know. The staff here is warned not to admit you. Dreadfully sorry. I guess you're struck at your father's house for a few days, at least.

But come round, please, I want to hear the story of how you bearded the lion in his den!

Your friend,
Claude MacDonald

Annoyed, Dylan walked away from his father and looked out the windows. Still gray, still drizzling, the light fading, rainwater running down the glass, blurring his vision. Tomorrow is a new beginning, he reminded himself.

He wondered why his father was so bitter, so sure life would turn to ashes in the mouth. Yes, two wives dead, that was part of it, and his illness, and a sinking business, all part of it. Even his housekeeper, Philomene, had disappointed him. For years Dylan hadn't known about their secret relationship. Then, suddenly one morning six weeks ago, they were acting like rejected lovers. That was when

Dylan moved out. It seemed clear that Philomene's love would be the last in his father's life. Yet all that was not excuse enough for bitterness, not to Dylan. If Ian Hugh Campbell wanted to give up, why did he have to ruin his son's life?

His father didn't pursue the questions. He'd asked in order to nettle, not to get an answer. Dylan tried to shock him with the reply.

"No, Father, I've quit."

Campbell sniffed his disapproval.

Dylan wondered whether his father heard. "Don't you believe me?"

"I believe you're a fool for moods, like your mother." It was a theme of his growing up. To Ian Campbell, as to Dugald MacDonald, the Scots were rough and ready and up to snuff. The Welsh were poetic, which meant moody, which meant weak, not up to the harsh business of life.

"Hiraeth," muttered Ian Campbell, like grinding nuts in his teeth. Dylan knew his thought—give me fine Scots, not melancholy Welshmen.

The pedal point of his childhood again. Whenever Dylan was sad, Ian said he suffered from *hiraeth,* like his Welsh mother.

It was Welsh for melancholy—according to his father, not just ordinary dejection, but a kind of world-despair that only a foolishly poetic people like the Welsh could be capable of. Dylan wondered why Ian Campbell had married Gwyneth, née Davis, if he despised the Welsh.

Don Coldsmith's
THE SPANISH BIT SAGA
The acclaimed chronicle of the Great Plains' native people.

THUNDERSTICK

Singing Wolf has reached his seventeenth summer—
and manhood. But a stranger has come, bringing to the
People a weapon of extraordinary power, magic, and
danger: the thunderstick. Together, Wolf and the
stranger may save the Elk-dog People.

❑ 26397-8	**TRAIL OF THE SPANISH BIT**	$3.99
❑ 26412-5	**THE ELK-DOG HERITAGE**	$3.99
❑ 26806-6	**FOLLOW THE WIND**	$3.99
❑ 26938-0	**BUFFALO MEDICINE**	$3.99
❑ 27067-2	**MAN OF THE SHADOWS**	$3.99
❑ 27209-8	**THE DAUGHTER OF THE EAGLE**	$3.99
❑ 27344-2	**MOON OF THUNDER**	$3.99
❑ 27460-0	**SACRED HILLS**	$3.99
❑ 27604-2	**PALE STAR**	$3.50
❑ 27708-1	**RIVER OF SWANS**	$3.99
❑ 28163-1	**RETURN TO THE RIVER**	$3.50
❑ 28318-9	**THE MEDICINE KNIFE**	$3.99
❑ 28538-6	**THE FLOWER IN THE MOUNTAINS**	$3.99
❑ 28760-5	**TRAIL FROM TAOS**	$3.99
❑ 29123-8	**SONG OF THE ROCK**	$3.99
❑ 29419-9	**FORT DE CHASTAIGNE**	$4.50
❑ 29862-3	**QUEST FOR THE WHITE BULL**	$4.50
❑ 29681-7	**RETURN OF THE SPANISH**	$4.50
❑ 29467-9	**BRIDE OF THE MORNING STAR**	$4.99
❑ 28334-0	**THE CHANGING WIND**	$4.50
❑ 28868-7	**THE TRAVELER**	$4.99
❑ 28945-4	**WORLD OF SILENCE**	$4.50
❑ 08262-0	**WALKS IN THE SUN** (hardcover)	$12.50
❑ 47026-6	**THUNDERSTICK** (hardcover)	$15.00
❑ 28012-0	**THE SMOKY HILL**	$4.50

Available at your local bookstore or use this page to order.